DON'T TURN
YOUR BACK ON
THE OCEAN

DON'T TURN YOUR BACK ON THE OCEAN

A JERI HOWARD MYSTERY

JANET DAWSON

Fawcett Columbine • New York

A Fawcett Columbine Book
Published by Ballantine Books

Copyright © 1994 by Janet Dawson

Library of Congress Cataloging-in-Publication Data

Dawson, Janet.
  Don't turn your back on the ocean / Janet Dawson.
    p.   cm.
  ISBN 0-449-90766-X
  1. Howard, Jeri (Fictitious character)—Fiction.   2. Private investigators—
California, Northern—Fiction.   3. Women detectives—California, Northern—
Fiction.   I. Title.
PS3554.A949D66   1994
813'.54—dc20   94-9781
                                                                    CIP

Manufactured in the United States of America

First Edition: November 1994

10 9 8 7 6 5 4 3 2 1

For Dawn and Alan in Monterey,
for Anne and Chuck in Morro Bay,
and for Barbara,
who stayed home so I could travel.

ACKNOWLEDGMENTS

I picked the brains of a great many people while researching and writing *Don't Turn Your Back on the Ocean*. Any errors are mine alone.

Bob Leos of the Monterey office of the California Department of Fish and Game and William H. Munger of the Monterey County Department of Health were extremely helpful and I am grateful for their assistance. I am also thankful for the help provided by Lisa A. Hoefler, Operations Manager and State Humane Officer, Monterey SPCA; Kathy Johannes, North County Wildlife Rehabilitation and Education Center, Paso Robles; George Isaac and Deborah Johnston of the Monterey office of the California Department of Fish and Game; John C. Ramirez of the Monterey County Department of Health; Sergeant Terry L. Kaiser, Investigations Division, Monterey County Sheriff's Department; Jim Hlavaty, United States Coast Guard; Brooks Bowhay, Harbormaster, City of Monterey; Frank Siino, Monterey Bay Boatworks; Frank Sollecito, Monterey Police Department; Robert M. Jones, National Marine Fisheries Service; Andy Russo and Sal Tringale for the tour of the *Sea Wave*; Bob Hurford, California Regional Water Quality Board, San Luis Obispo; Florence Rapp; Mary Swift; Cynthia and Haig Krikorian of Lalime's in Berkeley; and Philip and Nancy Chu of Nan Yang in Oakland.

DON'T TURN
YOUR BACK ON
THE OCEAN

O N LAND, THE BROWN PELICAN LOOKED BIG AND UN-
gainly. This one perched on a fence near the end of the
Coast Guard jetty, a bundle of gray-brown feathers dwarfed by its
huge dark bill and the loose dark brown throat pouch beneath.
The pelican stared at me with one round unblinking eye, set high
in its white-feathered head, then spread its powerful wings and
took flight. I marveled at the bird's unexpected grace as it glided
with military precision between the turquoise water of Monterey
Bay and the clear blue September sky.

Suddenly the pelican altered course and plunged some twenty
feet into the water, breaking the smooth glassy surface. I counted
the seconds until the bird emerged from the water, a silvery fish
wriggling in its beak. The bird straightened its S-shaped neck and
swallowed its prey.

"We've got some sicko at it again," Donna Doyle said, joining
me near the fence. "Just like back in 1984 and 1987. The creep
catches the pelicans, cuts off their beaks or slashes their pouches.
Or both. Then he releases them. Pelicans can't fish without their
beaks, so the birds starve to death."

I shuddered at the image, chilled despite the warm late-
September sun. I turned to look at my cousin. As a private investigator, I'm well aware that there are a great many evil people loose
in the world. Quite often they treat their fellow human beings the
way they treat animals.

"Who's involved in the investigation this time?" I asked.

"We are, of course." In this case, *we* meant the California Department of Fish and Game. My cousin is a biologist who studies and monitors seabirds, specifically the brown pelican, a thirty-million-year-old species that is on the endangered list. Blame DDT and a host of other pollutants.

Donna grasped the mesh of the chain-link fence separating us and other human observers from the rocks that formed the breakwater at the end of the jetty. Dozens of California sea lions sprawled unconcernedly in the early-afternoon sun, their companions an assortment of seagulls, cormorants, and pelicans.

"Also the Monterey County SPCA and the National Marine Fisheries Service, since pelicans are protected. But I thought maybe you could help."

"Me?" I stared at my cousin. She was three years older than me, thirty-six, and a few inches shorter than my own five feet eight inches. Her round fair face was full of freckles, splashed across a snub nose. "What makes you think a private investigator from Oakland can help?"

"The outside observer," Donna said. She ran a hand through her short unruly blond hair. "Another pair of eyes that might see something we've missed. These incidents are similar to the earlier ones, but there are some differences, too. Think about it. I have to talk to someone."

Earlier I'd wondered why my cousin had asked me to meet her here. Now she walked toward the inward side of the jetty, where the vessels of Coast Guard Group Monterey were tied up. Donna went through the gate and boarded the gleaming white cutter. I took a seat on the low concrete wall on the bay side of the jetty, just to the right of two elderly men who'd cast fishing lines into the blue water.

I heard sea lions barking in the distance, beyond the end of the jetty. The creatures congregated under Commercial Wharf Two, farther to the east, where the fishing boats unloaded their day's catch. Fisherman's Wharf was closer, several hundred yards distant. The wharf jutted over the water, buildings and planks balanced on a forest of thick pilings pounded into the bay floor. A number of small boats rode the water in between, at anchor, a picturesque sight for the customers of the restaurants whose broad glass windows sparkled in the afternoon sun.

I shifted, tucking my blue-jean-clad knees under my chin, and gazed out at Monterey Bay, a marvelous sight on this clear autumn day. As the bay curved to the east toward the coastal hills, it was edged by the smooth sand of Del Monte Beach and the mounded dunes along Highway 1, where huge breakers rolled foaming onto the beach. Farther north, past the Salinas River and Castroville, the self-proclaimed artichoke capital of the world, I saw the tower of the Pacific Gas & Electric generating plant at Moss Landing. Beyond that, distance and haze made the shoreline and the coastal hills indistinct as they circled north, then west, past Watsonville, Capitola, and Santa Cruz.

The blue-green water glittered like a jewel, dotted here and there with white foam and froth, moving with tide and current, waves and backwash from the boats that rode its surface. The bay was alive with fish and sleek black sea otters, barking sea lions and harbor seals, white seagulls, brown pelicans, the darker cormorants. Beneath the water's surface kelp drifted gently, hiding place for octopus, squid and rays, schools of fish and thousands of tiny sea creatures, all depending on one another for survival.

The first whale I ever saw was in Monterey Bay. I was five years old, walking hand in hand with my grandfather on the bluff overlooking the rocky shore at Lovers' Point. Suddenly Grandpa pointed at the water. My eyes followed the direction of his hand and I saw a whale breach, close to shore. The creature's enormous gray bulk lifted impossibly high, majestic in slow motion. Then it returned to the mother ocean with a mighty splash as I stood openmouthed, awed, entranced, clinging to Grandpa's hand.

"Well, that was a dead end." Donna tapped me on the shoulder and brought me to the present. "I thought one of the Coasties had a lead, but it didn't pan out. Did you think about what I said?"

"No," I admitted. I'd been drowsing in the sun, and Donna's mutilated pelicans had been far from my mind. "I'm on vacation. I'm here to loll about on Mother's deck, with a can of beer and a paperback, soaking up the sun. A week's respite from personal injury cases and digging information out of tax records at the assessor's office. Even private investigators take vacations."

Not very often, though. I was the sole owner and investigator of J. Howard Investigations. If I took time off, J. Howard didn't get paid. It was different from my five years as an operative for the Errol Seville Agency. Back then I had health and dental insurance provided by the company. But Errol had retired to Carmel eighteen months ago, sidelined by health and age, so I set out on my own.

My cousin tilted her head to one side, a challenge in her blue eyes. "Come on, Jeri, you know you can't resist a puzzle. Meet me this afternoon at the SPCA and talk to my friend Marsha. She's their investigator."

"Okay, okay. Now can we get some lunch? I'm hungry."

"Well ..." Donna's voice trailed off as we continued up the jetty, to where it intersected Cannery Row. Now we walked along the paved Recreation Trail that edged the bay, all the way from Del Monte Beach to Point Pinos at the tip of the Monterey peninsula. The Rec Trail was crowded with people, though it was a weekday, people walking, running, roller-skating, on bikes, or pedaling one of the two-seater jitneys tourists rented down on the Row.

Something else was on Donna's mind, something other than the most recent spate of pelican mutilations. I'd known her all my life and I could pick up on her moods. More than relatives, she and I were friends, similar in age, temperament, and personality. Her father and my mother are siblings, so she is my first cousin, one twig on my extensive maternal family tree. The tree is quite large, with lots of roots here on the peninsula.

I guessed Donna would tell me what was bothering her, in her own good time. "Where are we going for lunch?" I asked.

"The wharf. Ravella's."

"Got the urge for squid. I know you. Fine with me. I just got here yesterday, so I haven't seen Nick or Tina yet."

My family, on my mother's side, is Irish and Italian. Grandpa Dennis Doyle was a big black-haired, blue-eyed Irishman from County Mayo, a fiddle-footed fellow who wandered from Ireland all the way across America, finally lured to Monterey by the work offered by the canneries. He married Angelina Ravella, daughter of a Sicilian who'd been fishing the bay since the turn of the century. And so my two families were linked.

The Ravellas were additional and numerous branches on the

family tree. Granny Doyle's brother Dominic and Dom's sons Nick and Sal carried on the Ravella fishing tradition. Nick was now retired from the fishing fleet. He and his wife Tina operated Ravella's Fish Market, a fixture on the wharf almost as long as there has been a wharf.

A man and woman pedaled toward us in a jitney, weaving from one side of the Rec Trail to the other. A little towheaded boy sat in front of them in the bike's basket, his face beaming in the sunshine. We got out of their way, then Donna stepped off the path, heading for a bluff overlooking this sheltered part of the harbor between the wharf and the shore, where an unoccupied picnic table stood under the shade of a Monterey pine. Below us a sea otter did what otters seem to do best, eating as it floated on its back, oblivious to all but the sun and the water. The otter was close enough to shore that I heard the sound it made as it broke a clamshell on the rock resting on its chest.

"I need to talk with you," Donna said, "before we get to Ravella's."

I turned my gaze from the otter to my cousin's face. Her sandy eyebrows were drawn together, emphasizing her frown. "What else is going on besides these pelican mutilations?" Now I frowned. "Is it family stuff?"

Donna nodded. "Cousin Bobby."

"Of course. Cousin Bobby. In trouble again?"

"Actually he's cleaned up his act. Hasn't been in trouble for a while. Until now."

We stood in silence as the otter below us submerged and swam toward the wharf, the tip of its head visible above the water. Bobby was the youngest of Nick Ravella's brood, the only boy, preceded by three girls. He was twenty-nine, the same age as my own brother Brian. I pictured Bobby, seeing a tough wiry body honed by years of hard work aboard his father's fishing boat, a head of curly black hair atop a lean brown face. He had big brown eyes curtained by long lashes, and a cheeky infectious grin that made sure he never lacked for female companionship.

Bobby was a charmer, all right. He also drank too much, and his reputation as a hell-raiser was legendary. When he had a snootful he got belligerent and argumentative and got into fights.

Even worse, he sometimes climbed into the driver's seat of the lovingly restored classic 1957 T-bird that had once been Nick's, and drove while drunk. As a result he had a couple of DWIs on his driving record and the attention of law enforcement all over Monterey County.

"How and why has Bobby cleaned up his act?" I asked Donna. She and Bobby had always been close, despite the difference in their ages, so she'd certainly be in a position to know.

"The how is AA. He's been going to meetings and staying sober." Donna stepped away from the edge of the bluff. We climbed back up the slope and rejoined the walkers and roller skaters on the Rec Trail. "The why is Ariel Logan."

"A woman," I said. It wouldn't be the first time someone was redeemed by another person's faith. "She must be special."

"Yes. I introduced them, so I feel rather proprietary about the whole thing. It was just over a year ago, last August. She was buying fish at Ravella's. Bobby and I were there. They looked at each other—sparks."

"How did you know Ariel?"

"Her family lives in Carmel. She's a grad student at Cal Poly in San Luis Obispo, studying environmental engineering. She toured our marine pollution lab down at Granite Canyon that summer, so that's how I met her. All this past year Ariel and Bobby were seeing a lot of each other. I know she was bothered by his drinking, because she mentioned it to me. I think she gave him an ultimatum of some sort, last spring. Whatever happened, it took. All of a sudden Bobby straightened out. He's made a real change for the better. I've noticed it. So have his parents. Even his ex-wife noticed it."

"So what's wrong now? You're walking so slow I know you want to tell me before we get to Ravella's."

Donna turned and faced me, her frown deepening. "Ariel Logan is missing."

CHAPTER 2

NEAR FISHERMAN'S WHARF A TREE-SHADED CLEARING held a statue of Santa Rosalia, patron saint of Italian fishermen. A woman in long flowing robes, she stood looking out at the harbor, her hands outstretched, all smooth curving lines. Donna and I stopped near the statue and looked down at the water, washing onto the sandy sliver of beach edging this portion of the shoreline. A young couple had staked out a spot on the beach. They were eating sandwiches and fending off bold seagulls who aimed to part them from their lunch.

I spotted a bench under the stand of Monterey pines and claimed it. Once seated, I stretched my legs out in front of me, staring at the dusty toes of my formerly white athletic shoes. Then I raised my eyes and looked out toward the Coast Guard jetty, watching the progress of a man and a large dog in a dinghy, threading through the larger boats.

"Everyone around here knows I'm Bobby's cousin," Donna said. "I got a call yesterday from someone I know at the sheriff's department. They want to question Bobby."

"Why?"

"Bobby and Ariel quarreled at the Rose and Crown on Alvarado Street, last Friday afternoon. The barmaid and several customers saw them." Donna's hand clawed at her blond curls. "No one has seen Ariel Logan since. Or at least no one will admit to it."

"There must be more to it than that. What else did your source at the sheriff's department tell you?"

"Our old friend the anonymous telephone caller. Something along the lines of, 'If you want to know what happened to Ariel Logan, ask Bobby Ravella.'"

"Could be some wiseass who saw the argument and is trying to be funny."

"Or it could be more serious than that. My friend Marsha at the SPCA has been getting anonymous calls about the pelicans, too. With much the same message."

I sat up straight. "Implicating Bobby in the pelican mutilations? I can't believe that. Not Bobby. He's a fisherman. He loves the sea—and everything about it."

"You and I know that. The fishermen watch the seabirds to find out where the fish are. During the last run of the pelican mutilations several years ago, the fishermen formed a coalition to find out who was doing it. They didn't want to be tarred by that brush. Trouble is, when something like this happens people are quick to point the finger at the fleet." Donna shook her head.

"Now and then we have an incident, someone shooting at sea lions and otters. Fishermen know the animals are protected but they can get exemptions from the Marine Mammals Protection Act. If a sea lion is after a fishermen's catch, he's allowed to use reasonable means to protect it. I don't know that anyone has defined *reasonable means*. Depending on the circumstances, the fisherman can shoot at a sea lion."

"Bobby wouldn't do that," I repeated. "I've been aboard the boat. He uses those noisemakers, those sea-lion bombs, to scare the critters off."

"Right. But he also has a thirty-caliber rifle aboard, just in case." Donna sat beside me on the bench.

I stared out at the water, thinking about my cousin Bobby. He didn't strike me as a guy with a mean streak. He was rowdy, but he had charm and kindness and his grin was quick and ever-present. On the job he was serious and capable. Alcohol was the kicker here, the drug that could change a human being into a monster. His misadventures with alcohol seemed confined to weekends, that period from Friday night to Sunday, when Bobby wasn't out fishing, when he was likely to hoist a few with the guys. It occurred to me now that it had been a while since I'd seen my cousin. I didn't know whether he was caught in the grip of alcoholism, or just a guy who had too many beers on a Saturday night. When does a person cross that boundary?

"There's a line between shooting at a sea lion to scare it away from the catch and someone catching and mutilating pelicans. It takes planning and deliberate cruelty to catch a seabird and cut off its beak. I can't believe Bobby would do that."

Donna shook her head. "Neither can I. Even at his worst. It's just these damned anonymous calls about the pelicans and now Ariel. I don't know what to think, Jeri."

"I think someone's making a big effort to get Cousin Bobby in trouble. When was Ariel reported missing? By whom?"

"Her parents filed the report. They'd been in Europe, didn't get home till Sunday evening. The sheriff's department put out an APB for her car. They found it yesterday, in the parking lot of the Rocky Point Restaurant, down on Highway One."

I watched the couple on the beach below us toss bread crusts to the seagulls. One big white gull caught a crust and took to the air, with his compatriots in pursuit. "You say Ariel's a student at Cal Poly. It's the last week in September. Surely the fall term has started."

Donna nodded. "She should have been in class Friday. Ariel's college roommate says she left San Luis Obispo early Friday morning. The roommate's the one who alerted the Logans that Ariel wasn't where she was supposed to be."

"She cut classes to come up to Monterey," I said, "to see Bobby or for something else. I wonder if she left here on Sunday, on her way back to school. Maybe she was taking the scenic route."

There are two ways to drive from Monterey to San Luis Obispo, a central coast city a hundred and fifty miles farther south, known to its residents as "SLO," an accurate description of the pleasant, unhurried pace of life. If Ariel Logan had been returning to her classes at California Polytechnic University, the faster route would have been to take California 68 northeast from Monterey to Salinas. There she could connect with U.S. 101, a four-lane freeway that ran the length of California, approximating the route of El Camino Real, the King's Highway of the days when California was an outpost of Spain. Depending on how lead-footed she was, and how many stops she made on her way south, Ariel Logan could have made the trip in three hours or less.

The scenic route was down Highway 1, also known as the Coast or Cabrillo Highway. The two-lane road hugged the rocky cliffs and headlands where California crashed into the Pacific Ocean, past some of the most spectacular scenery found anywhere in the world. It was a beautiful drive, good for the soul, a drive a young woman might want to take if she'd had a quarrel with the man in her life. But it was much slower. The narrow two-lane road is popular with tourists in all but winter months, so traffic on Highway 1 usually moves at a glacial pace, which is wise, given the curves. Again, depending on the number of pit stops, Ariel Logan could have made it to SLO in five or six hours. But she never got there.

"What was she doing at the Rocky Point Restaurant?" I wondered aloud. The site where Ariel's car had been found was about ten or eleven miles south of Carmel. The restaurant itself was about half a mile off the road, down a drive leading to the edge of the headland.

"I don't know," Donna said. "Maybe Ariel wasn't on her way back to SLO, Jeri. Which means she could have driven down to Rocky Point anytime after she left Bobby on Alvarado Street."

"Maybe she just needed to stare at the ocean for a while, to sort out that argument with Bobby. There's a beautiful view from the bar, or anywhere on the point. Would she have gone walking on those headlands?"

"I hope not." Donna looked grim. "It's dangerous on this coast. You just don't turn your back on the ocean, not around here. Even when you think you're a safe distance away, one of those waves can suddenly leap up and snatch you right off the face of the earth."

I nodded, recalling something that happened several years ago, when two local women went walking on the ocean's edge, accompanied by a dog. A wave must have swept them out into the Pacific, which doesn't often live up to its name. The dog—or what was left of it—washed ashore several weeks later. I don't think anyone ever found the remains of the women.

Sometimes the ocean lulls you into a false sense of security, even on a broad sandy sweep, like Monastery Beach just south of Carmel. The locals call it Mortuary Beach, with good reason. Here on the Pacific side, the continent ends abruptly. The ocean floor doesn't deepen gradually, like it does on Atlantic beaches. Just under the surface of all that lovely blue-green water is a vicious undertow and an undersea cliff that plunges suddenly deep. Mortuary Beach has claimed its share of victims.

"I hate talking about Ariel in the past tense," Donna said, her voice quiet. "But I'm afraid she went into the water."

"What if she was meeting someone at Rocky Point? Does anyone at the restaurant recall seeing her?"

"I would hope that the sheriff's department has asked that question. Whether they've gotten any answers, I don't know."

"I assume you have a reason for telling me all this. What do you want me to do?"

Donna fixed me with a gaze from her blue eyes. "Talk to Bobby. After my friend at the sheriff's department called yesterday, I went to see Bobby. He seemed surprised, shocked, upset. He didn't know Ariel was missing. He'd tried to call her at her parents' house several times over the weekend and kept getting the answering machine. So he figured she'd gone back to school. He tried to reach her at her apartment down there, with no luck. Couldn't even get Ariel's roommate. Bobby says he hadn't seen or talked with Ariel since Friday, when they had the argument. But he wouldn't say what they were arguing about."

"You and Bobby have always been close. If he won't tell you, what makes you think he'll tell me?"

"I figure if we both work on him, maybe one of us will get him to talk." Donna shrugged. "You know how stubborn he can be. Tuesday it was just Ariel missing. But those phone calls give me a bad feeling. Anyone could have seen Bobby and Ariel arguing at the Rose and Crown. Obviously whoever is making those anonymous calls did."

I got to my feet and stepped back onto the Rec Trail. "Okay, I'll talk to him. Is he likely to be at Ravella's this afternoon?"

"Why do you think I suggested a late lunch there?" Donna said as she joined me on the path.

I grinned. "I thought it was a sudden urge for squid and chips."

"Nick and Tina don't know anything about this," she warned as we walked toward Fisherman's Wharf. "At least not yet. But they will soon. The rumor mill is already working overtime. You can't keep a secret in a small town. And despite the population figures and the big-city pretensions, Monterey's a small town."

CHAPTER 3

A T ONE TIME, THE BUILDINGS ON FISHERMAN'S WHARF were a jumble of restaurants, warehouses, supply shops, most of these one- and two-story wooden structures weathered to a soft silvery gray. The restaurants and fish markets are still there, purveyors of the freshest seafood from Monterey Bay. But the warehouses and supply shops have been replaced by souvenir emporiums full of T-shirts and seashells, decorative spoons and pottery mugs, racks of film for the visitors' cameras and postcards, in case those pictures don't turn out. On Fisherman's Wharf, the catch of the day is tourists.

An organ grinder and his monkey held court at the entrance to the wharf, drawing a crowd of adults and children. To our right were the Old Custom House and the new maritime museum, the municipal parking lot, and beyond that, the two-story harbormaster's office. In front of us, between the two wharves, was a marina, where pleasure craft were interspersed with larger boats fitted for commercial fishing.

I listened to the giggles of the children next to me as they watched the organ grinder's monkey, my eyes taking pleasure in familiar sights. My nose caught the salt tang from the bay, but this was quickly overwhelmed by other smells. As Donna and I headed up the wharf I identified the mix of odors. We passed a restaurant and I caught the smell of grease from french fries, then an outdoor stand provided the warm lure of popcorn and fat soft pretzels with mustard. Farther on, my nostrils were tickled by the sweet spun sugar of pink cotton candy.

Toward the end the wharf is shaped like a stubby H, with a crossbar leading to two shorter piers to the east. Just past the crossbar and to our left was the entrance to Ravella's. It's a deli and a fish market, the front open to the wharf, the back a small dining room with big picture windows looking down at the sheltered portion of the harbor Donna and I had passed on our walk from the Coast Guard jetty.

The fish-market counter was spread with chipped ice. Fish and crabs, both whole and in sections, reposed on the ice and behind the counter was a huge steamer and a rack spread with smoked salmon. Presiding over the fish market was a dark-haired man dressed in khaki pants and short-sleeved white shirt. Over this he wore a sky-blue apron with RAVELLA's embroidered in red script. He'd just wrapped a fish for a customer and now he stepped over to the cash register at the deli counter to ring up the woman's purchase. She handed him a twenty and he made change. Then he looked up and grinned.

"Hey, Jeri, I heard you were here."

"Hi, Nick."

The customer departed with her fish. Nick Ravella wiped his hands on his apron and put his arms around Donna and me, hugging us both in a warm, fish-scented embrace. Just then his wife Tina returned from the dining room, where she'd delivered some sandwiches to a quartet of customers. She wore the same sky-blue apron, only hers was cleaner than Nick's. Before she resumed her station behind the deli counter, she joined in the familial hug.

Nick and Tina were a matched set, both short, their dark hair now gone salt-and-pepper gray, smiling faces showing the lines of nearly sixty years of living. Nick walked with a slight hitch in his left hip, the legacy of a back injury incurred during his years as a fisherman. He's my mother's cousin and contemporary. If I traced Tina's lineage she'd turn out to be related as well, since her family, like the Ravellas, originated in Sicily. All the old fishing families are intertwined.

"You had lunch?" Tina asked us.

"I feel the urgent call of squid and chips," Donna said, not even bothering to look at the menu items chalked on the board behind Tina. "What about you, Jeri?"

I glanced over my shoulder at the salmon on the smoker. "I can't resist that smoked salmon."

"You want cream cheese on it?" Tina asked, reaching for a sourdough roll. I nodded. She picked up a serrated knife and deftly sliced the roll lengthwise, then, without missing a beat, turned to the fryer and lowered the squid and the french fries into their respective pools of hot oil.

"Cholesterol," I said.

Donna gave me the evil eye. "Cream cheese?" She pointed across the deli counter as Tina spread a thick layer on the roll.

"What'll you have to drink?" Nick moved behind the deli counter and opened a refrigerated case.

"Got any mineral water?" He nodded and handed me a cold bottle of Calistoga. Donna opted for the same. Nick helped himself to a can of diet root beer, popped it open, and gulped down a couple of swallows.

"How are Uncle Dom and Aunt Teresa?" I asked, unscrewing the top of my Calistoga. Nick's father was Granny Doyle's younger brother, now in his eighties, the Ravella family patriarch. His wife Teresa was a few years younger and they were both still vigorous and active, powers to be reckoned with in Monterey's large Italian-American community.

"Pop's great," Nick said. "He's probably over at the customhouse plaza right now, playing bocce and solving the problems of the world. Mom was real disappointed you didn't make it down for our picnic on Labor Day. We had Ravellas and Doyles and all the other branches of the family, more'n you could shake a stick at."

I'd been sorry to miss the family get-together, too. But at the time I was embroiled in the Raynor case, something that began as a divorce matter and wound up in murder. Private investigators don't normally get involved in homicides, but lately I'd had more encounters with death than usual. That's why I was looking forward to a week in Monterey with nothing more pressing than visiting relatives and friends. I planned to take a lot of long walks on the Rec Trail interspersed with equally long periods of staring at the ocean, working my way through the stack of paperbacks I'd brought with me. Of course, now that I'd agreed to meet Donna at the SPCA later today, it looked as though I'd do a bit of investigating.

"When did you get in?" Tina asked.

"Yesterday." I'd risen early the day before, Wednesday, and packed my bag under the disapproving eye of my cat Abigail, who didn't like to be left alone. My friend Cassie had an extra key to my Oakland apartment and she would stop each day on her way home from work to feed the cat and take in my mail. It was about a two-hour drive from Oakland to Monterey. I timed my departure after the morning rush hour, hoping to avoid the worst of the traffic, especially through San Jose. Of course, the only time I've never seen traffic in San Jose is at two A.M. The greater San Francisco Bay Area has grown so much that I didn't leave urban sprawl until I got through San Jose and past Morgan Hill and Gilroy. As I drove south on 101, I listened to the radio, flipping stations. An extraterrestrial studying the American airwaves would no doubt be astounded by the time, energy, and money devoted to extolling the merits of diet cola. I know I was.

Tina finished making my sandwich and set the plate on the counter. She turned and piled another plate high with hot squid and chips. "You want anything else?" she asked. "How about some fries?"

"I'll help myself to Donna's."

"The hell you will." Donna picked up her plate and a plastic bottle of ketchup, crossing one arm over her lunch in mock defense.

"This looks like more than enough food," I said, taking my wallet from my jeans. "How much?"

"You're family." Tina waved away my money.

"Half the people in Monterey are family. You'll go broke if you treat them all." I consulted the prices on the menu board and laid several bills on the counter. "Besides, I'd promised to buy Donna lunch."

"All right." Tina shrugged, took the cash, and made change.

"Thanks," Donna said. "I guess I'll let you have a couple of fries after all." She led the way to the first table in the dining room, close enough to the deli counter so we could continue talking with Nick and Tina. Donna tucked a paper napkin into the collar of her shirt, doused her french fries with ketchup, and picked up a morsel of squid. I bit into my sandwich, savoring the flavor of salmon mixed with cream cheese.

Nick went off to wait on a customer at the fish-market counter while Tina gave us a report on the Ravella offspring. Elena, the youngest daughter who lived with her husband in Santa Cruz, was pregnant again, which would increase her brood to three and bring the total grandchild count to six. Bobby and his ex-wife Linda had one son, Nicky. Sally was the oldest daughter, Donna's age. She and her husband had lived right here in Monterey with their two kids. Angie, the daughter who was my age, thirty-three, had no children. She and her husband Stan lived in Morro Bay, near San Luis Obispo, where Angie taught at a community college and Stan worked at the Pacific Gas & Electric plant.

"How's business?" I swallowed a mouthful of salmon and took a hit from my bottle of mineral water.

"Pretty good," Tina said. "Especially during tourist season. All the businesses here on the wharf do well. We're not as fancy as your mom's place, but we do all right."

I filched a couple of Donna's french fries and took another mouthful of my sandwich. My mother's place was an upscale restaurant in downtown Monterey, called Café Marie. She'd opened it six years ago, after she and my father were divorced, using her portion of the settlement for starter capital. It was rather late in life for someone to decide to be a gourmet chef, but she'd always had a talent for cooking. Before the divorce she'd done some catering, then she'd spent sixteen months and a large sum of money attending the extensive course at the California Culinary Academy in San Francisco. From all reports Mother and Café Marie were doing well. The café was now the kind of place that gets four stars from fussy restaurant reviewers who pick apart ambience and service as well as the menu. As a result, on weekends and throughout the tourist season, she had plenty of reservations.

"I hear she hired an assistant," I said, wiping my mouth on a napkin. Admitting that she couldn't do it all herself during one of her twenty-hour days must have been difficult for my mother, who, as far as I was concerned, was obsessed by her restaurant. "That surprised the hell out of me. I didn't think she could stand to have another chef on her turf."

"I told Marie she was wearing herself out," Nick said, returning from the fish market. "She's at that restaurant eighteen, twenty hours a day. Getting dark circles under her eyes. I said she'd better get somebody in there to help her and quit trying to do it all herself. She's my age, neither of us getting any younger. She interviewed a bunch of people before she hired this guy. But she's still putting in those eighteen-hour days. I think she's working the assistant just as hard as she works herself. You oughta talk to her, Jeri."

"Sure," I said, trading looks with Donna. As if I could talk to Mother about anything. Well, I could talk, but she probably wouldn't listen.

"Summer's such a busy time, for all of us," Tina commented. "I know it's nearly October, but as long as the weather's good it's tourist season."

As if to underscore her words, a man and a woman stepped up to the deli counter. The man had a camera bag draped over his shoulder and both customers wore Monterey Bay Aquarium T-shirts over their cotton shorts. They inspected the menu board above Tina's head and ordered. Nick spotted a customer inspecting the fish spread out on the ice, so he moved back over to the fish-market side of Ravella's.

"I hope the assistant chef is young, strong, and patient." I took a long drink of my mineral water.

Donna laughed and rolled her eyes. "Have you seen him?"

"No. I haven't been near the place. I just got here yesterday, remember?" I reached for one of Donna's fried squid tentacles and dipped it into a puddle of ketchup. She retaliated by filching a chunk of smoked salmon from my sandwich. "So tell me about this assistant. Judging from the glint in your baby blues, there's a story here."

"Heathcliff, all dark and brooding and compelling, with dozens of peninsula females longing to be his Cathy." Donna snorted derisively and waggled her bottle of mineral water for emphasis.

"Been reading the Brontës again? Just what is this fellow's name? Is he a refugee from the Yorkshire moors or somewhere else?"

"Julian Surtees. He's a refugee from Los Angeles."

I repeated the name. "Sounds like he made it up. Maybe he's an unemployed actor. Of course, you know he had to have impeccable credentials before my mother would let him into her kitchen. You don't suppose he's charmed Mother?"

"Oh, Marie's been dating someone."

"Indeed," I said, picking up my sandwich again. This was news to me. But I'd barely seen my mother since arriving the afternoon before. When I parked my car along the curb outside her two-bedroom house on Larkin Street, she'd been on her way to the restaurant. She had greeted me with a quick distracted peck on the cheek and her extra key before departing. I rustled up my own dinner from her refrigerator and cupboards, which were as minimally stocked as my own. You'd think a woman who runs a classy restaurant would have some food in the house.

Donna didn't elaborate on my mother's social life. She occupied the ensuing gap in the conversation by reducing the pile of squid on her plate. I whittled down my sandwich and watched the two customers file past us, drinks in hand. They took a table at the big picture window that looked out on the harbor. The woman pointed at something. The man barely glanced in the direction of her hand as he busied himself with his camera. I looked toward the front of Ravella's and saw Tina busy behind the counter as Nick rang up a purchase on the cash register. Then he rejoined us.

"Your mom tell you about what's been going on at the restaurant?" he asked.

I finished chewing my mouthful of salmon and washed it down with mineral water. Everyone seemed to think that on my arrival in Monterey for my long-delayed visit, Mother and I had immediately launched into a long motherly-daughterly talk. That was rarely the case. I don't get along with my mother. She doesn't get along with me. On those few occasions when we do converse, we don't veer into dangerous subjects, like my choice of profession or her walking out on my father. If we tread on that ground, the conversation becomes an argument.

"I didn't talk to Mother at all last night, Nick. She was on her way to work when I drove in. I was in bed before she got home." I picked up my mineral water, wondering if Mother had been planning to tell me about the man she'd been dating, or what Nick just brought up. It was typical that I'd hear it from someone else first. "What's been happening at the restaurant?"

Nick and Donna looked at each other, then Nick shrugged and plunged right in. "Well, accidents, I guess you'd call it."

"I wouldn't call it that," Donna said, squirting more ketchup on her remaining french fries. "At first it looked like accidents. But the last, those had to be deliberate."

I waited for them to explain but they didn't get the chance. Nick looked past me and I followed the direction of his eyes. A man approached us from the wharf. He wore faded blue jeans, a stained ocher T-shirt, and thick-soled shoes. He looked tired as he walked slowly past a middle-aged woman who stared intently at a fish on the iced counter. He had a slender wiry frame, muscles visible along his shoulders and forearms, and a head of thick black curls. His olive skin had been burned even darker by the sun and chapped by the ocean spray, making him look older than his years. His shoulders were slumped and his head was down. He moved as though he were on automatic pilot and he didn't look up until he was about six feet from the table where Donna and I sat. Then he saw us and the smile that broke out dissipated whatever cloud lowered on his face.

"Look who's here," Bobby said, hands on the hips of his Levi's. "My good-lookin' cuz from Oakland. Give me a kiss."

I wiped my hands on a napkin and rose to meet him. Bobby was about five-ten, just a couple of inches taller than me. He gave me a quick peck on the cheek, then put his strong arms around my waist and squeezed. He smelled of fish and sweat and salt spray. As we embraced, Donna leaned back in her chair and surveyed us both. "What about me?" Her voice held a bantering tone. "Don't I get a kiss?"

"I see you all the time," Bobby said. He released me and leaned over, brushing Donna's forehead with his lips. Then he gave his father a companionable slap on the shoulder. "Hey, Pop. How's business?"

"Pretty good," Nick said. "How about you? You have a good day? How many tons?" Bobby shrugged and named a figure. Nick frowned. "That's not a full load."

Bobby grinned and shrugged again. "The squid seem to be vacationing elsewhere, ladies. Down in Morro Bay, maybe. We're having to go out farther and longer. Pop, it looks like I'm gonna have to overhaul that fish pump."

He was referring to a vital piece of equipment used to move all those tons of squid from the nets into the hold. My cousin's boat is a purse seiner called the *Nicky II*, named for his son. It was a successor to the *Nicky I*, which was Uncle Dom's boat back in the early days. Bobby fishes for squid, mackerel, anchovies, and sardines, though at the moment it seemed he was concentrating on squid.

I knew the squid fishery was regulated and Monterey's fishermen could catch the tentacled delicacies from midnight to noon. That means the boats go out at ten or ten-thirty in order to be in position by midnight. Then they come back around noon to unload their holds. Even then, there were other things to occupy the crew, such as cleaning up the boat, repairing a torn net, seeing to machinery that needed maintenance or repair. That's why Bobby looked exhausted. It was past one in the afternoon. He'd been working fourteen hours. From here, he'd go back to his apartment, shower, and try to get some sleep before starting all over again this evening.

Bobby stepped past Nick and gave Tina a brief kiss as she bustled out of the deli to the dining room, carrying two plates with sandwiches to the customers who sat next to the window. He opened the refrigerated case behind the counter. Immediately in front of him were several bottles of beer. His hand hovered near one, then he reached past it and pulled out a soda. He popped the top, tilted the can, and drank a good portion of its contents before setting it on the counter and wiping his lips with the back of his hand.

Tina looked at him severely as she returned to her station behind the deli counter. "You had anything to eat?" Bobby shook his head. "I'll fix you a sandwich. What do you want?"

"Pastrami," he told her.

"Okay. Get out of my way. Go talk to Jeri and Donna."

Banished from behind the counter, Bobby joined Nick, who stood near our table. "Say, Jeri," he said, with a wicked sparkle in his brown eyes. "I'm short a man. You want to go squid fishing?"

I groaned. "Not a chance." My chronic seasickness was a long-standing source of family merriment. How could a child with so many fishermen in her lineage get seasick? But I much prefer to admire the ocean from the shore. I'd gone out on the boat now and then. The memory makes me queasy.

"Why are you shorthanded?" Donna asked.

"I fired Frank in June. Then the guy I hired to take his place quit. Haven't been able to find anyone to replace him. Not as many fishermen around as there used to be."

What Bobby said about not being able to find another crewman surprised me. Monterey's fishing fleet is still a vital local industry, employing about two thousand people in its various aspects, not just fishing but processing.

"I keep hearing that fishing is in a decline," I said, "but the harbor looks just as busy as ever."

"According to Grandpa Dom, we're an endangered species, like the spotted owl." Bobby took another sip from his soda can. "He says the days of the independent operator are numbered."

Nick shook his head. "Pop and I disagree on that. Not here, not in Monterey. Besides, it depends on what kind of fish you're after. It's just the warm current this year. That's why the squid aren't coming into the bay."

"The salmon fishery is way down," Donna said. "Salmon depend on freshwater runoff. We had seven years of drought. Add to that all the problems from pollution, logging, agriculture. Clear-cutting of lumber silts up the streams and most of the freshwater flow goes to farmers and the cities. Not much left for fish."

"I hear there's a move afoot to put the coho salmon on the endangered list," I said, "for just those reasons."

"To hear the salmon fishermen tell it," Bobby said, "there's too much government regulation."

Donna shook her head and put on her Fish-and-Game persona. "If we didn't put quotas on salmon, they'd harvest as many as they could. If they overfish they'll kill the whole fishery. Remember the sardines."

How could anyone in Monterey forget the sardines? The little silver fish had fueled the canneries for nearly half a century. Then, in the early fifties, the sardines vanished from Monterey Bay. No one is sure why. Overfishing had much to do with it. Both fishermen and biologists speculate that it was due to a naturally occurring cycle that spans many years. Both theories may be correct. In recent years the sardines have come back to the bay, but in smaller numbers.

"How long you gonna be in town?" Bobby asked me.

"A week. We should get together and catch up."

"Sure thing," he told me. "Wait'll you see Nicky. The kid's growing like a weed."

Tina brought Bobby a loaded plate. He sat at the table opposite me and Donna, picked up his sandwich, and dug into it as though he hadn't eaten in a week. He was halfway through it when someone entered Ravella's. Donna spotted the new arrival before I did, her eyes narrowing as she looked over my shoulder. I turned in my seat and examined the newcomer.

Law enforcement, I thought, looking him over with a practiced eye. He was a tall man, big shoulders crowding the jacket of his lightweight gray suit. He appeared to be in his forties, with a craggy lined face and a lot of gray in his short sandy hair. His bushy eyebrows fanned over a pair of flinty gray eyes that swiveled around Ravella's and finally settled on Bobby.

"Bobby Ravella?" he asked.

Bobby put down his sandwich and wiped mustard from the corner of his mouth. "Yeah, I'm Bobby Ravella."

"Sergeant Mike Magruder, Monterey County Sheriff's Department." The man in the gray suit pulled out a folder and showed Bobby his badge. "I'd like to talk with you, Mr. Ravella."

"What about?" Bobby asked slowly, his brown eyes troubled.

"About a friend of yours who's been reported missing. A woman named Ariel Logan."

"I haven't seen her since Friday." Bobby stared past the sergeant at nothing in particular.

"That's what I hear," Magruder said.

"Any news?" Donna asked.

Magruder didn't answer right away. When he did, his eyes were glued on Bobby's face. So were mine. As the sergeant spoke Bobby's right hand tightened on the can he held. His jaw muscles tensed and he looked as if anyone touched him he would shatter like glass.

"County dive-and-rescue unit just went out," Magruder said, his voice even. "We got a report late this morning. A woman's body washed up on a beach near Rocky Creek Bridge. We think it's Ariel Logan."

CHAPTER 4

U NTIL SERGEANT MAGRUDER MENTIONED THE BODY, I
think everyone who knew her hoped that Ariel Logan had
simply gone somewhere, anywhere, for a few days. Ariel was just
cooling off after her argument with Bobby. Soon she would surface and things would get back to normal.

When I glanced at Donna, who had expressed the fear that
Ariel had gone into the water, I knew that even she had clung to
that hope. I looked at Bobby, slumped in his chair. His dark face
had gone white around his mouth, now tensed into a line as he
compressed his lips.

"How long will it take to identify that body?" I asked.

"Depends on how long it's been in the water." Magruder
scanned me carefully, as though wondering who I was. His face
revealed nothing. "And how difficult it is for the rescue team to retrieve it. We've asked Miss Logan's parents for her dental records,
just in case. I'm not saying it's her, but Miss Logan's car was
found in the lot at the Rocky Point Restaurant. That's close
enough to Rocky Creek to make it a possibility."

The sergeant's eyes were like chips of stone in his rough-hewn
face. After giving me a thorough once-over, he turned those eyes
back to Bobby. "You say you hadn't seen Miss Logan since
Friday."

"That's what I said." Bobby's voice was curt. As the sergeant
continued to probe I looked past him at Nick and Tina Ravella.
They both looked stunned, just now realizing that the sergeant was

questioning their son as though Bobby was suspected of having something to do with Ariel Logan's death.

Sergeant Magruder wasn't getting much from Bobby. No, he hadn't seen Ariel Logan since they'd parted on the sidewalk outside the Rose and Crown Friday afternoon. How many times did he have to say it? What he and Ariel had argued about was private, he told Magruder, and he wouldn't say anything more. Finally Bobby stood up, his movements abrupt and jerky. He walked out of Ravella's without a backward glance at his parents or the sergeant.

Magruder's flinty eyes followed my cousin as he walked up the wharf and finally disappeared from view. Then he excused himself and left what had been, until now, a pleasant waterfront café.

Donna had to get back to work. Before we left Ravella's I fought down my own feelings of disquiet and tried to reassure Nick and Tina that everything would be all right. But even as I said the words I wasn't sure. From the way Sergeant Magruder examined Bobby, he seemed to be fitting my cousin for a pair of handcuffs.

"I'm going say hello to Uncle Dom," I told Donna when we reached the entrance of Fisherman's Wharf, where the monkey capered in front of the organ grinder.

"Okay. I'll see you at four, at the SPCA." She waved and set off along the Rec Trail.

I walked past the Old Custom House, once the port of entry for Monterey Harbor, now a museum of Monterey's past, the rock-and-adobe walls filled with trade goods typical of those that came round the Horn in the 1830s. Across the sunny plaza I saw two sand-and-concrete courts where bocce was played.

I've never quite been able to understand the rules of this old Italian game, which involves bowling balls at other balls. Uncle Dom says my lack of knowledge is because my Italian blood has been diluted. According to him, that's also why I get seasick.

I spotted Uncle Dom at the end of one of the courts, his compact body attired in brown slacks and a checked shirt. Ball in hand, he prepared his shot, squinting down the court. This is how Bobby will look in fifty years, I thought, black hair silvered, olive face lined, muscles gone flaccid with age. Uncle Dom drew back his right hand and let go the ball, which found its mark, to mur-

murs of approval. The language here was Italian, all the players were men, and most of them were older, though I spotted a couple of youngsters my age. As another man readied his shot my great-uncle saw me and walked over to greet me. He threw his arms wide, enveloping me in an embrace.

"About time you came to see us," he boomed. He'd been born right here in Monterey but still his voice held the flavor of his parents' Sicilian tongue, the language spoken at home while he was growing up. "Why you stay away for so long?"

My protestations of being busy didn't cut any fish with Uncle Dom. He was of a generation and a culture where women stayed home and cared for husband and children. Even if he accepted the fact that things weren't like that today, family was still important. I should check in with them more often.

He led the way to a concrete retaining wall on the far side of the bocce courts and we sat down. I looked at him disapprovingly as he took a pack of cigarettes from his shirt pocket. "You shouldn't be smoking."

"I'm eighty years old," he retorted as he fired up his cigarette. "It hasn't killed me yet. You been down to the wharf, to see Nick and Tina?"

"Donna and I had lunch there. We saw Bobby."

I told Uncle Dom what had happened at Ravella's and his face darkened. He muttered something in Italian, no doubt a comment on Sergeant Magruder's antecedents.

"Why is this cop sniffing around Bobby?" Uncle Dom asked. "He's foolish. Bobby wouldn't hurt anyone, especially not his girl. He loves this girl. So they had a fight. Who doesn't? Me and your aunt Teresa, we fight all the time."

I smiled. Aunt Teresa could be a formidable opponent. "Maybe the body they found isn't even Ariel."

"If it is her, could have been an accident. Bodies go into the water all the time. Boats get swamped, someone gets washed overboard. A lot of good fishermen go that way. The ocean's a dangerous place. Don't I know?" He rubbed his left arm and I knew he was thinking about a bad break years ago, out on the fishing boat during a storm, when he'd gotten tangled in a line.

The old man sighed and puffed on his cigarette. "I hope it's not her. She's a nice girl, good for Bobby. That boy, he's got enough trouble right now. He's shorthanded, had to fire that no-good Frank, but he's better off without a man like that." Dom scowled. "That Frank, back when he was working salmon boats, he rammed another guy's boat."

And that, I knew, broke one of the sacred rules of conduct of the Monterey fleet. You never damage another guy's boat. You never make threats. And above all, you never say something bad about another man's family. Which would, of course, be like disparaging your own, since everyone was related by blood or marriage.

Uncle Dom winked at me. "If I can give Teresa the slip, I'll go out fishing with Bobby. Show him how we used to do it in the old days, before they had all that fancy equipment."

Giving Aunt Teresa the slip would be a slick trick indeed and I laughed at the picture of Uncle Dom's bride of nearly sixty years barring the door.

"I'd like to go fishing again," he said, "before it's all gone."

"You think it's disappearing."

"Hell, yes, just like the sardines. By the time young Nicky grows up, there won't be any fishing boats left. Just rich people's sailboats."

"Why?" I asked.

"Who knows? Maybe this girl of Bobby's, this Ariel, was right. She used to talk about passenger pigeons. How there were so many and now they're all gone. She said people are polluting the ocean too much, taking too many fish. Big commercial outfits with lots of boats and equipment, driving little operators out of business. I've seen those big foreign trawlers with their drift nets, sucking up everything for miles." The old man sighed and shook his head. "I'm telling you, Jeri, some days I feel like one of those pigeons. It's not like it used to be."

No, it wasn't. Things seldom are. As I walked back along the Rec Trail later, I felt the pull of the past, one I'd read about, heard about all my life.

I'd parked my car in a lot near the Coast Guard jetty, where it joined the street that used to be called Ocean View Drive. The city changed the name to Cannery Row in 1953, some eight years after John Steinbeck wrote the book describing that street as "a poem, a stink, a grating noise, a quality of light, a tone, a habit, a nostalgia, a dream."

Mother remembered the stink above all else. It came from fish in all stages of processing, being cleaned and cut, cooked and packed into cans. Added to that was the stench of fish meal and the rotting remains.

"You can't imagine," she'd say, when anyone colored the past with nostalgia. "It was indescribable."

I love old movies and there's one from 1952, *Clash by Night*, that's set in Monterey, on Cannery Row. It stars Barbara Stanwyck and a very young Marilyn Monroe. Marilyn's supposed to be a cannery worker, but she looks much too well scrubbed. When Mother and I watched the film, Mother was reduced to howls of laughter.

"It wasn't like that at all," she said. "Where's the muck and the fish oil? Where's the smell?"

The odor permeated Mother's childhood, since Dennis and Angelina Doyle began married life in a cannery worker's cottage on Foam Street. Most of these little houses have long since been torn down to make way for other structures. The canneries also added to the financial prosperity of the Doyle family, which grew in children and income, finally moving up the New Monterey hill to a larger house on Prescott Avenue.

Grandpa worked at the Hovden Cannery, producing Portola-brand sardines. The old black-and-white photos of the era show fishing boats unloading tons of silver sardines, and the huge canneries, smokestacks poking into the sky, that lined both sides of the Row, linked by walkways high above the street. The people who worked in the canneries are preserved, too, in photographs showing men and women in smocks and aprons, with kerchiefs or nets covering their hair, standing at the cutting and packing tables.

All of this I've learned secondhand, of course. By the time I was born the sardines had vanished from Monterey Bay. Through the fifties and sixties the canneries shut down one by one. Many of the derelict buildings were destroyed by fire, both accidental and, as local gossip would have it, deliberate. Grandpa Doyle retired and his visits to Cannery Row were limited to walking hand in hand with a small granddaughter named Jeri.

We went to the Row to visit the ghosts, as Grandpa called all those empty buildings with pilings stretching out into the bay. He'd recite the names of the defunct canneries—Del Vista, Edgewater, Aeneas, Enterprise, San Carlos—names still visible on the outer walls, lettering blurred by time and the elements.

Grandpa pointed out Doc Ricketts's lab and the Wing Chong Market and the shell of the Hovden Cannery, describing how the fishing fleet would tie up at the end of those pilings and unload their catch. Then we walked past the Hopkins Marine Laboratory, along the shore to Lovers' Point, looking out at the bay for breaching whales. Grandpa told me the names of the different birds we saw, explained why sea otters float on their backs, and taught me that sea lions have ears and harbor seals don't.

Grandpa wouldn't recognize the Hovden Cannery now. The Monterey Bay Aquarium rests on the Hovden foundation, and some of the cannery equipment is displayed inside. The aquarium wrought a change here, deep and fundamental, as eventful as the departure of the sardines. It seems half the world wants to look at fish and sea otters. Since its debut in 1984 a steady growing stream of people came to Monterey to visit the aquarium. The city seemed ill-prepared for the onslaught.

Now there are parking garages and shuttle buses to ferry visitors from the Wharf to the Row. The buildings where sardines were once packed into tins now pack in tourists, luring them with souvenirs and fast food. The common complaint voiced by locals is that you can't drive to Pacific Grove on Saturdays, because of the traffic heading for Cannery Row, and it's hard to get into the good restaurants.

All of this means jobs and revenue for the city. But it's changed Monterey's face forever. The city was learning, as others had over the years, that tourism has two hands, one taking as much as the other gives.

CHAPTER 5

ASALINAS-BOUND PICKUP TRUCK WHIZZED PAST ME ON
Highway 68 as I braked and made the right turn onto the
narrow asphalt ribbon that wound uphill through a meadow to the
Monterey County SPCA. The ducks and geese had the right of
way, roaming freely over the grassy area on either side of the road
and gliding on a nearby pond.

The road led first to a parking lot that bordered several low
buildings, then snaked farther up the hills. I spotted dog runs in
the back of one building. This was the animal shelter, where dogs
and cats without people were either adopted or put to death.
Whenever I visited such a place I always wanted to take the creatures home with me. That impulse had to be balanced by the reality of living in a one-bedroom apartment with an irascible cat
named Abigail who was quite sure she was the only cat in the
universe.

I saw Donna's Jeep Cherokee and pulled into the space next to
it. "Marsha's up at the wildlife center," she said, getting out and
slamming the door. "It's not far. We'll walk."

She led the way up the asphalt road to some outbuildings, waving a greeting at a young woman who was working on a truck.
The road forked and we took the path to the right, climbing farther
up the hillside covered with oaks and Monterey pines and brush to
the wildlife center, located in a wooded clearing, masked from the
view of people below.

As we approached the one-story wooden building I saw other

structures on the hillside to the left. Donna explained that these were holding tanks for marine mammals, such as harbor seals or sea lions. The center's purpose was to treat sick and injured animals and return them to the wild. Its isolation on this hillside was so the animals encountered as few humans as necessary.

When we entered the building I saw a large cage sitting just to the right of the door. At the moment it was empty, and so was the small office to the left of the entrance. Directly in front of us a door led to an L-shaped room full of large cages, some taller than others. Many of these wire-and-mesh enclosures were draped with sheets. Donna explained that this was to keep the occupants safe from prying eyes or, in the case of the nocturnal creatures, so they could sleep during the day. When I peered through the glass window next to the door I saw a rabbit in the nearest cage. It gazed back at me with wild wide eyes, its nose twitching.

"Marsha," Donna called, listening for a response. Down the hallway to our left I heard water running. We walked toward the sound. I followed Donna into a large concrete-floored room. Most of the room was fenced off with a large mesh screen and there was a pool of water in the center of the concrete floor. Seabirds clustered around the pool, including several gulls. I recognized a sleek black cormorant and saw the black heads and white breasts of two common murres.

There was no mistaking the big brown pelicans, two of them, as large as the one I'd seen earlier today at the Coast Guard jetty. They dwarfed the other residents of the enclosure. Both were mature adults, with grayish-brown feathers and white heads over their big dark bills and throat pouches. Their powerful wings were folded close to their bodies. To my uneducated eyes the pelicans didn't appear to be injured, but they must be at the wildlife center for a reason. They stared at me warily with black beaded eyes and moved farther away, toward the other side of the pond.

"Is that you, Donna?"

The voice came from just beyond a screen door opposite us, leading outside the building. The door opened and two women stepped through. The first was an older woman with curly gray hair and glasses. She was followed by a woman who appeared to be in her thirties. Her brown hair was short and pulled back from her face, showing a pair of tiny gold studs sparkling in her earlobes. Both women wore rubber-soled shoes, slacks, and shirts covered by pale blue smocks stained with water and soil. I saw a gray-brown feather caught in the seam that joined the pocket to the younger woman's smock, next to a reddish-brown splotch that could have been blood.

Donna made the introductions. The younger woman, as I'd guessed, was Marsha Landers, Donna's friend who worked at the SPCA. Helena, the older woman, was a volunteer, one of several who staffed the wildlife center. Now Helena excused herself. She passed us and opened the door we'd just come through, heading back up the hallway.

"What's with these two?" Donna asked, indicating the pelicans.

"The female got caught in a net," Marsha said. "The male has an injured wing. They should be ready for release in a few days." Donna nodded and I looked at the huge seabirds again, wondering how one sexed a pelican.

"I heard on the radio that a body was found down at Rocky Creek." Marsha opened the door that led to the hallway. "Do you think it's Ariel Logan?"

"I hope not." Donna followed Marsha down the corridor and I brought up the rear.

"How do you know Ariel?" I asked.

"I talked to her this summer, middle of August, I think. I'd have to look at my calendar. She'd seen a couple of sea lions in distress at Point Pinos."

"What was wrong with the animals?"

"I don't know. She was alone, walking along the Rec Trail. By the time she found a phone and called the SPCA, the animals were gone. From the way she described it, the animals were having seizures. It could have been something they'd ingested, something they swam through. Maybe they'd contracted some illness. But without examining the animals, I have nothing to go on."

Marsha frowned. "I haven't received any other reports about sea lions or seals, so I'm hoping those were isolated incidents. We've been so occupied with these pelican mutilations. In fact we found one the same day Ariel saw the sea lions."

Now Marsha looked at Donna. "We had another one this morning. The crew of the *Mary Esther* brought it in."

"Where is it?" Donna asked.

"It didn't make it." Marsha looked grim. "The beak had been hacked off and the throat pouch slashed. That's the eighth one."

Donna swore under her breath. When we reached the entry area I glanced through the window in the L-shaped room and saw Helena cleaning out cages. Marsha opened the office door. The room held a cluttered desk and a couple of filing cabinets and two chairs. All in all it was barely large enough to hold all three of us. Marsha sat down in the chair nearest the desk and waved me to the other, while Donna stood in the doorway.

"Donna said you might be able to help us," Marsha said.

"I don't know," I said frankly. "Donna tells me you're a state humane officer, and the National Marine Fisheries Service agent is investigating as well. That might be too many people messing around in the same patch."

Marsha nodded. "That's true. I thought maybe an outside observer could pick up on something we'd missed. I'm very frustrated by this, Jeri. It makes me angry and I'd like to nail whoever's responsible."

When I didn't answer right away, she reached into the open leather briefcase that took up much of the desk's surface. It held some file folders and a five-by-seven brown envelope. This she handed to me.

"Take a look at those pictures, from several years ago," Marsha said, "and you'll see why I'm angry that it's happening again."

I opened the envelope and pulled out the contents. All the words Donna and Marsha had used to describe the mutilations had not prepared me for the reality documented in these color photographs.

The first showed a pelican on an examining table, its feathers stained with blood from the bird's beak—or what was left of it. The long formidable-looking bill had been hacked off with an ax or a saw, and what remained was a ragged and truncated appendage that left the pelican helpless. The dark brown throat pouch, which expanded as the bird sucked up water and small fish to feed, hung in ribbons of flesh, slashed by some sharp instrument.

As I sifted through the photographs I grew more sickened and appalled. Bird after bird lay on the table, each with a variation of the same cruel injuries. Some of the pelicans were obviously dead, and I wondered how many had actually survived this treatment. I've seen what humans do to each other, but somehow this was worse. The pelicans didn't have any defense against the warped strength and design of the human predator who had done this to them.

"How many were attacked like this before?" I shoved the grotesque photos back into the envelope and handed it to Marsha.

"One hundred twenty-five birds in 1984. Sixty-three in 1987. Those are only the ones we know about," Marsha said. "Birds that were reported to us or caught and brought here. Most of them didn't survive. Pelicans can still fly when they're injured like that. But they can't catch fish without their beaks and pouches, so they starve. A lot of them weren't caught and brought in until they were too weak. We didn't have much luck with prosthetics on the beaks. They're a lot like a human fingernail. Once broken, they're hard to repair. We did have some success stitching pouches back together, if the wounds weren't too deep or necrotic."

I looked from her to Donna. "Are they that easy to catch?" Whenever I saw a pelican sitting on a railing at the wharf I never had the urge to walk up and touch it. With their size and those long bills, I'd always thought the birds looked rather fierce.

"Unfortunately, yes," Donna said, shifting position where she stood in the doorway. "They're trusting and easily tamed. And they've learned to associate people with food. When wild animals lose their fear of humans, that's an invitation to trouble."

Marsha nodded in agreement. "We had quite a problem with pelicans and sea lions on Fisherman's Wharf."

"That was a few years back, when people could still buy fish scraps to feed the sea lions and the birds," Donna added. "The sea lions started congregating on the marina, even climbing onto the boats berthed there. You get three or four sea lions in one place and we're talking a ton or so of extra weight. They actually broke some of the decking and swamped a couple of small boats. The pelicans were wandering into the shops and restaurants, looking for handouts. Eventually the merchants on the wharf stopped sell-ing fish scraps and the sea lions moved back to the Coast Guard jetty."

"So if I wanted to catch a pelican I could just lure it with some fish."

Donna nodded. "Throw a sheet over it to disorient the bird, and you've caught yourself a pelican."

I turned to Marsha. "When Donna told me about this earlier she said you thought this current spate of mutilations was different from the earlier ones. Why?"

"Sheer numbers, for one thing." Marsha tilted her head to one side. "In previous years, the number of injured or dead birds was overwhelming. Counting the one that died this morning, we've had eight mutilated pelicans. It's been sporadic, starting in June. That's another thing, the time of year. Both of the previous incidents started in the late fall."

"Most brown pelicans migrate from Southern California and Baja," Donna said. "They arrive in Monterey Bay in mid-September. But we do have a small resident colony that's here year-round. They stay where the food is and this is a rich fishery."

"According to Donna," I said, "the local fishermen formed a coalition last time. To find out who was attacking the pelicans, because they didn't want to be blamed. Who were your suspects the last time? Or did you have any?"

"There was clearly more than one person doing it," Marsha said. "We had all sorts of leads, but none of them panned out. I didn't view the commercial fishermen as suspects at all. They make their living from the sea and they know brown pelicans are protected. If anything, they have more problems with sea lions than seabirds. Sport fishermen are different. The last time I suspected a couple of men who crewed on one of those hire boats that take people out for a day's fishing. We had several tips about some juveniles as well. Couldn't prove either theory."

"I don't know what I can do," I said, "that you local people aren't already doing. Nose around, maybe, see if I hear anything. The differences in the time of year and the number of birds are interesting. May I have a list of the dates the birds were found? And while you're at it, a copy of the report Ariel Logan made about the sea lions." As Marsha complied with my request I turned to

Donna. "Maybe the person who is mutilating the pelicans has a different agenda."

"A copycat?" Donna asked. "But why?"

"To draw attention away from something else. Those earlier incidents got a lot of press. I read about them in the Bay Area papers. That could be how the current perpetrator knows what was done to the pelicans before. The injuries have been similar." I shook my head. "It's easy enough just to say that the person is sick or warped. Maybe there's another reason."

"Before, we contacted the press," Marsha said, "hoping for tips from the public. And we did get quite a few calls. We haven't yet publicized this current round of incidents. But if the numbers increase, the word will get out. The press did a good job of arousing public interest, but when it comes to pelicans we have to contend with the cute factor."

I nodded. "Pelicans aren't as pretty as otters."

"Exactly," Donna said. "When something bad is happening to wildlife, people get riled in proportion to how cute and cuddly the animal is. Otters are high on the adorable scale, above sea lions and harbor seals. Mammals are higher than birds and both are higher than fish. If you're a marine invertebrate, forget it."

"Are these crewmen who worked on the sport fishing boat still around? Maybe I can have a talk with them."

"I think so. If I recall, they were both local." Marsha consulted one of the file folders in her briefcase. "Yes, here are the names. Derry McCall and Frank Alviso."

Donna frowned. "McCall doesn't ring any bells, but Alviso does. Jeri, you remember what Bobby said at Ravella's earlier today? About firing a guy named Frank? I think that's the same Frank."

CHAPTER 6

MY MOTHER'S EVENING RITUAL IS ALWAYS THE SAME. By the time she comes home from her restaurant it's late evening. She strips off her clothing, runs a boiling-hot bubble bath, and soaks in the tub until the hot water cools. Then, in her sensible cotton nightgown and robe, feet scuffing along in her slippers, she moves tiredly to the kitchen, where she puts the teakettle on to boil. When the hot water and steam whistle through the spout, she makes herself a mug of peppermint tea and sits at the kitchen table, sipping the fragrant liquid and staring into space until she is sufficiently unwound from her long day to finally go to bed.

I operate best during the day. Unless the case I'm working on requires it, I go to bed before eleven. I've been known to doze off in front of the television or over a book while I read in bed. Last night, my first in Monterey, was no exception. I had gone to bed early, after a solitary dinner and phone calls to several people I wanted to see while I was in town. So when my mother emerged from her bath, she was surprised to see me in the kitchen. I'd already put the teakettle on the burner of the gas stove, and the water was making preliminary popping and squeaking noises as its temperature rose.

"You're up late," she said, glancing first at the digital clock on the microwave, then at me. Her gray-streaked black hair, damp from her bath, curled in tendrils around her long face and at the collar of her rose-colored terry-cloth bathrobe. I sat on a kitchen chair, one bare foot tucked under me, in my oversize T-shirt and a striped seersucker robe. I'd been reading in bed as I waited up for her.

"I thought we could talk while we have some tea."

"Sure." Mother's black eyebrows lifted a bit at this. We didn't usually talk much. She walked to one of the kitchen cupboards and opened it, taking out two bright pink ceramic mugs. Next to the stove was a painted tin. She pulled the lid off this and removed two tea bags, placing one in each mug. Then she left the mugs on the counter, pulled out a chair, and sat down, elbows on the surface of the round wooden table, her chin cradled in one hand.

I looked at her with my investigator's eyes, those of the objective observer. The woman who sat across from me looked exhausted, dark circles under her eyes, lines pulling her mouth down in a frown. She looked like a woman with a great deal on her plate. I wondered that I hadn't noticed it yesterday. Perhaps I hadn't been looking.

"What did you do today?" Mother asked.

"I met Donna for lunch. We went to Ravella's."

"I figured you two would get together as soon as possible." Mother mustered a brief smile, then her face settled back into its sober repose.

"Donna heard through the grapevine that the authorities wanted to talk to Bobby about Ariel Logan's disappearance, because of an argument he and Ariel had last Friday. While we were on the wharf a sergeant from the sheriff's department showed up. He told us a woman's body was found down by Rocky Creek Bridge. They think it's Ariel."

Mother pushed one strand of salt-and-pepper hair out of her eyes and tucked it behind one ear. "News travels fast. People were talking about it tonight at the restaurant. It must be some dreadful mistake."

The teakettle began whistling. I got up from my chair and turned off the gas burner, then poured boiling water in each of the mugs. "You know anything about this argument Bobby and Ariel had?"

"If the police arrested everyone who had an argument with someone they care about," Mother declared, "we'd all be in jail."

"No one's arrested Bobby. At least not yet." I set the mugs on the table. "This sergeant just wanted to talk with him."

Not that Bobby was in the least cooperative. And I had the feeling Magruder wanted to do more than question him. I hoped the dead woman whose body had been found would turn out to be someone else. But if it was someone else, Ariel was still missing.

"Did you know Ariel?" I asked. Steam wafted upward from my mug, redolent of peppermint. The tea was far too hot to drink. I blew on it, because that's what you do with tea.

"Bobby brought her to the restaurant for dinner one night. At first I was surprised they found each other. Bobby's a fisherman and Ariel—" Mother stopped.

"She's a rich girl from Carmel," I finished.

Mother nodded, toying with the string of her tea bag. "Her parents are Hollywood refugees. They moved to Carmel when Ariel was just a baby. The mother's an actress, or was, and the father is a writer. From what Nick and Tina have told me, Ariel's parents weren't too keen on her relationship with Bobby. But Ariel seemed very assured, very much her own person."

The Ariel Logan described by Donna and my mother certainly sounded different from the other young women who'd crossed Bobby's path over the past few years. His ex-wife Linda was his high-school sweetheart, a pleasant down-to-earth woman. But that early marriage hadn't lasted much past the birth of their son Nicky. Since his divorce several years ago Bobby had been involved with a succession of blow-dried tootsies, all similar in their penchant for thick layers of eye makeup and tight, flashy clothes, more body than brains. That's all Bobby was interested in, a quick roll in the hay and no entanglements, all in a pleasant alcoholic fog.

Ariel must have been special. She had to be if Bobby had put a lid on his drinking and was talking marriage. She sounded like a wonderful young woman, someone I would like to meet. I hoped that I'd have the opportunity to do so. Despite the fact that Ariel was missing and her car had been found, I hoped she'd show up and tell everyone it was all a mistake. But like my cousin Donna, I had an unpleasant feeling in the pit of my stomach, one that had gotten a whole lot worse this afternoon when we heard about the body that washed ashore near Rocky Creek.

Suddenly I didn't want to think about Ariel anymore, or think about Bobby under the scrutiny of the sheriff's department. I changed the subject.

"When am I going to meet your friend? Donna says you've been dating someone."

Two rose-colored spots appeared on my mother's cheeks, matching the terry-cloth robe. Her mouth curved upward in a smile and the result took years off her face. I hadn't seen her look like that in a very long time. Something rubbed across my personal antenna—the wrong way.

"I see you're up-to-date on all the family gossip. I've been seeing an old friend. Karl Beckman. He owns Beckman Boat Works over on Cannery Row. You can meet him tomorrow, if you come over to the restaurant. We're catering a luncheon and Karl will be there."

I nodded, a brief noncommittal movement. Was my hesitation due to Karl? I didn't know. I sipped my tea and set the mug back down on the table.

"Speaking of family gossip, were you planning to tell me about the incidents at the restaurant?"

"I hadn't made up my mind whether to mention it. What did Donna tell you?" Now she frowned and the worried exhausted look returned to her face.

I restrained myself from asking why she'd considered not telling me. "She said at first it looked like accidents, but the last few had to be deliberate. What happened, and when did it start?"

Mother didn't answer right away. She took temporary refuge in her tea, the raised mug hiding the lower part of her face. Then she sighed. "It started in June. Someone put salt in the sugar bowls. It only happened once. Unfortunately it was a busy Saturday night and a lot of customers were affected. It could have been an accident. It's an easy enough mistake to make. I assumed it was, until the next time, about two weeks later."

She stopped. We sipped tea in silence for a moment, then she continued. "Someone didn't tighten the lid on a container of olive oil. As a result it spilled, all over the kitchen floor. God, what a mess. One of my cooks fell and hurt her back. And some of the oil splashed into pots on the stove, ruining several dinners. It slowed us down considerably, on a Saturday night when the restaurant was packed. That could have been an accident, too."

"But you're not sure."

Mother shook her head. "Particularly in light of what's happened since. In July someone called the Immigration and Naturalization Service, claiming I'd hired undocumented workers."

"An anonymous tip?" It seemed a great many anonymous calls were burning up the telephone wires in Monterey County.

"I don't know. Anyway, Café Marie had an INS raid, late in the afternoon while we were preparing for dinner. On a Friday, with a full slate of reservations. It put us off schedule and it was extremely embarrassing. Of course Immigration didn't find anyone without the proper papers. I'm careful about who I hire. All my employees have been with me forever."

"Except your new assistant. Julian."

Mother dismissed this with a wave of her hand. "Julian's not illegal. He's from L.A."

That would cause a great many Northern Californians to consider him an alien, I thought, picking up my mug again.

"Then there was the knife," Mother said. "I suppose that could have been an accident, too, but by this time I was starting to wonder if someone was out to get Café Marie."

"What about the knife?"

Mother stretched out her right hand, palm up. The callused flesh already showed the nicks and burns of someone who spent the better part of the day in a restaurant kitchen. But now, running diagonally across the palm, I saw a new scar, about three inches long.

"How did this happen?" I asked, frowning. "You're always careful with knives."

"Yes, I am. I'm careful about cleaning them, where I set them down, where I keep them when they're not being used." Mother stared at the scar, then raised her eyes to mine. "The knife was in the wrong drawer, with the blade up. I was reaching for another utensil and I cut myself. Blood everywhere. I had to go to the emergency room for stitches."

"When did this happen?"

"The middle of August. Then it got worse." She curled her

hand around the handle of her mug and raised it, sipping the peppermint tea before she continued. "The week after that, on a Saturday. According to the reservation book, we had a full house. But less than half the people showed up. That's never happened before. Of course, since it was a summer weekend, we did have plenty of walk-ins. But I'm usually booked solid all weekend—Friday, Saturday, and Sunday."

Easy enough to do, I thought. I could call Café Marie and reserve tables under several assumed names. When those fictional parties don't show up, the result is a nearly empty restaurant. How inconvenient and vexing. Someone was quite adept at using the phone to create havoc for my mother.

"Then Karl got sick," she continued, mouth curved into a frown. "At my restaurant, about a week later. I've never had anyone get sick before, at least not to my knowledge. He and his sister-in-law Lacy were having dinner. He became terribly ill while he was having coffee and dessert. Pale and sweating, with stomach cramps. I thought it was a bout of flu, but Karl's doctor said it might have been food poisoning. Food poisoning!"

Tea splashed from the mug onto the wooden surface of the table as Mother set it down hard, her face full of indignation and worry. "A couple of days later the county health department pulled a surprise inspection at the restaurant. The inspector said they'd gotten an anonymous tip about unsafe food-handling practices. Absolute nonsense, of course. My people are meticulous, both in preparation and storage. I insist on it."

"Did they find anything?" I got up and reached for a dishrag, wiping up the spilled tea. Then I picked up the teakettle and topped off my mother's mug and my own. I didn't know much about food poisoning, but from what I'd read on the subject, I understood that it's often difficult to trace where the tainted food is ingested, because of the time lapse between consumption and illness. But Karl's unexplained illness, followed by the health-department inspection, would certainly imply that something was wrong at Café Marie.

"Yes," my mother said, speaking slowly, a perplexed look on her face. "The inspector found the controls in one of the refrigerators had been turned up. Everything that's refrigerated is supposed to be forty-five degrees or below. The food had to be thrown out. I don't know how it happened. I check temperatures frequently, and so does Julian."

"What else?" I asked, resuming my seat.

"I think someone called the *Herald*. I got a bad review, right before the Labor Day weekend. The review implied that the restaurant isn't as good as it used to be. It alluded to the health-department thing—didn't come right out and say it, but anyone could read between the lines, particularly the comment saying that things weren't up to Marie's usual high standards. I'm hearing a lot of talk around town. Business has fallen off. I don't think it's just because summer's over."

Mother tightened her hands around her mug. "This is very serious, Jeri. A restaurant lives or dies by its good name. I'm afraid someone is out to destroy mine."

Pelicans and bodies and now this. So much for my nice quiet vacation, I thought.

"Do you want me to look into it?"

CHAPTER 7

Once, when Mother was rhapsodizing about the quality of a particular goat cheese, I told her it was just food. This heresy earned me an incredulous stare. I love good food just as much as she does, but with Marie Doyle Howard, food is a religion. Her entire life seems to revolve around the purchase, preparation, and consumption of food.

Not at home, mind you. On Friday morning I searched the restaurant owner's cupboard and was hard-pressed to find anything worthy of being called breakfast. Yesterday I'd finished the last of a loaf of raisin bread. Now all I could find was a package of rice cakes, which didn't exactly appeal. Two bananas in the fruit bowl had long since entered the state of ripeness that made them appropriate only for banana bread.

There was only one sensible thing to do. I made a bagel run, heading for the Bagel Bakery on Lighthouse Avenue. After fortifying myself with coffee and an onion bagel slathered with walnut-and-olive cream cheese, I bought a dozen assorted bagels and several varieties of cream cheese, enough to keep me in breakfasts for the week I planned to be in Monterey.

My mother's house on Larkin Street is small, just two bedrooms, a wood-frame structure painted blue with gray trim, furnished with old oak pieces that belonged to her mother. Some of the furniture she brought with her from Monterey to the Bay Area, when she married Dad. Other items were added later, inherited when my Doyle grandparents died. After my parents split, the well-polished oak made the journey from the spacious Victorian in Alameda, where I grew up, back to Monterey, winding up in this little house not far from the house where my mother grew up.

It's located in a section of town that climbs a hillside steep enough that the front porch overlooks the wharf and the shifting blue water of the bay. She didn't buy the house for the view, however, but because of its proximity to downtown Monterey. She's no more than a few minutes from Café Marie, which is fine with her since the restaurant occupies most of her waking hours.

By the time I returned from the Bagel Bakery, Mother was out of bed, but still in her nightgown and robe. She stood in the kitchen, staring out the window over the sink as she waited for her teakettle to boil. Maybe she was looking at the hummingbird flitting around her overgrown garden, which canted steeply up the hillside behind the house, but I doubted it. Her face, still puffy from sleep, looked worried and preoccupied.

"Want a bagel?" I asked, waggling my paper sacks at her. The onion bagels were so pungent they rated their own sack. Everything else had been put into the larger bag.

"Sure." She inspected my purchases, selecting a cinnamon-raisin bagel. She took a large serrated knife from the block near the stove and expertly split the bagel. As she did so I thought of the scar on her hand and how she'd acquired it. Mother took a plate from the cupboard and set one bagel half on it, then spread it with a thin layer of plain cream cheese.

"Thanks for going after bagels," she said as her teakettle began to whistle.

"You don't have much in the way of supplies," I pointed out.

"I was going to get to the grocery store, but time got away from me." Mother poured hot water over her tea bag and carried plate and mug to the kitchen table. "It seems to do that lately."

"I'll pick up a few things today."

Mother glanced at the digital clock on the microwave. "I shouldn't have slept so late. I have to get to the restaurant."

"I thought your new assistant Julian is supposed to lighten your load."

"He does. But we've got that luncheon today. I know you have a lot of people you want to visit, but I hope you'll come by. I'd like you to meet Karl."

"I planned to. I want to interview your staff."

Mother didn't say anything. Instead she picked up her bagel and nibbled on it. "Interview the staff," she said finally, reaching for her tea. "I'm having all sorts of qualms about this."

I sighed. "I thought we agreed I'd look into those incidents. If you don't do anything about them, they'll continue. And possibly get worse. Just the fact that I'll be asking questions might be enough to convince whoever's responsible to stop."

"It's just that—" Mother stopped for another mouthful of tea. "The idea that any of my people could do such things. Except for Julian, they've all worked for me for several years, some of them since I opened the restaurant. I'm picky about who I hire, whether they work in the kitchen or in the dining room. I don't just take anyone off the street. I trust my staff. Having you talk to them is like saying I don't."

"I realize that. But interviewing employees is the logical place to start. An outsider doesn't have the kind of access required to pull these stunts. If a customer walked into the kitchen and started messing with your knives, you'd notice."

"Yes, you're right." Mother conceded this with a nod and took another bite from her bagel. "But I hope you'll be as careful—and diplomatic—as possible."

"I'm good at what I do," I told her.

She smiled. "Yes. I know."

Mother finished her bagel and went to her bedroom to, as she described it, put herself together. When she emerged she looked like a different person. Her salt-and-pepper hair was combed back into an attractive no-nonsense coif and she wore a pale rose dress with a shawl collar, made of lightweight washable silk. Around her neck was a strand of pearls, complemented by matching pearls in her earlobes. Her shoes were sensibly low-heeled. She'd play the hostess at the catered luncheon, then during the afternoon lull, she'd shift persona to the chef of Café Marie. Her cooking clothes, as she called them, were zipped into the black garment bag she carried.

She gave me a quick peck on the cheek on her way to the front door, tossing words and the garment bag over her shoulder. "I'll see you later." I watched her little Honda back out of the driveway onto Larkin Street, then drive off in the direction of downtown.

I surveyed the refrigerator and cupboards, made a list, and headed to the nearest grocery store. I had returned and was putting away my purchases when the phone rang. It was Donna.

"I just got off the phone with my source over at the sheriff's department," she said, sounding subdued.

"Any news?" I had the phone tucked under my chin as I stashed a half gallon of milk in the refrigerator.

"The sheriff's rescue unit recovered the body late yesterday afternoon. They made a positive identification this morning. It's Ariel Logan."

The bleakness of her voice radiated through the telephone wire. I had never met Ariel Logan, but now I felt a twinge of sadness at the confirmation of her death.

"I'm sorry to hear that," I said slowly. "How did she die? Does Bobby know?"

"At this point no one's sure if it's an accidental drowning or something else. The autopsy's in progress. I'll call you as soon as I know anything. Bobby probably doesn't know. It's after twelve now. I'm going down to the wharf to see if the *Nicky II* is in yet."

CAF⁰ MARIE IS LOCATED IN DOWNTOWN MONTEREY NEAR A HOUSE where Robert Louis Stevenson lived briefly in 1879. The tourist publications call the area Historic Old Monterey, the part of town that was a thriving seaport when this coast was Alta California, part of Spain and then Mexico. The restaurant began its life as a residence and evolved into a store. When Mother purchased the building it was empty, and the transformation she wrought was complete and costly.

Mother gutted the interior, stripping away the building's previous lives. She spared no expense in creating the high-tech kitchen or the inlaid wooden bar. The hardwood floors were polished to a warm buttery sheen. She chose the highest-quality linen for the white tablecloths and napkins in a shade of turquoise that reminded me of Monterey Bay. It took her months to decide on china and tableware and to pick out the glassware that graced the tables. As for the tables and chairs, they were treasures found in antique stores and secondhand shops, restored and refinished. Few of them matched, but this added to the charm of the dining room.

The walls were white, decorated with artwork from local artists. The subject of each painting was the ocean in its infinite variety. Some were calm, like the watercolor near the entrance, showing fishing boats on the bay, or angry and vital like the oil above the bar, with huge waves crashing onto the rocky coast.

In addition to picking out china and linen, Mother contended with contractors and workmen, inspectors and permits, and governmental entities, from the city of Monterey to the county health department to the state alcohol and beverage control board. All in all, with the dizzying array of hassles and mazes one encounters in opening a business, it was nearly a year from the time she closed on the building purchase until the gala opening of Café Marie.

After the time and money she'd poured into the endeavor, it was a good thing the business was a success. According to my brother Brian, Mother's start-up tab had been in excess of half a million and it had taken a lot of hard work over several years to put her into the black. She couldn't afford to be pushed precipitously into the red again.

Mother had removed the door and wide glass windows that fronted on the street, dating from the time when the rectangular building was a store. In their place were a series of smaller windows covered with turquoise shades. Under the windows were planter boxes full of bright colorful zinnias. A sidewalk led up the right side of the building to double doors, about midway into the lot. Next to this was a narrow strip of land planted with flowers that found their way onto Café Marie's table, and herbs that wound up in the food. Through the doors there was a small waiting area with chairs on the left side and a long carved wooden bench on the right. A chest-high wooden stand held a phone and the reservation book.

As I passed this the dining room was to my left, on two levels. Some of the tables shared floor space with the bar, but most of them were in a square area at the front of the restaurant, reached by a couple of shallow steps. I glanced around and saw a sea of white tablecloths set for the luncheon, turquoise napkins shaped and sticking out of glasses.

Several of the luncheon attendees milled about in the dining room, holding glasses, standing between the tables, but most clustered at the L-shaped bar, in front of me and slightly to the right. Beyond that was the kitchen, visible from the bar through a cutaway window. Through this I saw several members of the kitchen staff arrayed in front of the bank of stoves, grilling what looked like salmon.

I sidestepped a well-dressed couple and headed down a central hallway that led to the rear of the restaurant. The first doorway on my right led to a small cloakroom. The second was Mother's office and, beyond that, two doors opening onto the rest rooms. Past this the hall jogged to the left, facing a wide shelf where the cooks placed orders ready for the servers to pick up and deliver to customers. To the right of the shelf the passage led into the kitchen, stoves and grills on the left and sinks and storage on the right. Near the back door was a pantry and a huge refrigerator and freezer.

I stopped midway down the corridor and peered through the open door into Mother's office. She sat in front of a keyboard and monitor, a cordless phone tucked between ear and shoulder. The whole restaurant operation was computerized, from dinner checks to ordering supplies, bookkeeping to tracking employee hours. I was continually amazed at how complicated this business was. Café Marie was a fairly small restaurant, only sixty seats. But those sixty seats were usually full every night and Mother took every aspect of the business personally.

"It's like inviting people into my own home," she once told me.

Mother waved at me. At the moment the people she'd invited into her home were keeping the man behind the bar busy. They appeared to be middle-aged, well kept, and financially comfortable, if their clothes were any indicator. I slipped onto a just vacated stool and watched the bartender work. His name was Evan and he'd been with Café Marie since it opened. He recognized me, grinned, and fetched a cold bottle of Calistoga before I had a chance to ask for it.

Eavesdropping, while not socially acceptable, is often quite instructive. I put my antenna out as I sipped the mineral water. Mother hadn't mentioned what organization had scheduled the luncheon here at Café Marie, but it didn't take me long to deduce from the scraps of conversation I was overhearing that what all these people had in common was sailboats. They talked about marina berthing space, how limited and expensive it is, and they seemed to be planning a regatta.

Bottle in hand, I left the bar stool and drifted slowly, scanning voices as though tuning in an array of radio stations. I heard a woman giving her companion a review of the jazz festival that had just taken place at the Fairgrounds. The man on my left was raving about the thirty-six-foot Pearson he'd just bought. Must mean a boat. Another woman was grousing about those damned tourists.

"You can't even get to Carmel on a weekend," I heard her say. "The traffic is just incredible. And forget finding a place to park."

Her friend nodded. "It's the same with Pacific Grove. I'd like to blow up that damned aquarium."

I moved into another conversation, this one about local politics. "It's simple," a man in a business suit said. "You just have to know which palms to grease."

To my left I saw Mother step out of her office, heading back to the kitchen to check on the progress of her staff. When would the illustrious Karl put in an appearance? I wanted to get a good look at him.

I started to follow Mother down the hall, then I overheard something that made me stop. "I hope the food's all right." The speaker was a balding man in gray pinstripes, his listener a slender woman in a green dress. "I mean, I read that review in the *Herald*. It said this place wasn't as good as it used to be."

"Well, it's just salad and grilled salmon," the woman said. "What could go wrong with that?"

"Plenty," the man said. "Didn't you hear Karl Beckman got sick here? Food poisoning."

"Really?" The woman in the green dress frowned and looked toward the kitchen.

Mother was right, I thought. The rumor mill was active concerning the incidents at the restaurant. The quicker I could get to the source of the trouble, the better.

A woman entered the restaurant just then and stood near the reservation stand, tucking her sunglasses into a leather handbag. She looked around and spotted two other women at the bar, moving to join them. "I thought you'd bailed out," one of her friends said. "Where have you been?"

"I went to see Sylvie and Peter Logan. It's dreadful. They're just devastated. Ariel was their only child."

I examined this new arrival. She was in her late forties, wearing a magenta silk dress, a lot of chunky gold jewelry, and the cloying scent of too much overpriced perfume. Her helmet of silvery blond hair looked as though it would stay in place even during a hurricane. She joined her friends at the bar and asked Evan for a gin and tonic. "Sylvie and Peter have been in France," she continued, after a healthy swig of her drink. "Sylvie's mother is dying. Cancer. And now this."

Her friends leaned closer, making sympathetic clucks. One was older, a frail birdlike woman with white hair, dressed in a simple gray linen suit. The other was a redhead whose bright yellow dress made her look like a large canary.

"How could this happen?" the older woman asked.

"The boyfriend, of course." The blonde in the magenta dress didn't bother to lower her voice. "Who else? They had a fight in a bar. Peter is convinced this guy killed Ariel."

"Who is he?" The woman in yellow fingered the buttons on the front of her dress.

"A fisherman, for God's sake." The blonde sneered. "Strictly blue collar."

My mouth quirked at her display of snobbery. I wondered if the speaker would ever give a thought to the source of the salmon she was about to have for lunch.

"Why in the world did Ariel take up with a fisherman?" the woman in gray chimed in. "I thought she was seeing that nice young lawyer, Ryan something-or-other."

"Evidently not. Ariel and this fisherman had been seeing each other for several months. Sylvie and Peter didn't care for the relationship." The blonde took a sip of her drink and wrinkled her nose. "Maybe they'd finally talked some sense into her. Maybe the working-class guy was starting to pall and she wanted to end it. I'll bet that's what they were arguing about. I'll bet he didn't want to break up, and she did."

The two women who stood beside her nodded and murmured, putting their stamp of agreement on the blonde's theory. Had Ariel Logan been trying to end her relationship with Bobby? Not according to Donna. She said they had talked of getting married. But what about this lawyer the older woman had mentioned? I shook my head. If this was any example of the rumors flying around the peninsula, people would be blaming Bobby for Ariel's death. Apparently Ariel's father had already made up his mind.

As if responding to some hidden signal, people began moving away from the bar and into the dining room, pulling out chairs and sitting down. The blonde and her two companions drifted toward a nearby table. "There's Karl Beckman," the woman in yellow said. "But I don't see Lacy with him. You know, I heard the Boat Works may close down."

"Really?" The white-haired woman sounded surprised. "It's been there for years. And you'd think with all the people who own boats . . ."

I drifted out of the range of her voice, looking toward the entrance of Café Marie. I saw my mother coming down the hallway from the kitchen. She spotted the new arrival and her brisk businesslike demeanor changed before my eyes. A smile lit up her face and she smoothed the skirt of her rose silk dress.

He was tall, almost as tall as my father, with a big muscular frame dressed casually in dark blue slacks, a light blue shirt, and a sport jacket of muted plaid. He looked vital and vigorous and good-humored. When he reached my mother's side, he took her arm, then bent his blond head close to her dark one and whispered something in her ear. She leaned her head back and laughed. As he joined in her laughter I got a good look at his face. It was broad and square, with blunt features and plenty of laugh lines around his hazel eyes. He had to be in his forties, ten years younger than Mother, if not more.

So this was Karl Beckman. I wasn't prepared for the hostility I felt.

CHAPTER 8

THE ANTIPATHY I FELT FOR KARL BECKMAN WAS NOTHING compared with my reaction to Julian Surtees. Mother's new assistant must be damned brilliant in the kitchen. Otherwise I couldn't imagine how she put up with his arrogance.

Donna had described Surtees as dark and brooding, his good looks causing flutters among the peninsula's female population. And probably some of the males, I thought, looking at the handsome face that scowled at me across the cramped space of Mother's office.

Surtees looked lean and muscular in a pair of tight-fitting black jeans and a white T-shirt that showed off sinewy arms. He was in his midthirties, a few strands of gray in the black hair at his temples. The hair was brushed straight back off his high forehead, curling slightly around his ears. His left earlobe held a tiny gold stud. Opaque brown eyes glared at me from his olive-skinned face. His sensual lips turned down in a frown.

The luncheon in Café Marie's dining room was over. The guests had departed, leaving the staff to set up the dining room before the restaurant opened at its usual time of five-thirty. While the sailboat people wolfed down their grilled salmon and planned their regatta, I'd been in Mother's office, going through her files.

Café Marie had thirty-five employees, some of them part-time, all working various shifts. Many of these cooked, including a baker and a pastry chef who made all the breads and desserts served at the restaurant. Others waited on tables. Two alternated as bartenders, Evan and a woman named Lori. Others washed dishes and bused tables.

I looked at some of the schedules for the past month, trying to get a sense for the day-to-day staffing of both the kitchen and the dining room. Back in the kitchen, the baker came in early, about seven in the morning. Then the dishwashers arrived at ten. The chef, Julian, arrived at one in the afternoon, and the rest of the cooks at two. Whoever was tending bar showed up at four, as did those who waited and bused tables. And it seemed Mother was there eighteen hours a day. Not only did she cook, during the day she acted as restaurant owner, ordering supplies and keeping the books.

On any given night, it looked as though there would be a total of fifteen people on staff. Seven of these would be in the kitchen— the chef, three cooks who sautéed, grilled, and created salads, the pastry chef, and two dishwashers. In the dining room there would be the bartender, four waiters, two busers, and Rachel Donahoe, Mother's longtime dining-room manager, who handled the reservations.

I began my investigation in Mother's tiny office, looking through the employment records for both the kitchen staff and dining-room staff. Then I interviewed people, not an easy task since everyone was occupied with cleaning up after the luncheon and getting ready for dinner. Now, a couple of hours later, I'd gotten to Julian Surtees. He wasn't pleased about being questioned.

"This is a waste of time," Surtees said, curling his lip at me. "I have work to do."

"I told you why I'm here. I want to find out more about these incidents that have been happening here at the restaurant."

Surtees waved one long-fingered hand. "Marie's overreacting. Accidents happen all the time in restaurants. When I was in L.A.—"

That was the third time Surtees had prefaced a remark with the phrase about Los Angeles. Evidently he found the Monterey peninsula to be a tad provincial, not up to his big-city standards. If things were so terrific in L.A., why had he left?

His attitude, and he had lots of it, made me want to find out more about Julian Surtees. As Mother had told me last night, most of the people who worked for her had been at Café Marie for sev-

eral years. Other than Surtees, the most recent hire was a young
Hispanic man who worked busing tables and was training to be a
waiter. He'd been at the restaurant since before Thanksgiving of
last year. Surtees, on the other hand, arrived in May, a month before the incidents began.

I opened my mouth to ask him a question. The phone at my elbow rang and I looked down to see one of the three lights stop
flashing as someone answered. Then it blinked again as the call
was put on hold. A moment later Rachel Donahoe appeared in
the office doorway, looking over Surtees's shoulder. "Telephone,
Jeri," she said.

"We'll continue this later," I told Surtees, who did not look
thrilled at the prospect. He gave me a withering look from his
heavy-lidded eyes, pushed back his chair, and strolled toward the
kitchen, moving like a rangy tomcat.

As I watched him go I thought about the possibility that a dis-
gruntled former employee might be responsible for the sabotage at
Café Marie. But Mother hadn't fired anyone lately. There had
been one waiter that she'd asked to leave, because she didn't feel
his work was up to her standards. That was over two years ago,
according to her records. As far as she or any other members of
the staff knew, the guy had left the Monterey area. Still, it was
worth checking out. But how could someone who didn't work here
gain access to the kitchen to tamper with the knife storage drawer?

I liked Julian for it. He was a monumental egotist, quite un-
abashed in his admiration for his own skill as a chef. He thought
he could do everything better than Mother, except as far as he was
concerned, cooking for tourists and what passed for Monterey society was beneath his talents. In his words I detected condescen-
sion toward my mother, a woman who'd entered the restaurant
game late in life. So why had he left L.A. to come to work for her?
Was he escaping from his past, a lover, spouse, or loan shark? Did
he have a motive, like taking over the restaurant after driving
Mother out in disgrace? Julian just didn't fit, and I planned to find
out why.

I focused on the blinking phone extension and reached for the
receiver. "Jeri Howard," I said.

"Hi. It's Donna." My cousin sounded unusually subdued.

"What's up?"

"Just got a call from my source at the sheriff's department," Donna said, biting off the words. "The coroner finished the autopsy on Ariel Logan. She didn't drown. No salt water in the lungs. She was bashed over the head with something."

I leaned forward with a sigh, elbows on the desk. My eyes fell on a restaurant-supply catalog and I stared at the cover without registering what was on it.

"She could have hit her head on the rocks when she went into the water." For some reason I wanted Ariel's death to be an accident, and even as I said the words I knew she'd been murdered.

"The right side of her skull was caved in," Donna said wearily. "Listen, Jeri, I have a meeting. I can't get away. I couldn't find Bobby earlier. Talk to him, before anyone else does."

I left downtown Monterey, driving past the U-shaped lake called El Estero and St. Johns Cemetery, where my Doyle grandparents and several generations of Ravellas were buried. Bobby lived near Del Monte Beach and the wharf, in a one-bedroom apartment tucked into the eaves on the second floor of a wood-frame Victorian.

I parked on the street and walked up the double driveway where the T-bird was parked, its dark blue finish gleaming as always. I climbed the stairs at the back of the house. On the second-floor landing, a small porch held a mop stuck into a plastic pail, a stack of newspapers tied with twine, and a pair of filthy shoes that stank of fish.

I knocked on the door. I didn't hear any movement inside, so I knocked again and called his name. Finally the door opened. My cousin, barefoot and clad only in a pair of blue-striped boxer shorts, stood framed in the doorway.

"I was asleep," he mumbled, running his left hand through his black curls as he squinted at me. "What d'ya want, Jeri?"

"To talk."

"Christ, Jeri, it's—" He looked over his left shoulder. "It's damn near four o'clock. I've been up all night. We didn't get the boat unloaded and cleaned up until after two. I'm exhausted. Can't it wait?"

"I don't think so," I said quietly, looking at the lines of weariness on his face and the shadows under his dark eyes.

He released the door and rubbed the stubble on his chin. "Suit yourself," he said, moving away from the door.

I followed him through the small kitchen, with its speckled yellow linoleum floor and white-painted cabinets, into the living room. A door on the left led to the bathroom, and in front of me I saw into the bedroom, where the sheets on a queen-size bed were in disarray. The living-room windows looked down onto the driveway.

The apartment had hardwood floors, covered here in the living room with a brown-and-gold area rug. I recognized the dark brown sofa on the wall that divided the living room from the bedroom. It was a hand-me-down from Bobby's parents. His mother had crocheted the afghan draped over the back of a faded blue wing chair in front of the windows. A shelf on the opposite wall held TV, VCR and CD player, a stack of CDs, and a few books. Next to it was a round table with four chairs, unopened mail scattered on one of the place mats. A low table on this end of the sofa held a telephone, an answering machine, and an eight-by-ten-inch picture frame, facedown on the wood surface.

Bobby sat down on the sofa, leaning forward, his head in his hands, eyes staring at a spot on the rug. "What do you want to talk about, Jeri?"

"Ariel." He didn't say anything. His eyes moved to the frame on the end table. I picked it up. She was beautiful, with long blond hair and intelligent brown eyes, her face glowing with humor as she smiled into the lens of the camera. I set the picture on the table and looked down at my cousin.

"She's dead, isn't she?" Bobby's voice sounded dead, too.

"They identified the body this morning. It looks like she was murdered, Bobby."

Still he said nothing. He moved his head upward, so that his chin rested on his hands, and he looked at me with his brown eyes, blinking several times as he tried to control the tears now streaming down his face.

"Oh, no," he said finally, his voice a ragged cross between a whisper and a sob. He covered his face with his hands. I sat beside him on the sofa and put my arm around him. He leaned into my shoulder and cried.

The telephone began to ring, a jangling intrusion that stopped as the answering machine kicked in. It was Nick. He left a terse message for his son to call him. No sooner than he'd hung up, the phone rang again. This time whoever was calling didn't bother to leave a message. Bobby reached past me and jerked the phone cord from the wall.

"I loved her," he said, huddled on the sofa. He shivered as though he were cold. "We were talking about getting married. I mean, I asked her to marry me. She said yes, but she wanted to finish grad school first. This was her last year. We talked about it a lot. Where we were gonna live, and having babies, and—" His voice broke and quavered. "God, Jeri, I can't talk about this anymore."

"We have to talk." I tried to soften my words. Bobby needed time to grieve and he wasn't going to get much. "We have to find out who killed Ariel. You know you're a suspect. You knew it even before Sergeant Magruder showed up at the wharf yesterday. Now that the autopsy points to murder he'll come looking for you again. You and Ariel had an argument in a very public place. There's a lot of talk and finger-pointing going on. I heard some of it earlier today, over at Mother's restaurant. What were you and Ariel quarreling about?"

Bobby's jaw tightened. "I can't tell you."

"Did you kill Ariel?"

He jumped to his feet. His hands tightened into fists and his brown eyes blazed at me, suddenly hot and angry. "Hell no, I didn't kill her. Are you out of your fucking mind?"

"Then tell me about the fight."

Bobby smashed one fist into the palm of the other hand. "I can't, Jeri. I can't. I made a promise. I owe someone a favor and it's complicated. You have to understand that."

"Is the favor still owed, now that Ariel's dead?" I asked. He nodded. "So you owe somebody else. Can you tell me about it later?"

"Yeah. I have to look into a few things first."

"I'm a private investigator, remember? I can help you do whatever you have to do."

"It's something I have to do myself," he said, shaking his head, that stubborn look on his face.

"All right," I said slowly, not completely convinced this was the right path. "You do it your way. For now."

C HAPTER 9

MADE SLOW PROGRESS IN THE FRIDAY-AFTERNOON STOP-
and-go traffic on Del Monte Avenue. The four-lane road was
crowded with cars as locals contended with tourists arriving for a
weekend on the peninsula. Finally I escaped into the parking lot
that stretched between Wharf Two and Fisherman's Wharf. I
parked near the harbormaster's office and walked along the sidewalk past the marina, where sailboats and salmon boats bobbed on
the gently rocking water of the harbor.

Near the entrance to Fisherman's Wharf the organ grinder and
his monkey were packing up after a day's work, heading for home.
By now it was five-thirty in the evening, and many of the sight-
seers had dispersed, except those who sought a meal on the wharf.
I dodged a foursome of tourists, two men and two women, on just
such a quest, as they moved back and forth across the wharf, examining the menus posted at competing restaurants.

Ravella's closed at six. Since I'd been at Bobby's apartment
when Nick had called, I wanted to let him know that Bobby was
okay, even if that wasn't true. As I approached the deli and fish
market I saw Nick at the counter, clearing away ice. Tina was behind the counter on the deli side, putting supplies in cabinets.
They were talking to a man whose big frame filled the passageway
between the two counters. When I entered Ravella's he looked up
and I recognized the fair, blunt-featured face. It was Karl Beckman.

"Hello, Jeri," he said, greeting me with an easy grin and an outstretched hand. "We didn't get much of a chance to talk at the

luncheon. I feel as though I know you already. Marie's told me so much about you."

"Has she?"

I shook the hand he offered, wondering just what my mother had told him. Karl Beckman seemed to be a friendly, affable, and attractive man. I could see why Mother was attracted to him. There was no logical reason for me to dislike the man. Yet I did.

The illogical reason was that he was dating my mother. Was my reaction negative because he was so much younger? Why was I having such a problem with that particular detail? I had certainly dated men younger than I was. With just a few years between us, though, not ten. Karl Beckman was surely in his late forties, fifty at the most. Mother would be sixty on her next birthday.

Or was it because my relationship with my father was the closer, deeper one? I hadn't seen my mother's face light up that way around Dad, certainly not in the last years of their marriage.

Whatever the reason for my intense negative reaction to Karl Beckman, I'd have to mask my feelings. I knew Mother would mention him frequently during my week in Monterey, and I didn't want a confrontation with her.

I turned to Nick. "I was with Bobby when you called. He doesn't want to talk with anyone right now."

"Not even his own father?" Nick stopped cleaning the counter, sighed, and shook his head, wiping his hands on a rag. Tina's face mirrored her husband's concern.

"The boat was late getting in again today," Tina said. "After the crew unloaded and cleaned up, Bobby didn't even come over to see us like he usually does. He's so upset about Ariel."

I nodded. It wouldn't take long for the general knowledge that Ariel's death was murder rather than an accident to percolate through the community. And when it did, the suspicion I'd already overheard this afternoon at Café Marie would be underscored, with fingers pointed at my cousin. Why was Bobby being so damned closemouthed about his quarrel with Ariel?

"What a tragedy," Karl Beckman said in his pleasant bass, shaking his head. "Ariel was such a lovely young woman. She was just a few years older than my own daughter."

I filed his mention of a daughter in my mind for further investigation, asking a more immediate question. "You knew Ariel Logan?"

"Oh, yes." The laugh lines around his hazel eyes crinkled as he smiled. "Bobby introduced us. Brought her over to the boatyard in August. A lively, intelligent girl. She asked lots of questions about our day-to-day operations. She was curious about every aspect of the yard, from transporting boats to how we recycle our paint cans." He paused, and his face grew thoughtful. "It's a damned shame. She was good for Bobby. And he cared for her a great deal."

"Do you know my cousin well?" I asked him.

Now Beckman smiled again, the laugh lines deepening on his broad face. "Why, Bobby and I are good friends. I remember him as a youngster, going out on the boat with Nick. Beckman Boat Works has been repairing Ravella fishing boats as long as I can remember."

"How long has your family been in Monterey?" It sounded as though I were grilling him but he didn't seem to mind.

"Since the thirties," Beckman said. "Not quite as long as the Doyles and the Ravellas, but long enough. Pop and Mom came to this country right after the Nazis took over. Pop never talked about it much but I guess he saw the writing on the wall and decided to get out. He was an independent old cuss. The brownshirts would've thrown him into a concentration camp."

"Old Hans was a character, all right," Nick said, nodding his head. "A genuine original."

"Pop was a tough old salt," Beckman continued. "He grew up in Hamburg and knew his way around boats. So when he and Mom wound up here in Monterey, he started the boatyard down on Cannery Row. The canneries were going full bore by then. Mom had a bakery, right down there at the foot of Alvarado Street."

Beckman waved his thumb in the direction of downtown Monterey. The area he was talking about had long since been torn down, the old San Carlos Hotel, the pawnshops, cafés, and other small businesses replaced by chain hotels and the conference center.

"Mom was famous for her apple strudel." He shook his head. "I haven't tasted strudel like that since she died."

"I remember," Tina said. "Nobody could make strudel like Ella Beckman. My mother once asked her for that recipe but she wouldn't give it out. Said you had to be German to make strudel properly."

Beckman grinned. "That reminds me of the time Nick's dad tried to teach Pop how to play bocce. Dominic finally threw up his hands and gave up. Said you had to be Italian to figure it out."

As the three older people laughed over this memory I studied Karl Beckman, wanting to find out more about him. He had a daughter, but I assumed that my mother wouldn't be dating a married man. At least I hoped not. So Beckman must be divorced or widowed.

"Is your daughter here in Monterey?" I asked.

"Kristen? Oh, no. She's in her junior year up at Stanford."

Costs a lot of money to keep a kid in school at Stanford, I thought, recalling what the women at the luncheon had said about financial difficulties at Beckman Boat Works. They'd also mentioned Lacy. According to my mother, this was Karl Beckman's sister-in-law, his dining companion several weeks ago when he'd become sick while eating at Café Marie.

"I understand your sister-in-law is involved with the operation of the boatyard." Something flickered over Karl Beckman's face, enough to pique my curiosity.

"Lacy takes care of the office. She also transports boats." He glanced at Nick. "That's something new we started this summer, to bring in more revenue. Seems to be working out." Evidently Karl Beckman didn't feel like discussing his sister-in-law. He looked at his watch, then at me, his hazel eyes friendly. Had I imagined something in those eyes when I mentioned Lacy?

"I've got to go take care of a few things down at the yard. Jeri, it was nice seeing you again. I'm sure we'll see more of each other during your visit."

Now it was my turn to be noncommittal as I shook his hand. I watched while he said good-bye to Nick and Tina. When Karl had gone, Nick resumed cleaning the fish-market counter. "Karl's a nice man," Tina said, as though she knew what was going through my mind.

"How long have he and Mother known each other?"

"Oh, they've known each other for years." Tina picked up a sponge and began wiping countertops in the deli.

"That's not what I meant. How long have they been dating each other?" Though I couldn't imagine when my mother would find time to go out with anyone, given her schedule.

"I think they met at a New Year's Eve party. It does Marie good to get out once in a while. She spends so much time at that restaurant. He's a nice man. Marie enjoys his company."

Tina sounded as though she were warning me not to interfere in my mother's relationship. She had a point and I decided I'd make an effort. After all, I was only going to be in Monterey for a week. Still, I wanted to know more about the man Mother was seeing. It was only fair. I recalled that she'd had the same interest in my companions back when I'd started dating.

"So tell me about Karl," I said, leaning forward on the deli counter. "Is he divorced?"

"No, his wife's dead. He was married to Janine Harper, from King City. Maybe you've heard of the family. Her brother Charlie is a county commissioner."

I shook my head. I hadn't heard of the Harper family but I didn't keep up with Monterey County genealogy. King City was a good-sized town about fifty miles south of Salinas on U.S. 101, toward the bottom of the Salinas Valley, nestled in farming and ranching country between hills to the east and the Santa Lucia range to the west.

"Janine was killed in a car accident," Tina said, rinsing the sponge in the sink. "Karl's brother Gunter was driving."

That would explain how this sister-in-law had an interest in the boatyard. But it didn't explain the look in Karl Beckman's hazel eyes when I'd mentioned Lacy.

"Same accident? What happened?"

"No one knows." Tina paused and shook her head. "It was raining, a night in February, about eighteen months ago. The car skidded off the road, down by Hurricane Point, and went into ocean."

The ocean. *Don't turn your back on the ocean.* Donna's words echoed in my mind. I thought of the ocean's latest victim, Ariel Logan.

But the ocean had help this time. Ariel Logan had evidently turned her back on someone, or something, besides the ocean.

CHAPTER 10

Pacific Grove, or PG, as the locals call it, occupies the tip of the Monterey peninsula. It began life as a Methodist summer resort and has retained its reputation as a quiet, staid community. It's known for the well-kept Victorian houses lining its tree-shaded street—and the butterflies. Each September migrating Monarch butterflies return to Pacific Grove, swarming over the Spanish moss and the Monterey pines at the northwestern end of Lighthouse Avenue, near Point Pinos.

Donna and her lover Kay share a house on Thirteenth Street just off Ocean View Boulevard, a one-story Victorian facing a tiny park. I parked my car farther up the street, toward Central Avenue, and walked back toward the wood-frame house. It was a small two-bedroom structure, painted white, its shutters and gingerbread trim a contrasting blue. I heard waves crashing on the rocks half a block below and felt moisture in the air. Surrounded by the ocean and with pine-tree-covered hills at its landward boundary, Pacific Grove was often shrouded with a dense gray blanket of fog. Through the trees I could see it coming in, creeping over the water to embrace the land.

Kay opened the front door as I stepped onto the porch. She was in her early forties, a tiny slender woman, five feet tall at the most, her long dark hair rolled into a knot at the back of her neck. This evening she wore loose-fitting trousers and a short-sleeved shirt, both in a bright fuchsia set off by a jade-green sash. She carried a wineglass in one hand as she ushered me into the living room, which was furnished with an eclectic mix that included an ornately carved lamp table, a round plush ottoman that looked as though it needed to go back to the garage sale, a high-backed chintz sofa mounded with multihued silk and velvet pillows, and a bright green canvas sling-back chair right out of the fifties.

"Donna's changing clothes." Kay gave me a quick hug. "How are you, Jeri? You look wonderful. We haven't seen you in ages. Want a glass of wine?"

"I'm fine. And yes," I said, answering both questions.

I followed Kay through the dining room, where the round oak table was set for three, with gleaming silver and delicate flowered china. None of the pieces matched—they'd been unearthed from antique stores over the years and were now displayed as treasures on the white tablecloth and in the glass-fronted china cabinet that stood against one wall. In the narrow kitchen, Kay took a bottle of chardonnay from the refrigerator and poured me a glass.

As we walked back to the living room I noticed Kay's earrings, glittering as they moved in the light from the fixture overhead. They were constructed of tiny strands of gold combined with fire opals. No doubt she had made them herself. Kay designed and manufactured jewelry in her crowded studio on the back porch of the house.

"How's the jewelry business?" I moved a couple of pillows and took a seat on one end of the sofa. The other end was occupied by a calico cat curled atop a blue velvet pillow, nose tucked under her paws. The cat opened one eye and looked me over, then settled back into sleep.

"Terrific." Kay inserted herself into the sling-back chair and set her wineglass on an end table. "I've got pieces in galleries from Santa Cruz to Big Sur. From my standpoint, this is much better than Eureka."

Donna's last Fish-and-Game assignment had been in the Northern California town of Eureka, up in Humboldt County, more remote than the Monterey peninsula. Since she and Kay had been together for over seven years, Kay had moved whenever Donna moved, sometimes to the detriment of Kay's career, something I suppose any couple faces. Donna had transferred back to Monterey two years ago and they'd bought the house.

Donna came out of the bedroom, comfortably attired in a blue sweatsuit. "Hi, Jeri." She waved at me and detoured through the dining room, returning a moment later with a full wineglass and the bottle of chardonnay. "Anyone need topping off?" Kay held out her glass.

"How's the Doyle branch of the family tree?" I asked my cousin.

Donna set the wine bottle down on the coffee table and took a seat on the disreputable ottoman. "Mom and Dad are fine. You won't see them until next week. They've gone tootling off to Hawaii. Sister Judy still lives in Boston and loves it."

"Brother George?"

Donna shook her head. "George is a poop. He has been ever since he was a kid."

George was her older brother. He hadn't reacted well when Donna came out of the closet nearly fifteen years ago, and from all reports he still wasn't comfortable with the fact that his sister was a lesbian.

"He and Marilyn, a.k.a. the wife from hell, just built themselves an ostentatious house up at Fisherman's Flats," Donna was saying. "I've never been invited to darken the overpriced door. He's probably afraid it'll rub off." She and Kay both laughed, somewhat wryly. "We only see George at family gatherings, like Aunt Teresa's big do on Labor Day. He's always coldly polite."

His loss, I thought. "Is George still building hotels right and left?" Donna's brother was a developer, and according to the family information network he'd been involved in several of the resort hotels springing up like weeds all over the peninsula. George hasn't had much use for me since I asked if he and his cronies had anything to do with an arson fire on Cannery Row that conveniently vacated the lot where they'd later built a hotel. I was pulling his leg but George is devoid of humor.

"He's salivating over the closure of Fort Ord," Donna said, sipping her wine. "Now that the Army has pulled out, he'd love to build high-priced houses all over the firing range."

"The base closure's really going to affect the economy down here," I said, and they both nodded. In addition to a large transient military population, Fort Ord had provided jobs to many

Monterey County civilians, and now those jobs were gone. The base closure promised to boost the local unemployment rate, already high, to even steeper levels.

"This place has changed a lot since I was a kid." Donna reached for the wine bottle and poured more chardonnay into her glass. "Monterey used to be a blue-collar town, with the fishing and the canneries, which I barely remember. Now the collar's white."

"Oh, no," Kay interrupted, "it's not even a collar. It's a T-shirt, from one of those tourist shops down on Cannery Row."

We all laughed. "With a picture of an otter, floating on its back on a sea of white cotton," I added.

"They're such picturesque little buggers." As Donna shook her head I thought of yesterday's conversation at the SPCA, when Donna and Marsha Landers defined the cute factor. "No wonder the tourists like them. Otter-feeding time is the number-one attraction at the aquarium."

"I don't remember the canneries," I said. "But I can remember a time when you could roll a bowling ball down the middle of Cannery Row and not hit anyone."

"Before the aquarium," Donna said. "That's the way we date things nowadays."

"Good, bad, or indifferent, everyone has an opinion about the aquarium." I sipped my wine. "I've heard Mother complain about how tourism has changed this area, yet the tourists represent a big chunk of her business."

"People used to go down to Cannery Row to pay homage to John Steinbeck, because they'd read *Cannery Row* and *Tortilla Flat*, and they wanted to visit Doc Ricketts's lab," Donna said. "Now I'll bet most of the people who visit the Row have never even heard of Steinbeck, let alone read him. They go to visit the aquarium."

"And they visit the galleries and the shops where I display my jewelry," Kay said, reaching for the wine bottle. "Thus providing a source of income for this particular self-employed craftsperson."

"Mind you, I'm not totally putting the knock on the aquarium," Donna added. "Most of the exhibits focus on the marine life in Monterey Bay. It's a wonderfully unique marine environment and thank God we've now got sanctuary status. The people who visit the aquarium are getting some education about things like tidal pools and the creatures that live in them. They're finding out there's more living things out there besides otters."

"Which brings us right back to the cute factor," I said. "The last time I was at the aquarium, I overheard some woman going on about the otters. They're just so darling and so cute and who can relate to fish anyway?"

"But if people can see the diversity of marine life," Donna argued, "maybe they'll think before they pour paint thinner down a storm drain or toss trash off a cabin cruiser."

"Or mutilate a pelican."

At my words, Donna frowned. "If I ever get my hands on the person responsible for this . . ."

Her voice trailed off. We were silent for a moment, then Kay rose from the sling-back chair. "I can smell my lasagna. It's time to eat."

We followed Kay through the dining room to the kitchen. "Is there anything I can do to help?" Donna asked.

"Put the salad on the table." Kay handed her a big wood bowl full of tossed greens. She put on a couple of quilted oven mitts and opened the oven door. First she took out a foil-wrapped package that looked like a loaf of garlic bread and handed it to me as I hovered in the background. "Bread basket," she ordered. I looked around and spotted it near the sink. Then she carefully removed a huge glass baking dish full of spinach lasagna and set it on a couple of trivets. "I think I'd better serve in here."

Donna returned from the dining room with three plates. Kay deftly cut three portions of lasagna and transferred them to the plates. By then I had the garlic bread safely wrapped in a couple of napkins, nestled in the basket. Donna opened another bottle of wine and we seated ourselves at the table.

"Mother told me about what's been happening at the restaurant," I said, helping myself to the salad. "She wants me to look into it. Reluctantly, I might add. She doesn't want me to antagonize the staff. I've already managed to do that, where Julian Surtees is concerned."

"Oh, you met Julian, did you?" Donna grinned. "And what did you think?"

"Arrogant snob, cocky bastard, full of himself. Have I missed anything?"

Donna and Kay both laughed. "But he *is* good-looking." Kay tilted her head, so the gold and opal earrings swayed. "Just because I prefer women doesn't mean I can't appreciate the aesthetics of an attractive man. He's nicely put together."

"And he knows it," I finished. "Is he cutting a swath through the ranks of male or female admirers?"

"Julian's definitely heterosexual," Kay said. "Much to the dismay of a certain gallery owner over in Carmel. I've seen Julian squiring several women. There was that redhead whose name I can never remember. You know who I'm talking about, Donna. That horsey type from Carmel Valley. But lately he's been dating Lacy Beckman."

Beckman. The name I kept hearing, over and over, all day long. "Karl Beckman's sister-in-law? I haven't met her yet but I'm sure it's only a matter of time. Somehow I can't imagine Julian Surtees attracted to anyone but himself."

Kay laughed. Her next words fed my curiosity. "I thought Lacy was interested in her brother-in-law. But Karl's been dating Marie since New Year's. Since then I've seen Lacy with Julian Surtees several times."

Donna shrugged. "I don't know Lacy that well. She always seems rather chilly to me. Maybe Julian will warm her up."

"I don't know about that," Kay said. "Julian is like Jeri's mother. Married to the job."

"I got the impression he'd like to move in and take over Café Marie," I said.

"You don't think he's behind the incidents at the restaurant?" Donna frowned. "Why would he do that?"

"I don't know. But the things that you and Mother described had to have been done by someone with backstage access. The staff would certainly notice if a customer walked into the kitchen and started messing about. My best guess is that the saboteur is an employee. Julian Surtees is the most recent addition to the roster. He's certainly got the opportunity. Motivation I'll have to dig into."

"Speaking of digging into, it looks like you need some more

lasagna." Kay stood up and reached for my plate. "How about you, Donna?"

Donna shook her head, but I succumbed. "I shouldn't. But it's so good. I didn't have much lunch. Just a small portion, Kay."

"Did you talk to Bobby?" Donna asked me as Kay stepped into the kitchen. "How did he react to the news about the autopsy?"

"He's grieving for her. I don't know that the idea of murder has sunk in yet. And when it does . . ."

Donna sighed. "Something's bothering me. I'll have to check on this, but it seems to me if Ariel went into the water at Rocky Point, where her car was found, the current would have pushed her body north, toward Point Lobos. But it was found below the Rocky Creek Bridge. That's more than a mile south, and there are a lot of coves and inlets and underwater currents to consider. Of course, I could be wrong. When someone goes into the ocean, search-and-rescue looks for the body a half mile in either direction of the entry point."

"We don't know where she went into the water," I said. "She may have met someone at the restaurant. She could have been walking on the headland. Or her body could have been dumped right off the Rocky Creek Bridge." I played with my fork. "I overheard some women talking at Café Marie. Mother was catering a luncheon for a lot of sailboat owners. One of these women knows Ariel's parents. She was quite sure that Bobby's responsible for Ariel's death. Evidently the Logans feel the same way."

Kay returned from the kitchen and set my plate in front of me. "That kind of talk is all over town. Or towns," she said. "I heard the same remark this afternoon when I was visiting a client in Carmel."

Donna finished off the wine that remained in her glass. "People have been talking since Ariel was reported missing. It's because of that argument Bobby and Ariel had last week. They couldn't have picked a more public place to have a disagreement."

"I asked Bobby about the argument." I picked up my fork. "But he wouldn't tell me anything about it. Except that he'd made a promise. He owes someone a favor and it's complicated. It seems really important to him, almost as important as Ariel. Do you have any idea what or who he's talking about? Who else is close to him?"

Donna thought about it for a moment as she used a crust of garlic bread to mop up some remaining tomato sauce. "Karl Beckman. He and Karl seem to be good friends."

"Despite the difference in their ages?" This surprised me. Bobby was twenty-nine, probably twenty years younger than Beckman. It wasn't completely out of the ordinary that he'd have a friend older than he was. Certainly he knew and worked with people of all ages. But why Karl Beckman? "How close are they?"

"Maybe it's a business relationship," Kay suggested. "Bobby's a fisherman, Karl repairs boats. That sort of professional acquaintance does grow into friendship."

"I think it's more than that," Donna said, playing with her napkin. "I've seen them together, having what looked like deep serious conversations, not the sort of talk you'd get into if you wanted to have your hull repainted. Could be Karl views Bobby as the son he never had. He and his wife just had one child, a daughter."

"Yes, he mentioned her. I was at the wharf before I came over here. I went to see Nick and Tina. Karl Beckman was there, talking with them. Tina told me Beckman's wife died eighteen months ago, in a car accident with his brother. What's the story there?"

"No one knows," Donna said. "Gunter and Janine were headed south on Highway One. It was raining, and the car skidded and went off the road near Hurricane Point. I guess Lacy inherited Gunter's share of the business. She's the office manager."

"I overheard something else at the restaurant," I said. "Rumors of financial difficulties at Beckman Boat Works."

"That's news to me," Donna said, leaning back in her chair. "But it wouldn't surprise me. So many of the businesses in town are hurting in this recession. The only thing that's thriving seems to be the tourist industry."

"As long as they buy my jewelry," Kay said, "that's fine with me. Just so I don't have to go to Carmel on a weekend."

"Oh, good, let's trash Carmel." I laughed. Then I stopped and shook my head. "But I do have to go to Carmel on a weekend. Tomorrow, in fact, to see the Sevilles."

CHAPTER *11*

SHOULDN'T HAVE LAUGHED.

Getting to Carmel on a weekend is not a matter for mirth, particularly during tourist season, which on the Monterey peninsula is nearly year-round. I've never been fond of Carmel, more properly known as Carmel-by-the-Sea. I'll admit the physical setting is glorious, with the blue-green water of Carmel Bay washing onto the impossibly smooth white sand beach at the end of Ocean Avenue. The rocky coast and manicured greens of Pebble Beach lie to the north. To the south is the rugged beauty of Point Lobos.

The older part of Carmel and its downtown are shaded by a thick canopy of Monterey pines, and much of the architecture looks like a fantasy out of the Brothers Grimm. Between the inevitable stores catering to swarms of tourists are restaurants, clothing stores, and art galleries with merchandise too expensive for my taste. There are no street addresses. Carmel residents get their mail at the post office and businesses advertise their location, discreetly, of course, by using the nearest intersection, such as Monte Verde at Seventh. If you're going to visit someone you can spend the better part of an hour looking first for a parking place, then for a house camouflaged by foliage, with no distinguishing marks.

The place has a serious case of the quaints. Most of the time I find Carmel's studied atmosphere a bit much to suit me. Besides, it's such an enclave of money and privilege that my working-class roots rebel.

But Errol and Minna like it. Errol Seville is my mentor, the man who plucked me from my day-to-day toil as a paralegal and trained me as a private investigator. I worked for the Seville Agency for five years, until a heart attack forced Errol into retirement. That's when my investigating career became a solo act.

Saturday morning I pointed my Toyota south on Highway 1, up the slope called Carmel Hill. It was early in the day and Ocean Avenue, Carmel's main street, was not yet clogged with cars. As the day wore on, however, the street would become a nightmare of stop-and-go traffic.

The Sevilles live on San Antonio Avenue, in a patch of sun amid all the pine trees. They've owned the one-story house for years, visiting Carmel on weekends until Errol's health made them full-time residents. The house is whitewashed stone, its dark green shutters matching the bounty of flowers and foliage in the garden, where duties are divided between Minna's flowers and Errol's veggies. I pushed through the wooden gate and walked down a flagstone path lined with autumn lilies.

I've always thought Errol looked like Sam Spade. Not like Humphrey Bogart in the movie version of *The Maltese Falcon*, but Dashiell Hammett's description of Sam Spade in the opening paragraph of his classic novel.

"Samuel Spade's jaw was long and bony," Hammett writes, "his chin a jutting V under the more flexible V of his mouth. His nostrils curved back to make another, small, V. His yellow-grey eyes were horizontal. The V motif was picked up again by thick brows rising outward from twin creases above a hooked nose, and his pale brown hair grew down—from high flat temples—in a point on his forehead. He looked rather pleasantly like a blond satan."

Errol's hair, once auburn like mine, is silver now, forming a widow's peak above his long narrow intelligent face, and Hammett's Vs are evident in his pointed eyebrows and the shape of his mouth. Today he looked like a bemused satan, a large blue ceramic mug of black coffee in his hand as he greeted me with a foxy smile. I thought, as I had many times before, that Errol Seville looked sexier than a lot of men half his age.

This morning Errol wore loose-fitting khaki pants and a blue work shirt, but when I stepped into the living room it didn't look as though Errol intended to do any work. Two matching wing chairs, upholstered with a tapestry fabric, were arranged in front of the fireplace, with a table between them. The table was piled high with books, detective novels. He loves to read them, using his knowledge of investigative fact to dissect the fictional form.

"Want a cup of coffee?" Errol asked. He didn't wait for my answer, instead beckoning me through the living room to the kitchen, where a coffeemaker sat on the counter. Next to it a square pan held something with walnuts and cinnamon sprinkled liberally over the top. "How about some coffee cake? Minna made it this morning."

"It looks delicious," I told him, succumbing to the warm spicy scent.

"Whack off a chunk, then." He opened a cupboard and handed me a plate, then pulled out a drawer and removed a knife and fork. While I cut myself a square of coffee cake he reached for the coffeepot and poured a mug of coffee.

"Where's Minna?" I asked, peering through the French doors to the flagstone patio and the garden beyond.

"Gone to do the marketing. She likes to get it out of the way early." Errol headed back to the living room and I trailed behind, balancing my plate and my coffee. Errol settled into one of the wing chairs and waved his hand at the other. "Have a seat. Just shove Stinkpot off the chair."

Stinkpot glared at me as though he understood every word and was daring me to try. He must be fifteen or sixteen years old now, an enormous neutered tom, as big as the average beagle, with the disposition of a cranky pit bull. The cat's long black-and-white hair and pushed-in face indicated some Persian in his mixed ancestry. He sprawled on the second wing chair, draped over two pillows that had once been blue but were now grayed by a visible layer of black-and-white fur. Stinkpot's yellow eyes glittered at me and he growled low in his throat. He flexed his front paws, showing wicked-looking claws that would slash at my hand should I be so foolish as to shove him off his chair.

I bypassed the wing chair for the nearby sofa, setting my mug and plate on the coffee table. I knew better than to mess with Stinkpot. He had the most disagreeable disposition I'd ever seen in a cat. Maybe it was the result of going through life with a moniker like Stinkpot. His primacy established, the big tomcat rose majestically to all four paws, stretched luxuriously, and turned his back to us, sprawling across the chair seat, his tail trailing to the floor like a triumphant plume.

"So why was your cousin Bobby Ravella arguing with Ariel Logan at the Rose and Crown last Friday afternoon?" Errol asked, sipping coffee.

I swallowed a mouthful of the coffee cake, which tasted as good as it looked. "He won't tell me. Do you know everything?"

If he did, I wouldn't be at all surprised. Errol is a damned good investigator, one of the best. I feel fortunate to have learned the business under his tutelage and to count him and Minna as friends. I call Errol on the phone when I need his help, or just need someone to act as a sounding board for ideas and theories. He may be retired but his brain and instincts are still sharp. And sometimes it seems to me he knows everyone in law enforcement throughout California, local and state and even federal. It's as though he's plugged into an enormous intelligence grid, and all I have to do is connect with Errol to gain information.

"Just about. Carmel is rather gossipy. It's been a major topic of speculation all week, ever since the Logans got back from Europe and reported their daughter missing. We know the parents, not well. They live just around the corner. I don't recall having met the daughter."

"What have you heard?"

"The most persistent theory about the argument," Errol said, "is that Ariel had tired of the relationship with your cousin and that he didn't want to break it off. That's what I heard when she was reported missing. After her car was found down at Rocky Point, the rumor mill suspected foul play. By late yesterday afternoon everyone had heard the news about the autopsy. Since the cause of death was a blow to the head, it's a rather short jump to the theory that he killed her."

"Bobby wouldn't kill anyone. Especially not Ariel. He loved her."

Errol tilted his head to one side and diplomatically did not remind me that people very often kill people they love. "Then you'd better find someone else with a motive. Peter Logan has already asked the sheriff's department why they haven't arrested Bobby for Ariel's murder. Sergeant Magruder is supposed to be meticulous and methodical. Also relentless. That's the reason he's the head of the county investigations division."

"I need more details. When did Ariel die? No one admits to having seen her since Friday afternoon. Her car wasn't found until Wednesday. So presumably she was killed sometime between Friday evening and Wednesday morning. The coroner must have pinpointed the time of death. Is there any way you can get a copy of that autopsy report?"

"I can manage it. The Carmel police chief is a friend of mine."

"The only way to go about this is to do exactly what Magruder is doing. Reconstruct Ariel's last few days."

"And try not to get in Magruder's way," Errol added. "I hear he has a limited tolerance for private investigators. Particularly one with a vested interest. And you definitely have an agenda, Jeri. Are you positive your cousin had nothing to do with Ariel Logan's murder?"

"You always told me to trust my gut." I looked at Errol steadily over the coffee mug I held cradled in both hands. "My gut says no. If I find out otherwise, I'll do what has to be done."

Errol nodded slowly. "What exactly did Bobby tell you?"

I took a swallow of coffee before I answered. "He says he owes someone a favor. He can't tell me until he checks something out. My guess is he and Ariel were arguing about this debt. I'll check out the Rose and Crown, to see if any of the employees overheard the argument. Even if Ariel was killed shortly after she left Bobby, surely someone must have seen her. She'd cut her Friday classes at Cal Poly, so she must have had a reason for driving to Monterey. What time did she get here? Did anyone see her before she met Bobby at the Rose and Crown?"

"I can answer that question," a voice said behind us.

Errol and I both turned our heads and he smiled. "Hello, love."

Minna Seville walked into the living room from the kitchen, a slender woman in her late sixties, with gray hair cut short and swept back behind her ears in a no-nonsense style. She wore blue seersucker slacks and a white blouse, her feet in blue canvas shoes.

"Hi, Jeri. Good to see you again." She leaned over and kissed

Errol on his forehead. "Groceries, Errol. I buy 'em, you carry 'em."

"I'll help," I said as Errol got to his feet. We trooped through the kitchen to the side door that led to the driveway and ferried several canvas sacks of groceries into the kitchen, where we began unloading and storing provisions. I helped myself to another cup of coffee and poured one for Minna. "You were going to answer my question."

"The Logans employ a Mrs. Costello, who cleans and cooks." Minna took the mug I offered, thanked me, and took several cans from a bag. "She'd been off while Peter and Sylvie were in France, just dropping by periodically to check on things at the house and water the plants. In anticipation of their return on Sunday, she came to the house on Friday to make sure it was clean and the refrigerator stocked. She left to do the marketing, around two, and saw Ariel drive up just then. When Mrs. Costello returned later with the groceries, Ariel was gone. Her overnight bag was in her room, where Peter and Sylvie found it Sunday evening. It looks as though Ariel never came back to the house."

As Minna spoke I found myself wondering again which route Ariel had taken on her drive north from San Luis Obispo. If she'd left early, as her roommate said, and taken the coast highway, her arrival in Carmel at two was not that unusual. But the inland route, U.S. 101, takes about three hours. If she'd taken that highway, where had she gone before arriving at her parents' house?

"How do you know this, my love?" Errol smiled down at his wife and she responded by handing him a box of shredded wheat.

"Peter's sister, Glennis Braemer, from Pasadena. I ran into her at the grocery store. Of course I had to convey my condolences. We got to talking."

"Did she tell you whether the funeral has been scheduled?" I looked up from the bag I was emptying.

"Monday morning at eleven, at Carmel Mission. Glennis said people have been dropping by the house nonstop since the body was found."

"Where do the Logans live?" I asked.

"Scenic Road. The gray stucco with the red bougainvillea, just past Santa Lucia."

"With a view of Carmel Bay. Big bucks," I commented.

"Oh, yes," Errol chimed in. He was stacking cans of cat food on a lower shelf. "The Logans do not lack money."

"Mother described them as Hollywood refugees. The mother an actress, the father a writer."

"Ever hear of Sylvie Romillard?" Minna asked. I shook my head. "Before your time, really. Sylvie's about your mother's age, maybe younger. Peter's older, probably my age. Sylvie was in some of the French New Wave films. When she came to Hollywood, her career never really caught fire. She married Peter in the late sixties. He'd been married before. Ariel was born down in Los Angeles, but they moved to Carmel shortly afterward. Peter still writes, but I think most of their money comes from real estate. I know they own some rentals and I think Peter's involved in some hotel deals."

"How well do you know them?" I asked.

"We're friendly, but not close. I met them several years ago, before we moved down here for good." By now Minna had emptied all the canvas bags of their burden. She laid them on top of each other and rolled them into a neat bundle, then tucked them into a drawer. "I'd met Ariel. She seemed like a pleasant, intelligent young woman, the kind who's destined for great things." Her smile was sad.

"Bobby said they were planning to get married."

"If that was so," Minna said, "she hadn't told her parents. I think they were hoping your cousin Bobby was a phase Ariel would outgrow."

I nodded. "They didn't think the fisherman was good enough for their daughter."

"Of course not," Errol said. "There is definitely a social pecking order around here. Ariel and Bobby were on different levels."

"Ariel had another boyfriend, before she met Bobby. A lawyer."

"Ryan Trent," Minna said. "He has an office downtown. A rather brash young man. I hear he was extremely upset when Ariel broke off their relationship."

I mulled this over for a moment, thinking that it would be worth my while to talk with Trent. He wouldn't be the first old boyfriend who didn't want to let go of a relationship. Of course, that's what people were saying about Bobby, an irony not lost on me.

"Did Glennis say how her brother and his wife were handling their daughter's death?"

"She didn't have to. Peter and Sylvie Logan thought the sun rose and set in that girl. Now that she's dead they're devastated." Minna's words echoed those I'd heard yesterday at Café Marie. "They're eager to find someone to blame. Your cousin happens to be the likely target."

I told Errol and Minna about the incidents at my mother's restaurant, those accidents that looked more and more deliberate. As I laid the details before him I saw Errol's gray eyes sparkle at the prospect of a real puzzle rather than the fictional ones that now occupied most of his time. My mentor was bored with retirement and eager to help me with this particular problem. Minna was willing to let him, as long as his assistance didn't affect his health.

Errol agreed that the most likely saboteur was an employee. After all, who else would have the opportunity to move about freely in the kitchen? Who else would know enough about the placement of the knives to tamper with the drawer?

"I saw the unfavorable review in the *Herald*," Minna told me, "but I didn't really pay it any mind. Any restaurant can have an off day. I suppose it would be different if we'd had a bad experience ourselves. I can see why your mother's concerned, though. Gossip can really have a negative impact on business. Café Marie's been consistently excellent as far as I'm concerned. In fact, we're having dinner there this evening, at seven. Why don't you join us?"

"Good idea." Errol's mouth curved in a conspiratorial smile. "Then all of us can observe."

N EW MONTEREY IS SO CALLED BECAUSE IT WAS NEWER
than the downtown section near the waterfront, which was
the earliest settlement of the citizens of Spain and Mexico who
later called themselves *Californios*. The people who lived in New
Monterey were the fishermen and cannery workers like the Doyles
and Ravellas. The streets climb a steep hill above Lighthouse
Avenue, looking down on Cannery Row and the bay. The houses
are wood frame and stucco, larger than they look from the street,
now sharing space with apartment buildings and condos.

Linda Camacho Ravella came from a fishing family. That's how
she met my cousin Bobby. Their fathers and grandfathers knew
each other, fished together, their boats plying the rich fishing
grounds of Monterey Bay. Their mothers and grandmothers wor-
shiped at the same Catholic church and belonged to the same civic
organizations. The Ravellas even lived near the Camachos.

Linda and Bobby grew up together, attending the same schools
and graduating together from Monterey High. They'd dated all
through their senior year and it seemed natural that they'd ex-
changed marriage vows. Nicky came along three years later, but
the marriage fell apart after that. Linda got a job working in the
office of one of the chain hotels in downtown Monterey and
bought a house on Belden Street in New Monterey, a block or so
from Bay View Elementary, where Nicky had just started the third
grade.

I was startled to see a For Sale sign in front of Linda's little wood-frame house, so similar to my mother's place, with one story and two bedrooms. The house sat on the upslope side of the street, so Linda had a scrap of a view, the blue waters of the bay visible in the gap between the two houses across the street. There was a wooden glider on the porch, its seat covered with fat pillows. Next to it was a small rattan table and a large jade tree in a pot. Several smaller plants were arrayed along the porch railing. As I climbed the steps to the front door I saw a red plastic crate containing balls in various sizes and other items made of plastic that I could only guess were toys. It seemed quiet when I rang the bell. I guessed that eight-year-old Nicky Ravella wasn't home.

His mother was, though. It was just after noon and Linda was in the kitchen, fixing herself a big salad. She invited me to join her, sliced a few more carrots and cucumbers, and fetched another wineglass from the cupboard. After eating, we adjourned to the porch and the glider, slouching comfortably, pillows propped behind us as we talked and finished the bottle of wine.

Linda's hair was brown and curly, caught back with a red ribbon, and she had large brown eyes rimmed by long lashes. Her body looked trim in the blue jeans and pink T-shirt she wore. On the third finger of her left hand she wore a diamond engagement ring, which explained the For Sale sign in front of her house.

"Your parents are going to hate it when you leave." I looked past her to the framed photograph she'd set on the rattan table. Her fiancé was a tall blond fellow with close-cropped hair and blue eyes, broad shoulders straining the jacket of his green uniform. His name was Warren Everett and he was an Army master sergeant stationed at the Defense Language Institute at Monterey's Presidio. But not for long. He had orders to Washington, D.C.

"I know," Linda said, her fingers playing with the diamond setting. "I've got mixed feelings myself. I've lived in Monterey my whole life, never even traveled much. Going up to San Francisco is a big deal to me. Now I'll be living all the way across the country. It'll seem strange not seeing Mom and Dad two or three times a week. But I'm looking forward to seeing another part of the country. And Warren—"

Linda flashed a big warm smile. "He's got a daughter from his first marriage, so I'll have that little girl I always wanted. She's ten and kinda feisty. She and Nicky get along pretty good. Warren is really nice, Jeri. I can't wait for you to meet him. We're having dinner tonight at your mom's restaurant. Bobby's got Nicky this weekend."

"I'll be at the restaurant, too, with some friends. If you see us, bring Warren over. I'd like to meet him."

I sipped my wine and broached a subject that had been on my mind ever since Linda told me about her impending marriage and departure from Monterey. The first was scheduled to take place in October, the second before Thanksgiving. Bobby had always played an active role in Nicky's life, spending alternate weekends with the boy. When Linda moved from Monterey, he would not see his son as often. I knew that would bother him.

"How's Bobby taking this?"

"He hasn't said." Linda's smile dimmed. "Bobby's got a lot on his mind right now."

"I know. He said he and Ariel were planning to get married."

Linda nodded. "He told me, too, right after he asked her. They were going to wait until Ariel finished her degree. She was with him once, when he came to pick up Nicky, and Bobby introduced us. She seemed like such a nice girl, so good for Bobby. He really had changed for the better. After we were divorced he was pretty wild, drinking too much, hanging out with a rowdy crowd. What a terrible thing to happen. When Bobby picked up Nicky this morning, he looked like someone had punched him in the stomach."

Their usual arrangement was for Bobby to pick up Nicky Friday night and return him to his mother's house Sunday evening. But Bobby had been in no condition to see his son yesterday.

"There's a lot of talk around town," I said, "about Bobby and Ariel."

"People are blaming Bobby. My parents told me. Jeri, that's outrageous. If you could have seen them together. He loved her as much as I love Warren."

"I know you and Bobby have kept up a friendly relationship with each other, in spite of the divorce. Linda, did he say anything to you about what was going on between him and Ariel? I'm trying to find out what they were arguing about last week."

"I don't know." Linda paused and sipped wine, then set her

glass on the table next to the photograph. "You see, Bobby was supposed to have Nicky last weekend, Friday night to Sunday night. But he showed up at my office last Friday afternoon, about four, and asked if he could pick up Nicky Saturday morning instead. I was a bit put out, since Warren and I had plans. He's got child-care arrangements on his end, too, which makes it difficult. But Bobby said it was urgent. He looked worried, upset, like a thundercloud. He must have just come from the Rose and Crown, from his fight with Ariel."

"What was so important that he'd rearrange the schedule at the last minute?"

"At first he was closemouthed, but I told him if he was going to change things at the last minute, he'd better tell me why." Linda sipped her wine. "He said he had to find Karl Beckman. In fact, he was on his way over to Beckman Boat Works." She tilted her chin in the direction of the bay, where Cannery Row was hidden from our view by buildings.

Bobby had to see Karl Beckman? At this my eyebrows went up. This favor that weighed so heavily on my cousin's mind—could it be owed to Karl Beckman?

"And did he?"

"I don't know." Linda shrugged. "Next time I saw him, he didn't say."

I asked Linda about Bobby's relationship with Karl Beckman. Like Donna, she speculated that it held some father-son element. Yet Bobby was close to his own father, so Beckman didn't fill any evident gap. Or maybe he did. According to Linda, the friendship between the older boatyard owner and the young fisherman began sometime before Bobby met Ariel, when Bobby was exhibiting some of his wilder behavior. I knew that Nick and Tina had been worried about Bobby's drinking and the company he kept. Perhaps the counsel of Beckman, an outsider, got through to Bobby when his parents couldn't. But Donna's theory was that Bobby's turnaround was due to Ariel.

I tried to tell myself that it was logical to be suspicious of Karl Beckman. But something inside me argued that I wasn't giving the man the benefit of the doubt. And I knew why. It was because he was dating my mother.

* * *

WHEN I LEFT LINDA'S HOUSE, I DID WHAT SHE ASSUMED BOBBY HAD done, and headed down the slope of the New Monterey Hill toward Cannery Row, where the huge crane loomed near the aquarium. I found a parking space on Foam Street and shoved coins into the meter. As I walked toward my destination I saw another crane and a sign announcing the impending construction of yet another hotel.

I wondered how long Beckman Boat Works could hold out against this shifting tide. Years ago, when canneries crowded both sides of the street, Beckman's Cannery Row location was an advantage. Now the yard was crowded by hotels, one across the street and one right next door. On the other side was a beach popular with divers. It was a given that traffic was already a problem. And people who stayed at those hotels no doubt wanted to look off their balconies at the bay and the rocky shore. Would they think it picturesque to view a high fence surrounding a yard full of boats in various stages of repair, accompanied by banging hammers, the whine of power tools, and the spark of welding torches?

Added to this was the fact that Beckman Boat Works was smaller than its only local competitor, the Monterey Boat Works, a couple of blocks away, at the foot of the Coast Guard jetty. Could the economy of the Monterey peninsula support two boatyards? I recalled all those sailboat owners at the luncheon yesterday and shrugged. As long as people have boats, those boats will need repairs.

I wasn't sure the boatyard would be open this Saturday afternoon, but the gate yawned wide and there was activity inside. As I entered the yard I saw a Travel-Lift directly in front of me, its supports sunk into the bay floor. At the moment its straps were secured around the hull of a cabin cruiser, suspended in the air as several of the yard's employees hauled it out of the water.

To my right I counted seven boats, resting on blocks or hitches. The one closest to me was a metal-hulled barge; a welder in coveralls was applying a torch to a seam. The other vessels were constructed of wood or fiberglass, and each had something being done to it by one or more of the workers, wielding paintbrushes, hammers, or other tools. In the old days most of these vessels would have been commercial fishing boats, but now it looked as though half of them were pleasure craft.

To my left I saw a two-story building with several doors. The first door had a soda machine and a pay phone next to it. I peered inside. This was the chandlery, a marine supply shop. A few steps farther a second wide door opened onto the machine and wood-working shops. In here, chaos and noise reigned as a saw screamed somewhere in the back.

A third door, on the bay end, had a small wooden sign that read OFFICE. As I approached it I saw a white pickup truck with a blue logo on the driver's-side door. It was a stylized drawing of a sailboat and below this, in a half circle of capital letters, I saw the legend BECKMAN BOAT WORKS.

I went through the door and up the stairs to the second floor. A small office looked down on the yard. There was no one in sight. A utilitarian metal desk held a phone, a message pad, and several flyers advertising for bids on government boat repairs. Behind the desk was a row of four-drawer filing cabinets and on the wall to my left I saw a copy machine, a fax machine, and some cabinets containing office supplies.

Doors on either side of the filing cabinets led to two additional offices. The door nearest me was closed, the other stood open. I tried the closed door and discovered it was locked. I moved to the open doorway and decided this office belonged to Karl Beckman. The wooden desk and the padded leather chair had a clubby male feel to it, and I saw that the wall behind the desk held several framed photographs showing the tall fair-haired boatyard owner with a variety of people. Another photograph on his desk caught my eye and I moved closer, frowning as I recognized the face. It was my mother.

I heard footsteps climbing the stairs and I stepped out of Karl's office, just before someone entered from the landing. She was a tall, athletic-looking woman wearing olive-green slacks and a crisp white shirt. Her straight shoulder-length hair was the same gold as ripening wheat, and her eyes were an odd shade of yellow brown that reminded me of the stone called tigereye. She was an inch or so taller than my own five feet eight inches, and several years older. Late thirties, I thought, spotting a few wrinkles around her eyes that didn't look like laugh lines.

The woman looked startled to see me there. She stopped and I saw that she carried a paper sack in one hand and a slender brown leather bag slung over one shoulder. The fingers of one hand ran down the strap of the bag. Her oddly colored eyes looked wary as they examined me, but her voice was polite enough. "May I help you?"

"I'm looking for Lacy Beckman."

"I'm Lacy. What can I do for you?"

"My name's Jeri Howard."

"Ah, yes," Lacy Beckman said. Now she reached into the leather bag and pulled out a set of keys, unlocking the closed door. "Marie's daughter. The private investigator."

"You know what I do?" I asked.

"Oh, Marie's told us all about it."

I followed her into the office, which couldn't have been more unlike Karl's. Everything was high-tech and modern, from the white laminated desk to the bookshelves and cabinets behind it. A computer and printer sat on a mobile cart, ready to be wheeled into position for use.

Lacy Beckman took a seat on the gray office chair at the desk and opened the paper sack, taking out a large container with a lid and a crusty roll. She removed the lid and the aroma of strong coffee filled the room. The only other seat in the room was an un-comfortable-looking director's chair with a red canvas seat and back. I sat down in this.

"Is there something you wanted, Jeri?" Lacy Beckman raised the coffee to her lips.

"I'd like to ask you a few questions. It concerns Bobby Ravella."

She took a sip of her coffee and tore a chunk of the roll. "Bobby Ravella. Your cousin, isn't he? I heard about his friend Ariel. What a tragedy." She said the words without much feeling, as though she were saying it just because everyone else was. "You don't think he had anything to do with it, do you?"

"No. Do you?"

"Of course not," she assured me as she pinched off a smaller section of the roll. "But there's certainly a lot of talk making the rounds. Especially after that fight at the Rose and Crown."

"Bobby may have come over here late that afternoon, looking for Karl. Were you here?"

"Friday afternoon?" She took another swallow of coffee. The phone rang and she picked it up, saying, "Beckman Boat Works." She listened, reaching for one of the pencils that stood in a gray plastic cup near her hand. As she talked she scribbled some notes on a pad of paper.

"A forty-three foot Beneteau from Bodega Bay to Monterey? Certainly. We can haul it or sail it, whatever you'd prefer. Let me check my calendar." She and the caller talked figures and dates. When she hung up the phone she smiled again and reached for her coffee.

"Now, what was it you were asking? Was I here Friday, a week ago? Yes, as a matter of fact I was. Right here in the office, catching up on some paperwork. That's what I do, keep the books, pay the bills, that sort of thing."

"And transport boats," I said, nodding at the phone.

"That, too. I love to sail. This gives me a chance to do it, on all sorts of boats, without the expense of having one of my own."

Lacy Beckman had a way of tilting her head back and looking down her patrician nose when she spoke. Her tone wasn't exactly unfriendly, but I didn't think the woman and I were going to be best buddies either. She sounded as though she'd spent some time back east or in an upper-crust school. What was she doing here in Monterey, keeping the books and hauling boats from place to place? She looked as though she belonged on the deck of a yacht with a cocktail in her hand, not behind the desk of a boatyard office. Even if she had inherited her share from her deceased husband, this business partnership with her brother-in-law was an odd pairing. I recalled the curious shadow that had passed over Karl Beckman's face when I'd mentioned his sister-in-law.

"If Bobby was here," I said slowly, "it would have been four-thirty, five o'clock. Did you see him?"

She shook her head. "No, I didn't. We were probably getting ready to close. Several people worked late that day, finishing up a job, so someone else may have seen Bobby."

"And what about Karl?" I asked, trying to find a more comfortable position in the canvas chair.

"I don't know where Karl was," Lacy Beckman said. She popped another piece of roll into her mouth, chewed, and washed it down with coffee. "He was here earlier that morning, then he left and I didn't see him again until Monday. I thought maybe he and Marie had plans."

She smiled again. I looked at her sharply, wondering if she knew that it bothered me to hear her say anything about Karl's relationship with my mother. "Why don't you ask him?"

I intended to do just that. "Which of the employees were here finishing up that job?"

"Want to talk to them? To see if any of them saw Bobby? Sure, let me check the payroll records to see who worked that afternoon."

She stood and walked the few steps to the outer office, keys in hand, and I heard her unlock one of the filing cabinets. She returned a moment later with a file folder in hand. She opened it and rattled off several names of employees who'd been here last Friday, including those who'd worked late. I had hoped that she would let me prowl the yard on my own but she had other ideas, such as escorting me. She left the folder on her desk and locked her office before leading the way downstairs.

Outside two workers in coveralls stood near the soda machine next to the chandlery door, taking a break. When they saw Lacy Beckman they finished their cigarettes and sodas quickly and headed back toward a sailboat in the middle of the yard. First we talked to the man who clerked in the chandlery, who didn't recall seeing Bobby. Then we walked over to the Travel-Lift, where the cabin cruiser was now out of the water and up on supports. The employees knew Bobby but none of them had seen him.

Finally we headed for the shops where woodworking and machine repairs were done. The deafening whine of the saw had stopped and whoever had been running it was nowhere in sight. Then I saw a man in dark blue pants and a torn and stained T-shirt that had once been white, coming through a door at the back of the shop. It must have led to the rest room because he was zipping his pants as he walked.

He stopped when he saw us, and I looked him over. He was of medium build, lean, with stringy muscles visible in his arms, and long dark hair that looked like it needed a good wash. His upper lip was decorated with a thin mustache and now he tightened his thin-lipped mouth, narrowing a pair of muddy brown eyes. I had a feeling he didn't much care for the boss lady, as represented by Lacy Beckman, who looked out of place here in the middle of all the grease and dust.

"Frank, this is Jeri Howard," she said, smiling as though to reassure him. "She's Bobby Ravella's cousin. She'd like to ask you some questions about last Friday."

"Friday?" he repeated, frowning a furrow between his eyebrows, as wispy as his mustache. His eyes flicked to his right, at a closed door, then just as quickly back to Lacy.

"Yes, a week ago yesterday." I wished Lacy Beckman hadn't announced that I was Bobby Ravella's cousin.

"The day you were working on the Gradys' boat," Lacy prompted.

"Oh, yeah, that was Friday." He nodded, running a hand over his chin, then wiping it on his filthy shirt. Now he looked at me. "What about it?"

"Bobby says he came by here looking for Karl." I wished I could talk with the man without Lacy looming nearby in the role of the vigilant supervisor. "You know Bobby Ravella?"

He narrowed his eyes. "Yeah, I know him."

Frank's shifty look put me on guard. Why did he keep cutting his eyes toward that door, as though waiting for something to jump out at him? It made me want to look behind the door. Suddenly I guessed who he was. Lacy hadn't mentioned his last name, but something told me it was Alviso, the same Frank Alviso Bobby had fired this past summer. And who, according to Marsha Landers at the SPCA, may have had a part in the pelican mutilations several years ago.

Frank shook his head. "Nah, Bobby didn't come by here. Least not that I saw. You could ask the other guys."

I already had, receiving the same answer.

"The Gradys picked up their boat and we all split," Frank offered with a shrug of his shoulders. "If Bobby came by, it must have been after that." He shot me a look that made me distrust him even more and escaped to the machine shop. A moment later the saw was in full cry.

"Sorry we can't help you," Lacy said briskly, as though she'd like to return to her coffee before it was completely cold. Her smile didn't quite reach her tiger eyes. "I'll tell Karl you dropped by. Of course, he's been spending so much time with Marie, you may see him before I do."

CHAPTER 13

The Rose and Crown on Alvarado Street in downtown Monterey is long, narrow, and dark, with booths and tables to the left of the entrance, some of them on a raised level, and a bar and small kitchen to the right. Farther back are two large round tables and a hallway leading to the rest rooms and a rear entrance.

It was nearly three on a warm Saturday afternoon. I figured everyone would be out enjoying the sunshine, but the Rose and Crown had plenty of customers. Most of them were younger than me, in their twenties. A group of three young men in blue jeans and T-shirts were playing darts near the back, where a television set suspended from the ceiling displayed the California lottery's keno game. The rock music audible over customers' conversation seemed at odds with the British pub atmosphere.

I took a seat on a bar stool and scanned the list of beers and ales. Most were British, as was the young woman behind the bar. I guessed her accent originated in England's industrial north and she confirmed this, saying she was from Leeds.

"How long have you been in Monterey?" I asked, ordering a Samuel Smith's Pale Ale.

"Two years. Come all the way from England and wind up working in a pub. Fancy that." She was in her twenties, with a slender build inside the snowy-white T-shirt she wore, its front decorated with the Rose and Crown logo. Her short spiky blond hair was tipped with red, and several rows of earrings ranged up her earlobes.

I laid some bills on the bar and asked her if she'd been working Friday afternoon, a week ago. She squared her shoulders and narrowed her sharp blue eyes, a little less friendly than she had been a moment ago. "Who wants to know?"

"Jeri Howard. I'm Bobby Ravella's cousin. He was here that afternoon, with a friend of his. Ariel Logan."

As she considered this, one of the dart players stepped up to the bar and called, "Hey, Stella, bring me another Guinness." She complied with his order, then moved back to where I sat and leaned her elbows on the bar.

"Yeah, I was working. Cops already been in, asking questions."

"What did you tell them?" I poured some of the ale into the glass, watching the foam rise.

"Not much." Stella quirked her mouth in a little smile. "Bobby and Ariel were here, talking. Then they went outside. Heard enough to know they were havin' a row, but I don't know what about. That's what I told the cops."

Somehow I thought she'd heard more than that. At least I hoped so. "What will you tell me?"

"Bobby's cousin, eh? He's got a lot of relatives. Where you from?"

"Oakland. My mother's Marie Howard. She owns Café Marie."

Stella nodded. "Posh place. I had a drink there once. Can't afford to eat a meal, though. Not at those prices. Yeah, Bobby was here. Doesn't come in much anymore. Heard he stopped drinking."

"Did you know Ariel Logan?" I asked, sipping my ale.

"Just to speak to. She used to come in here when she was seeing that lawyer. Now, he was a flaming asshole. She was better off with Bobby. I don't think he'd hurt her. Never mind what the gossips are saying."

Stella pointed over my shoulder at a booth on the upper level of the pub, near the front. "Bobby and Ariel came in 'round three o'clock and sat there. Had mineral water, both of them. Guess Bobby really is on the wagon. He ordered a sandwich." Stella wrinkled her nose. "He smelled of fish. After they ordered, he went back to the loo for a wash."

At three in the afternoon, I thought, Bobby had just finished his day's work at the wharf. Unless he'd gone home first to clean up, he would be both hungry and dirty. "Did you hear any of their conversation?"

"They were talking low, like they didn't want to be overheard. But I did hear a scrap or two. Just words, mind you. Couldn't really put them together."

I raised the glass to my lips. "What were some of the words you heard?"

Stella frowned and thought hard. *"Solve,"* she said finally. "Like, maybe it doesn't solve anything. Ariel said something about having to report it."

Now it was my turn to frown. "Report what?"

"A boat. Ariel saw something." Stella shook her head. "Sorry. Makes no sense. Only time I heard anything was while I was delivering drinks, to their table and the ones around them."

"How did they look? Body language, I mean."

"Bobby was all tight-jawed. Ariel was doing most of the talking." Stella fingered one of her multiple earrings. "Then she stood up and walked out. I saw her, because I was heading toward the booth with Bobby's sandwich. He threw a twenty on the table and followed her out, didn't even have a chance to eat. I guess they went at it hammer and tongs outside."

"How do you know that, if they were outside? Was the door open?" I glanced to my right, at the entrance.

"Usually is when the weather's nice. Maybe I heard them." Stella shrugged. "No, that's not it. A fellow came in right after they went out. He remarked on it."

"Who was he?" I asked. "I'd like to talk to him."

"I don't know," Stella said apologetically. "He comes in now and then. I'm sure I'd recognize him if I saw him again."

I gave her my business card and wrote Mother's telephone number on the back. "If you think of anything else, or remember who this guy is, get in touch with me."

Stella nodded and moved off to wait on several people who stepped up to the bar. I finished my ale and left her a large tip, then stepped out onto the sidewalk in front of the Rose and Crown, where Bobby and Ariel had continued their argument that

Friday afternoon. What were they fighting about? Something serious, something important, something Ariel saw and wanted to report. The sea lions? She'd already reported that to the SPCA. It must be something else. Why didn't Bobby want her to say anything?

I worked my way down both sides of Alvarado Street, looking for someone who might have seen Ariel or Bobby that afternoon. It had been Friday, the end of the work week, and I was sure the street had been busy with people running errands on their way home, headed for dinner or a drink after work. Someone must have seen them. But I came up empty. Besides, Sergeant Magruder had been there before me, presumably with the same results.

I ARRIVED AT CAF⁰ MARIE BEFORE MY SEVEN O'CLOCK DATE WITH Errol and Minna Seville, wearing a pair of black slacks and a short-sleeved shirt in a pale turquoise that blended with Café Marie's ocean decor. I took a stool at the bar. Evan the bartender gave me a friendly hello, despite the fact I'd interviewed him yesterday about the incidents at the restaurant.

"Calistoga?" he inquired.

"Sherry."

I glanced toward the kitchen. Mother and Julian were both in the thick of it, activity swirling around them as the cooks chopped and sautéed and arranged things on plates for the waiters. I turned toward the dining room in time to see Rachel Donahoe escort Karl and Lacy Beckman to a table on the lower level, near Café Marie's front windows. If I hadn't known they were sister- and brother-in-law, I'd have thought they were a married couple, an oddly matched one. I watched with interest as they greeted their dining companions, an older couple who had already been seated. The man was nearly bald, with a thatch of white hair behind his ears. He stood to greet the Beckmans, slapping Karl on the shoulder as he shook hands with Lacy.

Errol and Minna arrived a moment later. Rachel greeted them with a big smile, succumbing to Errol's charm. Our table was in the middle of the crowded lower dining room. The Sevilles took the two seats facing me. When I looked to the right I could see right up the two shallow steps leading to the bar and the kitchen.

I saw Linda Ravella and her fiancé at a small table in the corner. I excused myself and walked to where they sat. They were holding hands, leaning toward each other across the table, no doubt talking about their wedding and their future life together. When Linda saw me, she introduced me to Warren, who immediately got to his feet and grabbed my hand instead, shaking it vigorously. He seemed like a big friendly bear of a man, his devotion to Linda evident in his eyes.

"Who was that?" Errol asked when I returned to the table.

"Bobby's ex-wife and her intended. He's an Army master sergeant." I settled into my chair, picked up my menu, and tilted my head to the left, in the direction of the foursome near the front. "Who's that with Karl and Lacy Beckman?" There were two other tables in between, impeding my view, and the muted light of the restaurant made serious observation more difficult.

Minna Seville slewed her eyes to her right. "The Gradys. Recently retired and moved here from San Mateo. They have a sailboat berthed at the marina."

Grady. That was the name I'd heard earlier at Beckman Boat Works. Our server stepped up to the table, bearing a basket of warm bread, and asked if we'd care to order drinks. Errol raked his eyes over the wine list and ordered a bottle of chardonnay.

When the server had gone, Errol peered at me over the top of his menu. "Why so interested in the Beckmans?"

I shrugged. "Karl seems to be good friends with Bobby. Besides, his name came up when I talked with Bobby's ex-wife today." I gave Errol and Minna a rundown of my conversation with Linda, wondering again why it was so important that Bobby track down Karl Beckman last weekend, after his argument with Ariel. According to Linda, he hadn't succeeded in doing so. Where was Karl, then?

"Would this have something to do with the fact that your mother has been dating Karl Beckman?"

I looked at Errol, exasperated by his ability to hit nails on the head. "Is there anything that goes on in Monterey County that you don't know?"

"I'm sure there is," he said modestly. "I just happen to know that particular tidbit. I take it you don't like the prospect that your mother has a social life." I stumbled around a bit, not quite answering. "Just don't let it color your judgment."

"It's not." I took refuge in my menu, trying to decide which of the alluring entrées I wanted. I once described the type of food available at Café Marie as "California cuisine" but Mother corrected me, rejecting this overused term.

"I just cook good food," she said. "Whatever's fresh and in season, prepared in an innovative fashion."

I had to admit, looking at the menu, which varied from day to day, that some of the dishes she and her staff created were remarkable. Sometimes there was a hint of a French accent in the offerings, and other times the flavor was Latin or Asian. Whatever wound up on the bill of fare, it was created from the best and freshest ingredients Monterey County had to offer. Calamari or sand dabs, caught that morning in the bay, grilled vegetables from farms near Salinas, artichokes from Castroville, strawberries from Watsonville, and wine from central coast vineyards.

I'd narrowed my menu choices down to three when the server returned with our wine and poured a small amount into Errol's glass, waiting for him to pronounce judgment. Errol savored a mouthful, then nodded, and the server poured each of us a glass.

"Are you ready to order?" he asked.

"I'll have the grilled swordfish," Minna said, handing her menu to the server. "And the arugula salad."

"Consistency, thy name is Minna." Errol gave his wife an affectionate glance. "I don't know why you bother to look at the menu. If they have swordfish, that's what you order."

"I know what I like," she retorted.

Errol snorted and closed the menu with a flourish. "The rack of lamb." Minna started to say something about cholesterol but he waved his hand. "All I get at home is fish and poultry. Life's too short not to indulge occasionally."

I grinned at the two of them. Errol may resemble Hammett's Sam Spade but sometimes he and Minna sound more like Nick and Nora Charles. Now the server was looking at me. I ordered a starter of mushrooms and polenta, and the panfried squid with scallions and ginger. Then I reached for a piece of bread before I continued our original conversation.

"Karl got sick eating here at the restaurant. He was with Lacy that night. And Lacy, according to my cousin Donna, has been seeing Julian Surtees, Mother's new assistant." I glanced up, looking to my right at the hallway leading to the kitchen.

"I met Lacy this afternoon at the boatyard," I said, briefly describing my visit. "She strikes me as a cold customer. What can you tell me about her?"

Errol deferred to Minna, who seemed to know as much about Monterey Bay citizenry as he did. But even Minna didn't have a full dossier on Lacy Beckman. "She's from San Francisco, supposedly a wealthy family. She certainly has all the Pacific Heights moves. I think she's been married before, but Lacy never volunteers any information. Everyone was quite surprised when she showed up on Gunter Beckman's arm four years ago. I don't know where they met, but Gunter was definitely not the marrying kind. If he hadn't died in that car accident, I wonder if he and Lacy would still be married."

"Was Gunter the younger brother?" I asked.

"Older. Gunter was the black sheep of the Beckman clan. He liked liquor and women, and he didn't much care for the responsibility of running the Boat Works."

"He had a serious falling-out with old Hans," Errol continued. "Went down to Los Angeles and worked in the aerospace industry. With all the defense cutbacks he lost his job about five years ago, moved back up here. I gather he still owned a half interest in the boatyard, so Karl took Gunter back into the firm."

"How did the two brothers get along?"

Errol thought about this for a moment as the server delivered our starters. "Karl's the worker. He's the one who has kept the Boat Works going all these years after his father died. He's the one who makes sure the boats get repaired and delivered on time. Gunter was more adept at customer contact, drumming up business. Whenever I think of Gunter I see him at a social gathering, chatting with people, a glass in his hand."

"In other words," I said, "Gunter didn't dirty his hands. Karl does."

Errol nodded. "But someone needs to make those contacts that can be made in the clubhouse at Pebble Beach. There are two boatyards left in Monterey, and they compete with one another for trade. I know they bid on repairs and overhauls to the Coast Guard boats. Used to be most of their work was commercial trade, like your cousin's fishing boat. Now it's about half, the other half being pleasure craft, those sailboats and cabin cruisers owned by the kind of people who play golf at Pebble Beach or Spanish Bay."

"People like the Gradys," Minna added, "who have a sloop that needs regular maintenance."

I digested this along with my polenta and sipped some more wine. "Did Lacy step into Gunter's role after he died?"

"I think so." Minna set aside her fork and reached for the breadbasket. "She has the social skills. She works as office manager, too."

"And moves boats from place to place. How's business at Beckman Boat Works? I've heard it's bad."

I looked to my left where a server was taking dinner orders from the Beckmans and the Gradys. As the server stepped away from the table Lacy Beckman rose from her chair and walked between the tables. She glanced at me before she stepped up to the next level. I watched her stroll up the hallway separating the bar from the cloakroom and office. She pushed open the door to one of the rest rooms farther down the corridor.

"I don't know," Errol said. "The recession has taken its toll on the peninsula. Lots of small businesses in trouble, or closing. The Fort Ord closure will take much economic adjustment. I'll keep my ear to the ground, and let you know if I hear anything specifically about Beckman Boat Works."

The server arrived with our entrées. Everything looked terrific. I wondered if these dishes were Mother's handiwork, or if they'd been prepared by the surly Julian.

As I picked up my fork I heard a loud burst of laughter and looked for its source, several people at a table on the upper level. Then I saw Lacy Beckman standing at the bar. She was looking through the window to the kitchen, apparently watching Julian Surtees at work, standing with her hand casually stuck into the pocket of her green slacks. Then she walked this way, returning to the table where Karl Beckman and the Gradys sat.

During dinner I told Errol and Minna about my visit to the

Rose and Crown and my conversation with the barmaid, Stella. "She said he smelled fishy, as though he'd just come off the boat. Whatever Ariel wanted to talk with him about, she must have gone to meet him at the wharf after the housekeeper saw her in Carmel."

Errol speared some of his lamb and waved his fork. "She wanted to report something that may have concerned Bobby. Fish?"

"Sea lions," I said. Errol and Minna looked at me expectantly. "Ariel filed a report with the SPCA in mid-August. She saw some sea lions in distress." I told them about yesterday's visit to the SPCA Wildlife Center and what Marsha Landers told me. "You've heard about the pelican mutilations."

Minna nodded. "That was six or seven years ago. You mean it's happening again?"

"I'm afraid so. Donna and Marsha Landers asked if I'd look into it, though I don't know what I can do."

"There are some thoroughly sick individuals in this world. But you and Errol know that." Minna reached for the wine bottle and poured a little into each of our glasses, the last few drops going into her own. "Well, that's a dead soldier."

After we'd finished our entrées, the server cleared the table and brought coffee, as well as dessert menus to tempt us. Errol and Minna debated the merits of strawberry rhubarb crisp and crème caramel, but I'd already decided. I had just ordered the lemon chocolate tart when Mrs. Grady screamed.

I turned and saw the gray-haired woman struggling to her feet, napkin clutched to her mouth. Both Mr. Grady and Karl Beckman looked startled as they pushed back their chairs. Lacy reached for Mrs. Grady, who shoved herself away from the table, the back of her chair banging against the chair at the table behind her.

Evan the bartender and Rachel the dining-room manager appeared at the top of the steps. Behind them I saw Mother running from the kitchen, her white coat flying around her. Two servers and a busboy moved quickly toward the table as Mrs. Grady screamed again.

I was on my feet now, certain the older woman was choking.

But you can't talk and choke at the same time. Mrs. Grady was talking. She spat out one word, over and over, as her husband put his arms around her.

"Disgusting! Disgusting!" Mrs. Grady repeated. Lacy Beckman and Mr. Grady led her away through the full dining room of patrons sitting or standing in shocked silence. The ones closest to the table were beginning to mutter, a sound that grew in volume. Karl Beckman, my mother, and I stared down at the table.

I don't know which of Café Marie's exquisitely prepared entrées Mrs. Grady had ordered, but I was quite sure it wasn't supposed to include a dead mouse.

CHAPTER 14

"IT DIDN'T COME FROM MY KITCHEN," MOTHER SAID, much later that evening.

She sat at a small table in the bar of Café Marie, holding a mug of peppermint tea. She looked as though she needed something stronger. Julian Surtees slumped on a nearby stool, elbows on the bar. He'd opted for straight scotch, consuming it with morose single-mindedness.

Mother looked from me, seated at the bar, to Errol and Minna Seville, who had joined her at the table. Behind us Evan the bartender was trying to be invisible and quiet. From the kitchen I heard the clatter of pots and pans as the dishwashers finished their evening cleanup.

"I just had the health inspectors in, for God's sake." Mother gulped down a mouthful of tea. "They didn't find any evidence of rodent infestation."

"Someone put it there," I said. "The question is who."

I looked up at Julian Surtees, who appeared to be more interested in downing the amber liquid in his glass. I had two other questions to go along with who—why and how.

"They'll be back," Mother said, worry lines creasing her tired face. "The Gradys will report it, first thing Monday morning. I'll have the health department breathing down my back."

I recalled the earlier tumult in the dining room of Café Marie after Mrs. Grady found the mouse. Mother moved quickly, doing what she could to salvage the situation in the face of this latest disaster. She tossed one of the turquoise napkins over the offending plate and waved at the nearest server and a busboy, directing them to clear the table. Karl Beckman escorted the rest of the party up the steps toward the bar. I saw Lacy Beckman put her arm around Mrs. Grady's shoulder, shepherding the older woman down the hallway to the rest room. Minna Seville was right behind them. I looked around for Errol and found him at my elbow.

"Save the mouse," he said.

I seized the plate before the busboy could whisk it away and carried it back to the kitchen.

"What the hell is all that commotion?" Julian growled. He had remained in the kitchen, poised over the stove with a sauté pan in one hand and a large fork in the other. Perspiration dampened his face beneath his chef's toque, causing his dark curly hair to stick to his skull.

"A mouse."

Julian frowned. "Running through the dining room?"

"In the middle of one of your entrées." I pointed at the napkin-covered plate I held.

"No way," he exploded. He set down the utensils with a clatter and strode toward me, lifting the napkin to examine the plate. "No bloody way."

"Save it," I told him. "The whole thing."

He looked at me like I'd taken leave of my senses, then pushed past me, heading for the storage area, where he grabbed a large plastic storage bag from a drawer. Together we slipped the plate—entrée, mouse, and all—into the bag. I sealed the bag and labeled it with a pen I found dangling from a ribbon near the kitchen telephone extension. Julian made room for the evidence in the refrigerator.

"Cover it with a napkin," he said abruptly. "So we don't have to look at the damn thing." One of the servers obliged with yet another square of turquoise linen.

By the time I returned to the dining room the table was clear and Mother stood in the reception area with Mr. Grady and Karl Beckman. Of course dinner was on the house, she told them, not knowing what else to say. Karl laid a sympathetic hand on Mother's arm and murmured something in her ear.

Finally Mrs. Grady came up the hallway from the rest room, still looking shaken. Lacy Beckman held her right arm and Minna Seville was on her left. When the Gradys and the Beckmans had departed, Minna and I returned to our table. Our server swooped down on us with a frown and the desserts we'd ordered before the drama began. "More coffee?" he asked in a subdued voice.

"By all means," Minna Seville said cheerfully, as though nothing had happened.

It was unfortunate that Mrs. Grady had been so vocal about the situation, not that one could blame her. After the initial shocked silence, voices buzzed and hummed, spreading news of the incident quickly throughout the restaurant. There was a noticeable exodus as people called for their checks. I saw several half-full plates cleared from nearby tables. As Errol, Minna, and I lingered over our coffee and dessert, it appeared to us that Café Marie emptied more rapidly than usual for a Saturday night.

Although Minna had headed for the rest rooms right behind Lacy and Mrs. Grady, she hadn't learned anything other than that the older woman was understandably revolted, vowing never to eat at Café Marie again.

"She said she just looked down and it was there," Minna said. "I should think if it had been sitting there like a garnish, everyone from the cook to the server would have noticed."

"Tucked under something, perhaps." Errol polished off his strawberry rhubarb crisp and helped himself to a bite of my dessert. "We should question the staff. And I want a closer look at that mouse."

"I'll skip the postmortem," Minna said. "Give me your wallet so I can pay for dinner. I'll wait for you at the bar."

Errol and I trooped back to the kitchen to examine the plate. Mrs. Grady's entrée was simple—a marinated chicken breast that had been grilled with spices, arranged on a pillow of fettuccine tossed with several varieties of mushrooms, circled by grilled vegetables. So the mouse hadn't fallen from a cupboard into a cooking pot. As Errol had suggested, the tiny rodent appeared to have been neatly slipped onto the plate at some point after its preparation. Design, not accident. But was the mouse's destination random or specific?

Random would mean that someone in the kitchen added the mouse to a plate—any plate—without any idea which unsuspecting customer would encounter the surprise. That could mean anyone who'd been in and out of the kitchen during the evening, from Julian down to the busboys. Specific meant Mrs. Grady was the target, and those in her party were suspects.

When the server brought our entrées, Errol, Minna, and I had been concentrating on our own dinners and conversation. So I hadn't been watching the movements of the Grady–Beckman foursome, other than to note their positions at the table. The Gradys sat next to the window and the Beckmans had taken the outside seats. Mr. Grady had faced his wife, but unless he had a hidden agenda or a warped sense of humor I couldn't see him reaching across the table to drop a mouse onto his wife's plate.

Karl Beckman sat right next to Mrs. Grady, on her left. He was the closest, the one with the best opportunity to deposit something on Mrs. Grady's plate. Lacy Beckman sat on Mr. Grady's left, diagonally opposite Mrs. Grady, a long and obvious stretch. Lacy had left the table for a few minutes. I'd seen her standing near the bar after she came out of the rest room. She'd been looking into the kitchen, at Julian. Or had I imagined that? I hadn't seen anyone else leave.

How could any of these people have slipped the mouse onto Mrs. Grady's plate without the others at the table noticing? And why? I didn't think Karl or Lacy Beckman were interested in alienating paying customers like the Gradys. I couldn't think of any motive other than to blacken Café Marie's reputation. Which led me right back to why.

As the evening fizzled out, Errol and I quizzed the entire staff but none of the fifteen people who were working tonight had any idea how the mouse came to its current resting place. Finally we came to this uneasy gathering in the bar.

Julian set down his glass and slipped off the bar stool. "Go home, Marie. I'll close up."

"I agree," I said, standing up. "We've done all we can tonight. We'll continue this tomorrow."

* * *

"The older woman did get up and leave the table," Linda Ravella told me Sunday.

It was just after noon. Linda, Warren, and I were having coffee on Linda's front porch. The sun sparkled on the blue water of Monterey Bay, dotted here and there with sailboats.

I wanted to know if Linda and her fiancé had seen anything of the Grady incident from their corner table at Café Marie the previous night. There had been three tables between theirs and the Grady–Beckman party, and Warren's back had been to the dining room, but Linda had a clear view. She recalled two things I hadn't seen, two things that helped me clarify the movements of the foursome.

"I don't know why I glanced up at that moment," Linda said, "but I saw her leave the table. She was dabbing at her dress with her napkin, as though she'd spilled something on it."

I mulled this over for a moment. "How long was this before she screamed?"

Linda shook her head. "I'm not sure. Five, ten minutes." She looked at Warren and smiled. He was seated next to her on the sofa, his right arm flung behind her, the fingers of his left hand twined with hers.

"What about the other people at the table?"

"I think Karl was leaning toward Lacy, as though they were whispering together. The older man—Mr. Grady—he wasn't there."

"He wasn't? When did he leave?"

Linda frowned and thought about it, as though she were playing the scene in her mind, at a slower speed. "He stood up when his wife did," she said. "Did he sit down again? No, he turned to speak to someone at another table."

That's the trouble with eyewitness testimony. Five different people can look at the same scene and see it five different ways. They will remember all of it or just bits and pieces of the whole. As an investigator it was often my task to distill these recollections and form a reconstruction of what happened. How accurate? Hard to say. I'd been in the restaurant last night and I hadn't seen Mrs. Grady leave the table.

Linda told me she thought the spill occurred before she and

Warren had been served, but she could have been mistaken. Saturday night had been busy at Café Marie, with the dining room full of customers, and the staff bustling in and out of the kitchen.

Gene, the server who'd waited on the foursome, told Errol and me last night that both Mr. and Mrs. Grady had gotten up to talk to some people at another table, but he thought that was before the Beckmans arrived. He hadn't said anything about a spill, though Linda assumed from Mrs. Grady's behavior that she'd gotten something on her dress. I'd ask him again when I got to Café Marie. I planned to go from here to the restaurant to continue the interviews Errol and I began last night.

A car door slammed and I heard voices, one deep, the other high-pitched. Linda disengaged her fingers from Warren's hand and stood up as Bobby came up the sidewalk with their son.

Nicky seemed to have grown six inches since the last time I'd seen him. He'd turned eight during the summer, a wiry little boy with Bobby's curly dark hair and lively brown eyes. I didn't think he'd remember who I was, but he did. I was Cousin Marie's girl Jeri. He grinned at me and chattered away, telling Linda about his Saturday night.

"Me and Dad went to Gianni's and had pizza. This morning we had breakfast with Grandma and Grandpa and we went to mass." Nicky's voice took away some of the awkwardness that had crept in when Bobby climbed the porch steps behind his son, acknowledging Linda's fiancé with a polite nod.

Bobby didn't look any better than he had when I left him at his apartment Friday afternoon. The dark circles under his eyes looked harsh in the bright afternoon sunlight. His mouth had a pinched, painful look.

Bobby knelt and gave Nicky a hug. "You take care of yourself, sport, and I'll see you next weekend."

"I'll walk you to your car," I said.

We went down the steps together. When we reached the curb where his dark blue T-bird was parked behind my Toyota, Bobby sighed and rubbed his eyes. It must have been difficult for him to mask his feelings from Nicky. Yet he'd wanted to spend some extra time with his son and with his parents. My cousin didn't want to be alone.

"You look exhausted," I told him. "You'd better get some sleep before you go take the boat out tonight."

"I'm not going fishing tonight," he said, opening the driver's-side door of the T-bird. "Ariel's funeral is tomorrow morning."

"You're not going?" I framed the words as a question, even though I knew the answer.

"Of course I am," he said quietly.

"Bobby, you know people have you pegged as a suspect in her murder." My words were blunt and I saw him wince. "Do you think it's wise to show up at the services?"

"Jeri, I loved Ariel. I don't care what people think, I didn't kill her. I have to say good-bye to her." Bobby smiled but it was a pale imitation of his usual grin. "Don't worry about me, cuz. Donna said she'd go with me, to protect me."

I sighed. "I'll go with you, too."

CHAPTER 15

"**F**OUR CANCELLATIONS ALREADY."

Mother was in her office when I arrived at Café Marie later that afternoon, her face tired above her loose melon-colored shirt. This fatigue wasn't surprising, since we'd both had less sleep than we needed. "Three dinner reservations and a catering job. And I'm sure there will be more. I told you it wouldn't take long for word to get out."

The phone rang and she reached for it. "I hope it's not another one."

I walked back toward the entrance and encountered Rachel Donahoe, sitting at the bar with the cordless phone. She was leafing through the reservation book as she drank a soda. "Marie told you about the cancellations?" I nodded. "This is bad news in the restaurant biz, Jeri."

"I know. Listen, we went over this last night, but tell me again what you saw."

"The reservation was for seven o'clock," Rachel said, pushing the reservation book aside. "The Gradys were early. Their table wasn't quite ready, so Mr. and Mrs. Grady sat right about here and ordered drinks from the bar. When the table was cleared, I seated them."

"Who left the table, and when?" I asked.

"I can't say for sure." Rachel frowned. "I was back and forth to the kitchen, and waiting on other customers. Mrs. Beckman left. I assume she went to the rest room. And Mr. and Mrs. Grady got up to talk to some people at another table." Rachel added that she hadn't seen anything get spilled, nor had she seen the older woman go to the rest room. Last night the server who'd waited on the party had told me much the same thing.

The phone rang and Rachel picked it up. I left the bar and went down the steps into the main dining room, empty of people, ghostly with its array of white tablecloths, the twisted turquoise napkins like sentinels rising from the wineglasses at each place setting. I stopped at the table where the Gradys and Beckmans had been seated last night, mentally placing people in the now vacated chairs, then moving those phantoms according to what information I'd gleaned so far.

Both Lacy Beckman and Mrs. Grady had gone to the rest room, at different times. Mr. Grady had either turned away from the table or stood up to talk to someone. And what about Karl Beckman? Did he leave the table?

I went back up the shallow steps to the entryway and the bar, then down the hallway to the rest-room doors. I surveyed the layout of the hallway and the doors. The rest rooms were just a few steps from the kitchen entrance, with its wide shelf where the cooks placed food ready for pickup by the servers. The restaurant staff needed access to the toilet facilities. But it also meant that anyone who went to the rest rooms might gain access to the kitchen or the waiting plates.

The staff would notice if someone strolled into the kitchen, someone who didn't belong there, someone who wasn't wearing a white coat. Wouldn't they? The servers didn't dress like cooks. Nor did the bartender.

All along I'd been assuming that the saboteur was a member of the staff. It was the logical place to start looking. After last night I wasn't so sure. There were three opportunities for that mouse to come to its final resting place on Mrs. Grady's plate. One was while the entrée was in the kitchen. The second was while it sat on the shelf, waiting to be picked up. The third was after it had been served, which meant one of Mrs. Grady's dining companions put it there. I shook my head slowly as I considered each scenario, none of them entirely satisfactory, each with flaws.

I heard the *thunk-thunk-thunk* of the knife against the cutting board. Following the sound, I walked through the doorway, glancing to my left. One of the cooks was chopping vegetables, head down, eyes intent on the swiftly moving knife blade as it sliced through the deep purple skin of an eggplant. Bright orange carrots were piled to her left, and I saw a colander full of deep red onions in front of her. She glanced up, recognized me, and smiled, then returned to her task.

As I stood in the doorway I saw Julian enter the kitchen from the storage area at the back of the restaurant, dressed as I'd seen him before, in black jeans and a white T-shirt. He didn't look happy to see me. My presence meant more questions. Julian didn't like to answer questions.

"May I have a cup of coffee?" I asked him.

"There's a pot in the bar," he said, barely civil as he snapped off the words. "Help yourself."

I nodded and went back the way I'd come, stepping into the bartender's domain, where I poured a cup of black brew and looked at desserts the pastry chef had created for this evening's menu. Then I walked back to Mother's office, where she gave me the news about the cancellations.

"The employee files," I told Mother. "I glanced through them on Friday, before talking to the staff about the earlier incidents. Now I want to take a closer look."

"You still think it's one of my people?"

"At this point I'm open to all possibilities."

I'd done background investigations before. It's not unusual for a person to inflate qualifications on a résumé or smooth over the reasons for leaving a prior job. I suppose it's normal to want to present yourself in the best light if you're angling for a new position. And the reason for leaving a job may be interpreted differently by employer and employee.

But hiring the wrong person can cause a lot of problems for a company, as I'd discovered a couple of years ago when an Oakland firm asked me to find out who was embezzling funds. If they'd looked past the sterling qualities listed on the résumé of one of their accountants, they'd have found what I ultimately did—a felony conviction for grand theft.

Checking references in an era when people like to hire lawyers to fight their battles means that former employers are wary of giving information beyond confirming the dates of employment. Getting at the truth sometimes requires much digging and persuasion, to find that someone who resigned on paper may have done so because he was about to be booted out the door.

Mother slipped on the white coat that had been hanging behind the door and headed for the kitchen. I opened the file drawer containing employee records and pulled out the first folder. My reading was interrupted only by occasional forays to the bar for more coffee.

When one checks references, the rule of thumb is to get up-to-date verifiable information back three years from the date of application. Most of Mother's employees met that criterion. I saw notes here and there in her handwriting, indicating that she had called former employers. There was one busboy with a lot of gaps in his employment history and one of the servers, a young woman, hired last year, who seemed to have jumped from job to job.

But I kept coming back to Julian Surtees. He was the most recent hire, and as Mother's assistant, he was her second in command, a person in a position of authority. He also had the worst attitude. His attitude was enough to make me want to scrutinize his references.

Mother hired him in mid-May, after two interviews. He'd attended a cooking school in New York and had also studied in France before working in both New York and Los Angeles. There were two letters of recommendation in his file and Mother had called his previous employers. There was also a three-month gap between the time he'd left his last job and his first day here at Café Marie. He could have taken some time off between jobs. But there could be another reason.

I reached for the phone at my right elbow and punched one of the extensions that wasn't lit. Doing a background check on a Sunday might not be easy in a lot of businesses, but restaurants were usually open Sunday and closed on Monday, if they closed at all. I called the restaurant in Los Angeles where Surtees had worked for a year before he left last spring. Busy signal. I tried the place where he'd worked before that, and got a recording telling me the number was no longer in service.

I went to the bar for more coffee and found that some nice person had made a fresh pot. When I returned I tried the Los Angeles number again. This time someone answered the phone. When I asked for the manager he put me on hold. Finally someone picked up the line, a man who identified himself as Mr. Chase and sounded busy and harried. I explained my reason for calling.

"This is really a bad time," Chase said. "We do a Sunday brunch and we're swamped."

"I know, but this is important. Why did Julian Surtees leave your employment?"

He didn't answer right away. I thought I was going to get the official line about how he couldn't give out that information.

"We had a difference of opinion."

"That's a very elastic description, Mr. Chase. Just why did you differ?"

Again I got silence. Then Chase spoke up. "Oh, hell, Julian had a difference of opinion with everyone in the kitchen. You've met the man?"

When I assured Chase that I had, he continued. "He's got the personality of a rattlesnake. Julian's a monumental pain in the butt. He's good, but not that good. He thinks he's the only one who can cook and everyone else is an amateur. While he was here he antagonized everyone in the kitchen and rubbed the owner the wrong way. So I bounced Julian. You didn't hear this from me, of course, but since then, I've heard on the grapevine that Julian's left several jobs for the same reason. The man is just plain hard to get along with."

That didn't surprise me. "While Julian was working for you, did you ever have anything go wrong at the restaurant? A series of accidents, perhaps?"

Chase laughed. "Anything can go wrong at a restaurant. Yes, we had our share of disasters."

"Disasters tend to be random. I'm wondering about things that seemed to have a pattern, as though they were engineered rather than accidental."

"Well . . ." Chase drew out the word. "A couple of things last fall, that happened in the space of six or eight weeks. Salt in the sugar dispensers, stuff like that. Then a lid on an oil container was left loose, and someone dropped it. Made a horrendous mess. And some detergent that wound up in a pot of soup. Those could have been accidents but maybe not, since they happened so close together."

I thanked Chase and hung up the phone. At least two such accidents had happened at Café Marie. First the salt in the sugar dispensers, then the oil container.

I stood, stretched, and went looking for Julian Surtees. He was in the kitchen, where three cooks were lined up in front of the stove, readying the line for the evening's cooking. He was barking orders at them, now wearing his chef's coat over his T-shirt.

"I need to talk with you," I said.

"Can't this wait? I have work to do."

"No, it can't. Let's talk in the office." I gazed into his dark eyes, trying to read him.

He narrowed those eyes and left the line with an exasperated sigh, pushing past me out of the kitchen. He didn't say anything until we were in the cramped confines of Mother's office. I shut the door and leaned against the desk.

"I don't know anything about how the fucking mouse got onto the damn plate," he snarled. "We run a clean kitchen. Marie insists on it, and so do I."

I recalled Julian's reaction last night when I showed him the mouse on the plate. His outrage had seemed genuine. Unless he was a very good actor.

"Why did you leave your last job?"

"Is that any of your business?" He radiated edgy energy as he stood with his hands on his hips, his mouth curled into the sneer that seemed to be his usual expression.

I leaned toward him and sharpened my words. "It is if you're trying to shut down my mother's restaurant."

"Why the hell would I do that? I'd be out of a job."

"I don't know, Julian. You tell me. The manager of the restaurant where you used to work says you couldn't get along with your coworkers."

"You called Chase," he said. His jaw tightened. "If you already know the answers why do you bother asking the questions?"

"I don't know all the answers, Julian. That's why I'm asking you."

His lips thinned as he gave what passed for a smile. "Maybe Chase is exaggerating."

"I doubt it. You piss off everyone you meet, Julian. You're so damned disagreeable it shouldn't surprise you that no one has anything good to say about you."

"There are two sides to every story." Julian put his hands on his hips and glared at me, eye to eye. "Maybe my coworkers couldn't get along with me." I had to admit he was right about that. It was easy enough for two people to tell a different story and each be telling their own version of the truth. "I'm a good chef. That's all that matters. That's why Marie hired me."

I stared him down and shifted gears. "Chase told me there had been some incidents last fall at the restaurant in L.A. Salt in the sugar dispensers, the oil can with the loose lid, detergent in the soup. Sound familiar?"

Julian frowned. "Last fall? Listen, accidents happen all the time in this business. I don't know anything about the salt or the oil can thing. I remember the detergent in the soup. One of the waitresses saw a busboy fooling with a ladle. The chef figured it was him and fired him on the spot. We tossed the soup. Nobody got served any of it."

"What about here, at Café Marie? Two out of three, Julian. The salt in the sugar dispensers and the oil can with the loose lid. Then Karl Beckman got sick while eating dinner here. You don't see a pattern?"

"No, I don't." Julian tilted his head to one side and smoothed his black hair. "If you think I had anything to do with this, you're wrong."

"Did you tell anyone about what happened at the other restaurant?"

"Maybe." He shrugged. "Things like that happen everywhere. Putting salt in the sugar dispenser is the oldest trick in the damn book."

"But the oil can takes a little more finesse. So does adulterating the food." He didn't respond. Instead he glared at me. "How long have you known Lacy Beckman?"

Now Julian leaned forward again, his black eyes narrowed into two slits. "My personal life is none of your damn business," he hissed, hauling open the office door. "If you're finished with the interrogation, I've got things to do."

CHAPTER 16

I WENT LOOKING FOR MOTHER AND FOUND HER SEATED AT A
table between the bar and the railing separating the upper and
lower dining rooms of Café Marie. She wasn't alone. Karl
Beckman was seated across from her, his broad shoulders filling
his blue work shirt. They leaned toward one another, holding
hands, arms resting on the white linen tablecloth. I couldn't see
Karl's face, but two expressions warred in my mother's countenance. Worry about this latest incident at the restaurant etched a
frown, deepening the lines around her mouth and eyes. But the
eyes themselves reflected the fact that she was very glad to see this
man. I saw there the intimacy and ease that happens between
good friends—and lovers.

As I walked toward them I felt my mouth tense and I told myself that it wasn't logical or rational for me to respond this way.
My parents were divorced. They had marked out separate paths
for themselves during the years before the official legal sundering
ended their marriage. It was obvious Mother had strong feelings
for Karl Beckman, and that he felt the same way. If my mother
wanted to have a romance with this man, that was her business.
Maybe all my warning bells were going off because I was too close
to the situation.

So Karl Beckman was ten years younger than Mother. So what?
Did that really matter? But there was something about the man
that bothered me. I couldn't quite put my finger on the reason
why.

Something of my internal dialogue must have shown on my face as I approached the table. Mother looked up and a curtain whisked across her face, rearranging its lines. She released Karl's hand.

"Hi, Jeri." Karl greeted me with a smile, shifting in his chair. He was casually dressed in the blue shirt, blue jeans, and deck shoes. "Marie tells me you've been questioning the staff about this accident last night. I'm sure that's all it was, just an accident. Lacy and I tried to get the Gradys calmed down some, but Mrs. G was really in a state."

"Can't say I blame her," I said. A movement caught my eye and I turned to see Lori, the other bartender, arrive for her shift. She nodded in our direction and flipped on the radio set on the counter between the bar and the kitchen, keeping the music low as she tuned in a station. I heard Ella Fitzgerald singing "This Can't Be Love" over the clatter of metal in the kitchen as utensils came into contact with pans. The pungent odor of garlic and onions wafted into the dining room, a promise of food being prepared.

"You upset Julian," Mother said. The surly chef's exit from the office must have been quite visible.

"I'm sure he'll get over it." I took a seat on a bar stool and Lori left off readying the bar to ask if I wanted anything to drink. "Sure. An Anchor Steam. Don't bother with a glass." When she'd brought the beer, I took a swallow and looked down at Karl Beckman. "I met Lacy yesterday at the boatyard."

I saw that look again, the one that had passed over his face on Friday at Ravella's. Shutters closed in his hazel eyes. It made me very curious.

"Really? She didn't mention that you'd dropped by. Why were you at the yard?"

I decided not to tell him right away. On the radio behind us Mel Torme took over from Ella, accompanied by a counterpoint of conversation from the kitchen staff and the sizzle of meat in a sauté pan.

I turned to Mother. "How closely did you check Julian Surtees's references when you hired him? Why did he come to apply for this job, out of Los Angeles and into the sticks of Monterey?"

"Surely you don't think Julian had anything to do with it," Karl said. "He seems like a straight arrow to me."

I ignored Karl's remarks and waited for Mother to respond. She frowned.

"Julian was recommended by someone I know down in Los Angeles. Creative, innovative, that's what I was looking for. And this friend knew that Julian was looking for a change of scene. I called three restaurants where he'd worked. One had closed, but the other two gave him excellent recommendations."

I took another sip of my beer. "The manager at the last place told me he bounced Julian because Julian couldn't get along with any of the other employees. Maybe those people who gave excellent recommendations were trying to get rid of him. He's not the most personable individual I've ever encountered."

"I suppose you could say he lacks some people skills," Mother began.

"Lacks? He doesn't have any."

"He's good in the kitchen." Mother's words were sharp. "That's what I wanted. I get along with him just fine."

"The manager of the last restaurant told me something else." I repeated what Chase had said about the incidents last fall that bore a resemblance to what had happened this summer at Café Marie.

"It must be a coincidence," Mother said stubbornly, but she didn't look wholly convinced. "Things can happen in the kitchen of any restaurant."

"But it's different when it's your own restaurant," I told her. "I think I need to dig a little deeper into Julian's past. He certainly has both the skill and the opportunity." Mother looked appalled at the prospect that Julian topped my suspect list. The possibility of being betrayed by someone you trust is always disturbing. "Look, do you want to find out who's doing this or not?"

"Of course I want to find out," she said slowly. "But if it is Julian, why would he do such a thing?"

"I don't know. Maybe he's got his own agenda. One that makes sense only to him." Now I turned to Karl Beckman, looking straight into his hazel eyes. "I understand Julian has been dating your sister-in-law. What do you know about their relationship?"

The boatyard owner looked momentarily taken aback at my directness. "I don't know anything about it, just that they've gone out a few times. Hard enough to do, with Julian's schedule. I know that, from trying to find time to spend with Marie." He gave my mother a sidelong glance. "Lacy's personal life is her own. You'll have to talk with her."

"I will." I pushed back the stool and stood. "There is something else, Mr. Beckman. I've learned that after my cousin Bobby left Ariel Logan that Friday afternoon before she was killed, he told someone that he needed to find you. That he had something he wanted to discuss with you. Did he find you?"

Karl Beckman looked as though this information was a complete surprise. "Why, no. I didn't see Bobby until the following week, when Ariel was reported missing. If he came by the boatyard, surely he would have talked with Lacy, and she didn't mention it."

"I gather what he wanted to talk about was urgent. Any idea what that might be?" The big blond man shook his head slowly as I fired another question at him. "Where were you that weekend, Mr. Beckman?"

By now it had occurred to Karl Beckman that he was being grilled. He didn't like it. Neither did Mother. I saw a frown gathering strength in her knotted eyebrows.

"I was out of town," he said finally. "On business." Before I could ask any more questions he raised a big hand as though to forestall me. "And as to what, I don't think that's any of your business."

It is if it had anything to do with Ariel Logan's murder, I thought. But I didn't say it. At least not then.

The music from the radio changed again. Nat King Cole's velvety tones filled the uncomfortable silence, singing to "Sweet Lorraine." Suddenly I wrinkled my nose. Something in the kitchen had overpowered the pleasant cooking odors that had earlier wafted into the bar. And it wasn't charred California cuisine.

My eyes began to water. "What the hell is that?"

Mother and Karl pushed back their chairs as the smell grew in intensity, moving quickly from merely unpleasant to an overpowering stench that now made me gag.

Rotten meat? Decaying fish? No, it didn't have that sickly-sweet odor that went with food gone bad. It didn't smell like a backed-up toilet in the rest rooms or a skunk that had strayed into this urban environment and let loose with its protective musk. Chemical, I thought, something that choked and burned my nose and throat.

"Get out," I told Mother, gasping. My eyes streamed tears. I pulled the neck of my T-shirt up to cover my nose and mouth and pushed my mother in Karl's direction. He seized her arm and pulled her toward the entrance of Café Marie. Lori pelted from behind the bar, following them. Rachel went through the door after her, reservation book and the cordless phone in one hand, followed by two of the servers who'd been in the dining room.

From the kitchen I heard someone shouting at the rest of the staff to get out. I ran down the hallway and saw Julian at the back door, a dish towel tied around his face. With one hand he shoved one of the cooks toward the open back door.

One of the dishwashers had been overcome. He was slumped on the floor near the sink. Quickly I knelt and grabbed his arm, struggling to get him on his feet. Then Julian took his other arm. Together we propelled the dishwasher out the back door, into the garden at the side of Café Marie.

Fresh air had never smelled sweeter.

Rachel must have called 911 because I heard sirens in the distance. Julian pulled the dish towel from his face and stared into the face of the woozy dishwasher.

"You gonna be okay?" he demanded. The other man nodded, gulping unadulterated air into his lungs.

The fire department arrived first, quickly followed by the police. Within a few minutes we were ushered from the garden to a spot farther down the alley. We stood watching the chaos that now enveloped Café Marie, replete with flashing red lights, emergency vehicles, and shouting voices. Genderless figures swathed in protective clothing looked like they'd dropped in from another planet. Several of these space invaders were now unwinding yellow barrier tape around what they were already calling a hot zone.

Out in the street a crowd had gathered, drawn by the sirens and red lights. I located Mother by looking for her bright melon-colored blouse. She was here in the alley, raking one hand through her hair as she talked with a police officer and a round-faced fellow in tan slacks. Karl Beckman loomed behind her, hands on his hips and his wide face creased by a frown. I walked over to them.

Mother introduced me to Sergeant Smith of the Monterey Police Department, who identified himself as the incident commander. The civilian was Eric Lopez, a county environmental health specialist.

"Is all this routine?" I asked, sweeping my hand around to encompass the activity. "The fire trucks, the protective suits, the perimeter tape? It seems like overkill for a bad smell."

"We don't know what we're dealing with," Lopez said. "Could be hazardous, toxic. We always cordon off the zones. Now, I need to ask you some questions—" He turned to Mother first and I stepped back to await my turn.

Julian Surtees stood to one side, watching this exchange. He still had the white dish towel draped around his neck. It made him look like a disconsolate bandit.

"I suppose you think I did this, too," he said.

"If you did, I'd sure as hell like to know how you pulled it off. It seemed to be coming from the kitchen. Any ideas?"

"The ventilators above the stoves, maybe." He shrugged. "They pull the heat and the cooking odors out of the kitchen. Pull, not push. This stink seemed to come out of nowhere and all of a sudden it was everywhere. Besides, the vents have been on since the bakers were here early this morning."

At that moment one of the space aliens exited the restaurant through the back door and trotted down the alley toward Sergeant Smith. The two men conferred and I saw the man in protective clothing gesture toward the roof of the one-story building. I looked in the direction he'd pointed.

"What's in that metal box up there?" I asked Julian.

"The motor for the ventilating system." He stared at it, as though trying to see something hidden in code.

The metal box was close to the roof's edge. The vents above the stoves were supposed to pull cooking odors out of the kitchen. Pull, not push, Julian had said. But the odor spread through the kitchen and out into the dining area. I didn't know much about motors but I was willing to bet someone had climbed up on the roof of Café Marie and tinkered with some electrical wires.

It would be easy enough to get up there. I saw a small Dumpster right next to the back door. The Dumpster lid, about chest high, was closed. If there weren't yellow tape and men in protective clothing between me and the building, I could take a running jump and haul myself up on top of the Dumpster. Another jump, and I could probably climb onto the roof to examine the metal box and the screws that held it in place, looking for some fresh scratch marks.

But that didn't account for the fact that the vents had been on since this morning. Of course not. The havoc caused by the smell wouldn't be as great while the baker was making rolls. The saboteur had waited until dinner preparation at Café Marie was well under way, when maximum damage could be inflicted. I wondered if this stink bomb had a timer attached.

I scowled at the metal box and the Dumpster. Then I turned my head to the right and saw Mother pacing back and forth at the perimeter, along the yellow tape barrier. Then she stopped next to Karl Beckman and he put his arms around her, pulling her close in an embrace.

I tried not to glare at him and didn't succeed. Julian, still at my side, intercepted my look and flashed me a sudden sardonic grin that said he knew exactly how I felt about the boatyard owner.

It wasn't just Beckman and his relationship with my mother, I told myself. It was also the fact that Beckman always seemed to be on the spot whenever there was trouble. Saturday night at the restaurant, when Mrs. Grady found the mouse on her plate. And here, now, at the scene of Mother's latest disaster.

Mother withdrew from Karl's arms as she saw me walking toward her. Just as I reached her the sergeant joined us. "Looks like there's something in one of the ventilating ducts," Smith reported. "The pH test paper shows it's an acid. You'll have to get it tested to find out exactly what it is."

The sergeant explained that now that the county hazardous response team had taken the sample, it was the property owner's responsibility to have it analyzed by a lab. The additional bad news, delivered by Lopez, was that Café Marie was closed until an industrial hygienist could determine the origin of the odor.

"How long will that take?" Mother ran a hand through her already disarranged hair. I saw the look in her eyes and knew she was tallying the cost in ruined food and canceled reservations. The lost revenue would hurt badly.

"Two weeks is the standard turnaround time," Lopez said. "But there's a lab in Seaside that'll do it in twenty-four hours. Of course, it costs quite a bit more, if you want to pay the price."

"I have to pay the price," Mother said, her voice grim. "I can't afford to be closed for two weeks. If I have any customers left after this."

CHAPTER *17*

CARMEL MISSION WAS INITIALLY FOUNDED IN 1770, IN Monterey, the second of the twenty-one missions scattered the length of what was then known as Alta California. But Father Junípero Serra didn't like being so close to the soldiers of the Monterey Presidio. The following year he found another site, where the Carmel River runs into the sea, closer to the Indian population he intended to Christianize.

Never mind that California's native population didn't particularly want to be Christianized. Civilization, brought to the Indians by the Spanish sword and cross, now recalled in the mission's paternalistic murals of saintly friars and little brown brothers, was the death of many of them. I think of that whenever I see any of the missions, and this morning was no exception.

It was warm and sunny this Monday morning, now the first week in October. The parking lot of the mission complex was full and cars overflowed onto Rio Road and Lausen Drive, the side street. I left my car a block up Rio Road and walked to the mission, wearing a blue dress and heels borrowed from Mother's closet. First I saw Bobby's T-bird. Then I saw him standing alone near the open gate that led under an archway of foliage to the mission's front courtyard. He wore a navy-blue suit. I couldn't recall the last time I'd seen him look so formal.

I took his arm. "Where's Donna?"

"She couldn't make it," Bobby said. "Can't get away from work. I guess you'll have to be my sole protector."

We went through the arch into the long narrow courtyard, its pebbled pavement edged in red brick. On our left was an adobe building with a red-tiled roof that now housed a museum. To our right, a garden was filled with fall blooms. A hummingbird darted among the blossoms, outmaneuvering the slower bees. Both the courtyard and the garden were crowded with people in sober clothing, the buzz of their voices nearly drowning the musical tinkle of water from the fountain in the center of the garden.

As we moved across the court toward the sandstone church, I saw heads turn in Bobby's direction. Once or twice I heard his name, audible above the muted murmur. I tightened my grip on Bobby's arm and kept walking toward the massive wooden doors that led into the sanctuary of the basilica. Directly above the doors, a star window pierced the church's sandstone facade, and the Moorish tower with its four bells loomed above and to the left. Finally we went through the doorway into the sanctuary, which was starting to fill. We found seats in a pew on the right, midway up the center aisle.

The whitewashed walls of the church's nave curve inward as they rise, forming an arch that frames the main altar. Father Serra is buried here under the stones at the foot of the altar, in front of a low railing. On this side of the railing I saw Ariel Logan's casket, its closed cover blanketed by roses with lush petals of pink, apricot, and yellow. Their scent competed with the candles that burned in holders on either side of the altar. Other flower tributes had been arrayed on either side of the casket. Somewhere an organ played.

This was the second funeral I'd attended in as many months, in both instances the funeral of a murder victim. The services last month had required my presence as an observer rather than a mourner. In addition to offering Bobby whatever support he needed, that was the case here as well.

I looked around for faces I recognized, and saw Errol and Minna Seville in a pew on the left side of the aisle. I could almost see Errol's antenna twitch as he swept his eyes over the assemblage. Our eyes met, he raised his silvery eyebrows, and his mouth curved into that foxy smile. Minna Seville had turned and was talking quietly with two people in the pew behind her. Karl and Lacy Beckman, I noted, looking, as usual, like a married couple.

My antenna was out, too. As was the case in the courtyard, I could feel people's eyes on Bobby, who sat on my right, head down, staring at the floor. My gaze met that of a couple across the aisle and they quickly dropped their eyes. But someone else was staring. I could feel it. I turned, looking for the source of the scrutiny. Sergeant Mike Magruder of the Monterey County Sheriff's Department stood at the rear of the nave, gazing at Bobby's back. He shifted his eyes to me, his face a mask. I had a feeling I'd be talking to the sergeant later.

The people gathered to bid good-bye to Ariel were a cross section of the Monterey peninsula. I had expected older people, contemporaries of Ariel's parents, but there were also a few children and young people in their teens and early twenties, reminding me that Ariel had gone to Carmel schools all her life. It was also likely that some of her classmates from Cal Poly in San Luis Obispo had made the trip up the coast for the funeral. I hoped that one of the young women I saw in the front pews was Ariel's roommate, the one who'd alerted the Logans to the fact that their daughter was missing.

I saw three people enter from the side, one a woman of medium height, wearing a black dress and a hat with a black veil that masked her features. On her left was a tall slender woman with silvery blond hair that fell to the collar of her black suit. She and the tall man who stood to the right of the veiled woman were two halves of a cameo. He had the same silvery blond hair smoothed back over his temples, the same chiseled features and patrician nose. This must be Peter Logan, Ariel's father, and the tall woman in the black suit his sister Glennis. It didn't take any deductive skills to guess that the veiled woman was Ariel's mother, Sylvie Romillard Logan.

The woman I'd identified as Glennis Braemer turned, surveying the assembled mourners. Her eyes paused briefly on Bobby. I wondered if she knew who he was.

The priest entered the sanctuary, formal in his vestments, and stood before the ornate red-and-gold altar. Candles burned all around him, illuminating the smaller statues of saints perched to the sides and above the center of the arch where a large crucified Christ hung against a blue background. The scent of incense filled my nose as the funeral mass began.

I'm not Catholic, nor am I particularly religious. I was here for Bobby, whose low voice repeated the responses. I felt his pain and loss and confusion at Ariel's death, and I knew deep in my gut that's usually right that he couldn't have had anything to do with her murder. But he was keeping something from me. Why? I raised my eyes and found Karl Beckman. It had something to do with the older man and I had to find out what it was.

When the service was over, the sound of bells was replaced by shuffling feet as people prepared to leave the sanctuary. The priest escorted the Logans toward the side entrance. Ariel's mother walked slowly, bent as though the black veil, a tangible expression of her grief, weighed upon her as much as her daughter's death. One black-gloved hand clutched a white handkerchief. The other gripped her husband's arm. Peter Logan's sister brought up the rear. Before exiting the church, she stopped to talk to a dark-suited man, giving him some directions accompanied by gestures.

People began to file out of the pews, heading down the central aisle to the church's doors, talking quietly among themselves as they moved into the midday sun that seemed incredibly bright compared with the mission's interior.

"Do you want to go to the cemetery? Or speak to the family?" I asked Bobby, hoping he didn't. I could still feel the hostility some of those present were directing his way.

He shook his head and smiled, but it was a sad smile. "I can visit her grave later, when no one's around. Ariel's parents don't like me. There's no point in saying anything to them."

We walked across the courtyard, toward the gate leading to the parking lot. As we passed the fountain Errol and Minna joined us, greeting Bobby with handshakes. Errol leaned toward me, keeping his voice low. "Come by the house later. I have the autopsy report and some information."

I nodded. "Do you know whether Ariel's roommate is here? I'd like to talk with her."

"That young woman with the long black hair, in the gray dress with the white cuffs. Maggie Lim."

I glanced in the direction Errol had indicated, where a group of mourners was poised at the sanctuary door. I saw a young Asian woman, hair blowing loose around her shoulders. I started toward her. Maybe I could talk with her before she left.

Suddenly a man appeared from the garden to our left, cutting past Errol. He seized Bobby's arm and spun him around, then leaned toward him, his face full of fury, his voice a snarl.

"You murdering scumbag. You have a hell of a nerve showing up here."

All conversation in the courtyard stopped and people nearby turned to gape. Bobby's brown eyes smoldered with a rage that matched the other man's emotion. Then he banked the fire and shook off the hand that held his arm. He turned as though to leave but the other man moved closer, raising his hand again.

"You have a problem?" My voice was level as I stepped between the two men and stared into the other man's gray eyes.

He was six feet tall, maybe more, looking fit and tan in expensive gray pinstripes. His dark blond hair was short and combed back from his forehead. Right now he had a small tic to the left of his thin-lipped mouth. He stared back at me as though wondering what planet I'd dropped from. Somewhere behind him a redhead in a dark green dress hissed, "Ryan!"

Ryan Trent. The lawyer who used to date Ariel Logan. Minna Seville had described him as brash. No doubt about that, I thought as I stared him down. Maybe I looked intimidating, or he belatedly realized that the aftermath of Ariel Logan's funeral was not the best time to settle whatever score he felt needed settling. Trent dropped his hand.

Minna wrapped her arm through Bobby's and started for the gate, Errol a few paces behind. The woman who'd spoken to Trent tugged at his arm, alarm written all over her face.

"This isn't over." Trent snapped out the words, at me, his most convenient target.

"Not by a long shot." I favored him with my version of Errol's predator smile. The lawyer and his companion crossed the courtyard. By now Errol and Minna had escorted Bobby through the gate to the parking lot. I knew they'd accompany him to his T-bird. I looked around for Maggie Lim, Ariel's roommate. But she no longer stood at the church door. Instead I saw Sergeant Magruder standing in front of me, his bulk filling his dark suit, blue eyes cold in his rugged face.

"Sergeant Magruder," I said politely.

"Jeri Howard," he said. "You're Bobby Ravella's cousin. Private investigator out of Oakland. You used to work for Errol Seville." So the sergeant had checked me out. "What are you doing in Monterey?"

"Visiting family, Sergeant. Any objections?"

"None whatsoever," Magruder said, blinking his frosty eyes. "As long as it's just a family visit. But don't interfere in my investigation."

"What makes you think I'd interfere?"

He narrowed his eyes. "I know you've already talked to some people on Alvarado Street, including the barmaid at the Rose and Crown. Stay out of it."

I considered his words, weighing my own reply. "I'm a professional investigator, Sergeant. I make a point of cooperating with the authorities whenever possible. Sometimes I even help."

"Even if your own cousin's involved?" His tone made it obvious that he thought my family loyalty got in the way of any objectivity.

"Even then. I'm interested in finding out the truth, Sergeant."

"So am I. And I don't need any help."

"I'll keep that in mind." I turned and walked toward the courtyard gate.

At the end of the funeral service I'd heard some of the mourners mention that the Logans would be receiving people at their home after interment at the cemetery so Ariel's friends could offer their condolences. I drove down Santa Lucia Avenue, parked near Errol's house, and walked one block to Scenic Road, the thoroughfare that edged the broad sandy beach and the turquoise water of Carmel Bay.

I had no trouble locating the Logan residence. It was the only one with a funeral wreath on the front door. I stood for a moment on the sidewalk, studying the house. Like its neighbors, the house crowded its lot, a bit too large for its slice of prime Carmel estate. It was a two-story gray stucco, contemporary in design, with an upper-level balcony constructed to take advantage of the sweeping vista of the bay.

Two shiny, boxy cars, a Mercedes and a BMW, were parked in

the driveway in front of a closed garage tucked under the house. To the right of the driveway, curving steps climbed a slope landscaped with flowers and shrubbery rather than grass, leading to a front porch bracketed by two huge ceramic pots filled with succulents. The double front doors were carved wood, light in hue, with matching brass knockers.

The wreath was huge, white flowers overpowered by black ribbon. These stark colors contrasted with the bloodred blossoms scattering the bougainvillea vine. It had been planted at the lower right corner of the house and over the years it had grown diagonally upward, snaking across the pale gray stucco until it loomed over the front doors and grasped the balcony railing.

A door opened and someone walked out onto the balcony, a lone woman dressed in black. Ariel's mother. I recognized her from the funeral. She walked to the railing, looking out to sea. I watched her for a moment, hearing the constant voice of the ocean to my back, where the sandy beach gave way to rocky shore.

The door opened again and Glennis Braemer joined Mrs. Logan at the railing. She put her arms around her sister-in-law and shepherded her inside. Before she shut the door the tall woman looked down at me as I stood on the sidewalk, staring at the house. Our eyes met.

People began to arrive, trekking up the steps to the gray stucco's front doors. I waited about fifteen minutes, then walked up the stairs behind two well-dressed middle-aged ladies. We were greeted by a round gray-haired woman I guessed was the housekeeper.

"Is Maggie Lim here?" I asked after my two companions had entered the house. "Ariel's roommate?"

The housekeeper looked confused as she stood in the entryway. Then someone came up behind her, placing a hand on the door. Glennis Braemer looked out at me, her face as severe as the cut of her black suit, gray-blond hair straight and shiny as the gold jewelry she wore.

"I'll handle this, Mrs. Costello." The housekeeper nodded and disappeared. Mrs. Braemer stood in the doorway, a tough and fiercely protective sentry. "What do you want?"

"I'd like to speak with Ariel's roommate, Maggie Lim."

Mrs. Braemer narrowed her emerald-green eyes in her imperious face and looked me over as though I were carrying a concealed weapon. When she finally spoke, her voice was chilly.

"Maggie went back to San Luis Obispo. She left after the funeral." As I considered my next move she spoke again. This time anger heated her words. "I saw you with him at the funeral. I know who you are and why you're asking questions. But it won't do any good. Your cousin murdered my niece. He'll pay for it."

"Please convey my condolences to the family," I said as she closed the door in my face.

CHAPTER 18

"T HANKS FOR GETTING BOBBY OUT OF THERE," I TOLD
Errol when he opened the front door.

I'd walked back to the Sevilles' house after my encounter with
Glennis Braemer. Errol had changed clothes, discarding the suit
he'd worn to the funeral in favor of a pair of khaki slacks and a
checked shirt.

"I anticipated something like that," Errol said. "Minna and I
overheard plenty of comments at the funeral. Conventional wisdom says Bobby killed Ariel. A number of people were outraged
that he was there at all—and wondering why he's not already
in jail."

You could add Mrs. Braemer to that list, I thought, recalling the
implacable face of the woman guarding the door at the gray
stucco house. In fact, she looked as though she'd like to make the
arrest herself.

"Bobby insisted on going," I told him.

"Come on, you look like you need a glass of wine." Errol led
the way to the kitchen. Minna stood at the counter, she, too, in
slacks and shirt. She was spreading mayonnaise and mustard on
slices of sourdough bread.

"Turkey sandwich?" she asked as Errol took a wineglass from a
rack below one of the cabinets and filled it with wine from an
open bottle of Riesling. She didn't wait for my reply before taking
two more slices from the loaf. Stinkpot hovered near her feet,
winding his black-and-white body through her legs in hopes of get-

ting a nosh from the sliced turkey visible in its loose wrapping of white butcher paper.

"That was poor judgment on Mr. Trent's part," Minna said. "Not to mention execrable timing. I certainly hope he's not as impulsive in the courtroom."

Next to her, Errol sipped his own wine, then began piling turkey on the bread. He surreptitiously tore a strip off one of the slices and dropped his hand so that Stinkpot could reach it. The big tomcat wolfed down the turkey in two seconds flat and meowed for more even as he was licking the residue from his mouth.

"Errol, stop feeding that cat. He's spoiled enough as it is without you giving him smoked turkey from the deli. For which I paid an exorbitant price, I might add." Minna set down the kitchen knife and replaced the lids on the jars of mayo and mustard.

"I don't spoil him, you spoil him. You buy him that designer cat food from the pet boutique." Stinkpot realized he wasn't going to get any more turkey from Errol and went back to butting his head against Minna's legs.

Turkey sandwiches constructed, we carried plates and wineglasses to the kitchen table and pulled out chairs. Errol set down his plate and reached for a five-by-seven envelope in a nearby stack of envelopes and papers. "Want to take a look at the autopsy report?"

"Not while we're eating, Errol," Minna said. "It might not bother you or Jeri but it certainly would me."

It would bother me, too, I thought, sipping my wine, considering Ariel's body had been in the water for several days before it was found.

"I wonder if Ryan Trent is as impulsive as he seemed outside the mission," I said, after a few bites from my sandwich.

"You mean as a possible suspect in Ariel Logan's murder?" Errol tilted his head to one side. "Worth looking into."

"Trent appears to be a man who likes to have his own way. If his behavior after the funeral is any example, he can barely control his anger. Which could be genuine, I'll admit. But what if the scene was a dodge to divert attention to Bobby, and away from Trent? Minna, you told me on Saturday that you'd heard Ryan Trent was extremely upset with Ariel Logan for breaking off their relationship."

Minna nodded. "That's what the grapevine said."

"Would he do anything about it?"

"Trent has a short fuse. But if he were going to get back at Ariel for breaking up with him, I have a feeling he'd have done so immediately, rather than wait this long."

I nodded. Donna said she'd introduced Bobby and Ariel last August. Presumably Ryan Trent had been history for over a year. But some people do a slow burn.

"I don't know how long Ariel had been dating Trent," Minna continued. "Several months. But remember, she was in graduate school at Cal Poly. So any relationship would be long-distance, although San Luis Obispo is an easy enough trip for a weekend."

Errol's eyes met mine and I saw in them a warning. Don't be so eager to clear Bobby of Ariel's murder that I would stretch the circumstances to fit Ryan Trent. But Trent was an old boyfriend with a large chip on his well-tailored shoulder. I'd have to talk to him.

"I didn't get a chance to talk with Maggie Lim," I said. "Sergeant Magruder intercepted me. He knows I'm Bobby's cousin, that I'm a private investigator who used to work for you, and I've been asking questions. So I got the usual warning—stay clear of his investigation."

"He may also have found out that I obtained a copy of the autopsy report from the Carmel police chief." Errol indicated the envelope. "People in town know I'm an investigator."

"Retired," Minna interjected.

"Yes, love. No doubt that's why Peter Logan called me last night."

"What did he want?" I finished my sandwich, reached for a napkin, and wiped a trace of mustard from my hands.

"To put Bobby behind bars. He wants Bobby arrested and charged. He thinks Sergeant Magruder is moving far too slowly toward what to him is an obvious conclusion."

Logan's reaction didn't surprise me. If my daughter had been murdered I'd probably be eager to pin the crime on the first available suspect.

"Logan asked if I'd take on the case," Errol said. "I told him I was retired. Besides, I'm not as certain as he is that Bobby's guilty. After today in the mission courtyard, of course, the whole town will put me in the enemy camp. It's possible the Logans know about Bobby's cousin the private detective."

"They do. I went over to their house before coming here, looking for Maggie Lim. Mrs. Braemer informed me she was well aware of my identity."

"That may be their reason for upping the ante by hiring an investigator of their own," Errol said. "When I turned him down last night, Logan asked me to recommend someone. I gave him a couple of names. If he follows through, you may be facing an adversary other than the sergeant."

I shook my head. "Why hasn't Magruder made his move? He must not have enough evidence to charge Bobby. The only reason anyone has to suspect Bobby is the argument he and Ariel had before she disappeared. The one Bobby won't tell me about."

"So you have to get Bobby to talk, or go at it from another angle." Errol got up and cleared away the plates, which he then loaded into the dishwasher. "That means Ariel's roommate."

"I'll have to go to San Luis Obispo. Glennis Braemer told me Maggie Lim went back to school. I don't know if that's true but Mrs. Braemer is definitely guarding the door. No way was I getting past her to see for myself. She's quite a formidable woman. Tell me about her."

"Glennis lives in Pasadena and she's a widow. I gather her husband had money but I don't know how he acquired it." Minna reached for the wine bottle and topped off her glass. She waved it at me but I shook my head. "Glennis comes up here to visit Sylvie and Peter several times a year. She'll probably stay around for a while. From all reports, Sylvie is barely functioning. Not surprising when she's lost her only child, who was barely into her twenties. It's a tragedy. I don't think Bobby killed Ariel, Jeri, but I do hope you find out who did."

Errol wiped his hands on a dish towel. "Time to look at that autopsy report."

"In that case, I'll excuse myself." Minna got up from the table, wineglass in hand. "Come on, Stinkpot. Let's go pull weeds." The big cat must have thought food was in the offing. He rose from his crouch on a throw rug near the stove and followed Minna out the back door, tail stuck up in the air.

When she'd gone Errol sat down and opened the envelope. He pulled out a crisp photocopy, several pages long, and handed it to me. I leafed through it, then settled down to read the report of Ariel Logan's autopsy, attempting to make sense of her death from the words written on the pages.

I've watched an autopsy before and I don't recommend it for the fainthearted. Just reading the report brought back the memory of the sights and smells. I pushed back that recollection and focused on the words and the information they conveyed. Stripped of any humanity, the report was a purely scientific account of the condition of the remains that were once human and alive, and the coroner's educated guesses about what ended that life. I tried to look at it as the coroner would, as a puzzle to be solved, looking for clues in the body fluids and tissue, stomach contents and bone.

The coroner estimated that Ariel had been in the water five or six days before her body was spotted and recovered from the rugged coastal shore below Rocky Creek Bridge. That meant she died sometime on Friday or Saturday. There was some water in her lungs, but not much. So Ariel hadn't drowned. She'd been killed before her body went into the ocean, not long before. There was no evidence of insects or maggots in the remains.

The fact that she'd been in the cold ocean water had slowed the decomposition process somewhat, but there are other things that tear down the structure of the body. The sand, the rocks, and the crabs had all done their usual damage. Sand can strip the skin from a corpse in a very short time. The creatures that live in the ocean consume flesh and muscle. The body that the dive-and-rescue team recovered on Thursday was identifiable as a woman, but Ariel Logan's dentist had to provide his records for a positive identification.

The bones, the last to break down, provided clues. The crushed skull revealed traces of blood coagulated inside, which meant that the trauma had been inflicted before death, and not by the battering of the corpse against the unforgiving rocks. Someone who was probably right-handed struck Ariel Logan on the back and the right side of the head, several times, with something that left a sliver of metal embedded in the skull. This murder weapon had been wielded with great force, because Ariel had a subdural hematoma and a blown pupil on the right side of the skull.

She must have died immediately. That was a small mercy, since her body had been dumped into the ocean like so much trash. My guess was that the killer had also tossed the murder weapon into the sea, perhaps at another location, rather than risk it being found in the vicinity of the body.

"Magruder sent the metal fragment up to a crime lab in the Bay Area," Errol said as I looked up at him and frowned. "They may be able to identify what it came from."

"A tire iron," I speculated. "Part of a jack. A crowbar. A tool of some sort. It could have been anything. And you can bet it's somewhere in the water. They'll never find it."

"But if it's a specific tool, it may point to a specific person."

"Like something used on a fishing boat." Which would implicate Bobby. That prospect didn't make me feel any better. I reached for the wine and poured what remained into my own glass. The Riesling didn't do much to wash away the imagined scent of decay and formaldehyde.

"I don't see anything here that pinpoints a location," I said. "Can we assume she was killed near where her car was found, at Rocky Point? Or near where the body was found, at Rocky Creek Bridge?"

"Not necessarily," Errol pointed out. "It could have been moved a considerable distance on the current. There haven't been any storms in the past week, so I think the standard procedure is to assume the body shows up a half mile either side of the entry point."

"That's what Donna said. But she thought if Ariel's body had gone into the water at Rocky Point, the tidal current would have pushed the body north, toward Point Lobos. Instead the body was found a mile or so south of there, near the mouth of Rocky Creek. Of course, Ariel's body may have been wedged in the rocks, or trapped beneath the kelp, until the motion of the waves freed it."

"The Coast Guard might be able to give us more information on the tides and currents in that area," Errol said. "She could have been killed on a boat and pushed overboard."

I shook my head. "If I were going to kill someone on a boat, I'd be damn sure to get rid of the body farther out to sea, so it would never be found. I'd probably weight it with something, so the gases wouldn't bring it to the surface. I don't see any indication that the body was tied with line."

"Unless you were in a hurry and didn't have time to go out to sea. Or didn't have the right kind of boat to brave heavier seas. Or just wanted to get rid of the body as soon as possible." Errol shifted in his chair. "It's a disadvantage not knowing where she was killed. We can't examine physical evidence at the site. So we've got to trace her movements."

I nodded. "I think someone must have seen Ariel after she and Bobby quarreled at the Rose and Crown."

Errol tilted his head to one side. "You canvassed Alvarado Street?"

"After I talked to the barmaid at the Rose and Crown. But I haven't located anyone who'll admit to seeing them. I talked to the same people Magruder already interviewed, the owners of businesses nearby. And people on the street, where I could find them, like customers at the bookstore and coffeehouse on the other side of Alvarado, the one with tables on the sidewalks. The barmaid said the argument started inside, then Ariel and Bobby went outside and she heard them continue the quarrel. But if anyone on the street saw them, it's as though they looked away, to let them continue their argument in private."

"Do Alvarado Street again," Errol advised. "Maybe you can shake something loose."

I slipped the autopsy report back into its envelope. "Where did Ariel go? Back to her parents' house? Out to dinner? Is that why she went down to Rocky Point? I wouldn't go to that particular restaurant for a quick bite to eat. It's a spot for a romantic dinner, a place to watch the sunset. Maybe Ariel was meeting someone."

"The housekeeper saw her before her meeting with Bobby. And her parents were out of town." Errol leaned back in his chair and laced his fingers together. "From what I can glean by talking to the Carmel police the neighbors didn't even notice that Ariel was staying at her parents' house. She didn't announce her presence in any way, didn't call attention to herself, didn't phone or visit any friends. Except Bobby. What did he do after the fight?"

"He went looking for Karl Beckman. But first he went to see his ex-wife. He was supposed to have his son that weekend, but he asked Linda if he could pick up Nicky Saturday morning instead of Friday night. Linda thought he was headed for Beckman Boat Works right after he talked with her. But Karl Beckman says he didn't see Bobby until the next week, after Ariel had been reported missing. Nor will he tell me where he was."

"Did anyone at the Boat Works see Bobby?" Errol asked.

I shook my head. "I talked with Lacy Beckman and some employees on Saturday. No one recalls seeing Bobby. When he couldn't find Karl, he probably went home to get some sleep. Remember, he'd just brought the *Nicky II* in before he and Ariel went to the Rose and Crown, which meant he'd been up for close to eighteen hours. Normally he'd have gone home to sleep."

"Except Ariel showed up." Errol fingered his wineglass. "She cut her Friday classes at Cal Poly to drive up here to see Bobby. Whatever her reason, it must have been important. It comes back to Bobby. He's the key, Jeri. You must get him to talk."

"He can be pretty damn stubborn, even in the face of a murder investigation."

CHAPTER *19*

I WENT BACK TO MONTEREY, PAST READY TO CHANGE OUT OF the dress and heels I'd worn to the funeral. I was supposed to meet Mother later at Café Marie, where the industrial hygienist from Seaside was trying to sort out what had happened yesterday. The firm's lab was doing a rush job to identify the substance found in the ventilating system, promising a twenty-four-hour turnaround for which Mother was paying dearly.

Mother was paying in other ways, too. Sunday afternoon's disaster made the front page of this morning's *Herald.*

With a sigh of relief I kicked off the shoes and the dress and pulled on a white T-shirt and a well-worn pair of blue jeans. I carried my purse to the kitchen, dug out my address book, and used my telephone credit card to call an Oakland number.

Fortunately Cassie Taylor was in her office. We've known each other for years, since we were both secretaries in an Oakland law firm. Later I became a paralegal, then one of Errol Seville's investigators, and Cassie went to law school. Now she's a partner in the firm of Alwin, Taylor and Chao, which takes up the front suite on the third floor of a Franklin Street building, just down the hall from my own office.

"Your plants are fine," she told me. "Your cat, however, wishes you would hurry home."

I sighed. Abigail is a fat brown tabby, ten years old and imperious. She doesn't like it when I don't come home at the same time every night, let alone when I leave town for several days. My function in life, in cat terms, is to provide food and a lap on a regular basis. When I'm away, Cassie, who has my extra key, takes on daily cat-care duties. As far as Abigail is concerned it just isn't the same.

"Abigail will have to cope for a while longer. I hadn't been here twenty-four hours when my cousin Donna asked me to look into some pelican mutilations. But the pelicans got put on the back burner."

"Good lord," Cassie said when I'd finished telling her about Ariel's murder and the incidents at the restaurant. "Jeri goes to Monterey and all hell breaks loose."

I sighed. "Something like that. The incidents at the restaurant have been going on for a while. So have the pelican mutilations, for that matter. I've got to nail whoever is sabotaging the restaurant. Mother's losing business. But the most serious situation is Ariel Logan's murder. There's a sergeant in the sheriff's department who wants to pin that on my cousin Bobby."

"You'd better check the messages on your office answering machine," Cassie advised. "You're losing business, too. I've gotten calls from Bill Stanley and another attorney you've worked for, wondering where you are. As for Abigail, I'll just fuss over her more than I already do."

"Thanks. Before you hang up, get out your Martindale-Hubbell Law Directory and look up an attorney named Ryan Trent. He practices in Carmel."

Cassie set the phone down and went off in search of the thick volume that contained information on lawyers and their firms. "Trent, Trent. Here it is. Undergraduate work at UCLA, law school at USC. Business law, mergers and acquisitions, contracts, with some entertainment law thrown in. Before he was in Carmel he was in Los Angeles, at one of those huge law firms downtown."

Another Southern California refugee, I thought, just like the Logans.

"Office in Carmel," Cassie continued, "somewhere in the vicinity of Fifth and Lincoln. You'd think people down there would have street addresses. Locating someone must be like going on a treasure hunt. Why is Mr. Trent important?"

"Mr. Trent used to be Ariel Logan's boyfriend. And I had to step between him and Bobby after the funeral this morning."

"Sounds like you've got your hands full. Keep me posted, especially about when you'll be back. Remember, Eric and I are going away in a couple of weeks."

Which meant Cassie wouldn't be able to take care of my imperious cat. I fervently hoped it wouldn't take that long to sort things out in Monterey. After Cassie hung up I got a dial tone and called my office machine, punching the keys so it would play back my messages. I wrote them down and returned several phone calls. Cassie was right, I thought as I turned down a job. The longer I stayed in Monterey, I was losing business in Oakland. And I was working for free down here. So much for my vacation.

I made one more phone call, this one to Morro Bay. The phone on the other end rang several times. I was just about to hang up when my cousin Angie picked up the receiver, with a quick "hello" that sounded like she'd been running.

"Jeri! I just walked in the door," she said after I'd identified myself. "Let me catch my breath and sit down. It's great to hear from you. What's up?"

"I need a bed for the night, Angie." I planned to drive down to San Luis Obispo first thing tomorrow morning and I told her why.

"Murder? Oh, my God." The cheerfulness in Angie's voice turned into alarm. "I talked to Mom and Dad this weekend but they didn't say anything about murder. They just said Bobby's girlfriend had died and didn't go into details. I thought Ariel had been swept off the rocks and drowned."

"She was struck over the head and her body was dumped in the ocean." There was no way to soften the words or the images they brought forth.

"And the cops think Bobby had something to do with her death? Impossible," Angie declared. "Not my baby brother, not even on his worst day."

"I've got to find someone else with a reason to want Ariel dead. I didn't connect with her roommate at the funeral, so I'll have to track her down and hope she can give me some information. Ariel lived with another Cal Poly student, a woman named Maggie Lim. I assume they had an apartment together, somewhere in SLO."

"I've got the phone book right here. Let me see if there's a listing for Logan or Lim." Angie was quiet for a moment and I thought I heard the rustle of pages. "Well, several Logans, no Ariel, but one A. Logan, no address. And an M. Lim, no address, with the same phone number as A. Logan. That must be the Lim you're looking for."

"I'm sure it is. Give me the number." I quickly wrote it down. "She left Monterey after the funeral, so she won't be back in SLO until later this afternoon. This is a start. Now all I need is an address."

"I can find out where she lives. Our college admin office talks to the university admin office all the time." Angie taught at Cuesta College, between Morro Bay and San Luis Obispo. "I'll pull a few strings. What time do you think you'll get here? I've got classes in the morning but I'll plan to come home for lunch."

"Depends on when I get on the road. But I should be there by noon."

I looked at the digital clock on the microwave and grabbed my keys. The phone rang before I made it to the front door. When I picked up the receiver, I heard the voice of Stella the barmaid, her British accent competing with the fifties rock tunes blaring from the speakers at the Rose and Crown.

"You remember I told you about that fellow, came into the pub right after Bobby and Ariel left," she said. "He's the one who said they were going at it hammer and tongs outside."

"Is he there?"

"No, he's not here," Stella said. "But I think I've recalled his name. Last name, anyway. Porter. I flashed on it because he drinks Taddy Porter. I don't always remember names but I remember drinks."

"He hasn't shown up there since the day of the argument?" I asked.

"No. I think he's sort of a regular, been in a couple of times a month, over the past year or so. He must travel, comes here when he's in town. There's something else. I think his job's like his name. Can't tell you why that popped into my head, but it did, along with the Taddy Porter. Not a porter like in a train station. But transport. A truck driver."

If Mr. Porter was a truck driver that would explain why he hadn't been in the pub the past week. He could be on a run somewhere. I hoped the guy was a creature of habit, one who would show up at the Rose and Crown sooner or later for a glass of his favorite brew. For Bobby's sake, I hoped it was sooner.

"If he does come into the tavern, call me," I told Stella. "I have to talk to him."

"Rancid butter?"

Mother and I stared at the dark-haired man. His name was Leo Cumberly and he was the industrial hygienist from Seaside. He had twinkly blue eyes and the cheerful demeanor of someone who thoroughly enjoyed his work. He'd spent a good part of the morning combing through Café Marie's heat, ventilation, and air-conditioning system. Now he pulled out a chair, hitched up his stained and rumpled khaki slacks, and sat down. On the table in front of him was an open briefcase containing a pile of file folders and a portable phone.

"That awful smell was caused by rancid butter?" Mother repeated. She shook her head slowly and raked her left hand through her gray-streaked hair.

It was almost funny, I thought. Surely the stench that had shut down Café Marie Sunday afternoon had resulted from something more exotic than a stick of butter well past its time. Of course, the butter hadn't been left by accident on a kitchen counter.

"Butyric acid," Cumberly said. "It's not quite the same thing."

When I walked through the entrance of Café Marie fifteen minutes ago, I found Mother and Cumberly near the bar. She was in blue slacks and a pink shirt, looking tired as she watched the industrial hygienist talk into his phone. He was getting the results of the lab analysis. While Mother and I waited for him to finish the call I looked toward the kitchen and saw two people. One was Julian Surtees. The other was a round-faced man whose identity finally registered as Eric Lopez, the county environmental health specialist who'd been here last night.

Now Cumberly looked at the notes he'd scribbled, leaned back in the chair, and proceeded to give us a brief chemistry lesson.

"Butyric acid smells like rancid butter, only worse. It's a colorless liquid, soluble in water, combustible with a flash point of one-sixty-one Fahrenheit. It's also quite corrosive to metal and tissue.

Given time, it could have eaten a hole right through the ducts. It's definitely an environmentally hazardous substance."

"How would I obtain butyric acid?" I asked.

"You take a pound or so of butter, and leave it out in the sun until it's way past ripe. Then it becomes butyric acid. It's that simple." Cumberly shrugged and spread his hands wide. "You'd be astonished at the number of poisons and toxins you can produce using materials from your kitchen or garden."

All you need is a basic knowledge of chemistry, I thought. Or a reference book. "So I can cook up a batch of butyric acid in the comfort of my own home?"

Cumberly chuckled. "I wouldn't think you'd want to do it inside the house. Butyric acid is a real stinker, as you and Mrs. Howard discovered yesterday. It takes a while for the odor to dissipate."

The odor still lingered, faint but detectable. I'd noticed it as soon as I stepped into Café Marie.

"God, yes," Mother said. "This morning when my staff and I came here to clean up, it seemed as bad as it was yesterday. We've had the doors and windows open all day."

"It was in one location only, where the hazardous materials team found it yesterday. They cleaned it all out of there," Cumberly said. "As soon as the smell goes away I'm sure you'll be able to reopen the restaurant."

"You say butyric acid is corrosive, in addition to having such an awful smell," I said. "It had to be in some sort of container. How did it get from that to the ventilation system?"

"It was in a glass jar," Cumberly said, "right up there in that box on the roof. The jar was broken, though. It was rigged to a timing device. What we have, ladies, is a stink bomb. A very ingenious one."

So what happened last night was no accident, though I'd never really thought so. But a time bomb seemed like such a drastic escalation from the mouse on the plate.

"How was the timing device put together?" I asked.

The industrial hygienist pulled out a pencil and paper and quickly drew a sketch. "A lamp timer, with a dial and ridges for each hour of the day. Twenty-four-hour clock, twelve hours A.M., twelve hours P.M. You can buy them in any hardware store. You plug a lamp into the timer, connect the timer to an electrical out-let, and it turns on the lamp at whatever time you set. In this case, the timer was wired to some batteries and an explosive charge, set to go off at eight P.M."

I grimaced and so did Mother. Yesterday's incident was bad enough but it would have been even more disastrous if the restau-rant had been full of customers, as it would have been if the stink bomb had gone off on schedule.

"Something made it go off sooner," Cumberly continued. "Maybe the timer had a glitch. Or maybe the heat triggered it. I don't know. What broke the glass and released the butyric acid was that explosive. Clever little gizmo. I could have made it myself."

"What kind of explosive?" I asked, frowning.

Cumberly shook his head. "Small, but effective enough to smash a glass jar into fragments. I'm gonna have to analyze that further. I'll let you know. You and the cops. You've got yourself one mali-cious character at work here, ladies."

"Why would anyone do this?" Mother asked after Cumberly left. She slumped in her chair, her face etched with exhaustion. "I don't understand it."

"Neither do I." Was Café Marie in fact a deliberate target? Could this be just random meanness, done for the hell of doing it? There were certainly people in the world capable of such pure cussedness. But even as I considered this I shook my head.

No, there was an obvious intent at work here. Shut down the restaurant, ruin Mother financially, cause her a great deal of grief and pain. Marie Doyle Howard was the target. In my mind I echoed her questions. Why did the saboteur have such an animus against her? What had she done to warrant this—or what did the perpetrator think she had done?

I had hoped that the substance used to create the stink bomb at Café Marie would have some unique quality that would point a finger directly at its source. But it appeared that anyone with a grudge and a butter dish could manufacture butyric acid, as long as that individual stayed upwind of the stuff. Construction of the timing device required some technical knowledge; though, as Cum-berly had said, I could have put it together myself. More impor-tantly, whoever built the device had access to an explosive.

And access to the ventilating system works on the roof. I recalled the scene yesterday when I'd theorized that someone could have made it up to the roof by climbing on the Dumpster.

"The stink bomb must have been put in place after eight o'clock on Saturday," I told Mother, thinking out loud. "Since it was set to go off at eight o'clock on Sunday. Whoever put the device there did it during the night. Or early Sunday morning. I should think if it was broad daylight on Sunday, someone on the roof would have been noticed."

I looked up from my musings and saw Julian Surtees standing next to the bar, with an odd look on his saturnine face. I hadn't heard him approach. Suddenly I recalled that Julian had been looking at the Dumpster yesterday, drawing the same conclusion I had. Did he know something?

He tore his dark eyes from me and looked at Mother. "Marie? Can you come back to the kitchen?"

Mother got to her feet and we walked back to the kitchen, where Eric Lopez was examining Mrs. Grady's plate. He'd disinterred it from the plastic bag Julian and I had slipped it into Saturday night and he was using the end of a pencil to poke at the now congealed fettuccine as he examined the tiny brownish gray corpse that lay in the middle.

"Murine musculus," he said in a detached voice. "Common house mouse. Not a very big one at that." He looked up. "Thanks. You can toss it now."

With a barely concealed shudder, Julian swept up the offending plate and headed out the back door, toward the Dumpster.

Lopez turned to Mother. "They call it the common house mouse for a reason. You can find it anywhere. But I didn't find any here. You don't have a rodent infestation. No evidence of droppings, tracks, gnawing, or burrows outside. So somebody put it on the plate."

"So when can I reopen?" Mother asked.

"As soon as the place is fully ventilated," Lopez said. "Tomorrow's fine. You've got a clean bill of health as far as I'm concerned."

The question was, I thought, whether Café Marie's customers would agree.

C H A P T E R *20*

Tuesday morning I drove south, down the middle of the broad agricultural Salinas Valley, into San Luis Obispo County. At Paso Robles I left U.S. 101 and took Highway 46 west, over the hills toward the Pacific Ocean and the coast highway.

I rounded the curve just outside the beach town of Cayucos and saw Morro Rock looming in the distance, a granite sentinel marking the entrance to Morro Bay harbor. The ancient volcanic peak is the last in a chain of nine stretching from San Luis Obispo to the sea, lending their name not only to the town but to the strand of beach between Cayucos and Morro Bay. The rock dwarfed the triple stacks of the Pacific Gas & Electric steam plant where Angie's husband Stan worked.

I glanced to my right and saw a huge vessel rocking in the waves off Morro Strand. Offshore oil drilling, I thought, something the north coast had so far been able to stave off. At least Monterey Bay was safe now. The sanctuary's boundaries encompassed the coast from San Francisco down past San Simeon. There would be no offshore oil rigs there.

It was almost noon when I reached Morro Bay. My cousin's house was on Pacific Street, midway between the highway and the shoreline, near the downtown business section, a one-story wood-frame house painted white with dark green shutters. A huge pine tree stood in one corner of the small lot, shedding cones on the lawn. The flower beds along the front of the house were full of vibrant yellow-red marigolds, as warm as the midday sun burning through the coastal fog.

I parked the Toyota in front of the house and got out, carrying my overnight bag. Angie Ravella Sellers opened the front door as I came up the walk. I hadn't seen her in a couple of years but she looked the same, her curly hair cut short and tumbled around her face. She wore a flowered short-sleeved dress and low-heeled shoes. Angie and I were both thirty-three. She looked a lot like her younger brother Bobby, with his black hair and wide brown eyes.

"Great timing," she said, holding the screen door wide as I stepped into the living room. "I got here fifteen minutes ago and I'm fixing lunch. Just stash your bag in the back bedroom." She led the way down a hallway to my right. The small bedroom held a desk covered with papers, several bookshelves, and a daybed.

I detoured to the bathroom before walking back through the living room. It opened onto a big kitchen with space for a round oak dining table. Angie had set two cloth place mats on the table and now she stood at the counter, constructing a tossed salad from the array of fresh vegetables strewn on either side of the wooden cutting board.

Sunlight streamed through a back window, falling on an elderly beagle curled up on a throw rug just below. His name was Clyde and he'd been part of the package when Angie married Stan four years ago. I knelt and patted the old dog, noticing how white he was on the ears and muzzle.

"He's getting on, isn't he?" I straightened and looked out the window at the small backyard with herbs and vegetables growing in a plot along the fence.

"Just turned fourteen," Angie said, slicing mushrooms. "He has arthritis and he doesn't see very well. Stan will be devastated when Clyde goes. But you're hanging in there, aren't you, boy?" At the sound of her voice Clyde wagged his tail, slapping the linoleum on which the rug lay. Angie gathered the mushrooms and tossed them into the bowl, then turned her attention to a bell pepper.

"How are things at the college?" I asked as she cored the pepper.

"Fine. I'm teaching three classes this term. I've got one this afternoon, so I'll give you the extra key and leave you to your own devices." She picked up the tongs and tossed the salad, then set the ceramic bowl on the table, along with some bottled dressing and a bakery bag full of soft breadsticks. Then she turned and opened the refrigerator. "I have wine, beer, mineral water. What do you want?"

"Mineral water."

As we ate lunch I told Angie about the incidents at Café Marie and their escalating seriousness. "You don't have any idea who's behind it?" She stood up and carried our empty salad bowls to the kitchen sink.

"No. I have some theories but nothing concrete. Mother's frantic about it. That restaurant is her whole life."

"Mom hasn't mentioned any of this the last few times I've called. Of course, Mom's frantic about Bobby," Angie said, her face suddenly somber. "She thinks the sheriff is going to arrest Bobby for Ariel's murder."

I reached for the last breadstick and broke it into pieces. "I don't know. If the investigating sergeant had enough evidence I think he would arrest Bobby. But he hasn't. That means he doesn't have enough evidence. Did you ever meet Ariel?"

Angie nodded as she ran hot soapy water into the sink. "Bobby drove down to visit her several times last year. He brought her here for dinner. She was good for him. They seemed to fit together."

"Donna said Ariel was concerned about Bobby's drinking."

"We all were." Angie was quiet for a moment as she washed our dishes. "But he seems to have gotten that under control. Her influence, I'm sure. I hope he doesn't start again."

"Do you recall any specific time when he sobered up? Donna mentioned last spring."

Angie shook her head, rinsing the dishes and stacking them in the drainer. "Spring sounds about right. That was the end of the school year and I'm always up to my ears in work. I don't remember any specifics."

"Maybe Ariel's roommate can tell me. Were you able to find an address for Maggie Lim?"

My cousin's eyes twinkled. She dried her hands on a dish towel and reached for her handbag, hanging by its strap from the back of one of the chairs. She pulled out a sheet of paper. "I certainly did. Maggie Lim lives on Foothill Boulevard, not far from the campus. I don't know what sort of class schedule she has, but I would think if you hang around long enough, she'll come home eventually."

"Good work," I told her. "I may have to take you on as an operative."

"Does it pay more than an instructor's salary at Cuesta College?" When I shook my head, she laughed. "Then I'm not interested." Her demeanor turned more serious. "I just hope you can find out something that will prove Bobby's innocence."

THE COAST HIGHWAY TURNED INLAND THROUGH TWELVE MILES OF rolling hills until it reached San Luis Obispo. California Polytechnic State University, known as Cal Poly, was tucked at the bottom of the rolling hills northwest of town.

The highway turned into Santa Rosa Street and intersected with Foothill Boulevard. I kept one eye on the street and the other on the building numbers, finally spotting the address Angie had written on the paper. It was a two-story brown stucco with eight units that faced each other across a narrow central courtyard. The mailbox for number four held a strip of plastic tape that read LIM. Below it another strip of tape had been removed.

Number four was the upper rear unit on the right-hand building. I climbed the concrete stairs and knocked on the door but got no answer. I knocked on the opposite door. A moment later it . opened and a young man peered out.

"Hi, I'm looking for Maggie Lim," I said, favoring her neighbor with a big smile. SLO has a laid-back, mellow atmosphere and I was counting on the natives to be friendly. "Do you know where I can find her?"

He scratched his unruly brown hair. "You looking for a roommate? I know she put an ad in the paper." I cranked the smile up a couple of watts and didn't confirm or deny his assumption. "I guess she's in class or at the library. You could leave her a note or something. No, wait, it's Tuesday, right?" When I nodded he glanced at his watch. "She works at the bookstore, Tuesday and Thursday afternoons. She should be there."

"Which bookstore is that?" I prompted.

"Earthling, downtown on Higuera Street."

I thanked him and retraced my steps back to the curb, relieved that I wouldn't have to stake out the apartment. Stakeouts are excruciatingly boring. I headed downtown and I left my Toyota in a municipal lot just off Higuera Street, the main drag.

I walked a couple of blocks to Earthling, where customers browsed through the racks of books or sat round the upper-level fireplace perusing the *Coast Weekly* or potential purchases. Behind the counter, both cashiers were busy ringing up purchases. The man finished first and his customer departed with a stack of mystery paperbacks. I stepped up to the counter and asked if Maggie Lim was here.

He glanced at his watch. "She doesn't actually start work until three," he said. "It's just now two o'clock."

"She's early, then," the other cashier said. "I saw her back in the stockroom."

I thanked them and made my way to the rear of the store. I spotted my quarry, standing in the doorway to the stockroom, her face in profile as she spoke to someone I couldn't see. I'd only caught a glimpse of her at the funeral on Monday afternoon, looking subdued in her black dress. Now I examined her more closely. She was in her early twenties, maybe five feet two, and her long black hair hung straight down her back. Today she wore gray slacks and a white cotton shirt, with an oversized canvas bag slung over one shoulder. She was American-born, probably second or third generation, since she had no accent, unless one counted a slight flavor of San Fernando Valley Girl.

"Okay," she told her unseen companion, "I'll grab some lunch and be right back." She turned in my direction and saw me standing between two bookshelves.

"May I help you?" she asked with a ready smile. Then she looked at me again, as though she hadn't really seen me the first time. She frowned.

"I know you. You were at Ariel's funeral. With Bobby."

CHAPTER *21*

TOOK ONE OF MY BUSINESS CARDS FROM MY PURSE AND handed it to her. "My name is Jeri Howard. I'm Bobby's cousin."

Maggie Lim picked up the business card and stared at it. Then she looked up at me, black brows drawn down over her brown eyes. "Mr. and Mrs. Logan think Bobby killed Ariel." She spoke so softly that I had to lean forward to catch the words.

"What do you think?"

She thought for a moment before she answered. Then she shook her head. Her straight black hair flew back and forth, obscuring the collar of her white shirt. "No. I just can't buy that. They were in love. They were going to get married."

"Sometimes love goes bad," I said, playing devil's advocate.

Maggie shook her head again. "It wasn't like that."

"I'd really like to talk, Maggie."

"I was just going to lunch. You can come with me."

We left the bookstore through the front door and walked up Higuera Street, stopping at a deli where Maggie ordered a chicken salad sandwich and a diet soda. I asked for some mineral water and paid for all three.

"Thank you," Maggie said. "Let's go up to the mission."

We rounded the corner and walked up Chorro Street onto the grounds of the Mission San Luis Obispo de Tolosa, which occupies a wooded city block in the middle of the downtown area. A creek, liberated from the surrounding concrete, runs behind the shops, galleries, and restaurants fronting on Higuera Street. Children played on the banks of the stream, darting back and forth across a series of stepping-stones. Maggie and I walked along the path edging the creek, lured by the music of water running over the rocks. We found a vacant bench and sat down. Maggie spread a napkin on her lap and opened the paper sack containing her lunch. She opened her diet soda and set it on the bench next to her. Then she unwrapped her sandwich, staring at it as though she didn't remember what she ordered.

I waited until she'd eaten a few bites. "How long had you known Ariel?"

"We were roommates for two years." Maggie gave me a sidelong glance. "We met when I was a junior and she was a senior. I think we got to know each other pretty well."

That's what I'd hoped. "Tell me about her, the Ariel Logan you knew."

"She was really nice," Maggie said simply. "I'm going to miss her."

Tears brimmed up in her large brown eyes and she mopped them with a napkin. "I can't believe she's gone, that someone would kill her. She didn't have an enemy in the world. How could such a terrible thing happen?"

I didn't have any answers for her. Maggie took a deep breath, then bit into her sandwich again. I let her eat in silence. Then she began describing the Ariel she knew, someone who sounded like a normal young woman with goals and aspirations, hopes and dreams, the kinds of things that two roommates confide in each other, late at night in their off-campus apartment. Ariel was a student intern at the water board, a volunteer for several environmental organizations, and she liked to hike at Montaña de Oro State Park, on the rugged coast nearby.

"Do you remember when she met Bobby?" I asked.

"Oh, yes. That was a year ago August." Maggie nibbled at her sandwich. "When she came back to school she was buzzing about this guy she'd met, a fisherman. She said he was sweet, but a little bit wild."

That sounded like my cousin Bobby. "Were there any problems between them?"

"She thought he drank too much." Maggie sipped soda through the straw. "They dated during the fall, while she was home on weekends, or he'd drive down here. During the Christmas holidays she took him to meet her folks. I guess that was a disaster."

"Why? What happened?"

"I'm not sure." She tilted her head to one side. "I think maybe Bobby was nervous and he had too much wine, or spilled some wine. Ariel wouldn't give me all the details. Maybe Mr. and Mrs. Logan thought he was crude or unsuitable. I just don't know, other than things got off on the wrong foot. Later, at a New Year's party, Bobby did get drunk. Ariel got really upset with him and they argued, at the party. Then Ariel left without him."

I shook my head at the picture Maggie's words painted. I hadn't realized Bobby's consumption of alcohol had gotten that bad. "I'm surprised they didn't break up then."

Maggie continued her story between bites as she finished her sandwich. "Ariel was upset with him and she didn't see him for a couple of months. He'd call and I was supposed to tell him she wasn't home. I hated that. Then, on the long weekend in February, she went up to see her parents. She went out with Bobby and they started seeing each other again."

"Something happened in the spring," I said. "It had to do with Bobby's drinking."

"Ariel gave him an ultimatum." Maggie crumpled the napkin and the paper that had been wrapped around the sandwich and stuffed them into the bag. "The third weekend in April. He drove down here to see Ariel. Saturday night we went out, four of us. I was with a guy named Ted. We went to a club and Bobby got so drunk that Ted had to drive him back to our apartment in Bobby's T-bird. Ariel and I followed in Ted's car. All the way to our place Ariel was fuming. When Bobby dragged out of bed Sunday morning Ariel told him either he stopped drinking or she never wanted to see him again."

"What did he say?"

"He just left," Maggie said, shrugging her shoulders. "In a blue funk. I figured that was the last I'd see of him. But he did stop drinking. When the term ended, Ariel went back up to Carmel. I went with her, for two weeks. She was seeing him again. The three of us spent a lot of time together during those two weeks in June. And Bobby was different, like night and day. Even I noticed it. We'd go out for dinner, and he wouldn't have anything alcoholic. Then I came back here, for summer school. Ariel and I talked on the phone a lot. I went up to see her in Carmel a few times during the summer, and she came down here as well. The relationship between her and Bobby seemed to be working. He hadn't gone back to his old pattern."

What if he had? The thought came to my mind unbidden, unpleasant. This pattern of Bobby drinking too much, arguing with Ariel, breaking up with her. What if that was what they'd been fighting about at the Rose and Crown? But Stella, the barmaid, said he'd ordered lunch, with nothing to drink but mineral water. I shook my head. There were so many things I needed to ask Maggie Lim and the clock was ticking. I glanced at my watch and Maggie looked at hers.

"I know she cared about him and she wanted things to work out." Maggie stood and tossed the bag and the soda can into a nearby trash receptacle. "He brought up the subject of marriage during the summer. Ariel didn't exactly say yes, not at that point. It was more a case of waiting until she finished grad school before making any plans." She sighed. "I want an ice cream cone. Then I have to go to work."

Maggie led the way down the path through the mission grounds to a bridge that spanned the creek. "Did Ariel tell her parents any of this?" I asked as we crossed the bridge.

"I don't know." Maggie shrugged. We walked through a pedestrian mall that led to Higuera Street. "Mr. and Mrs. Logan didn't like Bobby. They made that plain whenever I was up in Carmel. I think they were hoping it was a phase Ariel was going through. They're, well, snobs. And awfully formal. Not like my folks at all. I think they liked the lawyer better, just because he was a lawyer."

"What did you think of Ryan Trent?"

I saw Maggie grimace and figured her opinion of the attorney was similar to mine. She opened the door and we stepped into an ice cream parlor called the SLO Maid. I studied the dizzying range of possibilities and settled on a variation of my old standby, chocolate, in this case chocolate and peanut butter chips. Maggie, on the other hand, was one of those who preferred fruit with her butterfat. She opted for peach. Waffle cones and napkins in hand, we left the SLO Maid and walked back outside, strolling toward the bookstore.

"Ryan Trent is a horse's ass." Maggie delicately licked a pale gold trickle of ice cream running down the side of her cone.

"You didn't like him."

"No, and it didn't take Ariel long to see through him, either. She had pretty good judgment when it came to people. She could see the good qualities in Bobby when her folks kept saying he's a fisherman who drinks too much. And she saw Ryan's bad side, in spite of the money and the fancy suits and the expensive car. Ryan Trent is pompous and possessive, a real 'I'm God's gift to women' type."

"Sometimes that type doesn't like to let go." We were halfway to the bookstore. I broke a piece off my waffle cone and popped it into my mouth.

"Well, yes, he kept calling her, even after she stopped dating him. That was after she met Bobby. Ryan knows her parents. He can be really ingratiating. I guess that's why they liked him so much." Maggie was quiet for a moment, working on her peach ice cream. "Ariel was beautiful. She always got lots of attention from men. When I was up in Carmel last June, Ryan kept calling and she kept shutting him down. Politely, of course. But she did say something about going to visit Ryan at his office, late in the summer. I thought that was odd."

So did I. Maggie shook her head when I asked if she knew why Ariel had gone to see Ryan Trent. We stood outside the bookstore and finished our ice cream cones. It was still a few minutes before three and I was reluctant to see Maggie go through the open door of the shop. I needed much more time with this particular source.

"Tell me about Ariel's parents," I said.

"Well, like I said, I thought they were formal, distant. Ariel was an only child and they were older when they had her. I think they had a lot of expectations for Ariel. But they loved her." Maggie's eyes grew wet again as she recalled yesterday's services at Carmel Mission.

"Poor Mrs. Logan, she's just overcome by grief. I didn't think she was going to make it through the funeral. Mr. Logan's really broken up about it. It's good Mrs. Braemer was there to take charge." Maggie looked through the window of the bookstore. "It's three. I have to go now."

I reached out and touched her sleeve. "Maggie, there's so much I don't know about Ariel, things that you can tell me."

"Why? How will that help Bobby?"

"I'm trying to trace Ariel's movements before she died. Why did she go up to Carmel that Friday? She must have cut class to do it. Did she tell you why?"

Maggie shook her head. "No, she didn't. And I didn't ask. I thought it was something about Bobby, their relationship. I didn't want to pry."

"Maybe it was something else, something that was important to Ariel, that led to that argument with Bobby. A project of some sort. I'd like to look at a diary, a desk calendar, anything that would help me find out where she went and who she saw that last week before she died."

Maggie sighed and edged closer to the doorway of the bookstore. "You're welcome to come by the apartment after I get off work this evening. I should be there by nine-thirty." She gave me the address. I didn't tell her I'd already been there earlier, looking for her.

"But I don't know if I can help you. Ariel's aunt stopped here Friday, on her way up to Carmel. She and I packed up all of Ariel's things and she took them with her. I doubt we missed anything."

CHAPTER 22

WHEN I RETURNED TO MORRO BAY ANGIE WAS HOME. We went for a hike at Montaña de Oro, the unspoiled coastal plain where the ocean surges against the rugged rocky coast. Not as unspoiled as all that. On our way back to the car we picked up litter caught in the foliage along the path. Diablo Canyon nuclear power plant lies just over the ridge to the east, near an earthquake fault. From the road we could see the long finger of the sand spit stretching north toward Morro Rock and the towers of the PG&E plant.

Back in Morro Bay we stopped at a market near the municipal pier on the Embarcadero and bought fresh fish. We took it home, where Stan grilled it outside. It was hard to tear myself away from this pleasant dinner and drive back to SLO.

The first thing that caught my eye when Maggie Lim let me into the apartment she had shared with Ariel Logan was a large framed poster of Van Gogh's mulberry tree, from the Norton Simon Museum in Pasadena. The poster's colors were not as vibrant as the original but nevertheless the blues, purples, and yellows, highlighted by a nearby floor lamp, added a much-needed splash of color to this apartment, with its beige carpet and beige walls.

"Some of the furniture is hers. Was hers." Maggie amended her statement as she switched on a lamp on a table next to the brown sofa in the living room. She walked to the window that looked down on the courtyard and closed the half-open blinds. Then she turned and ran her hand over an oak rocking chair with a flowered cushion.

"This rocker. The bookcase over in the corner. And all the furniture in Ariel's bedroom."

As Maggie spoke I nodded and moved slowly around the room, getting my bearings. As we'd entered the front door the living room was to my left, furnished with the sofa that looked like a castoff from someone else's den, bracketed by a couple of spindly and mismatched end tables. In addition to the rocking chair and bookcase Maggie had pointed out, there was a small television on a mobile stand, with a VCR on a shelf below. On top of the bookcase I saw a portable compact disc player and several CDs.

"Is the family going to collect the furniture?"

"That's what Mrs. Braemer, Ariel's aunt, said. Then, after the funeral Mr. Logan told me to keep the furniture. But I don't know if I can. It reminds me too much of Ariel. The only thing I want is the poster." With a raised hand, Maggie indicated the Van Gogh reproduction. "It was Ariel's favorite. I asked Mrs. Braemer if I could keep it and she said yes."

"So when you and Mrs. Braemer packed up Ariel's belongings," I said, "you mean personal items that would fit into her car."

"Yes." Maggie nodded. "Clothes, jewelry, photographs, her computer. Ariel had several plastic file boxes with schoolwork and personal papers. If I find anything else I'm supposed to ship it to them."

Maggie now moved through a dining area, where a round café table and four chairs stood, into the small kitchen that was separated from the living room by a counter. "Some of the dishes are Ariel's," she said distractedly, "and the blender. I keep seeing things that are hers. Like that cookie jar."

She pointed at a ceramic cookie jar in the shape of a fat red apple. A telephone rested atop a phone directory, next to a small white answering machine with its red light blinking. A large rectangular woven basket with a center divider held an assortment of mail.

I glanced at the contents of the basket. The envelopes on the left side had been opened and I saw bills, a magazine, and a couple of letters addressed to Maggie. The stack of mail on the right was larger, addressed to Ariel. I touched it with a finger, glancing at the envelopes. Most of them were envelopes with windows, either bills or pitches for money from the usual sources, including several environmental organizations. There were a couple of letters, both from women, one postmarked Boston, the other San Diego. Underneath all of this I saw a magazine, the monthly publication of one of the environmental organizations.

"I'm still getting her mail," Maggie said, looking at the basket. Then she stared at the blinking red light on the answering machine. "And phone calls. That's the worst. I have to tell people she's dead." She sighed and moved her eyes up to meet mine. "You want a cup of coffee?"

"Sure. Mind if I explore?"

"Go ahead." She put water on to boil and took coffee and filters from a cupboard. I walked farther into the apartment. The central hallway led to a bathroom and a closet, with bedrooms on either side. The front bedroom was Maggie's, I guessed, surveying the double bed with its green comforter pulled untidily over the sheets and pillow, the jewelry strewn on the dresser, the clothes hanging in the open closet. At the far end of the room I saw a white laminated student desk and a matching bookcase, its shelves crammed with books. The desk held a laptop computer and an inexpensive printer.

Ariel's bedroom, at the back of the apartment, looked as though it had been swept clean of any personal trace of its occupant. I looked it over carefully, just in case anything had been missed. The smooth pine desk was bare and mute, its drawers yielding only paper clips, pens, and pencils. The dresser was empty and so was the closet. The double mattress and box spring stood on a steel frame, covered by a blue flowered spread, and there was nothing on the bedside table except dust and a telephone extension.

When I returned to the living room Maggie had pressed the playback button on the answering machine. I heard a female voice inquiring about the apartment to share.

"I put an ad in the paper, advertising for a roommate," Maggie said, jotting down the caller's name and phone number. She had poured boiling water through coffee grounds and now it dripped from the filter into the pot. "I can't afford this place on my own.

I've had a couple of calls and someone's coming over to see it tomorrow afternoon. But it won't be the same without Ariel. God, I'm going to miss her."

"When did you realize she was missing?"

Maggie poured coffee into two mugs and asked if I took anything in mine. I shook my head and she handed a mug across the counter. She splashed some milk in hers. We settled on the sofa before she spoke.

"When Ariel left a week ago Friday, I was rushing around because I was late for my eight o'clock class. But I noticed her overnight bag there by the front door. She said she had to go up to Monterey, and she'd be back early Sunday afternoon."

"But she didn't say why? How did she act? Did you notice anything different?"

Maggie shook her head. "I assumed she was going to see Bobby. But she was frowning, like something was bothering her. I wondered if she and Bobby were having problems. Things had been going so well between them all summer. She had classes on Friday, plus her intern job at the water board. I was surprised that she was cutting. She didn't usually do that, so whatever it was had to be important. I didn't give it another thought until Sunday. When Ariel said she'd be back early Sunday afternoon, I thought she meant two or three o'clock. I figured she'd been delayed. So I called the Logans' house in Carmel. Mr. Logan answered the phone. They'd just got back from France that evening."

"What did he say when you told him about Ariel?"

"He sounded surprised that she'd gone up there for the weekend, but not worried, like it wasn't a big deal to him. I mean, who would think anything was wrong? Ariel had a key to her parents' house. She went up there all the time, to see them and to see Bobby."

"He didn't say that he'd seen Ariel?"

"No. Like I said, he sounded surprised. Then he said not to worry, she was probably on her way back to SLO. Just got a late start, or stopped somewhere for coffee or something to eat. But when she didn't show up here on Sunday night . . ." Maggie's voice trailed off and she sipped coffee before speaking again.

"When I woke up Monday morning, I went into Ariel's room,

hoping she'd come in sometime during the night. But she wasn't there. So I called the Logans. I even called Bobby, thinking maybe Ariel had stayed with him. I know he was probably out fishing when I called. I left a message on his answering machine." Maggie gnawed her lower lip and looked as though she were going to cry. "By the time anyone missed her, Ariel was already dead."

That Monday call to the Logans set the official wheels in motion. Ariel was reported missing on Monday morning. The APB on her car had gone out that afternoon and the vehicle had been found at the Rocky Point Restaurant Wednesday. Ariel's body was spotted on the rugged shore below Rocky Creek Bridge Thursday. How did she get from here to there?

"Did Ariel ever mention a friend of Bobby's, a man named Karl Beckman?"

"Oh, yes," Maggie said, brushing back a long strand of black hair. "In fact, I met him this summer when I was visiting Carmel. We went over to his house for a cookout. We met his daughter, who was home from school at Stanford, and his sister-in-law."

The ubiquitous Lacy, I thought, who is everywhere and seems to blend into the background. But not quite.

"Mr. Beckman took us on a tour of his boatyard. I didn't think it was particularly interesting, all those boats with their hulls being scraped and repainted, but Ariel did. I guess that's why she asked him to show us around."

"Why would Ariel want to see the boatyard?"

Maggie thought about this for a moment, sipping coffee, a frown on her face. "I'm not sure, but the night we had dinner with the Beckmans, she asked Mr. Beckman a lot of questions about what goes on in a boatyard and told him she'd love to tour the place. The next day, when he took us to the boatyard, she seemed fascinated, poking around and asking more questions."

"When was this?" I sat back against the sofa cushion. "Was there something specific that seemed to interest her?"

"August, I think," Maggie said. "Ariel was always interested in environmental stuff. Like, whether they recycled their paint containers and oil. And the types of chemicals used in the paints and glues. And how they got rid of the stuff when they were finished. Ariel asked Mr. Beckman about disposal of hazardous wastes. You know, that boatyard's right there on Cannery Row and the bay's a marine sanctuary now."

"Disposal of hazardous wastes," I repeated, thinking about August. When in August? "Everyone tells me Ariel loved the ocean."

"That's not surprising," Maggie said, "since she grew up in that house right there on Carmel Bay. To her, everything about the ocean was beautiful and fascinating."

And dangerous, I thought.

Maggie continued. "Ariel liked to walk along the beach with her sketch pad and pick up shells and pebbles. She had a big basket of them in her room. I should have kept some of them."

I thought of the sea lions in distress off Point Pinos and the report Ariel had filed with the Monterey SPCA. That was the middle of August. But when I questioned Maggie I discovered Ariel hadn't mentioned the sea lions to her roommate.

"So Ariel was very concerned about things like pollutants from boatyards," I said.

Maggie nodded vigorously. "Oil spills, she would get so upset about oil spills. When the Exxon Valdez disaster happened up in Alaska, she saw the TV reports about all the seabirds and otters covered with oil, and she'd cry and get angry. All it takes, she'd say, is just a little bit of stupidity and things are ruined for years to come. She hated offshore drilling. She used to go picket the refinery down in south county. She got arrested a couple of times during demonstrations, there and at Diablo Canyon."

"Maggie, you mentioned that Ariel went to see Ryan Trent this summer. Was that in August? Before or after her visit to the boatyard?"

"Yes, it was August," Maggie said. "It must have been after we went to the yard. Closer to Labor Day."

I mulled this over as I set the coffee mug on the table to my right and gestured toward the basket of mail on the counter separating living room from kitchen. "Ariel got a lot of mail from environmental organizations. Which groups did she belong to? Was she active in them?"

"Save Our Shores, Greenpeace, the Sierra Club," Maggie told me. "Friends of the Earth, Friends of the Sea Otter. She sent money to all of them. As for actually being a volunteer, there's one organization right here called Central Coastwatch. They have an office on Chorro Street. We walked right past it this afternoon."

"Did Ariel keep notes or files on things that were important to her?"

"Yes. I forgot to tell you that, but I just now thought of it. She'd keep the flyers and handouts from those groups and she was always clipping things out of the paper or magazines."

"Like an article about chemicals in boatyards," I commented. And all those files and notes were among the personal items that Ariel's aunt had packed in her car when she stopped here on the way to her niece's funeral. Could I persuade the Logan family to let me look through those files?

Maggie yawned, despite the coffee she'd been drinking, and I looked at the clock. It was nearly ten-thirty. "Just one other thing," I said. "Could I have a photo of Ariel? Surely you must have one. I'll send it back to you when this is over."

Maggie nodded and went back to her bedroom, returning with a snapshot of Ariel Logan. She looked so vital and alive, her blond hair blowing as she stood bracketed by her parents, her arms around both their waists. I thought again of Ariel's argument with Bobby, when she'd talked of reporting something.

What did you discover? I asked the photograph silently. What was so important that it made someone want to kill you?

CHAPTER 23

"I NEED TO LOOK AT ARIEL'S THINGS," I TOLD ERROL over the phone Wednesday morning after Angie and Stan left for work. "Glennis Braemer stopped in SLO on her way to the funeral. She and Maggie Lim packed up most of Ariel's possessions and Mrs. Braemer brought them with her to Carmel."

"So you want me to see if Peter and Sylvie Logan will let Bobby Ravella's cousin root around in their daughter's belongings." Errol laughed wryly. "I can tell you what their answer will be."

"You're probably right. But try."

"When will you be back?"

"Tomorrow. There are still some people I need to interview. Anything going on up there?"

"Nothing related to Bobby. Café Marie reopened last night. Minna and I had dinner there. The place was half-empty."

Parking was in short supply on the Cal Poly campus, so I left my car on a nearby side street and walked in. By now, professors and students were into the third week of fall-quarter classes and the campus was alive with people moving from classroom to library to gym, with arms of books or bags of athletic equipment. Students clustered on the patio at the University Union, and they all seemed to have that bustling, vigorous look of autumn renewal, ready to get back to work after the summer break.

I approached some of the students at the union, asking directions to the Engineering Building where Ariel Logan had spent much of her time. Once there, I found the office of the civil and environmental engineering department and spoke first with the department chair, then with several of Ariel's professors. I heard the same thing over and over—shock and disquiet over the murder of a promising student. What was the world coming to when a fine young woman like Ariel Logan could be bashed over the head with a blunt instrument, her body dumped into the ocean like so much garbage.

But it wouldn't take long for them to forget her. Nowhere did I get the sense that any of these people knew Ariel particularly well, despite the fact that she'd earned her undergraduate degree here. Ariel was just one more face in a classroom. They couldn't tell me much about the person behind the phrases *fine young woman* and *promising student.*

The professor who taught Advanced Wastewater Treatment was also Ariel's graduate adviser. He told me, as Maggie had, that Ariel spent several terms working as a student assistant at the regional office of the state water quality board in San Luis Obispo. This was a common practice, he said, giving both undergrads and graduate students the opportunity to get some hands-on training.

The water board was on South Higuera. When I got there shortly before noon, the receptionist located the engineer Ariel had worked with, a man named Belknap. He was burly and barrel-chested, dressed in a roomy pair of gray slacks and a blue shirt. I took him up on his offer of a cup of coffee.

"When Ariel didn't show up a week ago Friday, I called the engineering department," Belknap said. We had settled into chairs facing one another across his desk in a second-floor cubicle.

"What did the department tell you?"

"Not much. One of her professors called the following week and told me she was missing. Then later one of the other interns said she'd turned up dead." He shook his head. "What a shame. She was really a good student; sharp, you know. I told her she could probably get a position with the water board once she got her master's."

"Just what does the water board do?"

"Wastewater discharge," Belknap said succinctly. "We issue permits. The state's divided into nine regions and we're Region Three, Central Coast."

"And you cover Monterey Bay," I guessed.

Belknap nodded and reached toward the bookcase near his desk. He pulled out a handful of publications and showed me a map of the territory covered by this office. When people enjoy their work they like to talk about it. Belknap was no exception. I tried to make sense of his explanation of the difference between wastewater permits and the technical descriptions he used so easily, things like tertiary water treatment, suspended solids, and how to deal with pathogenic organisms and viruses. He described any usage of water as *waste*. That brought me up short with its logic.

One of the publications he'd hauled out of the bookcase was called the California Ocean Plan. It detailed what could and couldn't be discharged into the ocean. I leafed through the pages and stopped at a table about toxic materials limitations and objectives for protecting marine aquatic life and human health. My finger went down the list. Arsenic, lead, cyanide, benzene, carbon tetrachloride, and polychlorinated biphenyl, otherwise known as PCBs.

"You can discharge this stuff into the ocean?" I frowned, picturing the waves Angie and I had seen during our walk yesterday afternoon at Montaña de Oro.

"It's all monitored, of course." Belknap launched into an explanation of effluent limitations and units of measurement. I didn't understand most of what he was saying, and I wasn't sure I wanted to. Ariel would have. She was a graduate student in environmental engineering. This would have been quite clear to her.

"What about Monterey?" I asked. Surely, with the sanctuary now a reality, nothing was allowed to be discharged there.

Belknap disabused me of that notion. "There's a zone of prohibition that stretches from the mouth of the Salinas River to Point Pinos, at the tip of the peninsula. Monterey's outfall goes past the zone." I must have shown my confusion, so he explained that the Monterey Regional Treatment Plant processed about three million gallons of wastewater daily. Then I marveled at my own ignorance. The Monterey area had nearly a quarter of a million people. Did I think everything that went down a drain or a sewer pipe vanished magically?

"Right now we're concerned about heavy metals, like lead,"

Belknap was saying. "There's a hot spot right there in Monterey Harbor."

"Lead in the harbor? Where did it come from?"

"Slag. Years ago, when they built the railway from the main line to Cannery Row. They dumped the slag right there near the Coast Guard jetty."

I pictured the little cove between the jetty and Fisherman's Wharf, where the small boats were tied up, where Donna and I had seen the sea otters floating on their backs, drawing the eyes of tourists who walked along the recreation trail or the customers at the wharf restaurants like Ravella's. I hadn't known there was lead lurking under the surface of the blue water. The bay I thought was so pristine was more fragile than I'd imagined.

"Heavy metals are bad news," Belknap said. "They're bioaccumulative. They don't leave the organism's system. So we have the state mussel watch program. It's funded by the board and Fish and Game does the monitoring, up at Moss Landing. They set out some mussels, leave them in the water for three months, and then pull them out to check the muscle tissue for toxics."

"What would I expect to find in Monterey Bay?" I asked him, feeling more and more alarmed.

"Ariel asked me the same question. Thought it was odd at the time."

That caught my interest. "When? And why do you say it was odd?"

"First day of classes, three weeks ago. Her first day back here at the board. And it was odd because after working here last year, she knew what turns up in Monterey Bay. There's agricultural runoff because of all the farming, so there's always pesticide residue. With all the fishing boats and pleasure craft, there's bound to be fuel spills. When it rains, there's storm-drain runoff. Anything that gets spilled or dumped on a city street winds up in the bay. Maybe some bozo has a bunch of old batteries. He takes them out on a boat one night and deep-sixes them in Davy Jones's locker. It's not his problem anymore, but all that stuff from the batteries shows up in the food chain."

Was there any human activity that didn't generate pollution? I doubted it. Like slugs, wherever we go we leave slime, whether it's litter on the trail to Montaña de Oro or the sheen of oil floating on the surface of the ocean.

Why was Ariel asking these particular questions? Belknap didn't have any answers. If there was a particular pollutant or incident that worried Ariel, she hadn't shared that information.

After leaving the water board I had a sandwich at a nearby deli, then I headed downtown to Chorro Street, looking for the office of Central Coastwatch, one of the environmental groups that sent mail to Ariel Logan.

It was a narrow storefront a few doors down from the mission, with a window full of pamphlets and posters. Oil was the subject of the display—offshore oil drilling, tanker transport, and the need for conservation. I looked at a poster of a seabird coated with black sludge, then opened the door. The office was divided by partitions, the front half empty. Several chairs were grouped around a coffee table and a sofa. Farther back I saw a desk and a phone next to a large Rolodex.

"Hello?" I called.

A voice answered from the back. "Be right there." Then the phone rang. A tall woman came around the end of the partitions. "Be with you in a minute," she said briskly, reaching for the receiver. "Central Coastwatch."

I watched her as she talked with whoever was on the other end of the line, about something that seemed to amuse them both. She perched on one corner of the desk, a woman in her forties, I guessed, brown hair streaked with gray, tied back in a short ponytail that fell over the collar of her cotton shirt. She wore sandals and a baggy pair of blue painter's pants. Beads dangled from her earlobes, swinging each time she moved.

When she replaced the receiver in the cradle she smiled at me, laugh lines crinkling the skin around her brown eyes. "Hi. What can I do for you?"

"My name's Jeri Howard. I'm a private investigator from Oakland." While she'd been on the phone I had pulled one of my business cards from the case in my purse. Now I handed it to her. She held it between her thumb and forefinger as though it contained some toxic residue. I saw suspicion percolate into her brown eyes. "I'd like to talk about one of your volunteers, Ariel Logan."

Suspicion gave way to hostility and the woman glared at me. "I have nothing to say to you. Get out."

I'd made the wrong approach, I thought. Why was she so guarded? Had someone sicced an investigator on the organization at one time?

"Ariel Logan is dead. She was murdered, more than a week ago, up near Carmel. I'm trying to find out why."

Now she stared at me with consternation. "You're serious, aren't you?"

"I'm afraid so. If you don't believe me, you can call her roommate, Maggie Lim. She was at the funeral on Monday."

She strode past me to the coffee table, her hands sorting through a stack of newspapers bearing the masthead *San Luis Obispo Telegram-Tribune.* "I saw a headline, a couple of days ago, that said a Cal Poly student had been murdered. But with everything that's been going on, I didn't read the story."

She found the newspaper she sought and sat down on the sofa. As she read the story she shook her head in disbelief. Then she handed me the newspaper, Sunday's edition, with a small headline below the fold, near the bottom, and a few inches of type giving a bare minimum of facts.

"I wondered why I hadn't seen her. Particularly with the news about the oil company."

I sat down beside her, still holding the newspaper. "What news is that?"

She pointed at the banner headline that topped the newspaper. DA TO SEEK INDICTMENTS, it read. I quickly scanned the article. The oil company whose tanker I'd seen plying the waves between Cayucos and Morro Bay had been the subject of a lengthy investigation involving the San Luis Obispo County District Attorney's Office, Fish and Game, and the water quality board, as well as a number of federal, state, and local environmental agencies. The results made disturbing reading.

A huge amount of petroleum had leaked into groundwater and the ocean near the company's storage facility south of SLO. Evidently the leakage had been occurring for several years and nothing had been done to stop it. In fact, the company and several of its employees were accused of knowing about the leak and covering it up rather than notifying authorities. The DA's office had already filed misdemeanor charges and now things were about to move into the felony column.

"They deny it, of course," the woman said. I knew she meant the oil company. As she spoke her eyes sparked with the righteous anger of the truly committed.

"They always deny it. Or they point out that they've got a permit, issued by the water board. So they just keep spewing crap into the ocean. Arsenic, cyanide, mercury, lead, toxaphene, and PCBs, all of it legal, for Christ's sake. If people knew what gets dumped into the ocean just off those picturesque sandy beaches, they wouldn't stick a toe into the water."

Maybe she was right but I doubted it. We human beings have an enormous ability to ignore that which we do not wish to see or hear. I'm as guilty of it as the next person.

The woman continued to rail at the oil company. "And if they don't have a permit, they dump the stuff anyway. When they get caught, they get a slap on the wrist and a fine." She sneered. "Fines are peanuts to a large corporation. Maybe this time some of those executives and middle managers will get their corporate asses thrown in jail. That might get their attention." She stopped and shook her head in frustration. "I'm sorry, I get so angry. It's been going on for years. When I think about the seals, I get mad all over again."

"What about the seals? Ms.—?" I set the newspaper on top of the stack.

"Just call me Maya. You want to talk with a friend of mine, up in Paso Robles, about the seals." She leaned back against the sofa and waved away any more questions about marine mammals. "But please, tell me about Ariel. What happened? What's your connection with all of this? Did her family hire you?"

I shook my head. "They think my cousin had something to do with Ariel's death."

"She was involved with a fisherman, a guy named Bobby. Is that your cousin? Why is he supposed to have killed her?"

"They had an argument the day she died. Bobby won't tell me what it was about. The official theory is that Ariel wanted to break it off between them, and Bobby didn't, so he killed her. But that's not Bobby."

Maya crossed one leg over the other and cupped her hands together on her knee. "She did have her doubts about the relationship. They argued about a lot of things."

"How do you know this?"

She shrugged. "I'm not saying Ariel and I were best friends and confidantes. But she'd come in looking blue, so I'd ask her what was the matter, and she'd tell me. Earlier in the year, in the spring, she told me it was all over, because of his drinking. Then, during the summer, it was back on. She said he was going to AA."

"That much I know. What else did they argue about?"

"She had doubts about what he did for a living. Hell, she had doubts about her own career choice."

"She didn't like the fact that he was a fisherman?"

"It wasn't a class thing," Maya said. "Ariel wasn't like that. But she felt his way of life is disappearing and he'd better find something else to do. A lot of us think fishermen are like loggers. Overfishing is stripping the sea of life, just like the timber companies are stripping the forests."

"Some would say that's an extreme point of view." I thought about the Ravellas, three generations of fishermen, and knew what their reaction to this would be. On the other hand, the sardines disappeared from Monterey Bay back in the fifties. There were no more sardine canneries down on Cannery Row.

"Is it? The drought just about killed the salmon fishery. Too many demands on the existing supply of water. With the competition between agriculture and the cities, fish come out a distant third." Maya shook her head. "You should see what drift nets are doing. They're miles long, trapping everything in their path. A while back some Japanese vessels came through Morro Bay. They were hauling abalone out of the ocean by the dozens. Now the abalone fishermen are bitching because their catches are down. They blame the otters. What bullshit! Otters never take more than they need to survive. I can't say that about humans."

Environmentalists sometimes sound as though they're preaching. But they had much to preach about, particularly when I recalled the poster in the window and the newspaper headlines in front of me.

I steered her back to something she'd mentioned earlier. "You say Ariel had doubts about her career choice. I would have thought environmental engineering was a good field for her."

"Have you seen their ocean plan?" Maya's mouth twisted into a sardonic frown as she referred to the booklet Belknap had shown me. "Have you seen what they're allowed to dump? Heavy metals, carcinogens, toxins of all sorts. All perfectly legal. Oh, yes, it's monitored—by the wastewater discharger."

She flicked a disparaging finger at the headline about the oil-company indictments. "A bit like asking the fox to monitor the henhouse, if you ask me. That's what environmental engineers do, mitigate pollution. Damage control. And in my opinion they don't do a very good job of it. Ever since she started working at the water board, Ariel had doubts about whether she wanted to be a part of wastewater treatment and solid waste disposal."

"The people aren't going away," I said.

Maya shook her head. "No. The marine life will vanish first. Then there won't be any more fish for your cousin Bobby to catch."

I recalled something Bobby said, last week before Ariel's body was found, about how the squid weren't plentiful in the bay this year. The *Nicky II* had to go farther out to sea to make its catch. Were the squid going the way of the sardines?

"When was the last time you saw Ariel?"

She thought for a moment. "Three weeks ago, Wednesday, the week before classes started. We had a meeting here, then she and I went around the corner for coffee."

"A week ago Friday she cut classes. Her roommate says she left around eight that morning, to go up to Carmel. It's about three hours, if she took 101. But Ariel didn't show up at her parents' house in Carmel until that afternoon. She must have gone somewhere first. I have a hunch it may have something to do with what Ariel did during the summer. Did she say anything about how she'd spent her time?"

"Well, first she told me that her relationship with Bobby was back on," Maya said, "because he'd stopped drinking. Things were good between them. They were engaged but they were going to wait until she'd finished her master's. She hadn't told her folks yet and was wondering when to spring it on them."

Maya was quiet for a moment. "She was concerned about her grandmother. She had cancer. Ariel spent a year in France living with her grandmother, between high school and college. I guess she and the old woman are close. Ariel's parents went to Paris and Ariel would have gone with them if she hadn't been due back at school."

"Did she hint at anything else that was on her mind besides Bobby and her grandmother?"

"We talked about the oil-company investigation. It's been going on for a couple years and it looked like the DA was finally going to indict. Ariel would have been so pleased about the charges. Felonies as well as misdemeanors." Maya sighed, then she brightened, as though something had just occurred to her. "She asked questions about the seals. I sent her to my friend in Paso Robles."

"What happened to the seals?" I asked. This was the second time Maya had mentioned it. Could this have some connection with the report Ariel had filed with the Monterey SPCA?

"It was awful. Susan can give you the details." Maya leaped up from the sofa and crossed the office to the desk, flipping through the Rolodex. She quickly wrote a name and address on a telephone message pad and tore off the sheet. "I'll call and tell her to expect you."

CHAPTER 24

THE CENTRAL COAST LOCALS CALL IT PASO, SHORTHAND
for the town's name, which is Spanish for Pass of the Oaks.
The oak trees were indeed in great supply, covering the rolling
hills that surrounded Paso Robles, their dark green leaves contrasting with the brown grass under a blue October sun and shading
the sidewalks of the town's residential areas.

It was blistering hot in the midafternoon sun. One huge tree
shaded part of the asphalt lot in front of the veterinary clinic. I left
my car under the tree and walked into a reception area with a
linoleum floor and chairs against the walls. The air held the mixed
scents of wet dog and disinfectant. Next to the counter I saw an elderly woman with an equally geriatric Pomeranian sitting patiently
on her lap. Opposite her, a woman my own age sat with a little
girl about four, who kept squirming on her chair. On the floor in
front of them was a wooden carrier with a handle, containing a
calico cat who declaimed, in no uncertain yowl, her utter dismay
at being here.

I gave my name to the receptionist and asked for Susan Dailey.
"Oh, yes," she said, smiling distractedly as the phone rang. "Maya
called. Susan's expecting you."

She answered the phone, cutting off the insistent peal, listened
briefly, and made an appointment for Yazoo, without indicating
whether Yazoo was canine, feline, or something else entirely. I
picked up one of the clinic's cards and examined it. It listed not
only the animal hospital but the Daileys' wildlife rehab center,

which must be in a different location, judging from the photographs on the wall behind the receptionist. They showed a building in a wooded setting, and a variety of wild animals, including a raccoon, a badger, and a black bear cub.

I heard another dog barking somewhere at the back of the clinic. Then the door to one of the examining rooms across the hallway opened and a man came out holding a leash. At the end was a yellow lab puppy with enormous paws. He'd be huge when he grew into them. The pup made a beeline for the cat carrier. The calico hissed and spat in protest. The man stopped at the counter, pulling out his wallet. He tugged on the leash and the puppy galumphed over to snuffle my knees.

"Susan will see you now." The receptionist pointed down the hallway. The examination-room doors were closed, but one door was open, leading to an office. A desk with a computer stood against one wall and the rest were full of shelves lined with books. An open back door evidently led out to some dog runs, because the barking and the wet dog smell were prevalent here.

Susan Dailey was a small woman in her late forties, her short hair completely silver. She wore sensible shoes, khaki pants, a white lab coat over a checked shirt. Her eyes in her sharp-featured face were the same light gray as her hair. At the moment they held a somewhat skeptical expression.

"I only agreed to see you because Maya called," Susan Dailey said as she glanced at my business card, exhibiting the same suspicion her friend had. "I didn't know this Ariel Logan."

"But you did talk with her. Three weeks ago, before classes started at Cal Poly."

She nodded and waved me to a chair as she sat at the desk. "Yes, mid-September. She had some questions about the seals at Avila."

"What happened to the seals? Maya didn't give me any details."

Susan Dailey shrugged. "The oil company happened to the seals. Of course, I can't prove anything. I've been warned I shouldn't make accusations. But I just don't care."

She didn't elaborate about who'd been warning her off. But she cared very much about the seals, I thought, seeing fire in the gray eyes. There was much anger there and I was about to hear why.

"It happened about six years ago, down by Avila and Pismo," she said, referring to the two south-county beach towns. "Though some of them were reported as far north as Morro Bay. We—I mean, the wildlife center—started getting calls about seals in trouble. I was doing marine mammal rescues then, so off I'd go in my truck, all by myself. I picked up over a hundred animals in a three-month period. All adult females, all with grand mal seizures, on shore or just a few feet into the water."

I struggled with the image of this small woman hauling a seal off the beach or out of the water and into the back of her truck. Susan Dailey sighed and ran a hand through her hair.

"Some recovered," she continued, "if I got them back to the center fast enough. We'd cool down the body temp, give them something to relieve the seizures, and flush their systems with fluids. But some died, in the back of my truck, before I could get them here."

"What caused the seizures?"

"That's the part I can't prove," she said. "Probably a refined petroleum product, absorbed directly into the system. At the time I talked with several local surfers and fishermen. They said some days the ocean smelled like oil or chemicals. The surfers wouldn't go into the water. And the fishermen told me that the fish were migrating out of their usual grounds."

"How long did this go on?"

"It was sporadic for about four years. We'd get large numbers of seals, then it would stop, and start up again. The first two years were the worst."

"Did anyone do anything about it?" If she couldn't prove anything I doubted it, and her next words bore me out.

"Not a damn thing. Some guy from one of the state agencies did tell me I could pay for a toxicology scan to find out what was causing the seizures. A scan's expensive, about a thousand bucks. You have to specify exactly what toxin you're looking for, or it's useless. This same guy told me I'd have to prove the stuff came from the refinery and not some passing barge." Her laugh was bitter. "Fat chance."

"Is this still going on?"

"I haven't heard any reports since we had that oil spill two years ago. But by that time I wasn't doing any marine rescue work anymore."

"Why not?" I already knew the answer. The fire left her gray eyes. It had burned out.

"I couldn't stand to look at any more dead seals," Susan Dailey said matter-of-factly. "At the time I made the decision, I figured if I didn't pick up the animals, the whole coastline would be littered with carcasses. Maybe then someone would get angry and do something about it."

She shook her head. "It didn't work that way. Other people are doing what I don't have the heart to do anymore. They don't understand it's just like cleaning up after a drunk. That allows the drunk to escape the consequences of his actions. The oil companies are just like alkies, Ms. Howard. They don't accept responsibility for what they dump into the water—or what gets killed because of it. And the good citizens of this county are afraid of scaring off the tourists."

After talking with Maya and Susan Dailey, I wanted to haul out a picket sign and send money to some of those organizations that had Ariel Logan on their mailing lists. But Ariel was the reason I was here.

"Why was Ariel interested in this specific incident? Particularly if you're not doing rescue work anymore?"

Susan Dailey opened a desk drawer and took out a sheet of paper. "I took some notes when I talked with her. Today I reread them, to refresh my memory. In August she saw two sea lions in distress. In the water off Point Pinos. She went to call for help, but by the time she returned, the sea lions had disappeared."

I nodded. "I know about that. She reported it to the Monterey SPCA."

"Marsha Landers is a friend of mine," Susan Dailey said. "I called her after I talked with Ariel. She told me it appeared to be an isolated incident. Of course, she's been occupied by those damned pelican mutilations. They started about the same time."

I frowned, recalling the horrific pictures Marsha had shown me when I'd visited the Monterey wildlife center. Could one be connected with the other?

"Ariel had heard about the seals at Avila," Susan Dailey continued, "from my friend Maya at Coastwatch, and she knew I'd been involved in rescuing them. She described what she'd seen and asked if I had any theories about what caused it. I really couldn't say, based on her description, not having seen the sea lions myself."

"Did Ariel have any theories?"

"She wondered if it might be paint or some other chemical. I told her they'd probably gotten into something toxic. She already knew that. If she had any other theories she didn't share them with me." Susan Dailey sighed. "I told her it was damn near impossible to pin down what it was or where it came from. Look at what happened to me. All those seals, and I couldn't prove what it was or where it came from."

Susan Dailey kept talking about proof, as though her inability to nail the oil company for the dead and dying seals was eating away at her. What if Ariel had a hunch, I thought, one she'd tried to prove?

"The bay's a sanctuary now," I said, thinking out loud. "Does that mean it's safe?"

"Not as far as I'm concerned. Monterey's unique and fragile. It wouldn't take much to ruin the whole thing. A little human error goes a long way. Look at what happened up at Dunsmuir," she said, referring to an incident a couple of years ago in Northern California, when a railroad car dumped a load of herbicide and killed every living organism in a forty-five-mile stretch of the upper Sacramento River.

"According to the water quality control board," I said, "there's a zone of prohibition from the Salinas River to Point Pinos. Nothing goes into the bay inside that zone."

Susan Dailey shook her head. "It doesn't cover the whole bay. And the sanctuary's bigger than that. A lot of territory to cover. Who knows what gets dumped off a passing boat, where it can wash into the bay. All I know is that the ocean ecosystem wasn't designed to be a sewer. That's what we've made it. And it's about to reach the breaking point."

CHAPTER 25

AFTER BREAKFAST THURSDAY I DROVE NORTH ON COAST Highway 1, past Cambria, nestled in the tree-covered hills above the coast. The next town after that is San Simeon, the name serving both the tiny coastal village and the bay it faces. It's also the site of a rich man's indulgence.

In the nineteenth century George Hearst acquired huge parcels of what was originally mission land. He and his son, newspaper mogul William Randolph Hearst, added to their ranch until it covered fifty miles of coastline. On the hills above San Simeon, Hearst and architect Julia Morgan built the Casa Encantada—the Enchanted Castle. It's a vast bizarre palace, a warehouse for Hearst's collections of art and antiques. After the old man died his family deeded Hearst Castle to the state. Now the huge house is operated as a state historical monument, where visitors on guided tours can stare at the tapestries and the massive furniture. The castle's popularity among tourists accounts for the strip of motels clustered at the San Simeon turnoff.

As I passed this intersection I glanced to my right, spotting the castle as it stood bathed in the early-morning sun. Then I looked ahead and concentrated on the road, an absolute necessity if one is going to drive this route.

Here in northern San Luis Obispo County, the coastline is gentle, almost at sea level, but soon the road gains elevation. Crossing into Monterey County, the road climbs and twists along the dramatic hairpin curve at Salmon Creek, entering an area known as

Big Sur. Now the highway becomes a two-lane odyssey of hairpin curves and spectacular vistas, snaking nearly a hundred miles along the ledges carved from the Santa Lucia Mountains. The land plunges steeply into the Pacific Ocean. This is the end of the continent, a fact brought home to the driver who glances to the west and sees not so much as a guardrail, nothing, in fact, but air and water and jumbled rockscape.

Along the cliffs of Big Sur the Pacific Ocean is anything but peaceful. Riptides and dangerous currents, white foam on blue water, the ocean crashes incessantly against the rocky perimeter of land, carving sheer cliffs, offshore formations called sea stacks, and the occasional inaccessible curve of sandy beach. To the east the Santa Lucias rise steeply and abruptly, their rugged and isolated back country inhabited by mountain lions, wild pigs, forest rangers on horseback, and hardy individuals who choose to hike the trails of the Ventana Wilderness and the Los Padres National Forest.

I was in no hurry. This is not a road for haste. I drove at a slow steady pace, occasionally using a turnoff to let some idiot speed demon pass, now and then getting stuck behind a tourist in a large camper, moving even slower than I was. Several times that morning I stopped at one of the vista points to sample the breathtaking view, thankful that this stretch of ocean was protected by the sanctuary. Past Nepenthe and Ventana the highway moved inland to the little town of Big Sur. I stopped for lunch, then continued north, past the lighthouse at Point Sur and up the steep ledge of Hurricane Point.

This was where Gunter and Janine Beckman died eighteen months ago, when Gunter's car plunged off the cliff to my left. From the top of Hurricane Point I saw the spectacular curve of Bixby Bridge, towering over the steep canyon below. I drove slowly across the span, marveling as I always did, at both the spectacular view and the engineering feat required to construct this bridge.

Around the next curve was a relatively straight stretch of highway, then another bridge, not quite as high or as long as the one I'd just crossed. This bridge spanned Rocky Creek. I didn't drive across it. Instead I pulled my Toyota off the highway, onto the dirt verge. I turned off the engine, sitting for a moment as several cars passed. Then I got out of the car and crossed the two-lane strip of asphalt.

Rocky Creek Bridge has stone walls, about waist-high, with narrow sidewalks on both sides. A short guardrail stands at each of the approaches to the span. I walked about ten feet onto the bridge and peered over the stone wall. Below me a steep cliff plunged some hundred and fifty feet down to a sliver of beach at the mouth of Rocky Creek, visible now that the tide was out. I saw the backside of a blue station wagon, its metal skin pierced by rocks, scoured by sand and salt water. The irretrievable remains of an accident, it served as a reminder that when driving the coast road it doesn't pay to let your attention wander.

Had Ariel Logan let something distract her as a murderer stood behind her and slashed down at her head with a wrench or a tire iron? I retraced my steps along the bridge and walked past the guardrail to stand on a hump of earth near the south approach. There was nothing here to stop a body's plunge, just a few puny bushes tossing in the breeze, clinging to the rocky soil.

Ariel's body had washed up somewhere on the beach below, after several days in the water. Perhaps it had been caught in the kelp or wedged in the granite and basalt rocks that had long ago broken off these cliffs and were now scattered offshore. I moved a few steps closer to the cliff's edge, looking at the mute and unforgiving landscape. The tide was coming in now, and water surged forward over the rocks and sand, tasting the crushed metal of the old car wreck, a flavor it had sampled many times before.

Ariel had left her car at Rocky Point Restaurant. How did she get to this bridge? Had she gone into the water here? Or was she brought to this shore by the current?

I scanned the beach and the slopes above it, spotting a trail just visible below the private house on a small headland that jutted into the ocean on the north side of Rocky Creek Bridge. There were trails threading the headlands between here and the restaurant, but this was all private property. That made it more likely that Ariel had met someone at Rocky Point, or been killed there, and the body disposed of here or somewhere between. I peered at the surging ocean, hoping that something would leap out at me.

Instead it was I who jumped, startled by a blaring horn as a red convertible sailed by a few feet from me in the southbound lane of Highway 1. The soles of my sneakers slipped on the gravel. I reached for something to hold on to and grasped the comforting and solid metal side of the guardrail. It wouldn't take much, I realized, my heart beating rapidly, to tumble over the side and join the corpse of that station wagon.

There's a sign posted near a narrow path just below the Rocky Point Restaurant. It reads: CAUTION. HAZARDOUS WAVES. ROCKY POINT IS OCCASIONALLY HIT BY RANDOM WAVES OF GREAT SIZE WHICH CAN CARRY AN ADULT OFF THIS SHORELINE. ENTER AT YOUR OWN RISK.

Don't turn your back on the ocean. I heard voices off to my left and looked up. This warning hadn't deterred the three people climbing a rocky outcropping that jutted toward the sea. Farther to the south I saw the bridge I'd just left, floating above Rocky Creek.

I turned and walked back toward the building. The restaurant and bar were one story, painted gray, the seaward side nearly all glass, to take full advantage of the view. On this end of the building, the bar opened onto an outdoor terrace with chairs. There were two parking lots. The larger, where I'd left my Toyota, was several feet lower than the upper lot, just outside the restaurant's main entrance. It was the late end of lunch and the dining room with its sweeping vista was half-empty.

"The police were already here. Several times, in fact." The manager was a blunt-featured man in his forties, his sandy hair receding. "I don't know what else I can tell you."

I looked at him and didn't say anything, so he decided to fill the silence. "I noticed the car on Tuesday. White Honda Civic, sitting in the far corner of the lower lot. Who knows how long it had been there? When it was still there on Wednesday I called to have it towed. Next thing I know, the sheriff's department is out here. They said it belonged to some woman who was missing. I hear they pulled her body out of the water the next day, down by Rocky Creek."

I removed the photograph from my purse, the snapshot Maggie Lim had given me, which showed a smiling Ariel Logan standing between her parents. "Please take a look at this and tell me if you've ever seen the woman in the middle. She may have come in here on Friday or Saturday."

The manager's eyes flicked over the snapshot. "I know that's her, because the deputy showed me a picture. I never saw her. But Gina says she may have seen her Friday evening."

"May I talk with her?"

"Certainly." The manager peered into the dining room. "She's busy with some customers right now. Have a seat in the bar. I'll send her over as soon as she's free."

I cut through the dining room and took a seat on the nearest stool. "What'll it be?" the bartender asked. I ordered club soda. A few minutes later a slender dark-haired woman approached the bar.

"I'm Gina. You wanted something?"

"Information."

I laid my business card and the snapshot on the bar. She didn't pay any attention to my card. Instead she picked up the snapshot.

"This again. I talked to some sergeant twice already. He was here again yesterday. What's your angle?"

"Just trying to find out what happened."

"I did see her," Gina said, returning the photograph to the bar. "At least I think it was her."

"When?" I asked.

Gina brushed back a strand of hair. "Friday evening. I was out on the terrace having a smoke. I saw her sitting on the hood of a little white car in the lower lot. I thought she was watching the sunset. Then another car drove into the lot. She got off the hood, like maybe she was meeting someone in the other car."

"Can you describe the second car?"

"Oh, yeah," Gina said. "Couldn't miss a car like that. My brother had one just like it. A classic T-bird, fifty-seven or fifty-eight. Black or dark blue, maybe."

I stared at her. Bobby's car? How many others were there like it on the peninsula?

"Did she get into the other car?" I asked when I found my voice.

"I didn't see." Gina shrugged. "I finished my cigarette and came back inside."

The bartender had been listening to this exchange with interest.

Now he reached out and picked up the snapshot. "This is the girl that was killed? Who are those people with her?"

"Her parents. Did you see her Friday night?"

He shook his head. "I've never seen her," he said slowly, "but I have seen him. Same night, as a matter of fact." He pointed at Peter Logan.

"Friday night? Are you sure?"

"It's the same guy. I'm positive. A week ago Friday, same day everybody's asking about." The bartender tapped the photograph with his index finger. "He came in just as the sun was going down. Sat in the bar by himself, drank a couple of scotches."

"Did he act as though he were meeting someone?"

The bartender nodded. "Yeah. He sat at that stool over there." He pointed at the bar stool nearest the door that led to the terrace. "And he kept looking at his watch. I didn't see what time he left."

I slipped off my seat and walked to the bar stool the bartender had indicated, looking out through the glass. From here I could see the lower parking lot. My mind whirled as I thought about a car and a man. Neither of them should have been here that night.

The T-bird should have been parked in Bobby's driveway while my cousin slept before taking the fishing boat out later that evening. As for Peter Logan, he and his wife returned from Paris on Sunday. That's what everyone told me, that's what everyone thought.

So why was Peter Logan in the bar of the Rocky Point Restaurant on Friday, the same night his daughter was murdered? He'd been sitting right here at sundown, just a few yards from the last place anyone saw Ariel Logan alive.

CHAPTER *26*

I DROVE THE REMAINING MILES NORTH AS QUICKLY AS I dared, given the winding road and the usual traffic bottleneck through Carmel. Finally I sped down the grade of Carmel Hill, with the curving blue sweep of Monterey Bay below. I headed directly for the harbor, where I left my Toyota in a parking slot on Wharf Two and dropped a few coins in the meter.

Activity was winding down at the end of the commercial wharf, where sea gulls circled the Monterey Fish Company building, hoping for an easy meal. Sea lions who had the same goal crowded the water below the wharf pilings, barking incessantly. Those fishing boats who had gone in pursuit of sardines or anchovies had long since unloaded their holds. I stopped a rugged-looking old man who reeked of fish, salt water, and cigarettes. "Where's the *Nicky II*?" I asked. "Has her crew left for the day?"

For a moment he stared at me wordlessly, a female interloper in a male world. Finally the old man found his tongue. "Already unloaded. Moored out there." He pointed in the direction of the Coast Guard jetty. "I think that's the boys coming in now."

The blue hull of the *Nicky II* rode high on the waves, midway between the jetty and the wharf. I watched the skiff head toward the marina, counting seven men aboard. The remaining crew members of the purse seiner came up the float first, followed by Bobby. He moved tiredly, head bowed and shoulders slumped. Then he looked up and saw me waiting on the wharf and mustered a grin.

"Come to sign on my crew, cuz? I'm still short a man."

I smiled and shook my head. "I'm no fisherman. Couldn't stand the hours. Much less the nausea."

He shut the gate behind him. "Mom says you went down to SLO. You just get back?"

I took his arm. "Bobby, where did you go after you and Ariel had that argument? Besides looking for Karl Beckman. I know about that. Linda told me."

He sighed. "Why do you have to know?"

"Because a waitress at the Rocky Point Restaurant says she saw Ariel in the parking lot Friday evening. She also saw a classic T-bird drive in, one that looked a lot like yours, one that Ariel may have recognized."

Bobby stopped and put his hands on his hips. "Oh, no. That's impossible."

"Details, Bobby. You've got to level with me."

"Okay, okay." We walked up the wharf. "First I went over to Linda's office, to tell her that I couldn't take Nicky that night. Then I went to the boatyard."

"What time?" I interrupted.

He shrugged. "Four-thirty, quarter to five. I couldn't find Karl there, so I went to his house. That was about five-thirty. I waited outside for a while but he never came home. I even looked for him over at Café Marie, thinking he might be there. That must have been about six. But he wasn't there. I grabbed a sandwich at Casa Bodega around six-thirty. By that time I was real frustrated. So I went to a meeting. There's one every Friday night at seven."

"An AA meeting? Then you're in the clear. Surely one of the people at the meeting . . ."

Bobby shook his head. "We take this anonymity stuff seriously. I don't want to involve any of them. I was there for a couple of hours. After the meeting I went back to the apartment, to bed."

"So you were in your car or it was parked nearby."

"Yeah. At the church where the meeting was, for about two hours. After that, in the driveway at home."

"Does anyone besides you have keys?" I asked.

Before Bobby could answer, someone loomed in front of us, blocking the afternoon sun. Under his bushy brows Sergeant

Magruder's eyes looked as bleak as they had last week when he showed up at Ravella's to tell Bobby that Ariel's body had been found.

"Robert Ravella." The sergeant's voice was low and level, as it had been the day of Ariel's funeral, when he'd told me to butt out of his murder investigation. There was also a certain official formality in the way he addressed Bobby. I knew what that formality meant.

"Robert Ravella," Magruder repeated. "I have a warrant for your arrest, for the murder of Ariel Logan."

NICK AND TINA RAVELLA LIVED IN A ONE-STORY WOOD-FRAME HOUSE on Roosevelt Street, high on the pine-covered hill near the Presidio of Monterey. The picture window in front looked down, between two houses across the street, at a sliver of the bay. When I got there at five that afternoon, the driveway and curb were crowded with cars. I knocked but no one answered, so I opened the front door and walked into the fray.

A family summit was in full swing, the living room crowded with relatives, all of them talking at once. Worry etched lines deep in Tina's face as she sat on the sectional sofa. Aunt Teresa's wrinkled countenance frowned above her usual sober black dress as she sat next to her daughter-in-law, arm around Tina's shoulders. On the other side was Sally, Tina's oldest daughter. In the kitchen I saw Elena, the younger daughter, who had driven down from Santa Cruz. Elena was making coffee and talking over her shoulder with two women whose identities didn't immediately register. One wore a business suit, the other blue jeans.

Nick Ravella stood in one corner of the spacious living room, holding the phone in his right hand, his left hand cupped over his ear. Judging from the noise level that assaulted my ears, he must have been having trouble hearing what was being said on the other end of the line. Finally he took the phone, stretching its long cord, and disappeared into the hallway.

Uncle Dominic moved into view, a scowl on his weathered brown face, gesturing and talking full blast in Italian to Sal, Nick's older brother. Sal had his own fishing boat, the *Bellissima*, operated by his two sons, Joe and Leo, who now clustered around the two older men, adding their two cents' worth to the conversation, in English mostly, with the occasional dash of Italian.

The Doyle side of the family was represented as well. Directly in front of me I saw cousin George, the family stuffed shirt. At the moment George's florid blond face was even redder than usual. In fact, he looked decidedly uncomfortable, no doubt wishing devoutly to be in a meeting with some of his developer cronies, discussing the construction of yet another hotel on Cannery Row. But he always appeared to be out of place at family gatherings, as though he would like to divorce himself from his lineage, which reeked of fishing boats and sardine canneries.

My eyes moved to the right and I saw another reason for his discomfort. Kay was there, flamboyant in a fuchsia jumpsuit, a flowered silk scarf tied around her dark curls. George didn't like that fact that Kay and his sister Donna were a couple. It was ironic, I thought, since all the other people in the family accepted the relationship, even if he didn't.

Then I saw another Doyle and it was my turn to feel uncomfortable with someone else's relationship. Mother had deemed Bobby's arrest important enough to warrant a temporary absence from Café Marie. She'd brought Karl Beckman with her. I didn't think he should be at a family gathering. Nor did I like the proprietary way he stood behind the chair where Mother slumped tiredly, his big hands resting on her shoulders.

Donna swooped down on me like one of the pelicans she spent so much time studying. She opened her mouth to speak but it was so noisy in the living room I shook my head. I led the way through the kitchen, nodding to Elena and the other two women, who I now recalled were married to Joe and Leo.

"What the hell happened?" Donna demanded when we got out onto the deck.

"I went straight to the harbor when I got back to Monterey. I had to talk to Bobby about something I'd just found out. We were walking down the wharf when Magruder showed up and arrested Bobby."

I filled her in on the rest. While I tried to get the sergeant to tell me something, anything, the deputy accompanying him had shep-

herded Bobby into a waiting car. Magruder had told me again to
stay out of his investigation. When they'd left, I ran to Fisherman's
Wharf to tell Nick and Tina. Magruder and the deputy took
Bobby to the Monterey substation, at the courthouse on Aguajito
Road, where he was held until he was taken to jail in Salinas.

"What has Magruder got today that he didn't have earlier?"
Donna asked.

"He thinks he's got a witness who saw Bobby's car and Ariel in
the lot at the Rocky Point Restaurant, the same evening Ariel was
killed. But I think he's got a car and a girl, that's all."

I told Donna about stopping at the restaurant this afternoon
and the waitress who'd seen a young woman, possibly Ariel, and a
T-bird that looked like Bobby's. The sergeant must have figured
he had enough evidence to place Bobby at the scene. It was still
circumstantial, as far as I was concerned. There must be more
than one '57 T-bird on the peninsula. Even if the waitress did see
Ariel in the lot, it didn't have to be the combination the sergeant
wanted. The DA's office had forty-eight hours to review the file
and charge Bobby with murder. At that point he would be ar-
raigned and bail set.

When Donna and I went back inside, Nick was off the phone.
The roar of talk subsided as the people gathered in the living
room listened to what Nick had to say. He'd been talking with a
criminal lawyer who told him that if the DA charged Bobby with
Ariel's murder, bail would be high, maybe half a million dollars.

"Where are we going to come up with that kind of money?"
Tina asked, anguish coloring her voice.

"We could mortgage this place." Nick swept his hand around
the living room of the home he and Tina had worked so hard to
buy. It was more than just a house. It represented many hours
spent on a fishing boat or behind the counter of the fish market, a
home where they'd raised their children and cared for grand-
children.

"Not a good idea," George said, straightening his tie. "The real-
estate market is down, what with the closure of Fort Ord."

Donna scowled at him. "You're the big-time financier. Have
you got a better idea?"

"We all got money in the bank," Uncle Dom insisted in his

gravelly voice, moving into the role of family patriarch. "We're all family, we all kick in." He reached for a pad of paper and a pen near the phone. He wrote something on the paper and showed it to Aunt Teresa, who nodded.

Voices chimed in agreement as Sal Ravella took the paper and pen and consulted with his sons and their wives. Finally they agreed on an amount, which they wrote on the paper and passed to one of the cousins whose face didn't click in my memory.

"I'll talk to the guys on the wharf," Leo added. "And the fishermen's union. Maybe we can get some kind of a fund going."

The voices got louder as the paper went from person to person. I heard Sally and Elena, Bobby's sisters, say they'd have to discuss money with their husbands. Kay and Donna added to the line of figures on the paper. Then my mother reached for it and I heard her say she felt sure she could spare several thousand.

"Is business back to normal?" I asked her.

She shook her head. "Still way down. Thanks to the mouse and what happened Sunday."

So Mother didn't really have much to spare. She had salaries to pay but few paying customers. I could see the same thought on Karl Beckman's face as the boatyard owner leaned forward and intercepted the paper, adding his own pledge to Bobby's bail fund. Again I wondered at his relationship with my cousin, the much younger fisherman, remembering Bobby's statement that he owed Karl Beckman a favor, something he wouldn't discuss with me.

Karl handed the paper to Cousin George, who held it gingerly between two fingers and gazed at it as though it were radioactive. "So how much are you good for, George?" Kay asked, a wicked smile curving her lips.

George glowered at his sister's partner and took refuge in the same phrase Sally and Elena had used, except I knew they were sincere and George wasn't. "I really can't commit to this until I discuss it with Marilyn."

"Come on, George," Donna gibed. "You've got pots of money. If the rest of us can scrape up a few thousand you can probably spare three times that. I know how much you made off that last hotel deal. Marilyn was bragging about your take at the Labor Day picnic."

Her brother's face reddened. "My money's tied up right now. Besides, what if Bobby's guilty?"

He couldn't have gotten more attention if he'd suddenly started to disrobe. All conversation stopped and every eye in the room turned to gaze at George with varying degrees of consternation and hostility.

"What are you, crazy?" Nick bellowed. "My son didn't kill that girl. This is all some damn mistake."

Silence gave way to a mutter of censure. Then Uncle Dom snorted and said something in Italian that caused several of the assembled Ravellas to snicker. This lessened the tension George had created with his ill-timed question, but not by much. Tina glared at George. Nick looked as though he'd like to deck this particular Doyle cousin.

Kay leaned back and tugged the scarf tied around her head. "You'd better put your money where your mouth is, George. Either that, or your foot."

Her remark caused a titter of laughter that swept around the room, defusing the situation even more. The buzz began again and soon escalated into a roar. Suddenly I wanted out of this crowded room. I took my car keys from my pocket and made a quick exit out the front door. I don't think anyone missed me.

I liked my relatives, I told myself as I pointed my Toyota down the hill. In small doses. Too many of them at once caused my stress level to overwhelm the warmth of being in the family bosom.

Can't live with them, I thought, or without them. Especially if you're in jail and your relatives are passing the hat.

CHAPTER *27*

AFTER THE NOISE THAT ENVELOPED THE RAVELLA HOUSE, the garden of the Sevilles' whitewashed cottage seemed to be a quiet oasis. We sat on the flagstone patio, where two white-painted Adirondack chairs and a bench were arrayed around a low ceramic planter full of late-blooming asters and fall lilies. As the evening sun splashed across the garden one last time before sinking into the Pacific Ocean, we sipped sherry and talked, accompanied by the rush of waves breaking on Carmel Beach.

"When I left," I told Errol and Minna, "Uncle Dom was vowing to take the *Nicky II* out after squid tonight. He's spry for eighty, but not that spry. Aunt Teresa was giving him the evil eye. Trouble is, Bobby's shorthanded anyway. He fired someone this summer, a guy named Frank. With Bobby in jail, the crew is two men short."

"Will they be able to fish?" Minna asked. Stinkpot sprawled on her lap, his long tail pluming down her leg. Minna stroked the big cat and he stretched pleasurably, flexing his paws.

"They'll have to. No one in this business can afford to miss a night's fishing. Sal may skipper the *Nicky II* tonight while Joe and Leo take out the *Bellissima*. They said they'd see if they could come up with some extra men."

"I think Magruder's being hasty," Errol said, examining the rich amber in his sherry glass. "I know a man in Carmel Valley who has a T-bird just like Bobby's. Same color, same year. Unless Magruder has more, such as a full or partial plate number."

"I wonder if this arrest is due to pressure from the Logans," Minna said. She scratched the cat behind the ears. Suddenly Stinkpot perked up, as though he'd heard something. He leaped from her lap and went off to stalk some unfortunate creature in the garden.

Errol squinted at me in the dimming light. "What else did you find out in San Luis Obispo?"

I gave Errol a rundown of my interviews in SLO and Paso Robles, speculating about Ariel Logan's interest in the seals Susan Dailey had pulled off the beach near the oil refinery at Avila. Ariel's report to the SPCA about sea lions in trouble had to be connected. But how?

"If there had been any oil spills in the sanctuary there would be a hue and cry," Minna pointed out. "Something else must have caused those sea lions to behave oddly."

"Maggie Lim told me that Ariel seemed very interested in chemicals used at the Beckman boatyard here in Monterey," I said. "I read an article in one of the San Francisco newspapers a couple of years back, about workers in a boatyard who were getting sick because of the paints and solvents used there. What if Ariel discovered something going on at Beckman Boat Works?"

Errol tilted his head to one side. "Are you saying Karl Beckman, either deliberately or accidentally, is not complying with environmental regulations when it comes to toxic materials?"

"I don't know." I shrugged. "It's a stretch. She may simply have been curious, which wouldn't be surprising. She was an environmentalist, concerned about the ocean. And she'd seen those sea lions. But Errol, what about the argument with Bobby? Ariel mentioned reporting something. That *something* was important enough to send Bobby on a hunt for Karl."

Now Minna spoke up. "Do you think Karl Beckman killed Ariel?"

I didn't respond immediately. Karl Beckman certainly seemed like a personable, ordinary businessman. I wasn't quite ready to accuse him of murder. Still . . . "Bobby never found Karl," I said slowly. "And Karl won't tell me where he was. He says it's none of my business."

"Maybe it isn't," Minna said.

An uncomfortable silence stretched while I wondered again if my readiness to believe that Karl Beckman was hiding something had more to do with the way I felt about his relationship with my mother.

"So we're back to Ariel." I sighed. "What she knew or thought she knew. I think it was about those sea lions she saw in August. Evidently she wasn't planning to tell anyone until she'd had a chance to discuss it with Bobby. But maybe she kept some notes or wrote an account of what she saw." I glanced at Errol. "Did you ask the Logans if I could look through Ariel's things from school?"

"Yes. I talked with Peter this morning. Got an unequivocal no."

"Why should they?" Minna asked. "Now that there's a suspect in custody. If the DA doesn't charge Bobby, maybe the Logans will reconsider."

"I may have some leverage that will make Peter Logan change his mind," I said slowly. "When I was down at the Rocky Point Restaurant earlier today, I showed the staff a picture given to me by Maggie, a snapshot that shows Ariel with her parents. The bartender says he saw Peter Logan in the bar Friday evening, around dusk. He was there long enough to have two drinks."

"Curious," Errol commented. "Why would the Logans let it be known that they returned on Sunday if they came back sooner?"

"I'm sure Glennis said they arrived Sunday." Minna's frown was just visible in the fading light. "Why would she say otherwise?"

"Maybe Sylvie came back Sunday," I guessed, "and Peter earlier. How would they travel?"

"Sylvie's French," Minna said. "When she goes to Paris she always flies Air France out of San Francisco International. There's only one flight a day. You either have to drive to the city and leave your car in a lot, or catch a United shuttle out of Monterey." A streak of black-and-white fur shot across the garden and landed on Minna. She reached up and stroked Stinkpot as he settled onto her lap. "I can find out, Jeri. We use the same travel agent."

"I'll nose around the Monterey airport," I said, "to see if anyone remembers either Peter or Sylvie arriving. Is Glennis still here?" Minna nodded. "She's the gatekeeper. Maybe I can talk to her."

Errol spoke up now. "If the sergeant has Ariel's things the question's moot for now. In the interim, I think it's time I did a little background check on Peter Logan."

I had dinner with the Sevilles, then I headed back to Monterey and my mother's house on Larkin Street. I felt tired and travel weary, so I dumped my overnight case in the guest room without unpacking it and went to the bathroom to splash cold water on my face.

The phone rang as I was toweling myself dry. When I picked up the receiver I heard the unmistakable British voice of Stella, the barmaid at the Rose and Crown, sounding cheery over the rock music in the background.

"He's here, ducks."

"Who's there?" I asked, feeling foggy as I rubbed my neck with the hand towel.

"The fellow I told you about, the one that was here when Bobby and his girl had that row. He just walked in, not five minutes ago."

I shook my head and the fog lifted. "I'll be right down. Keep him there."

"No worry, love, he's having dinner."

The Rose and Crown was hopping when I got there, not surprising since it was almost eight o'clock on a Thursday night. As I walked past the counter that fronted the small kitchen, I saw that every stool at the bar was full and a serious dart game was in progress at the rear of the tavern. Most of the booths on the lower and upper levels were occupied. I spotted Stella delivering a round of drinks to a large group gathered around the big table in the back and waited for her to return to the bar.

"That's him." She pointed to a man in work clothes sitting alone at one of the upper-level booths. I thanked her and made my way to the booth. He was a broad-shouldered man in his middle thirties, his fair skin burned brown by the sun, his short brown hair receding from his high forehead. Until I approached him his attention had been occupied by the sandwich and french fries on the platter in front of him. Now he looked up at me, curious.

"May I join you?" I asked.

"Depends," he said, a tentative smile on his face. He reached for a napkin. I noticed a wedding band on his left hand.

I gave him my business card as I slipped into the booth opposite him. "You were here about two weeks ago, on a Friday afternoon. Right before you came in you saw a man and a woman outside, having an argument. You mentioned it to the barmaid when you came into the tavern."

"What's this about?" he asked, frowning now as he studied my card.

"The young woman was murdered. I'm trying to find out what happened after she left here."

"Murdered? No kidding?" He reached for the pint of porter near his left hand and took a large restorative swallow.

"What's your name?" I asked, trying to set him at ease.

"Don. Don Porter."

"Do you remember the people you saw? When did you first see them?"

"They were standing right there at the curb, just past the entrance to the pub here." Porter set his pint on the table surface and pointed his right thumb over his shoulder in the direction of Alvarado Street. "I left my truck over on Pearl, so I'd just turned the corner." He waved his hand to the right, indicating the street that intersected Alvarado, just to the south. "They were right in front of me. He was dark, curly black hair, with his back to me. She was a really pretty blonde. I could see her face over his shoulder."

"When you came inside the Rose and Crown you told Stella they were really going at it hammer and tongs," I said. "How could you tell they were arguing? Did you hear what they were saying?"

"Well, no," Porter said, picking up his sandwich with both hands. "I couldn't tell what they were fighting about. But I picked up on their body language. He had his hand on her arm. And she was frowning. Had both hands on her hips and was shaking her head all the time he was talking to her." He took a bite from his sandwich, chewed it thoroughly, and washed it down with another sip of porter.

I leaned against the wooden back of the booth. Somehow I'd hoped for more. The evidence linking Bobby to Ariel's death was tenuous, circumstantial, and a lot of speculation centered on the argument here at the Rose and Crown. I was trying to find out what happened after that and so far I'd come up empty. "So you didn't hear anything?"

Porter frowned. "There was a lot of traffic, it being Friday afternoon. And the door to the tavern was open. I could hear the music coming from inside. But maybe—" He stopped and shrugged. "Well, just a scrap comes to me. I couldn't even tell you which of them said it."

"Just tell me what you heard," I prompted, leaning forward with my arms on the table.

"Something about . . . give me some time, twenty-four hours."

It must have been Bobby, I thought, asking Ariel to give him time to contact Karl Beckman. Which brought me right back to the question of why it was so important for Bobby to talk with Karl. It had to have something to do with the boatyard.

"Were they still at the curb when you came inside the pub?" I asked Porter.

The big-shouldered man shook his head. "She left the guy standing there and went off across Alvarado, toward that bookstore."

"Maybe her car was parked on that side of the street."

"No, she went in."

"How do you know that? Did you see her go in?" I'd already talked to a clerk in the bookshop last Saturday when I was canvassing Alvarado Street. He didn't remember seeing Ariel Logan, but I might have talked to the wrong clerk.

Porter dipped a french fry into a puddle of ketchup and popped the strip of potato into his mouth. He looked at me quizzically. "I didn't see her go in. I must have seen her come out. Now that I think about it, I'm not sure what I saw."

"I'm confused," I said slowly. "You saw the blond woman later, after she left the man at the curb? How much later?"

"Yeah, that's it." Porter grinned and reached for his sandwich. "You see, I was over at the bar, and in comes this old guy I know. We got to talking and he wanted to see my new truck. So we finish our brews and go outside. Must have been thirty, forty minutes later. That's when I saw her again, standing in front of the bookstore, next to a pickup."

"Can you describe the pickup?"

"Of course I can. Beckman Boat Works," Porter said, as if there were no other answer. "Light blue with a boat and letters on both doors. Karl and Lacy both drive trucks just like that."

"You know the Beckmans?" I felt as though I were in the wrong play.

"Sure do. I know all the boatyards in this part of the state. I haul boats from one place to another. In fact, I'd just been down to the yard delivering a sailboat, before I came over here to the Rose and Crown."

Porter pulled out his wallet and gave me a business card. "I work all up and down the coast, pleasure craft and commercial. Say Beckman's got a sailboat needs to go from Monterey to Half Moon Bay. If it's small enough, he calls me, we put the boat on my trailer, and I haul it up there. Now, if a boat's too big, it would have to move under its own power. Lacy might sail it wherever it's supposed to go. She's a good sailor. Guess you'd have to be if you're gonna be in that business. In fact, I haven't been doing as much work for the Beckmans lately. Lacy's been handling most of the boat transport."

I nodded, recalling the phone call Lacy took while I was in her office. "Did it look as though the blond woman was talking to someone in the Beckman pickup?"

"Coulda been." Porter took another bite of his sandwich. "I just noticed her because I'd seen her before. She was leaning toward the pickup's window."

I let Porter eat his sandwich in peace while I digested the information he'd just given me. Ariel could have recognized the truck and leaned toward it to look into an empty driver's seat. Or she could have been talking to the driver.

Again I thought of last Saturday's visit to the boatyard. Lacy told me she'd been upstairs in the office that Friday afternoon and hadn't seen Bobby when he came by looking for Karl. But Karl was nowhere Bobby looked.

If what Porter told me was true, he'd placed either Karl or Lacy

Beckman on Alvarado Street about an hour after Ariel's argument with Bobby at the Rose and Crown.

Come on, Jeri, it didn't have to be one of the Beckmans. It could have been one of their employees. But if Karl, Lacy, or one of the people who worked in the boatyard had seen Ariel Logan late Friday afternoon, why hadn't that person come forward?

CHAPTER *28*

RYAN TRENT'S LAW FIRM WAS SANDWICHED BETWEEN two art galleries, in a two-story brown stucco building trying to look like a mission. According to the sign, so understated I almost missed it, the first floor was occupied by an accountant and a decorator. Silverberg and Trent were on the second floor.

It was about ten-thirty Friday morning. The front office had a dark clubby look, from the wainscoting on the walls to the blue-gray hues of the Oriental carpet on the floor. To my left towered a rubber plant in a huge black ceramic pot, glossy green leaves inches from the ceiling. On the right were two chairs and a sofa upholstered in the same subdued gray fabric. The sofa was occupied by a silver-haired man in a business suit. He favored me with the barest of glances, consulted his watch, and went back to reading his *Wall Street Journal.*

Directly in front of me I saw a wooden office desk with a computer workstation to one side. Seated at the desk was a sleek brunette, her purple silk dress a vibrant splash of color that drew the eye. She was on the telephone. Behind her an open door led to a room where filing cabinets and a copy machine were visible. On either side of her desk were two doors, both closed.

The receptionist finally hung up the phone and gave me a cool smile. "May I help you?"

"Jeri Howard to see Ryan Trent."

"Do you have an appointment?" Her eyes flicked over my slacks and cotton shirt, then down at the large leather-bound calendar on one corner of her desk.

"No. But I'm sure he'll see me."

The smile dimmed and her eyebrows raised. "Mr. Trent has a client due at eleven. And he's busy after that. Perhaps you'd like to make an appointment."

"Just tell him I'm here," I said firmly, taking up my immovable object stance in front of the desk.

She looked past me at the more presentable client with his nose in his newspaper and decided I was quite capable of making a scene. I was, if the situation warranted it. "Just a moment, please." She pushed the chair away from the desk and walked to one of the closed doors on the left. She tapped lightly, then she opened the door and stepped inside. A moment later she came out and resumed her seat without a word.

Ryan Trent opened the door of his office and glared at me as though he knew he'd seen me before and he was trying to remember who I was. His dark blond hair was combed back from his tanned face, as it had been when I'd encountered him Monday at Ariel Logan's funeral. His mouth compressed into a thin line and his gray eyes were cold. Finally he placed me and scowled.

"You were at the mission." His voice was low and its temperature wasn't any warmer than his eyes. "With Ravella."

"I'm a private investigator," I told him, voice even and face expressionless. "Bobby Ravella is my cousin."

"I have nothing to say to you." He dismissed me with a contemptuous sneer and turned. I moved quickly, my hand flat on the door he was attempting to shut. That surprised him. He was used to calling the shots. At the funeral I had noticed the tic at the left side of his mouth. Now it started to twitch and fury warmed the gray eyes.

"Get the hell out of my office."

"I don't think so."

"Sherry, call the police," he barked. From the corner of my eye I saw the receptionist reach for the phone.

I smiled. He wasn't expecting that either. "By all means, Mr. Trent. Call Sergeant Magruder while you're at it. You have as much motive for murdering Ariel Logan as Bobby did. I'd be happy to explain it to the sergeant. Or maybe you'd rather talk about it first."

The man waiting on the sofa peered over his *Wall Street Journal*, trying not to watch but unable to stop himself. Then the office door opened and his eyes swiveled from Trent's doorway to the newcomer, a sleek older woman who, oblivious to any other drama but her own, said, "I'm sorry I'm late. I simply couldn't find a parking place."

The older man folded the newspaper, left it on the sofa, and stood. "We'd like to see Mr. Silverberg now," he said, with just a touch of eagerness to get away from all this drama.

The receptionist, phone in hand, looked up at the client, then to Ryan Trent. He gestured abruptly. "Never mind, Sherry. Hold my calls."

Now he jerked open the door; at the same time he jerked his chin to the left. I took this for permission to enter, so I stepped inside. A neat freak, I thought, comparing this orderly space to the offices of some of the attorneys I'd worked with over the years. A place for everything and everything in its place. Even the files on the surface of the wide desk were stacked neatly, at right angles to the edge. So was the laptop computer on the other side. All the pens and pencils were uniformly arranged in a square container just above the desk blotter.

Trent remained standing near the door, ready to boot me out at the first opportunity. I settled into a chair. "Don't get comfortable," he snapped. "You've got sixty seconds to explain that crack about motives for murder. Then I'm tossing you out."

I laced my fingers together, crossed my legs, and didn't say anything. Instead I stared quite deliberately at the sweeping second hand on a round brass clock on the wall behind the desk. When sixty seconds had gone by I looked at the attorney.

"Get on with it," he said, taking a stance behind his desk. "I'm not interested in playing games with you."

"Murder's hardly a game. You're quite a martinet, Trent. Based on everything I've learned about Ariel I can't imagine what she saw in you."

He crossed his arms over his chest and favored me with an unpleasant smile. "What did she see in your alcoholic cousin? I had him checked out. I know about his drinking, his DWIs, his brushes with the law, his bimbo girlfriends."

"Come on, counselor. You can't tell me you haven't dated a few women whose attributes were physical rather than intellectual."

"I've never been arrested for drunk driving."

"So your quarrel with Bobby Ravella is that he wasn't good enough for Ariel." I uncrossed my legs and leaned toward him.

"Who the hell appointed you God? It was Ariel's decision. She was twenty-two years old and capable of making her own choices. No, what really makes you angry is that she didn't choose you. She bruised your ego."

Trent's thin mouth worked and his tic became more pronounced. "And that gives me a motive for murder?"

"Why not?" I shrugged. "Rejection is as good a motive as any. Ariel rejected you twice. She broke up with you a year ago and started dating Bobby. You didn't like that. This summer you kept calling her, but she wouldn't go out with you." He frowned at this, wondering how I knew. "The rumor mill says Ariel wanted to break off her relationship with Bobby and so he killed her. That's what the Logans think."

"Why not?" He flung my words back at me. "Your cousin's got a reputation. Maybe Ariel finally saw him for the loser he is. They were arguing about something at the Rose and Crown. And then she was dead. Murdered. Beaten over the head and dumped into the ocean." He glared at me, a trace of anguish visible behind his anger, hinting that what he'd felt for Ariel was perhaps deeper than I'd thought. "Christ, I wouldn't wish that on my worst enemy, let alone a twenty-two-year-old woman I cared about."

"Neither would Bobby," I said forcefully, believing it and willing him to do likewise. "He and Ariel were planning to get married. I have a hunch the subject of the argument at the Rose and Crown wasn't about the rumored breakup of their relationship."

"So what was it?" He pulled out his chair and sat down.

"Put your assumptions aside, Trent, and tell me why Ariel visited your office in August."

Trent looked startled for the blink of an eyelash, then he masked it. "What makes you think she did?"

"I went to SLO a few days ago. Maggie Lim told me she visited

Ariel in Carmel several times during the summer. In August Ariel came to see you. Maggie didn't know why, but I think I do. Ariel asked you to do something for her. What was it?"

"I can't tell you that." Trent scowled. He shook his head and waved away my words.

"I know all about attorney-client privilege. But Ariel's dead. She was concerned about something. It may have led to her murder. Did Ariel's request have something to do with Beckman Boat Works?"

The attorney's eyebrows went up. "How did you know that?"

"I'm a private investigator, remember? What was it? Karl Beckman's finances? Come on, Trent, you don't have to give me chapter and verse. Just confirm it."

He pulled a pen from the container on his desk and began fiddling with it. "She wanted to know if the boatyard was in financial difficulty," he said, reluctance in his voice. "It is. Dates back to a loan made to Gunter, the brother who died in the car wreck with Karl's wife. It was a large sum, using Beckman Boat Works as collateral. Gunter was behind in the payments. There was danger of a default, so Karl had to make good. It cleaned him out."

"Karl must have inherited something from Janine's estate. I'm surprised he'd be cash poor."

"That's what I thought," Trent said. "But I checked Janine Beckman's will in probate. It was dated just a couple of months before she died. Except for her share in the boatyard, everything was left to her daughter and her brother."

My ears pricked with interest. "Why would she do that? If Gunter was up to his ears in debt, what did he leave Lacy, besides a share of the business?"

"Not much. They had a fancy house here in Carmel. She had to sell it. Now she lives in an apartment in New Monterey. I don't think she's accustomed to living paycheck to paycheck."

I didn't ask Trent how he knew what lifestyle Lacy Beckman preferred. I was thinking about Karl Beckman's daughter Kristen, who was now at Stanford University, a place that ran up an enormous tab in tuition, fees, and all the expenses that normally accompany an education at a private university. Of course, according to her mother's will, she had her own money.

"What's Beckman's financial status now?"

"Still shaky." Trent tapped the pen on his desk blotter. "He was okay for a while, but the recession has hit everyone hard down here. Boats are expensive to maintain. I know several people who've decided to get rid of theirs for just that reason. That means fewer repair jobs for the boatyards. Business is bad. If he's going to stay afloat, Beckman needs capital."

What was he willing to do to get it? "Did Ariel tell you why she wanted this information? Surely you were curious."

"Of course I was." His fingers still twiddled the pen and he frowned, at the desk blotter rather than at me. "But she wouldn't tell me anything. She promised to fill me in later, she said, when she confirmed her suspicions. That's a direct quote. Suspicions about what?" He scowled again as a thought dawned on him. "Was Karl Beckman doing something illegal?"

"Maybe." I looked at him across the expanse of his desk. "Is Beckman's financial status desperate enough to make him do something illegal?"

"I hardly know the man. I wouldn't even describe his money situation as desperate. Serious, maybe."

But it wasn't just Karl Beckman's business. Half of it belonged to Lacy, who kept the books. She had to be aware of the boatyard's financial situation. If something illegal was going on at Beckman Boat Works, would Lacy know about it? Or was Karl keeping her in the dark?

"When you were looking into the boatyard's finances," I asked Trent, "what did you learn about Lacy Beckman?"

Trent was silent, still reluctant to talk. "She bought some property in Santa Cruz earlier this summer."

"Where did she get the money?"

He shrugged. "I assume she has money of her own. She's a Standish, from a wealthy family in San Francisco. She sold the Carmel house when Gunter died."

"How well do you know her?"

"Not well," he said, replacing the pen in its holder. He looked past me at the bookcase on the opposite wall.

The hell you don't, I thought. How else did he know her birth name? Trent's facial tic suddenly kicked in. Was that a sudden brief flush I saw under the lawyer's even tan? Had Lacy favored the lawyer with her affections before she took up with Julian Surtees?

I heard a brief tap on the door and then it opened. Trent's head swiveled in that direction. The receptionist appeared and hesitantly told the lawyer his eleven o'clock appointment had arrived. "I'll be right out," he said abruptly. When she'd closed the door again he looked at me, mouth tight again. "You'll have to leave."

I got to my feet. Neither of us offered to shake hands. "If you think of anything else Ariel told you during the summer, let me know." I took one of my business cards from my purse, wrote Mother's number on the back, and left it on Trent's desk blotter. He made no move to pick it up.

"If you find out who killed her . . ." he said, and didn't finish the sentence. He didn't have to.

CHAPTER 29

CHECKED THE PROBATE RECORDS MYSELF. I COULDN'T FIND a will for Gunter Beckman, so I guessed that he'd died intestate. Janine Harper Beckman's will was as Ryan Trent described it. She'd left her share of the boatyard to her husband Karl, not surprising since this was an asset she'd acquired by marrying him. Janine had owned a one-third interest in the Harper ranch in southern Monterey County. On her death this share had passed to her brother Charles. The rest of her estate was left to her daughter Kristen.

So Karl hadn't benefited significantly from his wife's death. He got what he already had—Beckman Boat Works—and that business was in financial trouble even then. This will had been signed in December, two months before Janine Beckman and her brother-in-law Gunter died in the car accident. What did her previous will contain? Did Janine have a reason for changing it? If so, was that reason a factor in her death?

At the Monterey Public Library I looked through copies of the *Herald* until I located the stories that dealt with the accident that killed Janine and Gunter. The information I found in the narrow columns of newsprint left me with more questions than answers.

The wreck had occurred on a rainy February evening at Hurricane Point, about twelve miles north of the village of Big Sur, above the beach where the Little Sur River runs into the ocean. No one was sure exactly what time the car went off the road, but Gunter Beckman had made a seven o'clock dinner reservation for two at Ventana, located about two miles south of Big Sur. He and his companion were no-shows. The accident had been reported around eight, when the driver of another car spotted something burning on the rocky marine terrace below Highway 1.

I recalled yesterday's drive up the coast and the tug of gusty winds that gave Hurricane Point its name. The road requires attention during daylight hours, even more so on a rainy night. After the accident, the wreckage of Gunter Beckman's BMW stayed where it was, where the waves and rocks would batter and grind it. It had taken the county rescue team two days to retrieve the badly burned bodies.

The authorities never determined why the car went off the road. Hurricane Point had claimed so many vehicles over the years that everyone assumed the driver of the BMW had failed to make the curve. A barmaid at the Hog's Breath Inn in Carmel reported that Gunter Beckman had been at the bar that afternoon, drinking steadily. It was his car, so everyone assumed he'd been driving. The bodies were so charred from the fire that the retrieval team couldn't tell who was behind the wheel or how much alcohol the deceased had consumed.

Why had Gunter and Janine planned dinner at Ventana? Was it just a friendly meeting between in-laws? Or did it have something to do with their respective spouses? I recalled Karl Beckman's reaction each time I mentioned Lacy. Something flickered in his eyes. I wondered about Karl's relationship with his brother's wife. Had they ever crossed the line from friends to lovers?

I also wanted to know where Karl Beckman was the weekend Ariel Logan died, and he wouldn't tell me. Why was he being so damned secretive?

I retrieved my car from the library parking lot and drove to the Monterey Peninsula Airport, where a clerk at the United counter looked at the snapshot of the Logans and told me he remembered Sylvie Logan's arrival a week ago. "Sunday evening," he said, "on the shuttle from San Francisco. She must have been coming from someplace else, because she had lots of luggage. I didn't think it would all fit in the cab."

"But you don't recall seeing the man?"

He shook his head. "Sorry, I don't. I think it was just her. You can check with the cabbie."

I went outside and questioned several cabdrivers waiting for fares. The cabbie I wanted to interview wasn't there. It was another half hour before he showed up, dropping off a passenger. He was a bulky Chicano who got out of his hack, leaned against the fender, and fired up a cigar redolent of wet garbage. I showed him the snapshot of the Logans. His memory improved greatly when I added a twenty-dollar bill to the equation.

"Yeah, I remember her. Fare to Carmel." He puffed on his stogie and I surreptitiously took a few steps upwind. "Older lady with an accent. Not like mine, though. No, she didn't have no man with her. But this guy—" He used the cigar as a pointer, waving the lighted end at the photographic image of Peter Logan. "This guy came out of the house in Carmel to help me with the luggage."

MINNA SEVILLE WAS IN THE FRONT YARD OF THE SEVILLES' HOUSE in Carmel, wielding a trowel at the base of a cluster of lilies. "Door's open," she told me. "Errol's on the patio." I went through the house and found Errol seated in one of the Adirondack chairs, reading a detective novel and drinking coffee.

I took a seat in the other chair. "Last night I had a talk with a man who hauls boats for a living."

Errol's eyes sparkled and he closed the book he was reading. "I assume you had a reason."

"I certainly did. He's the customer who walked into the Rose and Crown right after Bobby and Ariel left. He saw Ariel later, near the bookstore across the street. She appeared to be talking to someone in a Beckman Boat Works pickup truck. He couldn't see who was driving."

"That puts a different spin on things," Errol said. "Was it Karl, Lacy, or one of their employees?"

"This morning I went to see Ryan Trent."

"That must have been interesting. What did you find out?"

"Ariel's roommate Maggie told me Ariel went to see Trent while she was in Carmel this summer, despite the fact that she'd broken off their relationship the year before. Trent says Ariel asked him to look into the finances at Beckman Boat Works."

After I'd given him the details of Trent's inquiries, Errol leaned back in his chair and narrowed his eyes. "Interesting that Ariel went to such lengths to get information on Karl Beckman. Beckman Boat Works means a lot to Karl, since his father started it. But Gunter viewed it as a cash cow, a means of financing his lifestyle. So Gunter borrowed against the company's assets and Karl covered for him. Then both Gunter and Janine died. What did Karl and Lacy inherit?"

I told him about my excursion through the probate records, and the old newspaper articles about the accident. "I think I'll drive to King City tomorrow and talk with Janine's brother, Charlie Harper. Is everyone satisfied with the verdict that Gunter and Janine died accidentally?"

"As far as I know," Errol said. "It happened about the time we moved here permanently, so people were talking, assuming Gunter was driving. He liked his booze. The witness at the bar confirmed he'd been drinking earlier that afternoon. If he was going too fast, if he'd had too much alcohol . . . Hurricane Point is unforgiving of both vices."

"I'd like to look at that accident report."

"It should be on file at the sheriff's department since it happened in county jurisdiction. Stop in Salinas when you go to King City tomorrow."

Minna came through the gate lugging a basketful of gardening tools. She set them down and picked up Errol's coffee, taking a swallow. "Your coffee's cold, love. I'll make another pot. What are we talking about?" she asked as she sat down on the bench.

"Gunter and Janine Beckman," Errol said.

"Ah, that." Stinkpot appeared from the back of the garden. He leaped into Minna's lap and coiled himself into a large black-and-white ball, his feathery tail trailing to the flagstone patio. She stroked his back and I heard the cat's rumbling purr.

"I'd come down here the month before, to get the house ready while Errol finished closing up his office in Oakland." Minna rubbed the cat's chin. "There was plenty of talk, lots of speculation as to why Gunter and Janine were going down to Ventana for dinner. I heard the usual rumors that they'd been having an affair, but I didn't believe them. I met the Beckmans a few years earlier, while Errol and I were here for one of our long weekends. Janine didn't seem the type to stray, though Gunter certainly was. There are plenty of local women who had a fling with Gunter Beckman. He was a charming cad." She shook her head. "I never saw Gunter and Janine behave in a fashion that would give rise to such rumors. So either it wasn't true or they were good about covering their tracks. On the other hand, I wonder about Karl and Lacy."

"So do I," I said. "Janine Beckman made a new will two months before her death, which would have been shortly after Karl covered Gunter's loan default. That will essentially left Karl with what he had when they got married."

"I don't have anything specific to back up that impression about Karl and Lacy," Minna cautioned. "Gossip, mostly. People do love to talk and one can find out the most interesting things by listening. Lacy used to live in Carmel. She sold the house, so I guess Gunter's death left her finances lean."

"Not according to Ryan Trent. He thinks she has family money. What about Lacy? We know Gunter liked to play around. What about his wife?"

"Oh, yes. Plenty of rumors about that," Minna said. "When Lacy lived here, and even while she was married to Gunter, she cut a rather wide swath through the men in this area. Evidently she's not particular about whether they're married. In fact, I think lawyer Trent was one of her conquests, before he started dating Ariel Logan."

I had guessed as much. I needed more information on the icy blond with the tiger eyes. Especially since Julian Surtees seemed to be her current squeeze. If Lacy and Julian were involved, that might give her some access to the restaurant, I thought. But why would Lacy want to sabotage Café Marie?

I turned to Errol. "Were you able to get in touch with your colleague in Los Angeles?" I asked him.

Errol grinned. "Old private investigators never retire, they're just on hiatus. Yes, I talked to him. He said he'd be delighted to do a background check on Sylvie and Peter Logan. He'll call me this evening or tomorrow."

"I stopped at the Monterey airport before I came over here. The clerk at the United counter remembers Sylvie, and so does the cabbie who brought her home. She was alone."

"I talked with my travel agent," Minna said, stroking Stinkpot's back. "Sylvie and Peter Logan were booked on Air France Sunday from Charles de Gaulle Airport in Paris. That flight gets into San Francisco at three forty-five P.M. Then they were to take the United express from SFO, which arrives in Monterey at six thirty-five P.M."

"So if Peter came back early, on Friday," I said, "he must have gone straight from the airport to the Rocky Point Restaurant. But why? Unless the bartender who identified him from the snapshot is mistaken. But I don't think so."

"I also managed to talk with Mrs. Costello, the Logans' house-keeper." Minna shook her head. "She was no help, I'm afraid. She didn't see either Sylvie or Peter until she went to work Monday morning."

The phone rang and Errol went to answer it. A moment later he appeared at the French doors leading to the kitchen. "Jeri, it's for you. It's your cousin Donna."

I got up and walked into the house, taking the phone extension Errol held out for me.

"I've been calling around, trying to find you," Donna said, her voice revving with excitement. "Bobby's out of jail. The DA declined to press charges."

"WHAT HAPPENED?"

Bobby and I walked along the sidewalk between Fisherman's Wharf and Commercial Wharf Two. To our left, boats bobbed gently in the marina. We'd just left Ravella's and a tearful reunion between parents and son. Now Bobby wanted to check on the *Nicky II.*

"My AA group," Bobby said simply. "I thought they only knew me by my first name. But a couple of people from the group contacted the DA or the sheriff's office and said I was at the AA meeting two weeks ago. I guess Magruder was hot under the collar when they cut me loose. When Dad picked me up, he said he'd heard the sergeant had a partial plate number on the T-bird the waitress saw at Rocky Point. But it wasn't my car. Couldn't have been. That AA meeting is every Friday at seven. I got there before it started and I stayed till it broke up at nine."

"Maybe it was your car."

"How could that be?" Bobby shook his head as we passed the harbormaster's office and started up Wharf Two. "You're thinking somebody stole the T-bird. No way. I locked the car. Besides, it was sitting in the same spot when I left the meeting."

"Right before Magruder arrested you yesterday I asked if anyone besides you has a set of keys to your car."

"Only Dad." Bobby stopped and frowned. "But . . . back when I was drinking, I wasn't too careful about those keys. Or who borrowed the car."

Easy enough, I thought, for the borrower to stop at the nearest hardware store to have an extra set made. "Who's borrowed the T-bird over the past year?"

"Any one of the guys who work for me on the boat." He gestured toward the area between the wharf and the Coast Guard jetty where the *Nicky II* rode at anchor.

"Including Frank Alviso?"

Bobby looked at me, troubled. "Yeah, Frank borrowed the car a couple of times."

"Why did you fire Frank?" I asked.

"He's a fuckup," Bobby said. He stuck his hands in the pockets of his blue jeans and slowed his pace on the planked surface of the wharf. "He didn't pull his share of the load. He was always late. He was always messing up. He always had lots of excuses, and the more he talked, the lamer they sounded. Finally I had enough. So I canned him."

"Was he a friend?"

"I thought so." Bobby stared out at the boats. Beyond them, the sun inched its way toward the horizon. "Frank and I used to be drinking buddies. I put up with his crap for a long time, until I got sober. That's when the fog lifted. When I fired him, Frank told me I was more fun when I was drinking."

Bobby sighed. "My AA sponsor says this happens a lot. Sometimes your friends aren't your friends anymore. Because all you had in common was the booze."

We walked along in silence. When we reached the end of Wharf Two I stopped and leaned on the railing, watching a sleek sea lion swim from under the pilings. "Is Frank the kind of guy who would hold a grudge?"

"Yeah," Bobby admitted. "Big time. But it's one thing to hold a grudge and another to kill someone. I can't see Frank as a killer."

I could, I thought, recalling the shifty-eyed Alviso from our encounter at Beckman Boat Works. If he'd been involved in the pelican mutilations several years back, he was a killer, a very cruel one.

"Several years ago when those pelicans were being mutilated, Alviso and another guy named McCall were on the list of suspects. Did Frank ever do or say anything that could tie him to that?"

"He doesn't like cats," Bobby said. "He used to joke about running them down on the road. I guess if he'd mistreat one animal he'd mistreat another. But that's sort of an impulse thing. To cut off the pelican's bill you got to catch the bird first. Frank's not that organized. Hell, I don't know, Jeri. Maybe he's doing the birds. The guy's a jerk. He has been for years. I just couldn't see it until I sobered up."

"About sobering up," I said, turning to him. "When I was in San Luis Obispo earlier this week I talked to Ariel's roommate, Maggie. Tell me what happened last April, after Ariel gave you that ultimatum about your drinking."

He gave me a sideways glance and sighed. "I was pissed at Ariel. Me? I didn't have a problem with booze. I just got tanked every weekend. So I stomped out of Ariel's apartment and went steaming up 101 like a bat out of hell."

He shook his head, rubbing his chin wearily. "I stopped in Paso Robles, bought a six-pack, and guzzled beer all the way to King City. That's where I got pulled over. Not quite shit-faced, but almost, with an open container on the seat next to me. Failed the sobriety test. Next thing I knew I was being booked into the King City jail. I already had two DWIs on my record. I figured I was looking at serious jail time."

"You called Karl Beckman," I guessed.

Bobby nodded. "Yeah. Karl saved my ass, Jeri. He drove down to King City to get me. I don't know how he did it, but he got me out of that jam. They even deep-sixed the arrest report."

"So that's why you owe him. He kept you out of jail."

"It was more than that, Jeri. He kicked my butt when it needed kicking. After Karl got me out of jail he took me outside and backed me up against the T-bird. He said, 'This is between you and me. No one else needs to know. But it's the last time I'll help you. Next time you screw up, you're on your own.'"

Bobby stopped and sighed. "That was the second time in twelve hours someone I care about told me I'd better clean up my act. It got my attention."

"So you stopped drinking."

"Yeah. Quit cold turkey. Thank God I wasn't to the point I needed detox. But it was rough. The AA meetings are a lifesaver." He looked sideways at me and flashed a pale imitation of his usual wicked grin. "But you know, cuz, I've got such a bad reputation, I'm like the boy that cried wolf. Nobody believes anything good about me. Ariel's parents think I killed her, and so does that stony-faced sergeant."

"Karl must have called in some serious markers to keep you out of jail. Does he have that kind of clout in King City?"

"I don't know." Bobby shrugged. "Karl didn't say and I didn't ask."

"You just figured you owed him a big one."

"I do."

"I think I've guessed why you and Ariel were arguing, Bobby. Something's going on at Beckman Boat Works."

By now the sun had slipped to the horizon. Lights glowed in the windows of the restaurants on Fisherman's Wharf and streetlights went on all over the marina area. I looked at Bobby's face in the overhead light, trying to read it. He looked stubborn and he didn't respond to the question implied in my statement.

"Ariel loved the ocean and she was active in the environmental movement on the central coast. Sometime this summer, she got the idea that Beckman Boat Works is polluting the bay. She wanted to report it to someone. But you wanted to talk to Karl Beckman first. You asked her to give you twenty-four hours to have that conversation."

I paused and stared into my cousin's dark eyes. "Come on, Bobby. Level with me. I can't help you if you don't. Is Karl Beckman dumping toxic chemicals into Monterey Bay?"

"Karl wouldn't do something like that," Bobby said flatly, shaking his head for emphasis. "Any more than I would. He makes his living from the sea just like I do. We're all part of the same food chain."

"But you don't know for sure."

"Neither did Ariel." He clenched his fist and brought it down hard on the railing. "She didn't have any proof. Hell, there's always gonna be runoff from a boatyard. It's on the shore. Maybe one of the workers spills a little solvent and it gets washed into the bay. Just like every now and then I spill a little diesel fuel. Accidents happen."

"But Ariel wasn't talking about accidents, was she? She was afraid it was something larger, something deliberate."

"She didn't have any proof," Bobby repeated stubbornly. "All she had was this wild idea. I told her she couldn't put a guy out of business on suspicions."

"Where did she get those suspicions?"

"I took her out on the boat," Bobby said. "Last August. It was the night before she saw those sea lions. We saw a cabin cruiser. The *Marvella B.* It was off Point Pinos. I was busy in the wheelhouse but Ariel said she saw Lacy Beckman on the cruiser. I didn't think anything about it, but later, when Maggie was here for the weekend, Karl showed us around the yard. Lacy was there, and Ariel asked her about the *Marvella B.* Lacy said the yard just finished some woodworking on the interior and the night Ariel saw her she was taking it back to the owner in Santa Cruz. I didn't think anything about it. Then Ariel started asking Karl all sorts of questions about paint, solvents, and chemicals."

"Somehow Ariel connected that boat with what happened to the sea lions," I said. "And since the boat was at the yard . . ."

"I don't see the connection," Bobby said.

"She must have had more specific evidence. What was it?"

"She wouldn't say. Like she didn't trust me not to go spill my guts to Karl."

"You and Karl are pretty tight, despite the difference in your ages. And you're dead set against anything bad about him. Maybe that's why she was reluctant to give you the details. But she agreed to let you give him a heads up."

Now Bobby nodded. "Twenty-four hours, that's all I wanted, to confront him. I told her after that she could call anybody she wanted and report whatever evidence she had. I just wanted to talk to him, to watch his face to see if it was true. I owe him that much."

"But you never found him that weekend." I heard a splash nearby and caught a glimpse of two eyes reflected in the overhead light as a sea lion slipped by. "Did you ever discuss Ariel's accusations with Karl?"

"Yes. Monday. The day Ariel was reported missing. He said it was crazy, nonsense. I didn't pursue it any further. Ariel was missing. I couldn't think of anything else." Bobby sighed and leaned over the railing, staring down at the dark water.

I didn't say anything. Instead, I recalled my conversation with Karl Beckman on Sunday afternoon at Café Marie, before we'd been interrupted by the stink bomb. Not only had the boatyard owner refused to tell me where he was the weekend Ariel Logan disappeared, he also denied knowing why Bobby wanted to talk with him. Beckman was lying to me. I wanted to know why.

CHAPTER 31

I DETOURED PAST BECKMAN BOAT WORKS, CLOSED FOR THE night, though I saw a light on in the upstairs office. A small light-colored pickup truck with a logo on the driver's-side door was parked near the door. As I watched from my vantage point at the curb, the upstairs light went off. A moment later Lacy Beckman came through the door, locked it behind her, and got into the truck.

Catching up on paperwork? That's what Lacy told me she was doing that Friday afternoon when Bobby came looking for Karl. That seemed to give her an alibi for the time Ariel was seen near a Beckman truck. But had anyone seen Lacy up in the office?

I followed her as she drove down Foam Street and entered the parking lot of a grocery store. After twenty minutes inside, she returned to the truck, carrying a brown paper sack, which she deposited in the bed of the pickup. I kept several car lengths behind her as she took David Avenue up the New Monterey hill that overlooked the bay, turning left onto Pine Street. Midway along the block she parked on the curb in front of a house with an overgrown garden and no lights. As I passed her, she was still behind the wheel of the pickup and I couldn't tell whether she knew someone had been following her. I circled the block, but by the time I returned, Lacy was nowhere in sight. There were still no lights on in the house but I saw now that it had a small cottage in the back, light streaming through a front window.

I headed for downtown to Café Marie, intending to give

Mother an update on Bobby's release from jail. It was seven-thirty on a Friday night in Monterey and the restaurant should have been packed with diners and people waiting at the bar for a table, buzzing with conversation, and with the clink of tableware against plates. Instead it was half-empty and too quiet. I felt as though I'd walked into a chapel.

I spotted Rachel Donahoe escorting two people through too many empty tables, seating them near the window, at the table where the Beckmans and the Gradys had been last Saturday night. I walked up to the bar, where Evan looked glum and not busy enough. He perked up when he saw me, a potential customer. "You want something to drink?"

I shook my head, leaning my elbows on the bar. "Not right now. I'm looking for Mother." I peered past him at the kitchen, where Julian reigned in his white coat and toque, barking orders at one of the cooks. "Business is way down."

"Is this pathetic or what?" Evan swept the dining room with a glance. "Friday night we should be hopping, with locals and people in town for the weekend. We'd better get some customers in here or we're in deep trouble."

I glanced at Rachel's reservation book and saw a lot of gaps. Then I poked my head into the office but Mother wasn't there, so I walked back to the kitchen. I stopped at the counter where the servers picked up their orders, watching Julian work. He must have sensed my eyes on him. He looked up, saw me, and frowned.

"Where's Mother?" I asked him.

"She had a splitting headache. I told her to go home, take some drugs, and lie down. It isn't as though we're overwhelmed with customers."

That must have been some headache for Mother to leave the restaurant on a Friday. I jerked my head in the direction of the semideserted dining room. "Has it been like this ever since you re-opened?"

Julian's mouth thinned into a hard line and he gave me a curt nod. I stepped back as one of the cooks placed two entrées on the counter and the server came to collect them.

My mother's Honda was parked in the driveway of her house. Behind it was a small pickup. I left my Toyota along the curb and walked up to the truck. A Chevy, light blue, with the now familiar logo of a sailboat and lettering in dark blue.

So much for following Julian's advice, I thought as I went up the steps and opened the door. In the living room, Mother and Karl Beckman sat close together at one end of the sofa. His left arm was draped around her shoulders, his hand toying with a strand of her hair. His right hand held hers. I tried to keep my face blank but something of what I felt at seeing them in this intimate pose must have been abundantly clear. Mother dropped Karl's hand and he straightened, although he didn't removed his arm from her shoulders. He gave me a big smile instead.

"Bobby's out of jail," Mother said, reaching for the mug of peppermint tea on the coffee table. "The district attorney decided not to charge him."

"I know. I've been down at the wharf, talking with him." I paced restlessly in the small living room. "I went by the restaurant. Julian said you'd gone home."

Mother nodded over the rim of her mug. "I had a terrible headache. But it's better now." She set her tea back on the coffee table and pressed her hands against her temples. "I've been so worried. Business has been slow, since what happened Sunday was on the front page of the *Herald* Monday morning."

"Don't fret about that, Marie," Karl said, taking her hand again. "Once all the hoopla dies down, things will be back to normal."

So far I hadn't acknowledged Karl Beckman's presence, but that was about to change. As long as he was here, I intended to get some answers, to the questions he'd avoided on Sunday, as well as some new ones.

I fixed him with an unwavering gaze. "Mr. Beckman, on Sunday afternoon I asked you whether you knew why Bobby wanted to talk to you about the weekend Ariel Logan was killed. You said you didn't. But you do know why. You and Bobby talked about it Monday, the same day Ariel Logan was reported missing."

"What are you saying?" The thick blond eyebrows above Karl Beckman's hazel eyes came down as he frowned. I watched his face and detected a slight flush.

"I'm saying you lied to me. Why?"

"Jeri!" My mother's voice cut across the tension that linked me and Karl but did nothing to dissipate it.

"I thought there was no point in mentioning it." His voice was even. "It was so ludicrous I didn't give it much credence."

"Ludicrous," I repeated. "Those are some serious allegations. Bobby said you denied it."

"Denied what?" Mother demanded. Now she sat on the edge of the sofa as she looked from Karl Beckman to me, dismay and concern vying for primacy on her face.

"Toxic chemicals in Monterey Bay," I said, "and how they got there."

Karl's face reddened and his jaw tightened. He removed his arm from Mother's shoulders and leaned forward, staring right at me. "Absolutely absurd. And unfounded. My operation is in full compliance with environmental regulations. I wondered why Ariel was asking so many questions about the boatyard. At the time I just thought she was curious, interested. When Bobby told me she claimed to have some kind of evidence, I was flabbergasted. Where on earth could she get such an idea?"

"Did you ask her? When was the last time you saw Ariel Logan, Mr. Beckman?"

Now Karl's face became suffused with red, while most of the color drained from Mother's face. "What the hell kind of question is that?" Karl demanded, getting to his feet. Mother stood up, too, her hand on his arm.

"A fairly basic one. When did you last see Ariel Logan?"

"I hadn't seen her," he said, biting off the words as he stepped around the end of the coffee table and walked toward me. "Not since she went down to Cal Poly in the middle of September. I certainly didn't see her the weekend she was killed."

"You claim you were on a business trip but you won't say where you were." I put my hands on my hips and narrowed my eyes. "Ariel Logan was seen talking to someone that Friday afternoon, after she left Bobby, someone driving a pickup truck with a Beckman Boat Works logo. I've only seen two people driving those trucks. You're one of them."

Karl stared at me as though I'd taken leave of my senses. Then he shook his head.

"This is unbelievable. This is crazy. I don't have to put up with this inquisition." He turned and strode angrily toward the front door, yanking it open. "You were right about her, Marie."

His parting shot was a curious remark but I didn't give it more than a passing thought. I didn't have time to. As soon as Karl was out the door my mother whirled. She was scowling at me and her brown eyes glowed with outrage.

"What the hell is the matter with you?" she snapped, hands on her hips as she fired words at me. "Karl didn't have anything to do with Ariel Logan's murder."

"How can you be so sure?" I shot back. "I have reason to believe Ariel suspected him of something illegal. That makes him a suspect as far as I'm concerned."

Mother shook her head emphatically. "Don't be ridiculous. Karl wasn't even in town."

"How do you know that?"

"He told me he went to King City."

"And you believe him?"

"Why shouldn't I?" Mother threw up her hands in exasperation. "Good God, Jeri, I think you've been playing Sam Spade for too many years. Sometimes you take this detective stuff too far. You always act as though people are guilty of something. Everyone's a suspect to you."

Her disparaging tone grated on me. It always did, when she acted as though "the detective stuff" was a phase I was going through. That hadn't stopped her from asking me to look into the sabotage at her damned restaurant, I thought resentfully.

"I'm suspicious when people behave as though they have something to hide," I said, trying with an effort to keep my voice even. "Karl Beckman lied to me on Sunday, about something that's very important. What makes you think he's telling the truth now? You're awfully quick to defend him. How well do you really know him, aside from the fact that you've been dating him since New Year's Eve?"

"We grew up together." Mother dismissed my question with an irritated gesture. "I've known him all my life."

"Have you really?" I shook my head and walked a few steps

toward the dining room. Could she be so infatuated with this man that she was blind to a few facts?

"You left Monterey to go to college at Mills when you were eighteen. Karl wasn't even a teenager. The man's ten years younger than you are." Her lips compressed and I knew I was not the first person to point out the disparity in their ages. "How well did you know him then? You and Dad got married not long after you graduated. You lived in the Bay Area for over thirty years and only came to Monterey on visits until you divorced Dad six years ago. By the time you came back here to open your restaurant, Karl Beckman had a wife and daughter. You know very little about him."

Mother narrowed her eyes and her mouth twisted in a bitter smile. "This is about the divorce, isn't it? It's always been about the divorce."

Now it was my turn to put my hands on my hips and fire a salvo. "Well, I must admit I was somewhat shocked that you'd walk out on Dad after thirty-plus years of marriage."

"You blame me," she said. Anger mixed with resignation colored her voice. "You always have. Since you've been married and divorced yourself I should think you'd realize there was more to it than my leaving."

That hit home. I wasn't comfortable with my own failed marriage. It hadn't lasted very long and it had left a bitter taste in my mouth when it came to relationships with men. I would always wonder if I'd tried hard enough.

"Your father and I grew apart." Mother's voice sounded as though she were tired of explaining, tired of being required to explain. "He has his interests and I have mine."

"Oh, yes. The restaurant. Always the restaurant."

"Why is my restaurant less important than his historical research and his collection of Indian pottery? Or your desire to play Nancy Drew? I always thought you of all people would understand, be supportive of my need to finally do what I spent my whole life wanting to do."

"Did you have to do it at Dad's expense? At mine, and Brian's?"

"You and your brother were adults when I left, with your own lives. You were with Sid, your brother was married with children of his own. And your father has his dear friend and colleague Isabel Kovaleski. There was always more to that friendship than a mutual interest in history and Cal State Hayward politics, even when Tim and I were married. But you conveniently ignore that. You've been cold and rude to Karl ever since you got to Monterey. Don't think I don't know why. Your double standard grates, Jeri. Why is it okay for Tim to have a relationship but not Marie?"

She had a point, a good one, but I couldn't answer that question. I felt my own anger and resentment prickling behind my skull and I wanted to hurt her as she was hurting me. We'd been doing this to each other for years, usually with cold politeness, but I was too tired to stop.

"I thought you were married to your business." I said the words with a sneer.

She called me on it and we were back to the start of the argument. "And you're not? You can't stop being a detective, not even for a minute. People aren't people, they're suspects. You can't stop poking and prying and tearing off strips of skin."

"Ariel Logan was murdered." I said the words slowly, coldly, trying to get her to look at the seriousness of the situation. "That's more important than your friend's wounded feelings. And I should think you'd want to know whether Karl's involved."

"He's not involved," she shouted at me. "Just leave it alone." She stopped, as though taken aback by the loudness of her voice. "I don't know why I bother talking to you. God knows I've never been able to dictate to you. What gives you the right to tell me how to run my life?"

"Your life affects other people."

"And yours doesn't? I couldn't sleep nights when you got beat up."

"But you weren't there at the hospital."

Until I said it I didn't realize how much I'd resented her absence after the incident several years ago when I'd been pistol whipped by a couple of thugs. "Dad was. He was there every time I woke up. But you couldn't be bothered. You couldn't get away from your precious damn restaurant."

She wrapped her arms around herself and stared at me as

though she didn't know where I'd come from. "Yes, it is precious, something I gave birth to, like you and Brian. At least I can control and guide it. It needs me. You've gone your own way. You haven't needed me since you left grade school."

Suddenly neither of us had anything else to say. We glared at each other across a gulf of words that we couldn't take back and I felt drained of feeling and energy. I stalked past her, back to the second bedroom, where I grabbed my things from the bed and shoved them into my overnight bag. When I returned to the living room my mother was still standing where I'd left her.

I slammed the front door on my way out.

I T TOOK ME A MOMENT TO FIGURE OUT WHERE I WAS.
When I opened my eyes I saw wallpaper, a floral print in
blue and yellow. I lay on my right side on a single bed in a small
bedroom I didn't recognize. I shifted onto my back, yawning, and
tried to get my bearings. Sunlight streamed through pale yellow
curtains on the window near the foot of the bed. I glanced to the
left and saw the clothes I'd been wearing, tossed over the back of a
chair. My overnight bag and shoes were on the floor.

Errol's house. I remembered now. I was in the guest room at
the Sevilles' place in Carmel. I stretched my arms above my head
and let them fall onto the pale blue comforter that covered the
lower half of my body. The enticing smell of coffee wafted in from
the kitchen.

What time was it? Where was my watch? There it was, on the
chair seat. I could see the strap but not the dial. Better get up, I
told myself. But when I tried to move my feet toward the edge of
the bed I discovered that they were blocked by something heavy
and inert. I propped myself up on my elbows and looked for the
source of this impediment.

Stinkpot had joined me sometime during the night. Despite his
antipathy for anyone who wasn't Errol or Minna, I shouldn't be
surprised to see the big tomcat staking out a spot on the bed. After
all, it was his house. He figured he could sleep anywhere he damn
well pleased. Now he sprawled along the ridge formed by my legs,
his head pillowed on my feet. His long plumed tail stretched near

my hand. It twitched slightly, indicating he was awake. I wiggled my toes and tickled the end of the tail, which jerked away from my fingers and began slashing back and forth. Another wiggle of my feet, and he seized them with his forepaws, claws poking through the comforter to flesh beneath.

"Ouch! You ornery damn cat." I sat up and so did he, purring loudly, yellow eyes smug in his pugnacious wedge of a face. He stretched, yawned in my face, then jumped off the bed and sauntered out of the guest room.

I got out of bed and took a shower in the adjoining bathroom. When I was dressed I padded barefoot out to the kitchen, where Minna was emptying the dishwasher. The French doors leading to the patio were open and morning sun splashed on the flagstone patio.

"Good morning," I said.

"You look like you need lots of coffee." Minna took a large blue ceramic mug from the top of the dishwasher rack and filled it to the brim.

"I do. Thanks." I sipped the strong black brew and felt my synapses kick in. "Where's Errol?"

"He walked over to Katy's for breakfast." Katy's was a Carmel restaurant where Errol could linger over breakfast and get the day's news, the sort that never appears in the *Monterey Herald* or the *Carmel Pine Cone.* "Are you hungry? I've got cereal, or I can scramble some eggs."

I looked at her over the rim of the mug. "Oh, Minna, you don't have to wait on me."

"You're a guest," she said. She finished unloading the dishwasher and closed it. Stinkpot, who had gone outside to terrorize birds and small bugs, thundered across the patio, through the open doors, and into the kitchen, launching himself at Minna. She caught the big tomcat in her arms and hugged him tightly. "There's my boy. Isn't he a love?"

Depends on who's doing the loving. Every time I came near Stinkpot he either growled or took a swipe at me with his paws. But now he allowed Minna to hold him like a baby. His head rested blissfully on her shoulder and those lethal paws kneaded her arm gently as he purred like an engine.

"Why do you call him Stinkpot?" I asked, sipping the restorative coffee. I'd always been certain there was a connection between this moniker and the cat's disposition.

"It was Inkspot, because of his color. But Errol started calling him Stinkpot and it stuck." Minna laughed and shifted the enormous bulk of black-and-white fur in her arms. "He was eight weeks old and no bigger than a powder puff. I could hold him in the palm of one hand. As you can see, those days are long gone."

She released the cat. He thudded to the floor and strolled majestically toward the living room, his tail straight up like a flagpole. Minna topped off her own coffee mug and joined me at the kitchen table. "You want to talk about it?"

I remembered now, the argument with Mother. After stalking out of the house on Friday night, I'd headed for Pacific Grove, but Donna and Kay weren't home. I had a solitary dinner and contemplated checking into a motel. Instead I drove to Carmel, showing up at the Sevilles' doorstep with my overnight bag in hand. Minna had already gone to bed but Errol had opened the door, finger stuck in the book he'd been reading to mark his spot. When he saw me, he didn't ask for any explanation, but instead ushered me into the second bedroom.

"I had a fight with my mother," I said finally. "A nasty one."

I'd been working as an investigator for the Seville Agency when my parents went through their divorce, and Errol and Minna were well aware of the history of bad feelings between me and my mother. I told Minna what happened the night before, boiling it down to as few words as possible.

Finally I sighed. "Minna, I'm tired of this. I'm tired of living out of a suitcase and wondering how things are at home. I'm past ready to go home and sleep in my own bed, with my own cat. But I can't do that. I've started this thing and I'm going to finish it."

She smiled. "Have a bowl of cereal before you do. You need to keep your strength up." Then her lined face turned serious as she pushed a strand of silver-gray hair out of her eyes. "Jeri, what happens between you and your mother is none of my business."

"I guess it is if I'm sleeping in your extra bedroom." I looked at her, my hands wrapped around the mug.

"Nevertheless, I'm going to put in my two cents' worth. You

can tell me to butt out if you choose. You've always been closer to your father, ever since you were a child, and you and your mother have never seen eye to eye. That happens quite frequently between mothers and daughters."

Minna smiled again, the curve of her mouth tinged with something that made me wonder about the relationship between Errol and Minna and their children. The Sevilles had a son and daughter, both married and older than me. I'd met them occasionally when I was working for Errol and the Sevilles lived in Oakland. Those children, and their offspring, were more familiar to me through the framed photographs visible on various pieces of furniture.

"Your parents' divorce just exacerbated things," Minna continued. "You resent your mother's role in the breakup. This situation with Karl Beckman seems to be on several levels. Admittedly, he's being closemouthed about where he was the weekend Ariel was killed. That's a legitimate subject for investigation. But I think what really bothers you is that he's dating your mother."

Of course that was the reason. And I knew it. Karl Beckman was a nice enough person. If I'd met him under different circumstances I might have liked him. But I hadn't liked the idea of him since Donna told me my mother was dating someone. When I saw them together last night, seated on the sofa, Karl with his arm around Mother, it was obvious that their relationship had moved beyond dating. If I admitted it, grudgingly, I just didn't like the thought of my mother in bed with Karl Beckman.

I sighed over my coffee. It's certainly unreasonable for people of my generation to think that our parents don't have sex, that once past a certain age all those feelings and desires and needs disappear. I knew that Dad's relationship with Dr. Isabel Kovaleski, his colleague in the history department at Cal State Hayward, was more than just professional association and friendship. If it was okay for Dad, why wasn't it okay for Mother? When Mother fired that shot last night, she'd been right on target.

And so was Minna. I didn't have to tell her that. She knew. I'd always felt comfortable with Minna but never with my mother. Even when I was a kid and we lived in the Victorian house in Alameda, it was as though Mother and I were two strangers in the same house. I was closer to Dad and my nearby grandmother. Last night Mother said I hadn't needed her since I'd left grade school. It was true. I'd gone my own way, just as she had.

We don't have any common ground, I told myself. But that wasn't true either. My father once said Mother and I were too much alike. That was why we never got along. We'd probably never find any common ground, unless both of us made an effort.

"Enough talk," Minna said, as though she'd heard my interior dialogue. "Eat some breakfast. Errol will be back soon and the two of you will want to lay out the day's investigation."

"I wasn't supposed to let him get embroiled in this investigation," I said, mindful of Errol's age and heart condition.

"As though either of us could stop him." Minna's amused tone spoke of knowledge gained during more than forty years of marriage. "Retirement hasn't been easy for Errol. He loved being a private investigator and he was very good at it. He's thrilled to be in the thick of things again."

I was seated at the kitchen table eating a bowl of granola when Errol returned from his breakfast jaunt to downtown Carmel. He had the morning edition of the *Monterey Herald* tucked under one arm and a cat-that-ate-the-canary expression on his narrow face. He poured himself a mug of coffee and joined me.

"There is much speculation among the regulars at Katy's about why the district attorney refused to file charges against Bobby for the murder of Ariel Logan."

"How about because he didn't do it?" I retorted, swallowing a mouthful of cereal.

"Ah, but conventional wisdom says he did. Spurned lover and so forth."

I added more granola to the milk left in the bottom of my bowl. "Several people in Bobby's AA group came forward. He was at a meeting that night, between seven and nine."

Errol nodded. "That's what I heard. But my friend the Carmel police chief told me the reason Sergeant Magruder arrested Bobby is that he had a description of the T-bird as well as a partial plate number. Which means Magruder's witness was mistaken, or —"

"The T-bird *was* at the restaurant," I finished. "I asked Bobby about that last night. He says when he was drinking, he wasn't particular about who borrowed the car. Could be someone had an extra set of keys made."

"My thought exactly," Errol said. "But who?"

"Any one of those guys who work with him on the boat, including a man named Frank Alviso. Bobby fired him a while back and he looks like the type to hold a grudge. Alviso now works for Beckman Boat Works. That's where I encountered him. He's a shifty-eyed customer if I ever saw one."

"So either Karl or Lacy has access to Alviso." Errol got up and reached for the coffee carafe, refilling both our mugs. "You still think Karl has something to do with Ariel's death?"

"I don't know what to think." I leaned back and sipped the hot black brew. "According to Bobby, Ariel made some accusations involving toxics in the bay, implying that Beckman Boat Works was responsible. That's what she and Bobby were talking about at the Rose and Crown." I told Errol what Bobby had said yesterday at the wharf, about the boat called the *Marvella B*, the subsequent tour of the boatyard, and Ariel's pointed questions about chemicals.

"So Bobby went looking for Karl," Errol said as he settled back in his chair, "to get his side of the story."

"Right. Ariel gave him twenty-four hours to talk with Karl. But Bobby couldn't find Karl, not until Monday. At first Karl told me he didn't know why Bobby wanted to talk with him. But that's not true. Bobby told him. Karl denied Ariel's claims, first to Bobby, then to me last night, when I confronted him."

"So you backed him into a corner."

"Yes. And he was royally pissed, not only at me but at the idea that someone thinks he's polluting the bay. Of course, that could be an act, if he's covering his tracks." I stopped, shaking my head. "Something doesn't make sense. Donna told me last week, before Ariel's body was found, the cops had been getting anonymous calls implicating Bobby in her disappearance. Why would Karl do that to Bobby?"

I described what happened in King City back in April, when Bobby was arrested for drunk driving in King City. Karl Beckman not only called in some markers to get my cousin out of jail, but he had also given Bobby the push that finally got Bobby off the booze.

"If Karl cares enough about Bobby to rescue him in April, it doesn't make sense for him to kill Ariel and blame Bobby."

"It doesn't have to make sense," Errol pointed out. "There's nothing logical about murder or the emotions that lead to it. If Karl killed Ariel, he's more interested in saving his own neck."

"The pieces don't quite fit." I finished the granola, got up, and rinsed the bowl in the sink before putting it in the dishwasher.

"You just have to keep working with them until they do. Or you find another piece." Errol paused, then asked, "Is there anything else I need to know about what transpired last night?"

I smiled at his delicacy. "Minna will fill you in. Did your investigator friend in L.A. call with any information on Peter Logan?"

"Not yet. I'll phone him this morning. What are your plans this fine October Saturday? Are you going to lean on Frank Alviso?"

I reached for my coffee mug. "Eventually. But first I think I'll drive to King City."

CHAPTER 33

I LEFT CARMEL JUST AFTER ELEVEN AND COVERED THE DIS-
tance between the coast and Salinas in half an hour. In south
Salinas I drove through block after block of agricultural packing
warehouses until I reached U.S. 101, where I headed south for the
second time this week.

The highway cut down the broad flat middle of the valley, past
brown freshly turned earth contrasting with fields in varying
shades of green. The Salinas River meandered to my right, then
my left after I crossed it at Soledad. The dun-colored hills on both
sides of the highway were dotted with dark green trees.

An hour later I crossed the river again and took Broadway into
King City. Rows of buses waited in the parking lot of the big high
school for students who would be hauled in from outlying farms
and ranches on Monday. Today was a sunny Saturday in October
and downtown was busy.

I parked outside the post office and sought the nearest pay
phone. A tattered directory showed a listing for Charles Harper,
no address. I dropped some coins into the slot. The woman who
answered the phone identified herself as Mrs. Harper.

"May I speak to your husband?"

Her next words reminded me that Harper was a county commissioner. "Charlie went to town about an hour ago. Had a lunch
meeting with the mayor at Keefer's."

I headed for Canal Street. Keefer's is a restaurant—gas station—
motel on the west side of the highway, the kind of "easy-off, easy-

on" place that's popular with motorists who drive through King City rather than to it. The food's good, the service friendly, and during lunch the place was hopping. I asked a waitress to point out Harper.

"That's him, back there with the mayor. They're just getting ready to leave." One of the men she indicated was short and round-faced, wearing a suit. I pegged him for the mayor. The other man towered over him, rangy and broad-shouldered, face burned brown by the sun, his thinning hair sandy fading into gray. He wore boots, faded jeans, and a blue work shirt open at the collar. He looked the part of a rancher. In the Salinas valley that could mean he grew anything from cattle to tomatoes.

Harper covered the check with several bills. Before the two men left the table I intercepted them. "Mr. Harper? May I speak to you? Alone."

He had sharp eyes, as blue as the October sky. They narrowed as he looked me over. Then he nodded and told the other man, "I'll be in touch, Bill." When the mayor had departed, Harper smiled. "What can I do for you, young lady?"

I handed him one of my business cards. "I'm a private investigator out of Oakland, working on a case in Monterey. I'd like to ask you a few questions about your brother-in-law, Karl Beckman."

Charlie Harper's blue eyes turned wintery and several emotions wrestled across his face, so quickly I couldn't categorize them. When he spoke, his voice was no longer friendly, but harsh and abrupt.

"What's this all about?"

"It's about murder," I said, watching his face for a reaction. "The murder of a young woman named Ariel Logan."

Harper didn't say anything right away, and when he did, his eyes narrowed and his mouth curved down in a frown. "That body in the ocean, down off Rocky Point. I read about that in the papers. Everyone seems to think the boyfriend did it. But they cut him loose yesterday. Why do you want to talk about Karl? You think he had something to do with Ariel Logan's death?"

"Now, why would you leap to that conclusion?" I asked, but I thought I already knew the answer. It appeared that Charles Harper had a very large ax to grind with his brother-in-law.

When Harper didn't answer I plunged ahead. "I understand Karl Beckman came to visit you the weekend Ariel Logan died." I waited for some sort of confirmation and Harper gave it to me, a brief, almost undetectable nod. "I'd like to know what that visit was about, Mr. Harper."

He thought about it for a moment, then motioned me to the table he and the mayor had just vacated. By now it had been cleared and new settings were in place. As soon as we were seated another waitress appeared with water and a pot of coffee.

"What did Karl want?" I asked Harper, taking a sip of strong black coffee.

"Money." He snorted. "The damn fool. I'm not throwing good money after bad. If he can't keep that boatyard afloat on his own, he'll just have to let it sink. Besides, I pulled his chestnuts out of the fire before, when that no-account brother of his was still alive."

"When Gunter borrowed money against the assets of Beckman Boat Works."

"You've been digging around." Harper picked up his mug and swallowed a mouthful of coffee. "Why? Did somebody hire you?"

"Ariel's boyfriend, Bobby Ravella, is my cousin. I don't think he killed her and I'd like to find out who did."

"Ravella. That explains it."

I waited for Harper to explain these words he'd muttered, half to himself. He didn't offer any immediate enlightenment. I recalled what Bobby told me about his arrest in King City last April. Karl must have turned to his brother-in-law to keep Bobby out of jail, despite the fact that Harper didn't care much for Karl.

"Why did you loan Karl money two years ago?" I asked him.

"Because of Janine. She asked me to help him out. So I did." Harper's face darkened. "Of course, that was before we found out he was stepping out on her with his sister-in-law."

Somehow I'd known that, ever since I saw the look in Karl Beckman's eyes when I mentioned Lacy. Was it over between them? Did my mother know about it?

"Is that when Janine changed her will?"

"You *have* been busy." Harper sipped his coffee.

"How did Janine find out about Karl and Lacy?"

Harper flushed again. "Something I said. Purely by accident. I saw Karl and Lacy together in Carmel, a couple of months after I loaned Karl the money. I didn't even think anything about it. But when I mentioned it to Janine, she flew off the handle. Said Karl had lied to her about where he was that day. She'd suspected for some time he had a thing going on with Lacy. Who I hear is not particular about who she sleeps with. Neither was Gunter, for that matter."

He sighed and sipped his coffee. "Janine was thinking about divorcing Karl, but she wasn't sure how Kristen would take it. Kristen's real close to her dad. So she changed her will instead. Cut Karl out completely."

"How did Karl take that news?"

"He was mighty peeved, as I recall. But he didn't find out till after Janine died. As far as I could see, he seemed to be more concerned about the estate than he was about the way his wife died." Harper's face flushed under his tan. "I can't prove a thing, but damn it, Karl Beckman's responsible for my sister's death."

This underscored all those questions I'd had since I'd learned the details of the car accident that claimed the lives of Janine and Gunter Beckman. And since Karl Beckman was dating my mother, it also underscored several other disquieting feelings I had about the man.

"Why would Karl kill his wife?" I asked bluntly.

"Money," Harper said. "He'd have inherited most of Janine's estate if she hadn't changed her will. And it was a lot of money. Came to us both when our folks died."

"How do you know about the terms of the earlier will?"

"I was executor for both wills," Harper said. "I got a copy of the first one back at the house. I'll let you take a look at it."

I nodded. "Thanks. What motive would Karl have for killing Gunter?"

"Hell, I don't know. Gunter was irritating enough to make someone want to kill him. I know Karl was pretty damn ticked off at Gunter for borrowing that money against the boatyard's assets, and having to ask me for money to bail him out. Karl was sleeping with Lacy, maybe they were in it together. Hell, I don't know."

Harper balled his right fist and smashed it into his left palm, a gesture of frustration. "My wife says I'm crazy to go on about it like this. It's just a gut feeling. I can't prove a thing. But there's something odd about my sister's death. Why would she and Gunter be having dinner at Ventana? Unless it was to talk about Karl and Lacy. You know, the rescue team never could bring up what was left of Gunter's BMW. I'd be willing to bet someone tampered with the car."

"Does Karl know you suspect him of being involved in Janine's death?"

"I haven't told him," Harper said. "Not in so many words. But he knows I don't have any use for him."

"Then why would he drive down here a week ago Saturday to ask you for money?"

"Because he's desperate. He's been to bankers in Monterey and Salinas and they've all turned him down. Hell, he just paid off the last loan, back in April. He had another year to go on the payments, but he paid it off early, in return for a favor. Don't know where he got that money, but it was important to him."

"What was the favor?"

Harper shook his head. "I'm not supposed to say. That was part of the deal."

"You don't have to. Bobby told me he got arrested here in King City last April. He called Karl and Karl kept him out of jail. Why would you pull those kinds of strings for Karl, feeling the way you do about him?"

"Ranchers have cash-flow problems, same as anyone else," Harper said. "And I had a cash-flow problem last April. Karl had been paying back the loan regular, every month. At first I said I couldn't do anything for the boy. But Karl offered to pay me the whole balance owing if I'd help his friend. So I said yes."

"How much?" He told me and I whistled. It was a large sum to pull together on short notice. "If Beckman Boat Works is in trouble, where did Karl get that kind of money?"

"I didn't ask. I thought maybe he'd turned the business around. Or he got it from someone else. Something else occurred to me, after he showed up here a week ago, asking for more. Kristen's college money. He and Janine had set aside quite a bit for her education. Then Kristen got a scholarship to Stanford. So that money is sitting in a bank somewhere, drawing interest. I don't know where, or how he'd get to it, but that's something to look at."

I agreed. "When did Karl come to see you?"

"Saturday," Harper said. "When did Ariel Logan die?"

"The last time anyone saw her alive was Friday evening, about seven-thirty or eight. She could have been killed anytime after that."

"Karl got to the ranch a little before noon on Saturday," Harper said. "He didn't call or anything, just showed up as we were sitting down to eat lunch. My wife put another plate on the table. After we ate, he hit me up for a loan. That's when I told him I wasn't throwing good money after bad, no matter how deep a hole he'd dug himself. He left about one-thirty, quarter to two. Don't know if that helps you. I've got no idea where he was before he drove down here. But why would he kill Ariel Logan?"

"She may have had some information that would have closed down the boatyard."

"From the way he described it, business was so bad the boatyard was already sinking. I figured he was exaggerating. What if he did take Kristen's college money, and he needed to replace it?"

The waitress freshened our coffee, and I reflected on the contradictory pictures of Karl Beckman I had received. Karl had bought Bobby out of jail last April. He had money then. Where had it come from and why did he need more now?

Karl supposedly viewed Bobby as the son he'd never had, yet if Karl had killed Ariel he was willing to let Bobby take the blame. Errol said a man who killed was interested only in saving his neck. Desperate, I thought, repeating the word Harper had used to describe Karl's attempt to borrow more cash. Desperation might spur a man to do many things, including commit murder.

CHAPTER 34

I FOLLOWED HARPER BACK TO HIS RANCH SOUTHEAST OF King City, where he unearthed his sister's earlier will from a filing cabinet in his office. The yellowed paper was over ten years old, a fairly standard document in which Janine left everything to Karl except her interest in the Harper ranch. If Karl had died first, the estate went to Kristen, with Charles Harper named as the girl's guardian.

It was late afternoon when I returned to Carmel. Errol had given me a key since I now ranked as a houseguest. I found him on the patio, a detective novel in his lap and a glass of wine on the table next to him. When I came through the French doors from the kitchen, he glanced up and flashed his foxy grin. His eyes glittered and I recognized a certain look in his eyes, one I'd seen frequently during the years I worked for him as an investigator.

For a moment Errol was two people. The one his wife saw, and worried about, was a silver-haired man with a lined face and age spots, a man in his seventies who'd survived two heart attacks and retired on the advice of his doctor. The other person, the one I remembered behind that knowing smile, was the skilled and shrewd detective who took me under his wing years ago and taught me how to be a private investigator. Right now his motor seemed to be revving a few cycles above what it should be. I knew what would set him buzzing like this. Information. The old private eye had a hot tip.

"Your friend in L.A. came through," I guessed.

"With some interesting information about Peter Logan's last divorce."

"I thought he'd only been married once before."

"Twice, actually. The first one was so brief it barely counts."

"Let me make a pit stop," I told him. "Then I want to hear all about it."

"Call Donna while you're at it."

I detoured to the bathroom, then picked up the phone in the kitchen and dialed Donna's number in Pacific Grove. "Your mother called me this morning," my cousin said when she answered the phone. "She wanted to know if you were staying with Kay and me, or if I knew where you were. I figured you were at the Sevilles'. What happened?"

"We had a screaming match."

"What about?"

"The usual. Hell, Donna, I don't want to go into the details now. I'll tell you about it later." Resignation colored my voice. "Mother and I just don't get along. We never have. Arguments are inevitable. I'm surprised we lasted a week without one. This is why I don't come to Monterey very often. It raises my stress level too much."

"Usually you don't have murder and sabotage to worry about," Donna pointed out. "Maybe when all of this is sorted out . . ." She didn't finish and I didn't add what I was thinking. If it turned out that Karl Beckman had killed Ariel Logan, that would solve nothing as far as my mother was concerned. She would think I'd proved it just to get back at her.

I rang off and helped myself to some wine. Then I joined Errol on the patio. Stinkpot ambled toward us from the garden, yawned, stretched, and sprawled on a couple of flagstones warmed by the sun that was preparing its daily descent into the Pacific Ocean. In the distance I heard the rush of the waves against Carmel Beach.

"Where's Minna?" I asked.

"Minna gets tired of being cooped up here with the old man." Errol grinned, setting his book on the table. "So every now and then she escapes for dinner and a movie with a friend. Being able to go off on one's own is the secret to marital longevity. I can fix us some dinner here or we can walk downtown."

"Either sounds good to me." I settled into the other chair and sipped my wine.

"If it's any consolation," Errol said, "Minna never got along with her mother either." I shot him a look over the rim of my glass. "Minna was from a rich old San Francisco family with a mansion in Pacific Heights. She went to the best schools and summered up at Lake Tahoe in a big stone pile they called a cottage. Then she went off to Bryn Mawr to major in English literature. Not that she was going to do anything with her degree. I think the plan was for her to snag some presentable scion of an equally wealthy family."

Errol punctuated this recitation with a wicked laugh. "She certainly was supposed to do far better than marry a rather rakish private investigator from Oakland. I think that's what grated on them the most, that I was from Oakland."

"Rakish, huh?" I grinned at him. "I'll bet you wore a trench coat and a fedora and had a bottle of scotch in your desk drawer."

"I always favored bourbon." His mouth curved upward. "I was somewhat of a ladies' man in those days."

Now I laughed. "I'll bet you were." I looked at him fondly. Sometimes I thought if Errol were twenty years younger . . . well, so much for idle speculation. Besides, the man adored his wife.

"When I met Minna," he was saying, "all that changed. Her father and I became friends over time. I never could win over my mother-in-law, though. She barely tolerated me, until the day she died. Anyway, mothers and daughters are an odd combination. Our own daughter—" He stopped and narrowed his eyes. "You don't want to hear this now. I'm maundering, not focusing on the business at hand."

"You tell me what your friend found out about Peter Logan," I said. "Then I'll tell you about my conversation with Charles Harper."

Errol nodded. "Logan's first marriage was very brief, to what they used to call a starlet, back in the fifties when Peter was a new arrival in Hollywood. He married again in the early sixties, to a costume designer who'd also been married before. This woman had a daughter by her first marriage. She and Peter were still married when he wrote the script for a movie starring Sylvie Romillard. They met on the set and romance blossomed."

"So Logan had an affair with Sylvie while he was still married to his second wife," I said. "Seems to me that's a common enough occurrence, in Hollywood or elsewhere."

"It was a fairly ugly divorce," Errol said, sipping his wine. "Marked by some unsavory allegations about Peter's behavior with his teenage stepdaughter. The second wife told the court he'd molested the girl, which Peter denied. At the time the girl was fourteen. At first she said he did it, then she recanted."

"So the charge was never proven. But still, it was made." I shook my head and set my glass down on the table. All of a sudden the wine didn't taste very good. "Is Peter Logan a child molester who got away with it, or the victim of his second wife's revenge?"

"No one knows, but there are many opinions, according to my friend." Errol leaned forward. "Those allegations hung over Peter's head like the sword of Damocles. If he'd been a bit more important than a middle-aged, middle-ranked screenwriter, perhaps it wouldn't have mattered. As it was, the incident was enough to make a few people turn their backs on Peter and Sylvie. According to my friend, the Logans didn't so much get burned out on Hollywood as Hollywood burned out on them. That's why Sylvie retired from acting. Her career wasn't going anywhere before she became involved with Peter. And afterward the parts simply evaporated. As for Peter, my friend says he hasn't had a screenplay produced in years."

"How do they get by financially in a place like Carmel?"

"Real estate, of course." Errol saluted Carmel and its high-priced environs with his glass. "Land is the big cash cow around here and over the years Peter acquired several properties. Rentals, commercial, and I think he may have been involved in some hotel construction with your cousin George the developer. Plus he writes a series of action-adventure thrillers. So Peter and Sylvie Logan are not hurting for money."

I frowned. Allegations of Peter Logan's sexual misconduct with his stepdaughter years ago was a potent piece of information, but where did it fit in the puzzle? Was it even part of this puzzle at all? If this story, decades old, was true, how did it fit with the man who had so obviously been grieving at his daughter's funeral? Had Peter Logan done something to his own daughter?

The picture that thought conjured up was grotesque. I'd wanted some leverage to get the Logans to let me look at Ariel's things from the apartment in San Luis Obispo and now I had it. Thing was, using this as leverage made me feel soiled. It's a good thing Minna wasn't here. She wouldn't like any of this. In addition to being worried about Errol for getting embroiled in this investigation, because of his health, she knew the Logans. She wouldn't like hearing about the skeletons in Peter Logan's closet.

"Of course it's unpleasant," Errol said, as though he'd read my mind. His expression was as serious as my thoughts.

"An investigator encounters sleaze and venality all the time, Jeri. You knew that when you came to work for me and you've certainly confronted your share of corruption since then. You're the one who says that anyone who turns over rocks for a living should be prepared for what crawls out."

Stinkpot got up and stretched, then his attention was caught by something moving at the back of the garden. He lowered his head and began stalking it, moving insidiously toward his prey.

"It still holds true," I said slowly, wondering what effect my share of corruption had on my soul. "I also think it's important to be bothered by the sleaze and venality when I encounter it. I've met too many investigators who've let their shells harden so that nothing—good or bad—can get through the protective armor."

"I hope I'm not one of them," Errol said.

I reached for his hand, still strong even if the flesh was loose and crepey and discolored by spots. "Not you, Errol. Never you."

We sat in silence. Stinkpot pounced on whatever he'd been stalking. As I watched the big cat I hoped that whatever it was would get away. I felt relieved when I saw a bird escape in flight.

"All we have here is the implication. We don't know whether there's any truth to these rumors about Peter Logan. I'm not out to prove or disprove them. I just want to examine Ariel's things." I sighed. "The man buried his daughter on Monday."

"What if he had something to do with her death?" Errol reminded me. "After all, he was seen at the Rocky Point Restaurant the same day she was killed and he's evidently lying about when he returned from Paris. He came back early. Why?"

What possible explanation could there be for Peter's early return? My mind began playing "what if" games. What if there was a connection between Peter and Karl Beckman? There could be, a tenuous one. Beckman Boat Works was in financial difficulty and the boatyard occupied some prime real estate on Monterey's Cannery Row. What if Karl Beckman was planning to sell out to some developer? While I was asking myself questions, what if Peter Logan killed his own daughter?

When I thought developer I thought of my pompous cousin George, who'd built a couple of hotels on the Row. He would know if something was in the works. In fact, if my speculation were true, he was probably in it up to his avaricious fingertips. Which meant it would take a crowbar to pry any information out of him.

"What did you find out in King City?" Errol sensed that I needed time to mull over the Logan information, so he changed the subject. "What does Charlie Harper think about his sister's death?"

"He thinks his brother-in-law had something to do with it." I gave Errol the details of my conversation with Harper. "Karl had an affair with Lacy, which is really no surprise. His face closes up every time her name is mentioned. Janine found out and changed her will. Then she and Gunter died in the car wreck."

"I wonder about Lacy," Errol said, "and her ice-maiden exterior. I've heard rumors about her sexual escapades, ever since she married Gunter. And Gunter never made any secret about his exploits, before or after the ceremony. They had what used to be called an open marriage, so much so that I'm surprised they bothered making it legal. Fidelity wasn't an issue. But it would be with Karl and Janine."

"I think it's time I took a closer look at Lacy." I finished the wine in my glass. "She's intimately involved with the business of Beckman Boat Works. Ryan Trent told me her family name was Standish, and she's from San Francisco. Ring any bells?"

Errol shook his head. "Not with me. But Minna probably knows. Her sister's still living in the Pacific Heights manse. Are you hungry? I am, and I don't feel like cooking."

"Errol, I love you, but I've sampled your cooking. Meal preparation is Minna's forte, not yours. Where shall we go?"

He grinned as he got out of his chair. "There's this pleasant little bistro at Fifth and Monte Verde."

We walked downtown. The restaurant was tucked into an out-of-the-way courtyard. Errol led the way up a path and held open the door. As we stepped into the foyer we came face-to-face with the people we'd been discussing half an hour earlier.

Peter and Sylvie Logan sat on a short bench opposite the door, their bodies close together, their hands entwined. Glennis Braemer stood at her brother's left shoulder, next to a large potted orchid. Three pairs of eyes swiveled toward us. Sylvie's eyes were brown and red-rimmed and she looked as haggard as she had at the funeral earlier in the week. She quickly turned her gaze away and I saw her hand tighten on Peter's.

Her husband glared at Errol as though he'd been betrayed by a friend. No doubt he felt that he had, although Minna Seville knew the Logans better than Errol did. Peter had asked Errol to use his investigative skills to get evidence that would prove Bobby had killed Ariel Logan, and Errol had declined. Then Errol had compounded his affront by showing up in the enemy camp at the funeral, and by asking the Logans if I could examine Ariel's things. The Logans knew I was Bobby's cousin and a private investigator who once worked for Errol. Their eyes were full of hostility.

Glennis Braemer started to say something, then thought better of it. She swept both Errol and me with a withering glare. But Peter Logan stood, his face contorted with fury, his anger directed not at me, but at Errol.

"I know what you've been doing. A friend of mine called from L.A. He said some private eye's been digging around, asking questions about me. You instigated that, didn't you? Prying around in things that are none of your business. Admit it, damn it."

Errol looked at the other man, head tilted to one side, his expression bland. Then he nodded.

"Good God, Errol." Peter's voice was laced with bitterness. "I thought we were friends. Why are you doing this?"

"I was an investigator for more than forty years," Errol said, sounding thoughtful. "I suppose I always will be. Yes, Peter, I did a background check on you. I know about the divorce, and the charges made against you at the time."

Peter Logan drew back from him, as though from a blow. Glennis Braemer narrowed her eyes and opened her mouth. But Sylvie spoke first.

"I will never think of you and Minna in the same way." Sylvie Logan's voice was low and sad. She still had a French accent, even after all her years in the United States. Her words held a tinge of regret at the irretrievable loss of friends. "Why have you done this?"

I stepped forward. "Because I need to examine Ariel's things from college."

"That's out of the question." Glennis Braemer dismissed me with a curt wave.

"Those boxes you brought up from San Luis Obispo might hold a few clues to why Ariel was killed."

"I won't have you pawing around in my daughter's belongings," Peter raged. "Your cousin murdered Ariel. Sooner or later he'll pay for it, even if the DA let him out of jail."

"Fine," I said. It was time to play the trump card. "Let's talk about your return from Paris, Mr. Logan. Everyone seems to think you and Mrs. Logan came back together on Sunday."

Peter Logan stood very still, as though rooted to the wooden floor of the restaurant foyer. I thought his face looked paler than usual. But it could have been the glow of a nearby street lamp.

"Someone saw you at the Rocky Point Restaurant Friday night, identified you from a photograph, in fact. You were there the night your daughter was killed. Do you want to tell me about that? Or should I pass this information on to Sergeant Magruder?"

CHAPTER 35

GLENNIS BRAEMER CALLED SUNDAY MORNING WHILE I lingered over coffee and breakfast with Errol and Minna. She didn't waste any words. Lunch, one o'clock, the Tuck Box on Dolores. When I agreed to meet her, she hung up without any further niceties. I didn't expect any after the ugly scene at the restaurant.

That incident left a bad taste in my mouth. Errol's, too. He'd been subdued last night when he gave Minna a report. She wasn't pleased with what he'd had to say.

Perhaps Mrs. Braemer's call meant my words to Peter Logan would have the desired result. Leverage, that was the word Errol and I had used. I wanted a chance to examine Ariel's possessions from her apartment in San Luis Obispo. Maybe I'd gained the access I needed. In doing so I'd also earned the enmity of the Logan family.

But Bobby was still in trouble, and he was part of my family. I doubted Sergeant Magruder would back off his investigation, even though the DA had declined to charge Bobby with Ariel's murder. That just meant Magruder would redouble his efforts to come up with a stronger case against my cousin. My family, I thought, picturing that large, noisy, and exasperating conglomeration of Doyles and Ravellas, those relatives I didn't visit often enough.

So it came down to family. I could only tolerate them in small groups or for a limited amount of time. But when I saw Donna, Nick and Tina, or Uncle Dom and Aunt Teresa, there was the instant recognition of shared blood and heritage, tied to this place.

In a contest between my family and someone else's I knew where my loyalties lay. Besides, I wanted to find out who killed Ariel. Had she lived, she would have joined my family.

At twelve-thirty I walked downtown, savoring the early-October sunshine that splashed through the trees as houses gave way to inns, shops, and galleries. The Tuck Box is quaint and touristy, though Minna tells me the locals like to meet there over big cups of English Breakfast tea. With its oddly shaped structure and steep-pitched roof it tries hard to be a thatched-roof cottage in the Cotswalds. Inside, the windows are curtained in red-and-pink flowered fabric. The young women waiting on tables are definitely California grown, tanned and leggy in their pink T-shirts and black shorts.

I'd eaten at the tearoom before. The food wasn't all that remarkable. But then, British cuisine, such as it is, has limits. One doesn't go to the Tuck Box for the food but for the experience.

Glennis Braemer stood near the entrance of the Tuck Box, wearing a gray raw-silk pantsuit enlivened only by a magenta scarf in the breast pocket of the jacket. He mouth was a thin line with just a hint of lipstick. The blue eyes were masked by a pair of oversized sunglasses.

She acknowledged my arrival with a curt nod and swept past a trio of girls who'd stopped to peer into the tearoom's front window. I followed her through the front door into the postage-stamp-size waiting area, which was full of people in shorts with cameras slung around their necks. We had to wait about twenty minutes for a free table. During that time she said nothing to me. She appeared to be staring resolutely ahead of her, but I couldn't tell because of the sunglasses. I amused myself by watching tourists, which Carmel always has in great supply.

Finally we were seated at a small table next to the fireplace on the other side of the tiny dining room. I found myself facing a picture of flowers on the wall. Mrs. Braemer sat next to the window that looked out at the courtyard next to the tearoom, which held several tables and a little shop where customers could purchase orange marmalade, scone mix, and the inevitable T-shirts.

Looking out the window was evidently preferable to looking at me. She removed her sunglasses, stowed them in the slim gray leather bag she carried, and occupied the next few minutes gazing at the occupants of an outside table. When the server appeared at our table she ordered scones and tea without ever glancing at the menu that lay unopened before her.

"I'll have the Welsh rarebit," I said, handing the menu to the young woman who stood at our table. "And a pot of English Breakfast." I waited until the server left. "You wanted to talk to me, Mrs. Braemer. Suppose you lead off."

She turned her head from the window and fixed me with her angry blue eyes. "Why are you harassing my brother and his wife?"

"I'm not harassing anyone."

The server returned with our tea and Glennis Braemer waited before speaking again. Instead she picked up the pot and the strainer and poured herself a full cup of dark brown tea. She raised the cup to her lips and took a mouthful. Then she set the cup in the saucer with a firm clink.

"You are a ghoul," she said, her voice a low-pitched whip. "How dare you intrude on my family's grief? They've lost their only child, for God's sake. You are prying into things that are none of your business. First you went to San Luis Obispo to talk to Maggie, then Ryan Trent. And your former employer, Mr. Seville, had the audacity to set one of his cronies rooting around in my brother's past. Private investigator—" She said this last with a sneer. "How can you lower yourself to do what you do? Invading privacy, peeking in keyholes."

"Uncovering other people's trash," I added helpfully. I'd been in the business long enough to hear all the accusations. I'd even turned over some rocks I wished I hadn't. "Everyone has something to hide. Often with good reason."

"Yes, Peter had a messy divorce." She stopped while the server set our food in front of us, looking at the plate of scones without appetite. When the young woman had departed she continued. "His ex-wife made some horrible accusations against him. Even set one of your ilk on him. But those accusations were never proved. Because he didn't do it."

"Accusations made," I said quietly, "but not proved. The same could also be said of Bobby Ravella."

Glennis Braemer didn't make the connection. Or she didn't

want to. She picked up her knife and held it as though she wanted to stab me with it. "Stop this now. Or I'll go to the authorities and swear out a complaint."

I don't take well to threats. They just spur me on. My eyes grew equally cold over the cup of hot tea that I held. I set the cup down and leaned toward Glennis Braemer.

"So I'm a ghoul. I've been called worse. You and your family are so eager to blame someone for Ariel's death that you've developed tunnel vision. You and Sylvie and Peter don't like Bobby. He's a little too rough around the edges for you, isn't he? Working class, never went to college, spends twelve, fourteen hours a day on a fishing boat. He's divorced, he used to drink too much. It's very convenient to call him a murderer."

She drew in a sharp breath. Then her mouth thinned and she glared at me.

"No, he wasn't right for Ariel. She was special. You can't imagine how special she was." I saw Mrs. Braemer's lip quiver but she fought back the emotion. "You accuse us of tunnel vision. Aren't you prey to the same malady? He's your cousin. Doesn't that blind you to the possibility that he could be a killer?"

"It could. I'll admit that." I picked up my fork and cut into the Welsh rarebit. "I feel about my family the way you feel about yours. I also believe in justice. If Bobby killed Ariel, I'll turn over that evidence to the authorities and let the chips fall. I don't know whether I can convince you of that. But it's the truth."

She didn't respond. Instead she dumped a spoonful of orange marmalade on a wedge of scone and lifted it to her mouth. "Why don't you think he killed Ariel?" she asked a moment later.

"I've been an investigator for a number of years, Mrs. Braemer. I'm good at it. I've developed some instincts, some intuition, and I've learned to trust them. There's nothing scientific about it." I poured myself another cup of tea and took a sip.

"Bobby didn't kill Ariel, but someone's going to a lot of trouble to make it look like he did. When I see someone being fitted for a frame, it makes me suspicious." She didn't say anything and I filled the silence by asking a question. "Why did your brother come back early from Paris?"

"He had nothing to do with Ariel's death." Her face looked as grim as her voice.

"I'm not saying he did." I'd toyed with the possibility, of course, after I'd heard that Peter Logan had been accused of molesting his stepdaughter so many years ago. But the same gut instinct that told me Bobby hadn't killed Ariel made me also dismiss Logan as a suspect. "But why was he at the Rocky Point Restaurant, the same night his daughter was there?"

"He was meeting someone. Someone who never showed up."

"Who? And why?"

"It has nothing to do with Ariel," she repeated. I waited and she knew I'd wait until she explained. Finally she sighed. "I'm going to tell you a little story about Hollywood. You know Peter was a screenwriter. Still is, when he can get someone to buy a script. People in Hollywood have long memories."

She brushed her hand over her face, suddenly looking tired. "Sylvie and Peter just didn't decide to move to Carmel because of the scenery. When Peter was accused of molesting his stepdaughter, he couldn't sell any scripts. Sylvie couldn't get work either. So they left town. If it weren't for the money Sylvie's father left her, they wouldn't have been able to survive. Peter made some smart real-estate investments. And he writes adventure novels."

"But not screenplays?"

"Occasionally," she said, signaling for more tea. "Sometimes he collaborates with other writers. But now he has a different problem. These days, all the movers and shakers in the industry are children barely out of the UCLA film school. They don't buy scripts from elderly people over the age of thirty. The man Peter was meeting at the restaurant was one of those Hollywood youngsters he's had to deal with recently."

Her smile was humorless. "Peter had a business arrangement with this person, one that involved his name going on Peter's script, in the hopes the script could be sold. Peter's done it before and he's not proud of it. He's embarrassed by it. Like any writer, he'd much prefer to have his name on his own work. That's the only reason he was at the restaurant. To meet someone who didn't show up."

She took a creased business card from her handbag and placed it on the table between us. "This is the other writer, his name and phone number. Maybe he can at least verify that the appointment was made, if not kept."

I took the card and looked at it, noting the address in Carmel Valley. Another Hollywood refugee, one who could probably eliminate Peter Logan as a suspect. Was Ariel's father then a witness, who might have seen something important without realizing its value?

"Did he see anything? Ariel, the car?"

Mrs. Braemer let out a sigh. "No. He's agonized about this over and over, wondering whether he could have prevented what happened. If he'd seen Ariel or who she was with, maybe we wouldn't be sitting here."

This had the ring of truth. If Logan had been nearby while his daughter was murdered and realized it later, his guilt at not being able to prevent her murder might explain his eagerness to blame Bobby, the convenient suspect he didn't like anyway.

I looked at the tea leaves floating in the bottom of my cup and wished they would provide me with all the answers I sought. "I like Ariel. I wish I'd known her. I do want to find out who killed her. To do that I need to know what she was investigating."

"What makes you think she was investigating anything?" Glennis Braemer drew her eyebrows together.

"As you pointed out, I've been to San Luis Obispo. I talked to a number of other people there, as well as Maggie Lim. Ryan Trent also provided me with a lead. We've both mentioned accusations which were made but not proved. Perhaps Ariel was about to make a few accusations of her own, and it got her killed."

"Accusations against whom?"

"It may have something to do with the environment."

"She was studying to be an environmental engineer."

"More than that," I said. "Ariel was also an environmentalist. She was active in a group called Central Coastwatch. Maggie told me Ariel used to demonstrate at the nuclear power plant at Diablo Canyon and the oil refinery."

Glennis Braemer laughed, an unexpected and pleasant sound. Her face softened.

"Oh, yes. Tankers and derricks and spills. Oil. That's how my late husband made his money. We had lively arguments when Ariel came to visit. I will miss those arguments." Her eyes turned bleak again as she turned to me. "Can you find out who killed her?"

"I've been working on it since the body was found. I have a lot of pieces of the puzzle, Mrs. Braemer, but I haven't found the pattern yet."

"You think the pieces are in Ariel's life," she said, looking at me speculatively as the server brought the check and cleared away the dishes. "The leftovers, represented by all those books and papers and computer disks I brought with me from San Luis Obispo. But the sheriff's people looked through those things and returned them. What makes you think you'll find anything they missed?"

"Maybe they didn't know what to look for. I'm not saying I do. But I have a hunch. I'd like to play it out."

"I'll talk to my brother and his wife," Glennis Braemer said. "But I can't promise anything."

CHAPTER 36

THE PHONE DIRECTORY GAVE ME AN ADDRESS FOR FRANK Alviso, one half of a down-at-the-heels duplex on Alcalde, a short street just off Fremont Street in north Monterey. I went by the place three times Sunday afternoon. There was a beat-up, rusted Ford in the driveway, but Alviso wasn't there. His neighbors in the other half of the duplex got more curious each time I knocked on the door.

When Alviso finally came home I heard him before I saw him. The rap music on his car radio vibrated the immediate neighborhood. He was driving a shiny red Pontiac Grand Am that looked as though it was not long off the lot. He pulled into the drive behind the Ford and cut the engine. When he saw me standing between him and his front door he stared at me as though he couldn't place me. Then recognition narrowed the muddy brown eyes.

"What d'you want?"

"Answers, Frank."

"Already told you I didn't see Bobby that day." He stepped past me onto the porch, keys in hand.

"Great-looking car, Frank. Looks new. How long have you had it?"

"Coupla months. What's it to you?"

"I thought maybe you were hurting for money, since Bobby fired you this summer."

Alviso cut his eyes toward me, then away. "Yeah, well, I got hired on by Beckman right away. Pay's good, regular hours. I don't need Bobby or his damned boat. I'm doing just fine without him."

"You used to be friends."

"Before he got to be Mr. High-and-Mighty," Frank snarled. "So goddamn critical he wouldn't cut a guy any slack."

"You'd like to get back at him, wouldn't you?" Alviso's eyes smoldered but he didn't respond. Not with words, anyway. "Is Lacy Beckman easier to work for?"

"Hell, yes. She appreciates a guy who can do a job. Karl, too." This last was almost an afterthought.

"You used to borrow Bobby's T-bird."

Alviso's eyes narrowed again. "So?"

"Borrow it lately?"

"Hey, I haven't talked to Bobby since he canned me."

"That's not what I asked." I looked at the key ring Alviso held. "You ever borrow the T-bird without asking Bobby first?"

"Dunno what you're talking about." Alviso threw the words from the side of his thin mouth as his eyes glanced off me. He unlocked his front door. "Dunno anything, so leave me the hell alone." He shoved open the door, eager to get away from me.

"I hear you and Derry McCall used to catch pelicans. Caught any recently?"

Alviso froze, turned his head, and looked at me. Then he stepped inside his apartment and shut the door. I walked back to my car, marveling at the way his eyes never stayed in one place very long. Bobby was well rid of this clown. Or was he rid of him at all? Frank Alviso was nursing a grudge against Bobby. I recalled the resentment that flared in Alviso's eyes when he spoke of being fired from the crew of the *Nicky II*. He was going to get even. Maybe he was already doing it.

I found a pay phone and called Minna Seville to ask if there was anything she needed in the way of groceries. She gave me a short list of items. By the time I got back to the house on San Antonio Avenue, dinner preparations were under way. I unloaded the groceries and pitched in by setting the table.

"I need to check Lacy Beckman's background," I told Minna as I opened drawers, looking for napkins. "She's a Standish from San

Francisco. You said she had all the Pacific Heights moves. Errol said you or your sister might be able to help me."

Minna didn't say anything as she basted the chicken she was roasting in the oven. I didn't know whether Errol had told her of the conversation he and I had Saturday afternoon, when he told me that Minna had bucked her family's disapproval to marry him. Then she closed the oven door, straightened, and hung the oven mitts on a hook near the stove.

"I'm never quite sure whether San Francisco's a big city or a small town. My sister's one of the Old Guard, as people call it. Her social circle is small. It consists of people who wear expensive clothing and lots of jewels to the symphony and opera openings. Then they fall asleep in the third act."

I smiled at this description and so did Minna. "The name Standish isn't familiar to me," she continued. "But I haven't lived in that world for a long time. I don't know whether Celeste can help you. I'll certainly call her."

THE FOG ROLLED IN WITH THE DAWN MONDAY MORNING. FOR THE first time this year it felt as though winter was coming. Glennis Braemer called shortly after eight with the Logans' decision.

"Peter and Sylvie have agreed to let you examine Ariel's things. But they don't want to talk to you."

I might need to talk with them, I thought. That could come later, though. At least this was a foot in the door. "I'll be right over."

I borrowed a sweater from Minna and walked the short distance from the Sevilles' home to the gray stucco house on Scenic Drive. The bloodred bougainvillea climbing the outer wall provided a beacon of color, visible through the shroud of gray fog that obscured the horizon, masking the tops of the Monterey pines and the curve of land around Carmel Bay. On my right the surf whispered across the sand of Carmel Beach, dark blue water and white froth rushing out of the fog bank. I felt the chill of the thick salty air and pulled the sweater tighter around me as I mounted the stairs and rang the bell. The huge black-and-white wreath still hung on one of the double wood doors, the white flowers looking wilted after a week.

Mrs. Braemer answered the door, looking poised as usual in her taupe slacks and a matching pullover. "Everything's in the garage," she said. She turned and led the way down shallow carpeted steps to a door opening onto a double garage.

The overhead light didn't do much to penetrate the gloom of the windowless space. On the back wall, opposite the garage doors, I saw floor-to-ceiling storage cabinets, each door labeled with a white adhesive strip and a handwritten legend I couldn't make out. The BMW and the big boxy Mercedes I'd seen before had been pulled into the stalls, leaving space on the cold concrete floor for the stack of boxes piled between its grille and the cabinets.

I counted at least eight cardboard cartons, as well as six plastic file boxes with handles, the kind you can buy in any office-supply store, each a different color. Several garment bags hung from the door handles of the cabinets. To the right of the door where Mrs. Braemer and I stood was a set of luggage, three suitcases in varying sizes, all the same shade of blue.

"You must have had your car crammed full," I commented, guessing the Mercedes was hers.

"It's a big car. I didn't think everything would fit but you'd be surprised how much that trunk will hold." She sighed, folding her arms in front of her as she stared at the pyramid.

"I thought stopping in San Luis Obispo to pick up Ariel's things would save Peter and Sylvie the chore of having to go down there. Now that the stuff is here, no one has the heart to go through it. I'm sure someone could use the clothing. But . . ." Her voice trailed away.

"As I told you yesterday, Sergeant Magruder's people looked through all of this. They didn't find anything of interest. Presumably you're looking for something they may have missed. Do you have any idea what that might be?"

"I think so." I walked toward the cartons, looking to see if they were labeled. Some were, some weren't. "It has something to do with some sea lions having seizures. Ariel saw them in August, off Point Pinos, and filed a report with the Monterey SPCA. She may have kept some sort of account of what she saw and why it was important. Correspondence, journals, notes of some sort. I think these file boxes will be a good place to start."

As I reached for the first one, bright red in the inadequate overhead light, Glennis Braemer shivered. "It's cold," she said. "I'll send Mrs. Costello out with some coffee."

I saw a step stool near the storage cabinets. That would do as a chair, since the thought of sitting on the floor didn't appeal to me at all. I walked to it. Now I could see the labels on the cabinet doors, things like CHRISTMAS DECORATIONS and CAMPING EQUIPMENT, that evoked the change of seasons and the time when the Logan family was whole, not irreparably torn by Ariel's death. I positioned the stool as close as possible to the light. The housekeeper opened the door leading to the house. She carried a wooden tray holding an oversized white ceramic cup and an insulated carafe.

"Do you take anything in it?" she asked. "Mrs. Braemer didn't say."

"This is fine, thanks." I filled the cup and sipped the coffee, strong and hot, warming my fingers as they circled the cup.

When she'd gone, I opened the red file box. The array of manila folders that confronted me reminded me of a case I'd had earlier this year, when I spent hours going through the files of a dead professor from Cal State Hayward, where my father taught. Then I had no idea what to look for, but now I did. Or I thought I did. I was acting on a hunch and I could be wrong.

I knew the contents of the cartons had been packed hastily and haphazardly by Mrs. Braemer and Maggie Lim, as the professor's things had been by his nephews. The sheriff's deputies had no doubt been equally haphazard. But as I looked through the file boxes I discerned some organization, probably Ariel's. The one I sorted through now contained bank statements and bill receipts, both of which told me that Ariel kept good records, at least as far as her finances were concerned. After examining the folders I closed the red box and reached for another. I worked my way through all six file boxes. Lavender contained old letters, birthday cards, and photographs, snapshots and negatives in photo-processing envelopes, the flaps labeled with the subject. No journal or diary, though. The orange and yellow boxes contained school things, papers from Ariel's environmental engineering classes as well as her French-language studies.

The green and blue boxes were devoted to Ariel's environmental interests. Some folders contained pamphlets and publications, others were full of clippings from newspapers and magazines, notes in Ariel's handwriting scribbled in the margins in blue ink. Several of these had business cards clipped to them, as did the papers in another folder, one I found in the green file box. It was filled with copies of letters Ariel had written. She had aired her opinions on a regular basis, firing off thoughtful missives to people and agencies at the state and federal level, expressing her concerns about the Diablo Canyon nuclear plant and offshore oil drilling, as well as other issues. Any responses she'd received had been clipped to the original letter, as had various business cards.

But nothing here pointed either to the earlier incidents concerning the seals off Avila Beach in San Luis Obispo, or the sea lions she had reported to the Monterey SPCA in August. I wasn't surprised, though. Ariel hadn't contacted Susan Dailey about the seals until after she'd seen the sea lions. The letters in the file folder spanned several years but seemed to end in May, when Ariel had finished her most recent term at Cal Poly. She'd been here in Carmel all summer.

By now I'd drained the carafe of coffee and was in need of draining myself. I opened the door to the house and looked around. To my right were the stairs Mrs. Braemer and I had descended from the foyer. To my left an open doorway led to a larger space that appeared to span the back of the house. I could see a low sofa and a coffee table. A recreation room? Maybe I'd have some luck in that direction.

"Do you need more coffee?" a voice said above me. I turned and saw Mrs. Braemer standing on the steps, surveying me with wintry blue eyes. She must have heard me open the door. Was the woman hovering on the landing above, listening to my every movement, afraid I might storm the rest of the house?

"More coffee would be appreciated," I said. "But first I need a bathroom."

"Of course. Through Peter's office, on the right. I'll refill the carafe."

I walked toward the back of the house, past the sofa I'd seen, and saw in the far corner a long L-shaped surface on which rested a computer, a small copier, and a fax machine. There were bookshelves everywhere. I found the bathroom just beyond, and past that an open door leading to an extra bedroom. A few minutes later I returned to the door leading to the garage, just as Mrs. Braemer descended from the upper regions of the house, carrying the carafe.

"Have you found anything?" she asked.

"Not in the file boxes. Did Ariel have a computer?"

"Yes, a notebook." She looked past me at the cardboard cartons in the garage. "It's in one of those boxes, along with some of those little disks."

"I'll have to plug the computer into a grounded outlet. Somewhere with better light than this," I told her, pointing at the ineffectual fixture on the garage ceiling.

"All right. You can come into Peter's office."

She helped me look for the computer, opening boxes until we found the notebook in its padded nylon case. Tucked into the same carton was a smaller box, a clear plastic container with its lid secured with a strip of masking tape. Inside were half a dozen 3.5-inch computer disks.

I carried the computer and the disk holder into the house. Mrs. Braemer followed, switching on the overhead light in the room that served as her brother's work space. In the corner near the sofa I saw a lamp and I turned this on, following its cord to the nearest electrical outlet. Then I set the case on the coffee table and unzipped it, pulling out a slim notebook computer and its cord. I plugged it into the outlet and turned on the computer. Then I checked the directory to see what Ariel had on her hard drive. While I was looking at the list Mrs. Braemer brought me the coffee cup and the carafe.

"I'll be upstairs," she said.

I was familiar with some of the programs. I called up each in turn, getting used to the machine. It was fairly new, with a color screen and lots of power. I began working my way through the disks from the little plastic box. All of them bore adhesive labels, and on some of them Ariel had written the names of classes. One was simply labeled COR.

Correspondence, I thought, shoving the disk into the A-drive. I checked the directory list as it scrolled onto the screen, trying to decipher whatever system Ariel had used to file each document. It seemed to involve initials, no doubt referring to the recipient of the letter, and numbers, probably dates. I called up the word-processing program and went through each document in turn.

I'd seen some of these letters before, the hard signed copies in the correspondence folder I'd found in the green file box. But some had been written during the summer while the author was here in Carmel. Evidently she hadn't photocopied these, so the only record was here on this disk.

The next piece of Ariel Logan's puzzle were two letters, both dated August 23. The first was to a paint manufacturer in Ohio, asking for an analysis of a certain product. The other was to an environmental testing lab in San Jose, dated late August, asking for an analysis of the enclosed samples, to be paid for by the attached check. The letter didn't say what was contained in the samples but I had a feeling it was water, from the ocean off Point Pinos.

I felt like yelling "Eureka," but I hadn't struck gold, at least not yet. What I saw in front of me was the glimmer of color in the stream. If I followed it maybe I'd find the nugget.

I got up and headed for the garage, leaving the door open as I sifted through the green and blue file boxes once more. Earlier I'd seen business cards among the other papers in Ariel's files. The name of the firm at the head of the letter now on the computer screen fit with something I'd seen before. Here it was, stapled to a firm résumé.

Head down, eyes on the papers in my hand, I walked back through the door into the house and smack into Glennis Braemer. She'd appeared at the bottom of the stairs, lured by the sound of my movements. Her eyes narrowed when she saw my face.

"You've found something," she said.

"Yes. Two letters. Written a month before Ariel died."

She followed me to the office and sat on the sofa, peering at the little computer on the coffee table. She read the letter over my shoulder as I examined the résumé of the environmental testing lab Ariel had contacted. The chain of events took shape in my mind. Just as my mother had paid for an analysis of the substance that closed down her restaurant Sunday afternoon, Ariel had paid for an analysis of the water where she'd seen the sea lions having seizures. But where was the response?

"I need to call these people," I told Mrs. Braemer, looking up from the firm résumé.

She frowned, more at the computer screen than at me. "Use the extension on Peter's desk."

I dialed the number on the business card. Then I talked my way through several people until I found someone who told me the work had been completed on Wednesday of the week Ariel Logan died.

"Did you mail a report?" I asked. "Or did Ms. Logan pick it up?"

The woman on the other end of the line paused, as though she were checking a log entry or a file folder. "Let me see. Looks like she called the week before. But the work hadn't been completed. So she asked to be called as soon as it was ready. She was, the following week. She picked it up herself. On Friday, around noon."

The timing was right. Ariel left San Luis Obispo before eight that morning and she drove straight up to San Jose. It would have taken her about four hours. What she read in the report sent her back down to Monterey, to talk to Bobby. But she came here first.

I set the phone back in its cradle and looked across the room at Peter Logan's copier, then at Glennis Braemer. She was perched warily on the edge of the sofa. The look on her elegant face said she didn't quite understand the significance of the letter she'd read. But she was putting it together with what she'd overheard on my end of the phone call. She wasn't far behind me.

"I have to find this report. It's somewhere in this house."

"W HAT IS *SHE* DOING UP HERE?" PETER LOGAN DE-
manded harshly as I came up the stairs from the
foyer, into the spacious living room.

He sat on a long white sectional sofa facing the front windows.
The thick white drapes were open but there was little to see on the
other side of the moisture-beaded glass but the occasional car with
the lights on or a determined clothing-swathed pedestrian, making
slow progress through the fog. An oval wooden tray holding two
coffee cups rested on the glass-topped table in front of the sofa,
along with this morning's copy of the *Herald*. Behind Logan I saw
a wide doorway leading to a formal dining room and the kitchen
beyond.

Logan's question had been addressed to his sister, who'd led the
way up the stairs, but I answered him. "I have to look for something in Ariel's room."

Ariel's father got to his feet, face haggard below his uncombed
silver-blond hair. His clothes seemed to hang loosely on his tall
frame. He glared at me with hostility, mouth twisted bitterly as he
spoke.

"No. I won't allow it. I don't want you in this house, pawing
through my daughter's belongings, touching her clothes."

"Peter." Mrs. Braemer sighed. At the end of her beige cashmere
sleeves her hands clenched and unclenched. "Peter, it's very important."

He shook his head violently and started toward us. Then he

stopped and looked up, past me at the stairs leading to the second floor. Sylvie Logan stood there, still dressed in black, this time wool pants and a sweater. Her dark hair was swept back from her face, which looked serene until I saw the grief in her brown eyes. Hand on the banister, she walked the rest of the way down the stairs.

"You have found something, Miss Howard?" she asked me in her low French-accented voice.

"Yes, I have." Quickly I told them about the letter, the sea lions, and the report that brought Ariel from San Luis Obispo to Monterey the day she died.

"Ariel said nothing of this to me." Sylvie frowned. "I remember the night she went out on the fishing boat. The next day we learned of my mother's illness. I was trying to decide when to go to Paris, and whether I would stay long enough to bury my mother. Instead I came home to bury my daughter." She stopped and looked across the living room at her husband. "Perhaps Ariel did not want to trouble us."

"Maybe. At that point she was speculating. She had nothing but theories, until . . ."

"Until right before she died," she finished. "You think this knowledge led to her death. But what is it?"

"I won't know until I find that report. Even then, I may have to have someone explain it to me. But it was important enough to make Ariel cut classes that Friday and drive all the way to San Jose to pick it up."

"Then we must find it," Ariel's mother said, but not to me. She took her husband's hand in both of hers. "Where shall we look?"

"All she brought with her was an overnight bag," Peter said slowly, his voice becoming progressively more ragged as he spoke. "I saw it sitting at the foot of her bed when I got home that night. I thought she was out with . . . him. But she was dead."

"The sheriff's people examined the bag," Glennis Braemer said. "I can't imagine they would have missed the report if it were there."

"Let's look again."

Sylvie Logan led the way up the stairs to a bedroom that seemed to be waiting for Ariel to return. The mission-style double

bed against one wall was made of oak, as were the matching night-
stands on either side. A chest of drawers and a dresser with an
oval mirror bracketed the closet. A bright patchwork quilt covered
the bed. Against the pillows at the head I saw a plush brown bear
with only one black beady eye and a black-haired porcelain-faced
doll in a frilly pink gown and slippers. A small bookcase made of
dark wood sat next to the window that looked down on the ocean,
its shelves filled with books and knickknacks, like the chipped
china cat that had some significance to Ariel alone.

No one said anything as I surveyed the room. I spotted the
overnight bag, a match for the blue suitcases down in the garage.
It was on the floor at the foot of the bed, zipper closed. I set it on
the bed and began removing the contents. There was a striped
cotton robe and a matching nightshirt, several changes of under-
wear and socks, a T-shirt and a pair of jeans. I also found a blue-
and-yellow floral-print toiletry bag containing little plastic bottles
of shampoo, rinse, and lotion, a toothbrush and toothpaste, a small
container of vitamins, some makeup and tampons, and a zippered
cloth coin purse that held a pair of earrings and a gold chain.

I emptied the toiletry bag and felt its compartments to see if
there was anything else concealed there, but I found nothing. I returned to the overnight bag, which had several interior and exterior zippers, but I found nothing more than the items I'd already
removed.

"I'm going to search the room," I told the Logans as I returned
Ariel's things to the bag and set it back on the floor. They said
nothing, only stared at me in fascination as I opened the top
drawer of the dresser.

"I'll help you," Mrs. Braemer said, pushing up her sleeves. "Or
this will take forever."

It took more than an hour, during which time I stripped the bed
to see if Ariel had hidden the report between the mattress and box
spring. She hadn't. Nor had she hidden it in the closet, in or under the dresser and chest of drawers, or in any of the books on the
shelves.

I sat cross-legged on the floor in front of the bookcase. After
partially emptying it, I'd tipped it to one side to see if there was
anything underneath. Now I shoved the last volume onto the shelf

and scrambled to my feet, wishing Ariel had hidden the report in
a more accessible location. I wasn't looking forward to searching
the remainder of the Logans' large house. There were all sorts of
nooks and crannies in a home this size and I envisioned poking my
nose into attic and crawl space. That would take the rest of the
day and it was already edging toward noon.

Maybe I was wrong, and it wasn't here at all. Maybe she'd had
it with her when she died and it was now in the possession of her
killer.

"What about the car?" I asked. I'd seen the autopsy report but
that didn't tell me what the sheriff's investigative team found at the
scene. "Did they find her purse?"

"I don't think so," Mrs. Braemer said wearily, sitting on the
edge of the remade bed. "It hasn't been returned to us, at any
rate. You'll have to ask Sergeant Magruder and I have a feeling he
won't tell you."

Peter scowled at me as though the futile search was proof that I
didn't know what I was doing. He and Sylvie were replacing the
contents of the closet. Suddenly Sylvie dropped a hatbox. A straw
hat rolled onto the carpet at her feet.

"*Bien sûr,*" she said. "*Evidemment . . .*"

"You thought of something." I certainly hoped so.

"A place where Ariel used to hide things, when she was living at
home."

She whirled and headed out to the hallway between the bedrooms, with me and the others at her heels. She opened a door to
what turned out to be a large, deep linen closet and began pulling
towels off the middle shelf, shoving them into her husband's arms.
When the shelf was empty she pulled me toward it and pointed at
the back.

"Do you see it?" she asked. "I found it one day when I was
putting away laundry. When I opened it, I found some treasures
Ariel had put there."

"I see it."

It was a sliding door, a rectangle about twelve by eighteen inches.
I reached for the little knob on the left side. The door slid easily to
the right. The little compartment was about four inches deep, just

right for hiding a young girl's treasures. At the moment the only thing inside the cubbyhole was a white business-size envelope.

When I opened it, I found three sheets of paper. The first was rectangular, with ragged edges, as though it had been torn from something. It was a label, waterlogged and now dried, but readable. I read the lettering. Paint, manufactured by the same firm that Ariel had written to in August. There was a note in the margin, printed in black ink. It read, "8/17, *Marvella B*, Santa Cruz, Beckman."

The two larger sheets of paper were the report from the environmental testing lab. A staple had been removed from the upper left corner, probably so that Ariel could make a copy. I read through it twice. The samples Ariel referred to in her August 23 letter were water, from the surf off Point Pinos on August 18, the day she saw the sea lions having seizures.

There were things in the water that caused those sea lions to become ill. But it would take someone with more scientific knowledge than me to understand what and how toxic they were. I was fairly certain, however, that the substances listed on this report had no business being in Monterey Bay.

"I have to go to San Jose," I said. "I don't want to take the original. You have a copy machine downstairs."

Peter Logan reached for the report. "The label, too?" he asked, holding the sheets gingerly. I nodded. Sylvie, Glennis Braemer, and I waited for him in the living room. When he returned I took the copy and folded it.

"Put the original back where you found it," I said, heading down the stairs to the foyer. "Don't tell anyone about it, not until I get back."

CHAPTER 38

RICHARD SANTIAGO WAS LEAN AND BONY-FACED, LOOK-ing younger than the gray hair at his temples would indicate. At first he wasn't going to tell me anything about his analysis of Ariel's water samples. He changed his mind when I told him the young woman who picked up the report ten days ago was dead, murdered, perhaps because of the information contained in those pages.

His brown eyes gazed at me across the desk in his cramped office at the testing lab. The windowless cubicle wasn't much larger than the one at the Monterey SPCA and just as full of file cabinets. Santiago sat in a creaky wooden chair, elbows resting on the arms, hands tented in front of him. I was wedged into an armless version of the same piece of furniture, next to an overflowing bookcase.

"I found traces of solvents used in the manufacture of computer chips."

Santiago glanced at the photocopy I'd brought with me. Underneath was his own file folder containing more details about the analysis he'd done.

"They're highly toxic. We see a lot of solvents in groundwater contamination here in the Silicon Valley."

"So how did they wind up in Monterey Bay?"

"Good question. I asked Ms. Logan when she picked up the report. She didn't come right out and answer me but I got the impression she had some theories. I thought she was going to turn the information over to the authorities."

"She was. But someone killed her first. Do you have any theories?"

Santiago shrugged. "Someone's been dumping illegally. There's a whole network of laws against it. But they're broken all the time. Illegal disposal often goes undetected."

"Say I have half a dozen barrels of toxic waste I want to get rid of. What are my options? The illegal ones."

Santiago tugged on his earlobe and shifted in his chair. "If you dispose of the waste on land, sooner or later someone will notice. Maybe you bury those barrels in a landfill. Five years from now some developer decides to build an office park on that landfill, starts grading the site, and a bulldozer hits a barrel. Or you could pay some guy to haul them off and conveniently figure what he does with them afterward is his problem."

"What might he do with them?"

"Pour the stuff down the nearest storm drain," Santiago said. "It winds up in San Francisco Bay. Which is why I'm not about to eat any shellfish that comes out of the water around here. Or this midnight disposal service might haul those barrels out to the San Joaquin Valley and open 'em up on some out-of-the way country road, the kind that runs between two farms. The stuff gets poured into a borrow ditch that drains into an irrigation ditch when it rains. Or it just gets dumped onto the dirt road. Once it dries, the wind blows the contaminated dust around. You get the picture?"

"Yes. It's not a pleasant one. If I wanted to dispose of my toxic waste in the ocean?"

"That's easier. And in many cases legal. People think the ocean is some big cesspool that flushes all our waste and magically makes it disappear. But it doesn't. It goes into the food chain. Hell, the government dumped a whole bunch of barrels of nuclear waste out by the Farallon Islands. They've been sitting on the ocean floor for years, and they're leaking."

"So I haul my barrels of toxic waste far enough out to sea and push them overboard."

"Who's gonna know?" Santiago finished. "Sure, the barrels may corrode and leak, but the chemicals get diluted by the water and the currents move the stuff around. How can anyone be sure how much was dumped? Or where? You deep-six your waste in the ocean, you may never get caught because no one knows it's there.

Unless you see some results, like those sea lions Ms. Logan saw. Having seizures, probably because they absorbed a toxin."

"What if someone sees you do it?" Had Ariel Logan seen something else besides those sea lions, something that tied the act to the perpetrator?

Now I knew why Ariel was so interested in Karl Beckman's business. If I were going to dump barrels of toxic materials in the ocean I'd need a boat. Where better to find one than a boatyard?

It wasn't the everyday runoff of paints, chemicals, and oil from Beckman Boat Works that started Ariel wondering. It was the boats, out of their owners' custody, away from their normal marina berths, accessible to any one of the yard's employees. If one of those boats took an unauthorized voyage, or even an authorized one, in Santiago's words, who's gonna know?

"If I were operating a midnight disposal service, as you put it, would I be making a lot of money?"

Santiago laughed. "Oh, yeah. You'd better believe it."

I nodded. "Any ideas who might have some waste to get rid of?"

"None of the big firms would risk it."

"Are you sure about that? They've all got deep pockets. Don't they just pay the fines and go on with business as usual?"

He moved back a bit, uncomfortable with the question. "I'm sure the local authorities can tell you more about that than I can. I just hear things, around the edges, you know."

"I know. And you've heard some rumors, haven't you?" I stared at him across the desk, doing my best immovable object impersonation. "You say the big firms wouldn't risk getting caught disposing of waste illegally. What about the small firms?"

"Well," he said reluctantly. "There are a few companies that have been cited over the past couple of years. They've cut corners on regulations—occupational health and safety, wastewater discharge. If you're planning to stick your nose in, you could start there."

"Names?" He gave me four possibilities, all companies he'd heard rumors about.

"But you'd be better off going to the DA. All the counties have someone who prosecutes environmental violations."

But I didn't have enough to go to the DA. I had a lot of threads that needed tying together. Sergeant Magruder would probably boot me out of the sheriff's office, unless I gave him more evidence than this.

According to what Bobby told me, Ariel suspected that Beckman Boat Works had been dumping chemicals into the ocean. But Bobby said she didn't have any proof. By the time she met my cousin at the Rose and Crown, Ariel had already picked up the report from this testing lab. But she hadn't shared the details with Bobby. If Ariel was so convinced that Beckman was involved, she must have had another link in the chain, one that I was presently missing.

"I NEED HELP, NORM. AND I NEED IT FAST."

"Tell me about it," he said in his gravelly voice as he poured me a cup of coffee.

My friend and colleague Norman Gerrity is a retired Boston cop who got tired of inactivity and hung out his shingle as a private investigator. We help each other out now and again. I sipped the strong black brew and I told Norm what I'd been doing for the past two weeks.

"You're up to your eyeballs," Norm said. "I thought you were going to Monterey for a little downtime."

"Life intervened." I sighed. "I'll be glad to wrap this up and get back to my normal routine. Maybe then I can get some rest. But I feel like Sergeant Magruder is just waiting to slap Bobby back in jail unless I can come up with more evidence. I think it's possible both the Beckmans are involved in this. Their firm is in financial difficulty. Karl won't say where he was that Friday, the evening Ariel was killed. Lacy's got an alibi but it's thin. I'm going to run a background check on her."

"You've still got to draw lines between a lot of dots," Norm pointed out.

"That's where I need your help. Santiago at the lab gave me some names I'd like to check out, firms that have had violations here in Santa Clara County. Could be that would make it more attractive to import the waste to another county and pay someone very well to dispose of it."

"How do you figure to get in the door, much less get anyone to talk?"

I grinned. "It's always a good idea to call first."

Norm played the phone like a virtuoso.

Whether cajoling information out of his Silicon Valley contacts, or pretending to be a man with something to get rid of, Norm Gerrity could persuade people to tell him things they hadn't planned to relate. I was good at it myself, but Norm amazed me. Between the two of us, we used both Norm's extensions to separate wheat from chaff. Daylight darkened to dusk and we consumed most of the pizza I'd had delivered. Finally we connected with a man at a Sunnyvale number who sounded as though he was talking through a handkerchief.

Not to worry, he said. He would provide the containers, the transport, the disposal. For this he wanted an enormous sum of money. I pretended to be reluctant to spend so much, seeking assurances that our "problem" wouldn't come back to haunt us.

"Not to worry," he said again. "Your problem will be deep-sixed in Davy Jones's locker."

I recognized that term. The same words had been used by Belknap at the water board in San Luis Obispo and Santiago at the testing lab. Hell, I'd heard most of the fishermen in my family use it, from Uncle Dom to Bobby.

If you want to dump something in the ocean, you deep-six it.

CHAPTER 39

IT HAD BEEN NEARLY TWO WEEKS SINCE I'D SPENT A NIGHT in my own bed. It felt better than I ever could have imagined. Before getting between the sheets, however, I received a thorough dressing-down from Abigail.

As I unlocked the front door of my apartment in Oakland's Adams Point district, my fat and vocal tabby greeted me, questioning my wisdom at having been gone. My friend Cassie had been over every evening to provide food and fresh water and clean out the cat box. But it just wasn't the same, Abigail informed me in nonstop meows, as having one's own person about.

"I hate to tell you this," I said after I dished up a redolent concoction from a newly opened can, "but I have to go back tomorrow. I'll be home soon, though."

Abigail's meows subsided into huffy grunts as she inhaled her dinner. I sorted through the mail Cassie had left on the dining-room table, tossing most of it into the wastebasket. Then I checked the messages on my answering machine. Alex Tongco, the Navy lieutenant commander I'd been dating for the past few months, wanted to know if I planned to keep our date this coming weekend. I called and explained the situation. Then I brought Cassie up to speed. As I talked on the phone Abigail settled into my lap, washed herself, and began a rumbling purr.

Finally I called Errol in Carmel. After finding the report at the Logans' late this morning, I'd gone back to the Sevilles' house for

a quick report before driving to San Jose to locate the environmental testing firm.

"Your mother phoned," he said. "Maybe you ought to call her."

"I'll think about it." I had put the quarrel with Mother on the
back burner, telling myself I had more critical priorities. Truth was
I just didn't want to deal with it right now.

I stroked Abigail's back and she purred even louder. "I'm at
home in Oakland. I'll spend the night here, then call Minna's sister in San Francisco tomorrow. I should be back in Carmel tomorrow afternoon."

"The Logans have called twice, wanting to know what you
found out in San Jose," he said. "What should I tell them?"

"The water samples Ariel sent to that lab were contaminated
with solvents used in making computer chips. Someone's dumping
toxics in the bay. Ariel found out." I told him how Norm Gerrity
and I spent the afternoon. "It's possible the guy we spoke with is
the source. He must be hauling the stuff over the Santa Cruz hills.
We know Ariel suspected Beckman Boat Works. Karl, Lacy, or
someone who works there. If that's the case, how is it getting to
the boatyard? Norm's going to see if he can nail down some
specifics on the Sunnyvale end."

"I'll do the same down here," Errol said, before I could ask.

"Be careful."

I got up from the chair and carried Abigail to the bedroom. As
soon as I was in bed the cat deposited herself on my stomach as
though her bulk would prevent me from leaving again.

Tuesday morning, fortified by coffee and a bowl of cereal, I
went to my office on Franklin Street in downtown Oakland and
spent some time playing catch-up. There were bills to be paid and
phone calls to return, some of them from people who wanted to
hire me. Or they had a week ago. I felt frustrated at the paying
customers who wouldn't or couldn't wait because I was embroiled
in something in Monterey, something I couldn't walk away from.

When I called Minna Seville's sister she suggested tea at the
Garden Court. It was past one when I headed across the Bay
Bridge to San Francisco and deposited my Toyota in the garage of
the Palace Hotel.

The Garden Court just off the lobby sparkles, whether from

sunlight through the domed glass roof or electric light from the many ornate glass chandeliers. The marble surrounding the elegant dining room is a rosy beige, its columns topped with dark gold accents. Large pots of palms and ivy dot the blue-and-purple Oriental carpet. Scattered throughout the room are tables with dark green tops and comfortable chairs with striped upholstery.

On the phone Celeste Bainbridge told me she looked a lot like her sister. Minna was a good deal more down-to-earth and casual than this slender woman with her impeccably coiffed white hair. Minna had told me Celeste was ten years older than she was, which meant Mrs. Bainbridge was seventy-eight. She wore a stylish dark blue suit, accented by a hat and gloves. In my usual slacks and shirt, I felt underdressed.

"Minna tells me you want some information on the Born and Raised," Mrs. Bainbridge said when we were seated at one of the green tables. She removed her gloves, smiling at me. At that moment she looked very much like her younger sister.

"Just one in particular," I told her. "Lacy Standish."

The Born and Raised she referred to were those who had entered life and spent most of their years in San Francisco. Not just within its city limits, mind you, but a specific territory made up of both geography and society. They lived their lives according to old and well-established patterns, attended certain schools from kindergarten to college, spent their summers at Lake Tahoe, and finally went into certain professions. They married each other and produced offspring who would repeat the patterns. To their credit, they were also the backbone of institutions like the symphony, the opera, and the city's museums.

"Lacy Standish. I won't ask why. Other than to comment that I always thought that girl would come to a bad end."

"Why?"

"Blood will tell, whether people nowadays like to admit it or not."

The elegant Mrs. Bainbridge's eyes now had a wicked twinkle, as though she were looking forward to a good gossip. So was I. Our server loomed at the table. We ordered tea with sandwiches and pastries, which was quickly delivered. I poured myself a cup of Earl Grey.

"Lacy Standish," Mrs. Bainbridge said, adding cream and sugar to her Russian Caravan. "Her mother was Margaret Victor. The Victors were related to the Crockers but that was years and several generations ago. Doesn't count for much now. Of course there aren't any Victors left. They lost a lot of money in the Crash and never really recovered. Lacy's grandfather was an executive at Crocker Bank. When there was a Crocker Bank." Mrs. Bainbridge's mouth quirked at the passing of that institution.

"Lacy's father was a man named Lawrence Standish. He was what used to be called a remittance man. Do you know what that is, Miss Howard?"

"Someone whose family pays him an allowance to get out of town and stay out." I helped myself to a bit of bread decorated with a sliver of smoked salmon.

"Exactly." Mrs. Bainbridge nodded and nibbled on a cucumber sandwich. "In this case the family was British. Lawrence was from Southampton and he came over to the States after the war. Dined out for years on his plummy accent and his Royal Navy record, which I'm sure he embellished. He loved to sail, ride, and shoot, and he taught Lacy all three. In those days he was a fixture down at the St. Francis yacht club and at the Meadow Club up in Marin. He attached himself to Peggy Victor, who could have done better, God knows. She wasn't bad-looking. The family had some status, and a little money, as well as a house in Pacific Heights."

"Is that why Lawrence was interested?" I asked.

"I think so." Mrs. Bainbridge nodded sagely and sipped her tea. "Peggy was the sole heir. Her brother was killed at Guadalcanal. So she married Lawrence. They had a big wedding at St. Mary the Virgin on Union Street. The reception was right here at the Garden Court." She looked at the opulent surroundings and smiled. "So was mine. But that was a long time ago."

"Where did Peggy and Lawrence live after they married?" I asked, reaching for another sandwich.

"With Peggy's father, in the Victor house on Divisadero. Peggy's mother died during the war, so Mr. Victor was alone except for his staff. Peggy played hostess and Lawrence went to work for his father-in-law down at the bank. They even made him a vice-president. Things went on that way for about fifteen years before the scandal."

"What scandal?" I leaned forward, caught up in the tale.

Mrs. Bainbridge freshened her tea and chose another sandwich before continuing. "He embezzled," she said, her voice tart. "Quite a sum, I understand, over a period of years. Old Mr. Victor kept Lawrence out of jail but fired him. He even gave Peggy an ultimatum, telling her to leave Lawrence or he'd cut her off." She sighed and shook her head.

"Peggy wouldn't, of course. She genuinely loved the man. Lacy was about twelve or thirteen at the time. Spoiled rotten, she was. Daddy's little girl, and she had no use for her mother."

Why should these last words make me uncomfortable? I wasn't Lacy Standish.

"What happened to Lawrence and Peggy? Did Mr. Victor make good on his threat?"

"Yes, he did. Peggy, Lawrence, and Lacy moved out of the Victor house and into an apartment near Union Street. Still Pacific Heights, of course."

"So Lacy was barely into her teens when this happened. It must have hit her hard."

"Oh, yes." Mrs. Bainbridge nodded sagely. "Lacy had been going to Katherine Burke's school but her parents could no longer afford the tuition. So she transferred to Grant. Public school but very good. I believe she went on to Lowell High. All her friends were taking dancing lessons at Frank Kitchen's school. But Lacy couldn't get in. He was very particular about who he took. She didn't have access to the sailing and horseback riding, except as someone's guest."

"What happened to her parents?"

"Mr. Victor left most of his money to a foundation," Mrs. Bainbridge said. "Peggy had some money from her grandmother's estate but she and Lawrence went through it fairly fast. Lawrence drank himself to death. Peggy used the last of her trust fund to send Lacy off to school at Lone Mountain."

I knew of the school, a Catholic college in San Francisco.

Mrs. Bainbridge narrowed her eyes. "There's something about

Lacy's last year in high school." She paused. "Goodness, I can't quite recall the details. I must be getting old." She smiled ruefully.

"Anyway, Lacy graduated from Lone Mountain and promptly got married, to someone she met up at Tahoe. He was from Eureka or some such place, up north on the coast. That didn't last. I heard he drank, too, just like Lawrence. They were married four or five years. Then Lacy divorced him and came back to San Francisco. That was right about the time Peggy died. She was living with one of her cousins on Jackson Street. Sort of a paid companion." She paused and reached for her teacup. "Sounds like one of those soap operas, doesn't it?"

I laughed. "That's why those stories are so popular. They're familiar, because things like that happen. What did Lacy do when she came back to the city?" We'd finished the sandwiches and had started on the pastries.

"She worked at a gallery on Union Street, lived in that area, too. I don't think she made a lot of money. She had a settlement from her first marriage. But Lacy always did have champagne taste, which made it difficult to live on a beer budget. She caused talk, by the way. Had an affair with a married man, whose wife finally used some leverage to rein in her husband."

Mrs. Bainbridge paused and spread lemon curd on a tiny scone. Then she continued. "Then I heard Lacy married again, this time to a man from Monterey, Gunter Beckman. She met him while she was down at Pebble one weekend, visiting some friends who have a place down there. I hear he had something to do with boats. I wondered if Mr. Beckman had money, because Lacy's always been a mercenary creature. Did he?"

"She may have thought he did." I popped a miniature éclair into my mouth. "Gunter Beckman and his brother Karl jointly owned a boat repair yard. Gunter died in a car wreck that also killed Karl's wife."

Mrs. Bainbridge raised her eyebrows at this. "What did Lacy inherit?"

"Gunter's share of the business, evidently a lot of debts as well. She had to sell their house in Carmel and now she works as office manager for the business. And she transports boats, sails them from port to port."

"Goodness, I can't imagine Lacy working in an office. Boats, yes. I recall seeing her up at Tahoe one summer when she was a teenager, piloting someone's Chris-Craft as though born to it."

I poured another cup of tea. "Have you remembered what happened in Lacy's senior year at Lowell?"

Mrs. Bainbridge thought a moment. "I believe she was expelled for some prank. She finished at the Wilkins School. That was the school you went to when no other school would take you. I can't recall what the prank was, though." She brightened. "Surely my granddaughter knows. She was a year or two behind Lacy at Lowell."

My elegant white-haired companion reached for her purse. To my great surprise she pulled out a small mobile phone. "A Christmas gift from one of my gadgety grandsons," she explained as she flipped through the pages of a leather-bound address book. "I must say, it does come in handy."

Mrs. Bainbridge's granddaughter was a broker who worked for a securities firm in San Francisco's financial district. Summoned to the phone by her grandmother, she described the incident that got Lacy Standish expelled from Lowell High School at the start of her senior year, an incident that had entered the realm of legend.

"The principal caught her stealing from someone's locker and suspended her. It was what she did afterward that got her expelled."

"Very ingenious," I said when the granddaughter recounted the details. "Why would she go to such trouble?"

"We learned early on never to cross Lacy Standish. She always got even."

I ARRIVED AT CAF⁰ MARIE ABOUT FOUR-THIRTY THAT AFTERNOON. Back in the kitchen dinner preparations were in full swing. Mother and Julian Surtees stood together, heads bent as they talked, accompanied by the clatter of cooking utensils and the swing music emanating from the radio in the bar. Mother looked up as I planted myself next to the row of stoves, my hands on my hips. A whole range of emotions crossed her face, from apprehension to welcome. I didn't say anything to her. Instead I focused on her assistant.

"Julian, you and I are going to have a talk."

The black eyebrows in Julian's saturnine face shot up. "Now? I'm busy."

"Get unbusy." I gestured toward the front of the restaurant. "The office." He hesitated for a moment. I narrowed my eyes and he decided not to push it. He stepped past me and I turned to follow.

"You couldn't say hello?" Mother said, frowning.

"I think I've found your saboteur."

"What? Who? Not Julian."

I walked toward the office with Mother at my heels. Julian waited in the doorway of the small cubicle, face resentful, hands balled into tight fists as he crossed his arms over his chest.

"This better be good," he said.

"We're going to talk about your relationship with Lacy Beckman, Julian." The office was so small there wasn't room for three people, so I stood in the doorway.

Now he glared at me. "I told you that was none of your damn business."

"Lacy was expelled from high school her senior year. The principal caught her stealing. That only earned her a suspension. She got the boot for setting off a stink bomb in the school office. The fire department evacuated the whole damn school. Sound familiar?"

I watched Julian's face. The dark eyes widened and his eyebrows drew together. Mother looked stunned, white around the mouth.

"Lacy was here at Café Marie almost every time something went wrong. The night Karl Beckman got sick, the night Mrs. Grady found the mouse on her plate. Probably the night the salt wound up in the sugar containers and when the oil-can lid came off and you had an oil spill back in the kitchen. As for the rest, the phantom reservations that never showed up and the anonymous calls to the health department, I'll bet she's responsible for those as well."

Julian's frown got even deeper until he looked like a hawk about to swoop down on its prey. Mother moved her head slowly, back and forth, trying to negate my words.

"She must have doctored Karl's food with something to make him ill," I said. "Easy enough if he left the table for a moment. She could have used anything. Detergent, rhubarb leaves. I saw some growing in the garden near her cottage. Getting the mouse onto Mrs. Grady's plate was tricky, but there were enough comings and goings at that table that she managed it. But I really want to know how she managed to get that butyric-acid time bomb into the ventilating system."

"That bitch," Julian snarled. Anger boiled into his dark eyes. "She used me. The knives, damn it. I showed her where the knives were kept. Then Marie cut her hand the next day. It could just as easily have been me."

I nodded. "Yes, she used you. And she didn't care who got hurt. If a customer strolled into the kitchen during the evening the staff would notice. But you were dating Lacy, so the staff was accustomed to seeing her. If she popped into the kitchen to say hello, it wasn't anything out of the ordinary. If she was hanging around in the bar waiting for you to finish up, well, that's just Lacy. So how did she get that stink bomb into the ventilating system, Julian? It was rigged to an ordinary twenty-four-hour lamp timer and it was set to go off at eight P.M. Sunday. So it had it to be in place after eight P.M. Saturday, probably before dawn Sunday morning. Did you see Lacy that night?"

Julian swore, ugly obscene words spilling from the tight line of his lips, one fist smashing into the palm of his hand.

"I closed up Saturday night. I told Marie to go home, remember? Lacy came back after she and Karl left with the Gradys. We had plans for the evening. She got there just as I was finishing up. Everyone else had gone—the servers, the busboys, the dishwashers. She came into the kitchen from the back door. She was parked in the alley."

"She used the Dumpster to climb up on the roof," I said. "Probably didn't take her long to remove the metal covering and set up the device. Then she strolled into the kitchen to keep her date."

Mother finally found her voice. "But why? Why would Lacy do this to me? She's always been friendly."

"The better to hide what's under the mask. But you've done something to make her angry, Mother. Maybe it's because you have some things she doesn't. A successful business. And Karl Beckman."

CHAPTER 40

WOULD HAVE PREFERRED TO CONFRONT KARL BECKMAN on my own but Mother insisted on going with me. She didn't say much on the way over to Beckman Boat Works. It was just after five when I drove my Toyota into the boatyard and parked to the left of a pickup with the boat logo.

"Is it Karl's, or Lacy's?" I looked over the hood of my own car to the half-open driver's-side window of the truck.

"Karl's." Mother glanced to her right as she shut the passenger door of the Toyota. "He's got a leather grip on the steering wheel. Lacy doesn't."

Where was Lacy? I swept my eyes around the yard but her truck was nowhere in sight. Nor did I see Frank Alviso's flashy new Grand Am.

Most of the boatyard employees were finishing up their day's work, ready to head for home. Two men stood near the Marine Travel-Lift. Inside the machine shop I saw a couple of workers, a man and a woman, putting away their tools. A young woman in blue jeans was locking the door to the chandlery.

We went up the stairs to the office where I'd first encountered Lacy. There was no one at the desk in the outer office and the door to Lacy's cubicle was closed. Karl Beckman was behind his wide wooden desk, leaning back in the padded leather chair as he talked on the phone. He chuckled at something the person on the other end of the phone said, then he looked up and saw me standing in the doorway, Mother crowding in at my side.

"I'll call you back," he said, laughter leaving his voice. He hung up the phone and got stiffly to his feet. His eyes fixed on Mother's face with a mixture of affection and apprehension. "Marie, it's good to see you. I've been meaning to call." Then he looked at me with no welcome at all. "To what do I owe this visit?"

"You have some explaining to do," Mother said. Not the best way to phrase it, but she jumped right in before I could speak.

Karl looked mystified. "About what?"

"About Lacy." Mother folded her arms in front of her and stuck out her chin.

"What about Lacy?" Now Karl's eyes got that shuttered look I'd seen before. But it was time to open the window and take a look at what was beyond.

"Lacy is responsible for the incidents at Café Marie. The stink bomb, the mouse on Mrs. Grady's plate, your getting sick the night you had dinner there, back in August." I watched his face as my words worked their way in.

"But why?" His question echoed the one Mother had asked earlier at Café Marie. I noticed that he didn't deny the accusation I'd lobbed at his sister-in-law.

"It's more than pure meanness. Lacy's a spoiler. If she can't have something, or it gets in her way, she'll destroy it. In this case what she can't have is you. Although she came close." Karl winced as though I'd slapped him. "I went down to King City on Saturday and had a talk with Charlie Harper. He told me you had an affair with your sister-in-law, two years ago."

I heard a sound from my mother, a little indrawn breath that meant she hadn't suspected this. Karl ran one big hand over his broad face as though he wanted to put the flesh between him and my words.

"It was a fling," he said, his voice sounding rusty and subdued. "An aberration, a god-awful mistake."

"More than you realized. Your brother Gunter probably didn't care. But your wife found out about it. She was so angry she changed her will. You didn't discover that until she and Gunter were killed in that car accident at Hurricane Point. Charlie Harper thinks you had something to do with his sister's death."

Karl slumped back on the edge of his desk. "Somehow I knew

that, although he's never come right out and said anything. I'm not surprised that he'd believe the worst of me. But he's wrong."

"If he dislikes you so much, why did you ask him for money?"

"He told you about that, too?"

I waved my hand impatiently. "I know about Gunter using the boatyard as collateral for a loan. He defaulted. You had to borrow money from Harper to bail yourself out. I also know how you helped Bobby when he was arrested in King City last April. I suspect the reason you were so unavailable the Friday Bobby was looking for you is that you were making the rounds of bankers, probably somewhere other than Monterey. You got turned down. That's why you went to your brother-in-law with your hat in hand. Come on, Karl, I've got most of the pieces but I need some answers from you. Why do you need money?"

"Because this business is in trouble." He shook his head slowly, then the words came tumbling out. "Because the recession has eaten this town alive. Even people who can afford boats are deferring maintenance and repairs. The people who have boats and can't afford the upkeep and the marina fees are getting rid of them. The fishermen are repairing their own craft. The cost of materials keeps going up. I'm not doing the same amount of business I was two, three years ago."

He gestured at the empty outer office. "I used to have a secretary working out there but now I don't because I can't afford to pay the salary. Had to let some other workers go, too. Damn it, I can't keep up with my competitor at the other end of the Row. I'm under pressure to sell out to the developers. For the past year, it's been all I can do to keep my head above water."

"Your difficulties are common knowledge around town," I told him. "Besides, Ariel Logan had someone look into the state of your finances."

"Good lord, why would she do that?" Now he looked stunned. "I hardly knew the girl."

I let him stew about that one a little longer. I had to keep him talking, to determine whether or not he was part of Lacy's scheme. "What happened after your wife died? Did Lacy wait the usual decent interval?"

Karl's face colored and he looked at Mother as though for help.

But she wasn't prepared to offer any. Instead she seated herself in one of the chairs in front of his desk, hands knotted in her lap, her jaw tight as she waited for his response.

"My daughter was really broken up by Janine's death," Karl said. "Kristen wanted to drop out of school for the next term, but I persuaded her to stay." He stopped and ran his hand over his face again.

"I'm not avoiding your question, Jeri. What I'm saying is, I concentrated on my daughter. Lacy didn't make any overtures until late last year. When she did, I ignored them. Finally she came right out with it. Christmas, as a matter of fact, with my daughter at home cooking dinner. Lacy said it had been nearly a year since Gunter and Janine died. Why didn't we get together?"

He stopped and his face colored again, reliving the scene. "I told her no. What happened between us was bad judgment. I succumbed to an impulse. I've regretted it since it happened. It wasn't worth it."

I could sympathize with his discomfort. I've succumbed to more than a few impulses in my time. "And how did Lacy react?"

"I didn't give her time to react." Karl shook his head. "I just walked away."

"You turned your back on her," I said. "Big mistake. Lacy likes to get even."

"But she's been cordial and businesslike ever since," Karl protested. "I was relieved, since she's my partner and we have to work together."

"She's very creative in her methods. And her timing." I glanced to my right, at my mother seated in the chair. "You two met at a party New Year's Eve. And started dating in January. It probably took some time for Lacy to figure out that you were an item. She decided to get back at Mother by destroying the restaurant. But she waited to play her games in the summer, when the tourists are here and Café Marie is always crowded. By then Mother had hired Julian. Lacy zeroed in on him, and she had an opportunity to be at the restaurant, where she could create some havoc."

Karl shook his head, disbelief in his eyes. "Hurt Marie because of me? That's fairly indirect. If Lacy wanted to get back at me I would think she'd attack me outright."

"How about destroying your business? Is that direct enough?"

"But it's her business, too," Karl said.

"I think she's found a more lucrative one." I reached into my bag for the photocopies I'd carried with me for the past two days and handed one page to Karl Beckman, the copy of the wrinkled paint-can label. "Recognize this?"

He examined the sheet of paper and looked up at me, confusion in his hazel eyes. "Paint. Certainly. We buy cases of this product, have for years."

"Where is it kept?"

"In the paint locker next to the chandlery."

"Not the storeroom behind the machine shop?"

"No. There aren't any supplies back there. Certainly not anything flammable. It's too close to the welding. Sparks from the torches might set off paint. That's why paint's kept in the locker."

"What do you do with the containers when they're empty?"

"We used to throw them out. But Lacy's recycling them now. She takes them to a place in Santa Cruz."

"Lacy's recycling program won't thrill the EPA," I said. "When did she start transporting boats regularly?"

"Early summer, June. What's this about? Where did you get this label?"

"Ariel Logan found it," I said, laying out the scenario as I'd pieced it together. "In the surf off Point Pinos. She took samples of the water and sent them to an environmental lab in San Jose. This is their report."

Karl took the other pages and read through them. Then he handed the report to Mother, who'd gotten up from her chair.

"I don't know what all these chemicals are," he said slowly. "But I have a feeling they're bad."

"You're right. They're solvents used in the manufacture of computer chips. Highly toxic and highly concentrated, according to the man who ran the analysis. Much more serious than pesticide runoff from the Salinas River. Or whatever your workers might spill into the bay here at the boatyard."

"How did they get into the water?" Mother asked. "What's this note in the margin, Jeri?"

"It says, '8/17, *Marvella B*, Santa Cruz.'" I took the report, folded it, and stuck it into my bag. "Bobby took Ariel out fishing with the *Nicky II* that night. They came across a cabin cruiser called the *Marvella B* near Point Pinos. Ariel saw Lacy aboard. She saw something that roused her curiosity. The next afternoon she went down to Point Pinos and saw two sea lions having seizures. I'm guessing she found the paint-can label at the same location. The following weekend you gave Ariel and her friend Maggie a tour of the yard. She asked lots of questions, about paint and chemicals and a boat called the *Marvella B*."

Karl furrowed his brow. "Yes, she did. We worked on that boat." He strode past me to the outer office and pulled open one of the filing cabinets. He riffled through the file folders, pulled one out, and flipped it open. "The *Marvella B*. Forty-five-foot Chris-Craft. Belongs to a couple from Santa Cruz. We had it in here second week in August, for some work on the hull."

"When did it leave?"

"August seventeenth." His voice was subdued. "Lacy took it to Santa Cruz under its own power."

"If I were heading for Santa Cruz, I wouldn't be hanging around Point Pinos in the middle of the night," I said. "Does she always take Frank Alviso with her?"

"Frank? I think so. I'll have to check. Why?"

"When I was here a week ago Saturday talking to Frank, he kept looking in the direction of that storeroom near the machine shop where you supposedly don't store any paint. It was obvious Lacy didn't want me to talk with him alone. Frank is Lacy's partner."

"In what?" Karl frowned, still trying to make the connection between the report I'd shown him and the fact that Lacy had sailed the *Marvella B* to Santa Cruz that night.

"Dumping toxic waste in the bay," I said. "Let's take a look at that storeroom."

Karl turned and went back into his office, hauled out one of the desk drawers, and poked at an assortment of keys. He pulled out a ring with several labeled keys on it and shoved it into his pocket. We followed him down the stairs, out to the yard. The workers in the machine shop looked startled as he hurried past them and gestured at the door.

"Is this the one?"

"That's it." I stopped near the workbench where I'd talked to Frank, Mother so close behind me that she trod on my heels. I reached out to steady her.

"There's nothing in here but spare parts, tools, and—" He stopped abruptly. The key in his hand wouldn't go into the door. He tried it again, then stared at the label on the key.

"When was the last time you were in that storeroom?" I asked him.

"It's been several months." He went down on one knee and examined the door. "Goddamn it, the lock's been changed." He scrambled to his feet and looked around, catching sight of the two workers who had been watching with avid curiosity. "Jo, Manuel, help me break down this door."

"Be careful," I said. "If I'm right about what's in there, it could be dangerous."

Mother backed up a few feet, to the doorway of the machine shop. I looked around for something we could use as a pry bar but Karl and the other two were already attacking the door with some tool I'd never seen before. It only took them a few minutes to haul the storeroom door off its hinges.

It was empty.

No tools, no spare parts, no containers of something that might be paint, or might not. But something had been stored in here, and recently.

"Flashlight," I said. Karl handed me one. I shone the beam on the concrete floor. Dampness glistened in the far corner. I inhaled and caught a faint scent of something chemical. It didn't smell like paint, but I was no expert.

"Do you have any idea where Lacy is right now?" I asked Karl, turning away from the now empty storeroom.

He shook his head. "I had to go up to Moss Landing to talk to a customer. When I got back, she was gone." He glanced at Jo and Manuel. "Either of you seen Lacy?"

"She and Frank left," Jo said, mystified. "I couldn't tell you when, but they were supposed to sail a boat to Half Moon Bay. That thirty-four-foot Targa. We finished working on it yesterday. They put it in the water and loaded some gear into it last night. Frank had to overhaul an engine today, so they planned to sail it tonight."

Tonight, because Lacy needed the cover of darkness. "Did you see what they loaded into it?" I asked, trying to keep the urgency out of my voice.

"No," Manuel said. "They did it last night after everyone left. I offered to help Frank close up. Now that I think about it, he seemed real anxious to get rid of me. And Lacy was upstairs in her office. She's up there at all hours."

I spun around, heading for the office. "I need a phone. And a description of that boat."

"**Y**OU'RE CRAZY, CUZ, YOU KNOW THAT?" BOBBY SAID. "What makes you think we can find that sailboat before the Coast Guard does? Besides, the Coasties won't like us interfering."

I fought down the nausea that began the minute I climbed onto the deck of the *Nicky II*. Now I sat on a bench in the wheelhouse, my hands gripping the edge of the chart table, as Bobby piloted the purse seiner into Monterey Bay. We were a skeleton crew this evening. And we weren't fishing for squid. Our prey was a sailboat called the *Windrunner*, with Lacy Beckman and Frank Alviso its only crew.

The *Nicky II* rolled as it hit a swell. My stomach rolled with it. I clutched the table and stared down at the nautical chart of the bay, at the network of lines that represented its depth in fathoms. Here and there were little circles designating buoys and other symbols marking hazards. There were several more charts underneath, one for the coast and ocean south of here, toward Big Sur, others for the area west and north of Monterey Bay.

"It's a big bay," I said, sucking salty air from the open hatch nearby. "I figure the Coast Guard needs all the help we can give it. How much daylight do we have?"

I waved one hand in the general direction of the spectacular sunset outside. The boat was heading northwest, the curve of the peninsula on our port side. The windows of the buildings on Cannery Row and along Ocean View Drive caught the reflected glare of the setting sun, sparkling like glass palaces arrayed along the shore on the port side.

"An hour, maybe more," Bobby said as the *Nicky II* chugged steadily toward Lovers' Point, then Point Pinos beyond that.

According to the chart on the table before me, Monterey Canyon was ahead of us, plunging some ten thousand feet down to the ocean floor. Beyond that were the rougher waters of the Pacific Ocean. The bright yellow sun hung low in the blue October sky, streaking the clouds with red and orange above the water that glittered gold in the reflected light.

Red sky at night, sailor's delight. But I was no sailor. Only the urgency of the situation could make me climb aboard a boat and face the unpleasant lurching of my stomach. Soon the sun would slip from sight behind the marine layer of fog forming a hazy line along the horizon. Day would plunge into night and the water and sky would be indistinguishable from one another.

"Lacy and Frank will dump that cargo as soon as it gets dark," I said. "Then she'll head for Half Moon Bay. Even if the Coast Guard catches up with her, there won't be any evidence aboard that sailboat. Besides—"

I didn't finish the sentence. The boat rolled again and I held my breath.

"Besides what?" Bobby said with a sidelong glance.

I released the breath I held and took another. "I'll tell you later."

Bobby looked exasperated as well as doubtful. "Good thing one of the guys at the marina saw the *Windrunner* leave the boatyard, or we wouldn't even know when they set out. But they've got at least an hour's start on us."

"I know that. But they're in a sailboat. We can outrun them in this. I hope," I added, looking at my cousin for confirmation.

"Hell, yes. Running empty at full bore I can do eight knots," Bobby said, looking out at the bow. "That Targa can do seven or eight knots in ideal conditions. But the bay's not ideal. They're probably making six knots. Damned lucky they aren't in some cabin cruiser with more horsepower."

The luck of the draw, I thought. Lacy's choice of vessel was dictated by which boats in the yard she'd contracted to transport. In this case, it was a thirty-four-foot sailboat with a center cabin.

"We gotta find them first," Bobby continued. "The sonar's good for three hundred, four hundred yards." He shook his head, still doubtful. "Lacy's a good sailor, Jeri. And so's Frank, for all he's a creep. They'll be listening to the radio. They'll know the Coast Guard's looking for them."

"But they won't know we are, if we use the radio the way we planned."

Knowing they were the object of a Coast Guard search might cause the two people sailing the *Windrunner* to make a mistake. Perhaps they'd make a run for it. Or they'd play cat and mouse with the cutter. Either way, though, they'd dump their cargo as soon as it got dark, poisoning the ocean with those solvents.

I glanced at the radio, its crackling lifeline an ally in our search. We could hear the Coast Guard cutter, and other vessels as well. If someone out there spotted the *Windrunner*, the *Nicky II* could set an intercept course.

We also had backup. Sal Ravella and his sons Joe and Leo were readying the *Bellissima*, planning to follow us out into the bay. All the Ravellas could communicate in Italian, but according to Bobby, Frank Alviso didn't speak or understand the language. I hoped Lacy Beckman couldn't either. We also planned to couch our radio communications in code. The *Windrunner* was, for all intents and purposes, a large school of sardines.

We were certainly far better equipped to find sardines than a renegade sailboat. An array of high-tech equipment occupied the console in front of Bobby. There was a sonar to scan for fish in front of the boat, a fathometer showing what was beneath us, and a small closed-circuit television set used to monitor the engine room below.

The radio crackled. I heard an exchange of voices between the Coast Guard cutter and another vessel. "What was that?"

"Coast Guard has both its patrol boats out in the bay," Bobby said. "The cutter is farther out in the shipping lanes. They were just talking to a container ship. Nobody's seen our fish so far. The wind's picked up. I think we may get some weather."

"Wonderful," I said grimly. "That will make the boat rock even more."

"I made some coffee." Donna climbed the ladder to the wheelhouse from the galley below. In one hand she carried a big ceramic mug that she handed to Bobby. "Good lord, Jeri, you should see your face. It's as green as this mug."

"Thank you for that observation." I tried not to think about my seasickness, focusing instead on the rapid succession of events that had brought the three of us aboard the *Nicky II.*

Lacy Beckman's plan was simple and straightforward, repeating a pattern she'd used several times over the summer. She would sail the *Windrunner* to Half Moon Bay and pick up another boat that Beckman Boat Works had contracted to repair. That was what she'd done back in August, when Ariel and Bobby had seen her aboard the *Marvella B.* On paper she was merely taking that boat to Santa Cruz, where she picked up another to sail back to Monterey.

But somewhere below the deck of the *Marvella B* she carried a cargo of solvents concealed in paint cans, ready to dump overboard as soon as it got dark. Lacy had made a mistake that night, by jettisoning the cargo too close to shore, too soon after her encounter with the *Nicky II.* She'd been seen by Ariel Logan, and Ariel was curious about Lacy's behavior. Even more curious the next day, when she saw the sea lions off Point Pinos. Apparently one of those paint cans smashed against some rocks and leaked its deadly contents, poisoning the creatures. Ariel had linked one image with the other.

Karl Beckman had difficulty believing this when I told him. I'd been in a rush, explaining between phone calls, finally telling him to go through his records and list the dates Lacy moved boats from one place to another. The Coast Guard duty officer sounded dubious, too, when I detailed what was still a theory, without much evidence to back it up. But I'd managed to convince him that something was up, and the cutter was out looking for the *Windrunner,* as were the two smaller patrol boats based in Monterey.

I was lucky to find Eric Lopez at his office. By now the county environmental health and safety specialist was at Beckman Boat

Works, taking a sample from the glistening traces of liquid left on the concrete floor of the storeroom.

I tried to reach Sergeant Magruder but the sheriff's office said he'd been called out to the scene of a double homicide east of Chualar. I left a message, then called Bobby and Donna, catching both of them at home. Leaving Mother and Karl at Beckman Boat Works, I headed for Wharf Two. By then Bobby had put his ear to the fishermen's grapevine, gleaning the information that the *Windrunner* had set out an hour before, under power rather than sail.

Normally the *Nicky II* had a crew of eight, but this wasn't a normal voyage. This evening we were in pursuit. All we needed was someone to steer the boat and someone to cast off the lines. Bobby had the first duty and Donna took care of the second. My role was to figure out what Lacy Beckman was going to do next, but at the moment I was trying not to throw up.

The radio came to life with several voices in English, as two vessels communicated with the Coast Guard cutter. Bobby listened intently, then told us the first transmission came from a salmon boat out of Moss Landing, now in the waters off Davenport. The second was a party boat, hired to take customers out fishing. They were somewhere in the bay between us and Santa Cruz. The party boat may have seen the *Windrunner*.

"Hand me those charts," Bobby ordered.

Donna grabbed the charts off the table and spread them on the console where Bobby could look at them. Then the radio spoke again, this time a rush of Italian. Bobby reached for the mike and replied. The *Bellissima* was now patrolling with us. So was another boat from the Monterey fleet, the *Guiliana*.

"Another purse seiner. The skipper's a friend of mine, a *paisan*," Bobby said as he translated the conversation for Donna and me.

"Busy out here," I said, looking out at the brilliantly colored horizon, watching daylight slip inexorably into the sea.

"It is. A lot of traffic moves up and down the coast at night. And when the fishing boats go out, it gets downright crowded." Bobby turned the wheel, changing the *Nicky II*'s heading. "So cuz, assuming we do find the *Windrunner*. What are we gonna do then?"

"I haven't figured that one out yet," I admitted.

The *Nicky II* hit a trough and bucked like a rodeo bronc. I grabbed the chart table and clamped my mouth shut.

"Come on down to the galley," Donna said, grabbing my arm. "Maybe you'll feel better. At least you'll be closer to the toilet."

I followed her down the ladder to the galley, a roomy and comfortable space, with a general air of musty male untidiness. At the bottom of the ladder I'd just descended was a hatch and another ladder leading down to the noisy room where diesel engines powered the *Nicky II* and everything on it.

I stepped past this hatch and steadied myself, left hand on the edge of the large square table. Its wooden surface was scratched and scarred and it was surrounded on three sides by padded benches. Above the table, built into the woodwork, were a TV and VCR, the latter with a couple of videotapes stuck into the space next to it. Stacked on one end of the table I saw several board games, a deck of cards, and some books and magazines. All these diversions occupied the crew on those nights when they had to travel several hours to get to the fishing grounds.

There were two bunkrooms, off the galley and under the wheelhouse, each with three berths, spread with blankets and sleeping bags. Toward the stern, where a door led out to the lower deck of the boat, was a small head. It contained a toilet and a shower, though at the moment the shower was occupied by several lengths of pipe and hose.

The *Nicky II* had a kitchen with a refrigerator, a four-burner stove, a microwave, and a coffeemaker. The stove had bars welded around the edges, to hold pots on the burners while the boat was under way. The stove could have used a good wipe-down and there were dirty dishes in the sink. Visible on one of the shelves above the counter were several boxes, most of them containing cereal. The one that didn't, according to its label, held sea-lion bombs, the small explosive devices used to scare the creatures away from the boat's catch.

Donna poured me a cup of strong black coffee. "Here. I hope this settles your stomach. Or maybe it will clean it out."

I took the mug from her, sipped the brew, and gave her a crooked smile. "Too early to tell."

"You didn't have to come with us."

"Of course I did. I have to get some answers from Lacy Beckman. If the Coast Guard gets to her first, I may not have the chance."

The boat rolled and I groped my way unsteadily toward one of the benches at the table. Donna remained standing. She had better sea legs than I did. She poured herself some coffee and looked at me with troubled blue eyes.

"You don't have this all put together, do you?"

"Not as much as I'd like. I've got lots of hunches, though." I reached for my handbag, which I'd discarded earlier on the bench. I pulled out my notebook and flipped through the pages.

"Lacy Beckman started transporting boats from one marina to another in June, according to Karl, who thought it was a good idea to bring in some additional income. But it looks like she's doing more than simply moving boats from one place to another. If she's dumping toxics in the ocean she's making a hell of a lot of money. Then we have Frank Alviso. Bobby fired Frank at the end of June and he went to work for the Beckmans. Frank's definitely the kind of guy who holds a grudge."

"Why are the dates important?" Donna asked.

"Timing. And those pelican mutilations that you and the SPCA are so concerned about." I tapped the page where I'd made notes.

"The mutilations began in June. You know about eight birds so far. Marsha Landers said one bird was found August eighteenth, the same day Ariel saw the sea lions. The day after the *Marvella B* supposedly went back to Santa Cruz, sailed by Lacy and Frank. We know Frank was suspected of mutilating pelicans a few years back. As for Lacy, I wouldn't turn my back on the woman. What if the two of them have been hurting the birds to divert attention from their dumping scheme? Remember, Marsha said she hadn't focused on Ariel's report about the sea lions because she was occupied with the pelicans."

Donna swore under her breath. "How would we prove something like that?"

"Check the dates the pelicans were found. Then go back through the records at Beckman Boat Works, and see if Lacy sailed boats to different ports on or around those days. Better to catch them in the act, though. Just as I'd rather catch them with those paint cans still aboard that sailboat."

"Otherwise you can't prove it," Donna said.

I nodded over the rim of the coffee mug. "Maybe not. Norm Gerrity and I spent a lot of time on the phone yesterday, pretending that we had a few barrels to get rid of. We smoked out a guy in Sunnyvale who said he could 'deep-six the stuff in Davy Jones's locker.' That phrase has ocean disposal written all over it. When we leaned on him we got some details. He trucks it over the mountains to Santa Cruz, reportedly looking for people with boats who are interested in making some ready cash. When Ryan Trent looked into Lacy's finances, he discovered she'd bought a place in Santa Cruz. My guess is she's using it as a holding facility. I'd really like to catch her red-handed. That would make it so much easier."

Donna was silent for a moment. "You think Lacy killed Ariel, don't you?"

Before I could answer, the boat rolled and the coffee mug went flying from my hand. Cleaning up the spill was the least of my worries. I made a dash for the head and retched over the toilet, tears of misery springing to my eyes as the contents of my stomach came up. When I finally flushed the toilet and hauled myself into an unsteady upright position, Donna stood there with a dishcloth that was as wet and wrung out as I felt. I took it from her, mopped my face, and tried to smile.

"It's just as well I got that over with."

Donna laughed. Then Bobby called down from the wheelhouse, a note of excitement in his voice.

"Jeri, Donna, get up here."

We scrambled for the ladder.

CHAPTER 42

W̲E'D ONLY BEEN BELOW FIFTEEN OR TWENTY MINUTES but in that time the edge of the sun had dipped into the fog layer. Now the orb was a golden half circle suspended in the gray haze, staining the sky above with yellow as the sea below turned dark. I looked in the opposite direction, for a glimpse of land. There I saw twinkling lights too low to be stars, layered here and there in different concentrations and intensities. Except for that link to solid ground, I saw nothing but water and, above that, a sky that was already dark with night. I shivered. Now that the sun was gone it had cooled considerably.

"Did someone spot the *Windrunner?*" I asked, turning to Bobby. The diminishing daylight had raised my anxiety to a sharp pitch. We were running out of time.

"Maybe," Bobby said. "A research ship out of Moss Landing. They radioed the Coast Guard. Saw a sailboat, northwest of where the party boat saw one. We're closer than the cutter." He grinned. "And we've got plenty of help."

"What kind of help?" Donna asked.

"Uncle Dom's been on the horn. Sal says it was all they could do to keep the old man from coming with them. So Uncle Dom and one of the other old fishermen have been calling skippers in Monterey, Moss Landing, Santa Cruz, and Half Moon Bay." Bobby slapped the wheel. "We've got this coastline covered."

I smiled at the picture of Uncle Dom, ready to climb aboard the

Bellissima. "That gives us a better chance of catching up with the *Windrunner.* Good thing everyone's willing to help."

"Hell, these are our fishing grounds." Bobby's face turned grim as he looked out at the waves surrounding the boat. "It's hard enough to make a living at this business without some damn fool poisoning the ocean, killing the fish."

"I just hope they don't spook Lacy," Donna said with a frown, her eyes on the sun's downward progress. The glowing edge still visible in the fog was even narrower now. Soon it would disappear entirely.

Bobby nodded toward the radio, now crackling with transmissions, in English, Italian, Portuguese, Spanish, and the language of the newest immigrants to fish these waters, Vietnamese. Bobby identified the boats. A purse seiner from Moss Landing, a lampara from Santa Cruz, a salmon boat from Half Moon Bay, a trawler in the waters south of Año Nuevo, all hunting for the *Windrunner,* instead of anchovies, salmon, or squid.

"We're setting the purse," Bobby said, tossing his head back toward the stern where the *Nicky II*'s nets lay furled on the deck. "Soon we'll draw it tight, and we'll have our fish."

"Unlike squid, this fish will fight back," I warned him. "Better get your rifle."

Bobby looked at me for a moment, then nodded. "Here, take the wheel. Just hold it steady."

He might as well have asked me to dance naked on the flying bridge. Gingerly I stepped up to the helm of the *Nicky II* and grasped the wheel, conscious of the powerful engines whining below my feet. It wasn't as though I were going to run into anything. As far as I could see there was nothing around me but sky and water. The thin gold line on the western horizon was all that remained of daylight. Everything else was dark blue water, waves constantly moving and shifting and rolling.

I tightened my grip on the purse seiner's wheel. I remembered those sea stories I'd heard Uncle Dom tell about killer waves that could leap high, suddenly obliterating puny vessels on the ocean's surface. Old salts like Uncle Dom and Bobby no doubt thought it was calm tonight. But I was a fervent and confirmed landlubber. Even the slightest swell alarmed me.

I glanced back, anxiously looking for Bobby. He came out of

the captain's stateroom, which sounded far grander than the cubicle with a bunk that it was. In his right hand he carried a rifle, a box of shells in his left. He sat down at the chart table and loaded the weapon. When he finished, he handed the rifle to Donna and moved back to the wheel. I eagerly relinquished it to him.

"See, that wasn't so hard," he said, poking me in the ribs with an elbow. "How you feeling, cuz? Still seasick?"

"No." I shook my head, surprised. "Not anymore." Not since my hasty dash for the head. "Don't talk about it. You'll jinx me."

"You sound as superstitious as Uncle Dom." The radio came alive again, with a burst of Italian. I understood a few words, enough to know that the speaker was probably one of the Ravellas aboard the *Bellissima*. Bobby listened, then picked up the mike, responding in the same language as he consulted the charts. He looked up and frowned, scanning the water all around us. Another voice came on the radio, this one in English. The lampara from Santa Cruz, Bobby reported. Both vessels were heading for the area where the research ship had seen a sailboat.

"We should be getting close," Bobby said, his hands moving over the chart. "We should intercept them right about here."

"Where are we?" I asked.

Bobby pointed at the chart. We were roughly in the middle of Monterey Bay, northwest of the harbor we'd left and almost due west of Moss Landing. The boat rolled on the swells but to my amazement I felt no nausea.

"We're close to where I thought the sailboat might be," Bobby said. "But I'm not picking up anything on the sonar."

"If it's the right boat." Donna leaned over and looked at the charts. "Maybe they're running without lights."

Lights. The only ones I could see were right here on the *Nicky II*, which meant we were visible to the sailboat we were trying to locate. Outside the wheelhouse it was so black I couldn't tell the difference between the water and the sky. The last thin edge of sunlight slipped from view. To the east, where land curved around Monterey Bay like a reversed C, I saw lights sprinkled here and there along the coast. There were no other boats nearby, at least no mast lights visible to my eyes. How could anyone find anything on all this water?

Too late, I thought. Now that it was dark Lacy Beckman would dump her cargo. I shook my head, staring out at the void. "I don't see any lights."

"Time to provide some," Bobby said.

He told me to take the wheel again and hold it steady. Donna propped the rifle in the corner near the hatch leading to the captain's stateroom. Then she and Bobby left me alone in the wheelhouse, heading out the port hatch and down to the lower deck at the stern. I gripped the wheel of the *Nicky II* and felt the throb of the engines below. Then the boat hit a trough. My nerves screamed like a high-pitched violin and my gut danced to the discordant music. I hoped Bobby was coming back soon. Very soon.

Suddenly the ocean around me turned unnaturally bright. The halogen lights Bobby and his crew used to attract squid were rigged all around the *Nicky II*'s deck. Now they shone out on those dark rocking waves. A long way in front of me and to port I saw light reflect from something. The hull of a boat? The waves shifted and it disappeared, then glinted again.

"We got something." Bobby appeared suddenly at my side, his words more confident than my thoughts. He looked out at the object that kept appearing and disappearing in the swells, then pointed to the sonar. Now the object was showing at the edge of the range.

He turned the wheel. The bow of the *Nicky II* sliced the water between us and the object, eating up the distance. I reached for a nearby set of binoculars and joined Donna where she stood, at the hatch on the port side. I squinted through the glasses as we drew closer to the object. It resolved itself into a shape, a sailboat tossing on the waves, sails furled, its bow pointed toward us. There were no lights showing. I couldn't see any identifying marks on the hull. Nor did I see any sign of people aboard.

Donna took the glasses from me and looked at the sailboat. "Can't tell if it's got a center cabin," she called to Bobby. "Not at this angle."

"Did you figure out what we're gonna do, cuz?" Bobby asked as we bore down on the sailboat, its bow on our port side. "Or am I supposed to ram it?"

"We need to board it," I told him.

"Shit, you don't ask for much, do you?" Bobby shook his head. "That'll take some doing."

"I have faith in you."

Donna handed me the binoculars and I slung the cord around my neck, peering through the glass again as the other vessel loomed closer. I still didn't see any movement or light. Was it the *Windrunner*? Was it adrift? A sudden awful thought occurred to me. What if Lacy and Frank had dumped the cargo, then transferred to another boat to make their getaway? What if I was altogether wrong and they'd used another vessel?

I let the binoculars drop, so they hung heavy at my chest. It was the wrong boat. I was sure of it.

Bobby cut the throttle as we approached the smaller craft, easing the purse seiner closer. He closed the distance between the two boats, keeping the sailboat's sleek white hull off our port bow. I guessed the distance between us to be fifty or sixty feet. Finally we passed the sailboat and I could see that it did have a center cabin and there were two figures hunched low over the wheel. Suddenly over the shriek of the *Nicky II*'s engines I heard the unmistakable crack of gunfire.

Belay my last, I thought as Donna and I ducked into the wheelhouse. It's the right boat.

"Call for reinforcements, damn it," Donna yelled, scooping up the rifle from its corner resting place.

Bobby reached for the radio. He raised the Coast Guard cutter first, then called Sal Ravella on the *Bellissima*. The other purse seiner was a few miles east, Bobby reported. The lampara was to the north, on the other side of the *Windrunner*, with the trawler behind it. And the Coast Guard vessels, cutter and patrol boats, were south. It would take time for any of them to reach us. So we'd have to keep the sailboat here.

I heard gunfire again and something peppered the bow and the port side. I recalled what Mrs. Bainbridge had said about Lacy's upbringing, riding, sailing, and shooting with her father. She still knew how to handle a gun.

"Jesus," Bobby swore. "What have they got over there? Sounds like it's got more firepower than my Winchester. Still want to board her, Jeri?"

"I just want to get my hands on Lacy Beckman." At the moment the gulf between that desire and the reality loomed larger than the gap between the two boats.

I saw one figure leave the center cabin and move quickly toward the sailboat's stern. Then it ducked back into the sailboat's cabin as the smaller boat surged with sudden power, heading in the direction of our stern.

Bobby swore again. "They're gonna make a run for it." He turned the wheel to port and we began to circle. But the *Windrunner* had left something behind.

"They've set a raft adrift," I called, training the binoculars in the sailboat's wake. The orange rubber oval floated precariously on the waves. "It's full of paint cans. And water. They've scuttled it. It's sinking fast."

"Donna and I can get it with the nets," Bobby said. He slowed the engines as we approached the raft. "But I can't steer the boat at the same time." He took my hands and placed them on the wheel. "You got to hold it right there, Jeri. No matter what."

"Do it. Hurry."

Bobby and Donna vanished through the hatch, heading back toward the stern. Under my nervous hands the *Nicky II* circled the raft, floating on the port side. When I dared to glance at the raft I counted eight large paint cans like those I'd seen at Beckman Boat Works. Lacy and Frank must have slashed the rubber of the raft in several places. The normally buoyant sides were limp and flat. The bottom was rapidly filling with water. Soon the weight of those cans would swamp the raft. The cans and the solvent they contained would sink to the ocean floor.

Now I couldn't see the raft. It was off the port side of the purse seiner. I thought I heard Bobby's voice shouting at Donna, borne by the wind that now tossed the waves. I gripped the wheel tighter, determined not to deviate from the circle Bobby had set for me. What if Bobby and Donna didn't get the raft on the first pass? It would sink. We'd never catch up with the *Windrunner.*

Bobby suddenly appeared, racing up the outside ladder from the lower deck. He took the wheel and turned it hard to port. "Get down below and help Donna," he ordered.

I flew down the ladder to the deck where Donna stood. She and

Bobby had set one of the squid nets and now Bobby moved the boat in a tighter circle around the sinking raft, setting the purse. When we'd encircled our prey, we pulled the purse strings tight, with Bobby suddenly everywhere at once.

My heart sank with the raft, seeing the orange rubber disappear beneath the waves. "Don't worry, we've got it," my cousin said. Sure enough, the raft rose again as the winch hauled the net from the water. Bobby, Donna, and I guided it gently into the hold of the *Nicky II.*

We had it, but I'd lost track of the time it took to catch this particular fish. Once again, the *Windrunner* had a lead on us.

"Now let's see how fast this old bucket will go," Bobby said as we hurried back to the wheelhouse. "Donna, get on that radio."

The *Nicky II* left its circle and straightened its heading, power surging beneath our feet as the steel-hulled fishing boat once again became a pursuit vessel. As Donna broadcast a terse report to anyone who was listening, repeating the coordinates Bobby gave her, we headed in the direction the *Windrunner* had taken, running flat out as fast as Bobby could coax the engines.

I looked out at the black night sea. Where would Lacy go? We had three-hundred-sixty degrees of choices to make. And if she were monitoring the radio, she knew that everyone from the Coast Guard to the Monterey fishing fleet was out looking for her.

The radio crackled and spoke, a veritable party line of conversation. The Coast Guard, as Bobby predicted, was quite irked with us for being out here. But the rest of the fishing fleet was caught up in the hunt. No matter which way the *Windrunner* turned, there would be boats in Lacy Beckman's way.

"Lacy's got to have a contingency plan," I said. "She doesn't have enough fuel to run forever." I looked at the nautical charts as though they were tarot cards, revealing the future if I just knew how to interpret them. "She must have a car waiting at some port, just in case they need to escape on land. She has a house in Santa Cruz. That's my best guess."

"Has to be," Bobby said. He tapped his finger on the chart that showed the port on the northern rim of Monterey Bay. "She can't go back to Monterey. Moss Landing's farther east and too close to Monterey. If she heads south she'll run into the Coast Guard.

Davenport and Half Moon Bay are farther north and there's nothing west but open ocean."

He turned the *Nicky II* onto a new heading and reached for the mike, communicating with the *Bellissima* in short bursts of Italian. We were running full bore now. With the binoculars to my eyes I swept the waves in front of the boat. Minutes crawled by. We were approaching land.

Something appeared at the edge of my vision, enhanced by the binoculars and blurred by the edge of the lens. A boat, without running lights, illuminated by the halogens on the *Nicky II*. I called out a report to Bobby and he poured it on, cutting the distance between the vessels. It looked like the boat we'd seen earlier but I couldn't be sure. It was moving fast, though, without lights. Bobby brought the *Nicky II* closer still. The stern of the smaller boat grew as we raced toward it, now visible without the binoculars, ahead and to starboard. Still I peered into the glasses, looking for some identification. The lettering on the sailboat's hull was obscured by the boat's wake. Then the water shifted and I glimpsed the name I sought.

"It's the *Windrunner*," I reported.

"I can overtake her," Bobby said, "but she's got me on maneuverability. That'll work to her advantage in the harbor. That also means she can shoot at us from that cabin."

"We can shoot back." Donna glanced at the Winchester. "I don't know how accurate you can be at this speed. It would be better if we could slow them down."

"I have an idea," I said.

I went down the ladder to the galley, returning a moment later with the box I'd seen on the shelf above the sink. *Danger. Explosive,* read the lettering. *Do not hold in hand. Light and throw away.*

"Sea-lion bombs?" Bobby glanced at the box, then back at the sailboat, intent on shortening the distance between the *Nicky II's* bow and the *Windrunner's* stern. "They're not kidding about the light-and-throw-away part, cuz. Those suckers have a short fuse. They'll blow off your hand if you're not careful."

"But they've got a big bang," Donna said with a grin. "A couple of these lobbed into the cabin would certainly get their attention. How do we deliver the package?"

I opened the box and pulled out a couple of sea-lion bombs, fat short firecrackers with minimal fuses. "We'll just have to throw them. Got a lighter?"

"I saw one down in the galley." Donna quickly descended the ladder and returned a moment later with a butane lighter discarded by one of Bobby's crew.

"Jesus, Mary, and Joseph." The skipper of the *Nicky II* moved his eyes heavenward, then back down to his prey. "I'll try to get as close as I can. Just don't blow a hole in our hull, or we'll be swimming to shore."

If I had any sense, I thought, I'd be scared. Throwing sea-lion bombs at the *Windrunner* seemed simple, straightforward—and foolhardy. What if the wind blew the little firecrackers right back at us? Besides, the people aboard the sailboat had a gun. Donna and I made good targets out here on the *Nicky II*'s bow, holding a box of powerful explosives.

"How much delay do you suppose we have?" Donna asked as she examined one of the squat bombs.

"I guess we're about to find out."

I looked to starboard. Bobby was overtaking the *Windrunner* on the sailboat's port side. One of the figures in the sailboat's cabin steered to starboard, trying to get away from us. The other figure held the gun.

The bow of the *Nicky II* edged past the *Windrunner*'s stern now, gaining, then losing, then gaining again, all the while angling closer to the ketch. How close were we? Twenty feet? Close enough to get shot. I ran my fingers over the little firecracker. It had been years since I'd played softball. Could I throw this thing far enough to land it on a moving target?

Bobby edged closer to the sailboat. Now was my chance. I held out the sea-lion bomb and Donna flicked the lighter. The fuse sparked and caught. I threw it. The bomb hit the water and disappeared. I aimed the next one higher. It glanced off the furled sail at the rear of the sailboat and exploded in the air with a violent concussion and a flash of light.

Damn, these things had a kick.

I held out another bomb. Donna lit the fuse and I lobbed it toward the sailboat just as the *Nicky II* pulled ahead. The bomb landed on the *Windrunner*'s bow and exploded a few seconds later, taking some of the sailboat's rigging with it. The *Windrunner* slowed. The next bomb I threw landed just behind the cabin. I saw the two figures scramble for the bow as the firecracker exploded with a deafening crack. Now the sailboat slowed to a disoriented crawl.

"Now what?" Donna asked.

"Get inside. They've still got a gun."

We ducked back into the wheelhouse as Bobby brought the *Nicky II* across the bow of the disabled sailboat. "The *Bellissima*'s about ten minutes away, and so's that lampara. Do we sit here and wait for them?"

I gazed down at the sailboat, recalling what Bobby said about the smaller craft's maneuverability. It was moving again, slowly, heading straight toward us. What the hell were they doing? I saw two figures on the sailboat's deck. Why would Lacy and Frank aim their disabled boat at the *Nicky II*? What could they gain by ramming this larger vessel? Unless . . .

"They're trying to board us," I shouted.

I heard the thump as the sailboat banged against the purse seiner's hull, somewhere on the starboard side. Bobby swore and grabbed the rifle.

"Donna, get on that radio. Jeri, down through the galley." He dodged out the port hatch and headed down to the lower deck. I went down the ladder to the galley door that led out to the deck.

As I peered through the glass I saw movement near the fish pump. Frank Alviso climbed aboard the boat he used to help crew. He knew the layout. Behind him was Lacy Beckman, carrying a rifle.

Bobby was somewhere above and to port, looking down on the deck. I knew that because the Winchester spoke as he fired at the boarders. Frank and Lacy ducked behind the fish pump. It didn't offer much cover but Lacy fired in Bobby's direction. I opened the door and moved onto the deck, hidden by the winch housing and the elevated hatch that led to the holding tank. I looked around for something to use as a weapon. Here was a winch handle. I could do some damage with that. And on the deck at my feet I saw a brail, a large, long-handled net used to remove fish from the hold. I stuck the winch handle in the pocket of my jeans and reached for the net, pulling it toward me, holding the handle near the circle that held the net.

Lacy fired at Bobby. Then she and Frank left the shelter of the fish pump, each running in a different direction around the holding tank. I dodged around the winch housing with the brailing net in my hands, using the net end to knock Frank off his feet. He struggled to rise, hands fighting with the webbing of the net. I hit him with the winch handle and he stopped moving.

When I straightened I saw Lacy Beckman pointing the rifle at me.

"You might as well give it up," I said, with more bravado than I felt. I didn't doubt she'd use the gun. After all, she'd killed Ariel. I moved to my left, along the starboard side of the deck, toward the fish pump, and she moved, too. "There's no way you're taking over this boat. The Coast Guard's just a few minutes away."

She slashed words at me. "You think you've got it all figured out."

"I do." That wasn't entirely true but she didn't have to know that. I moved to my left again and nodded toward the *Nicky II*'s hold.

"We got the raft before it sank. The paint cans are in the hold and all three of us saw you and Frank trying to dump them. I know how the disposal scheme worked and I can tie you to the guy in Sunnyvale. I know you and Frank were mutilating the pelicans to draw attention away from it."

I moved past the fish pump now, and Lacy followed me. If Bobby was still up where I thought he was, Lacy was no longer hidden by the winch housing. He'd have a clear shot.

I continued with my half of the conversation. "I've even figured out how you killed Ariel Logan."

I heard a sound somewhere above as the impact of my words hit Bobby. Lacy heard it, too. She turned swiftly and raised the rifle, eyes searching for Bobby. I threw myself at her. The shot she fired went wild. Then she and the rifle went sprawling as I kicked her legs out from under her.

CHAPTER 43

"T'S A THEORY."

Sergeant Magruder scowled at me. I'd lost track of time. I was very tired and it seemed the sergeant and I kept going over the same ground. Of course he was irritated with me and my fellow crew members. I don't know who was angrier with us, Magruder or the Coast Guard.

The cutter had arrived about the same time as the *Bellissima*. The captain took everybody and everything into custody and told us we'd sort out the overlapping crimes and jurisdictions when we got back to Monterey. Everyone from the feds, the state and the local authorities wanted a crack at this one but the Monterey County Sheriff's Department was first in line. In fact, Magruder was waiting for us on Wharf Two when the *Nicky II* returned to the harbor. The homicide investigator's mood was way past testy. He refused to be mollified by the fact that I'd left a message for him.

"Maybe it is a theory. But I've given you enough to make it work." I took another sip of barely palatable coffee. Why was I drinking this stuff? It didn't even have enough caffeine to keep me from yawning. Not that I wanted to stay awake, if only this man would let me go find a bed.

"There's a damned good paper trail," I said, trying to sound more placating and less argumentative. "Started by Ariel Logan herself." I pointed at the now creased report from the environmental testing lab.

"Lacy Beckman transported boats from one marina to another, on the water and by highway. She started this little service last June. She'd take the empty paint cans from the boatyard up to Sunnyvale and leave them with her contact."

"This is the guy you and the other PI dug up?" Magruder interrupted. "The Sunnyvale cops picked him up. He denies everything."

"Of course he does. But he's dirty. If Gerrity and I could find the evidence, so can the Sunnyvale investigators. When he had stuff to get rid of, he filled the paint cans and hauled them to Lacy's house in Santa Cruz. She took them to Beckman Boat Works on whatever boat she was hauling by trailer and stored the stuff in that storeroom off the machine shop. Whenever she'd transport a boat by sea out of Monterey, Frank Alviso went with her and they'd dump the stuff."

Magruder gazed at me, not looking convinced. "You got anything to back this up?"

"Look, Karl Beckman put together a list of dates Lacy sailed boats to other harbors. I'm sure you'll find both Lacy's and Frank's bank accounts showed healthy increases coinciding with those dates. Besides, you've got three witnesses. Me, Bobby Ravella, and Donna Doyle. And eight paint cans full of solvents recovered by the *Nicky II*."

Magruder narrowed his eyes and used the end of his pencil to tap a tattoo on the desk. "Okay, I'll buy the dumping scam. But how do you tie Lacy Beckman to Ariel Logan's murder? No witness to the actual event."

"Here's where we get into theory," I conceded. "The boat hauler saw Ariel talking to someone in a Beckman pickup truck. My guess is Lacy was on Alvarado Street when Bobby and Ariel came out of the Rose and Crown. Perhaps Lacy heard enough of the argument to know what they were fighting about. She must have realized that Ariel got suspicious back in August, when she and Bobby were out on the *Nicky II* and encountered Lacy and Frank on the *Marvella B*. Ariel had been interested in the boatyard operations all along but that's when she began asking questions about the paint cans. She thought Karl was involved."

So had I. I was more than willing to believe the worst about the boatyard owner, for my own reasons. That was part of the unfinished business I had to take care of before I could go back to Oakland.

"So you think Lacy Beckman approached Ariel later that Friday afternoon," Magruder said.

I nodded. "She convinced Ariel to meet her that evening at the Rocky Point Restaurant. That would take some persuading, since Ariel was already sure the boatyard was involved in something illegal. My guess is Lacy lured Ariel by pointing the finger at Karl. Frank had keys to Bobby's T-bird and he must have mentioned this to Lacy. She took the keys and the T-bird. That's the only way to explain how that car got down to Rocky Point while Bobby was at the AA meeting. Easy enough to cast suspicion on Bobby, since everyone had him pegged as a suspect anyway."

I shrugged. "Frank Alviso will probably sing like Caruso. He signed onto this for the money, and to get even with Bobby for firing him. Just mention an accessory-to-murder charge and he'll talk."

"As long as you're doing my job for me," Magruder said, sarcasm edging his voice, "tell me how Lacy killed Ariel."

"Pure guesswork," I admitted. "Lacy drove into the parking lot in Bobby's T-bird. Ariel recognized the car. I don't know how Lacy explained why she was driving it. Maybe she implicated Bobby in the dumping scheme. That would have put Ariel off her guard." I reached for the coffee, then thought better of it.

"I think they walked out onto the headlands, out of sight of the restaurant. Then Lacy hit Ariel over the head, with a wrench or something small but heavy. Then she pushed Ariel's body over the nearest cliff and tossed the murder weapon, hoping the sea would take care of the evidence. Just as it had with the toxics. When Ariel was reported missing, Lacy made some anonymous phone calls, pointing the finger at Bobby, just for insurance."

"All for money," Magruder commented.

"Lacy doesn't like to be without money. Illegal dumping is very profitable, despite the risks."

"And this stuff at the restaurant, the mouse and the stink bomb, that was Lacy getting back at Karl Beckman for taking up with your mother?"

I nodded. "Everything points to Lacy. The only reason seems to be Karl's rejection. Mother was a target because of Karl's affection for her. As I told you, Charlie Harper thinks there's something suspicious about that car accident that killed Janine and Gunter Beckman. I wouldn't be surprised if Lacy had something to do with that car going off the road at Hurricane Point."

"We'll never know." Magruder shook his head. "The wreck's still down there on the rocks. What didn't burn has been pulverized by the waves and the sand. I'll look into it, but after this time . . ."

He didn't finish. I knew what he was thinking, because it was in my mind as well. Pinning a murder charge on Lacy Beckman for the deaths of Janine and Gunter was close to impossible, unless Lacy slipped up and said something to implicate herself. Right now she wasn't talking.

"Greed and revenge," I said quietly. "A couple of the best motives I know, Sergeant. They appear with great regularity in the cases I've worked."

Magruder narrowed his eyes. "I've worked homicide investigations for a long time. I know about motives. Do you butt into Oakland police matters with this much enthusiasm?"

I thought of my ex-husband, an Oakland homicide cop. His probable response to Magruder's question brought a smile to my lips. "Sometimes. They're about as thrilled with my participation as you are."

"Going back to Oakland soon?"

"You mean I can leave?"

"You'll have to ask the DA," he said. "But I'm finished with you. For now."

I got to my feet. "I've been off my home turf too long. This was supposed to be a week's vacation. I didn't expect all this to happen."

"And when it did," Magruder said, "you just jumped right in. Warn me the next time you come to Monterey."

IT WAS NEARLY MIDNIGHT. I DROVE BACK TO CARMEL, SHOOED Stinkpot off the guest-room bed, threw off my clothes, and took his place. I woke about eight-thirty the next morning, lured by the aroma of good coffee. After a quick shower and change of clothes, I made my way to the kitchen. Through the French doors I saw Errol and Minna working in the garden. I poured myself a cup of coffee and put two slices of bread into the toaster.

The doorbell rang at the front of the house. Coffee in hand, I walked through the living room and opened the door. Standing there were Sylvie and Peter Logan, with Glennis Braemer bringing up the rear. We stared at each other for a moment, then Ariel's mother said in her soft French-accented voice, "Tell us. We want to hear it from you."

"Okay." I ushered them into the house and called Errol and Minna. Then I buttered the toast and took a seat at the kitchen table while Errol offered everyone coffee. I told them everything that had happened from the time I left the Logans' house Monday until my conversation with Magruder late last night.

Peter Logan couldn't stay still. He paced around the confines of the Sevilles' kitchen, his haggard face a shifting study of emotions. Sylvie sat motionless as I talked. When I finished she looked at the coffee cup in front of her and then at me.

"Thank you," she said. "It helps to know that the person who killed our daughter has been caught." She stood and took her husband's arm, leading the way to the front door. Mrs. Braemer followed, then paused in the doorway. A tiny smile played briefly on her lips.

"I have become a reluctant admirer of your persistence, Ms. Howard."

"Some people view it as one of my negative character traits. They don't always like the results."

"Perhaps not. But at least you get results."

When they'd gone, I rinsed the coffee cup and plate and put them in the dishwasher. "Good work," Errol told me.

"If they charge Lacy. Oh, they'll get her for dumping toxics and a host of lesser crimes. But I want to see her charged with murder. There are holes in what Sergeant Magruder calls my theory. The evidence is circumstantial, even if Frank Alviso implicates her." I shook my head. "Lacy Beckman should pay for killing Ariel Logan. For the pain and grief in the Logans' eyes. And in Bobby's."

Errol nodded, understanding my anger. "It's been good seeing you. Heading back to Oakland?"

"As soon as I can say my good-byes." I walked to my mentor and wrapped him in a hug. Then I leaned over to kiss Minna, who was seated at the table with Stinkpot draped over her lap. "Thanks for everything."

"I hope you're going to see your mother before you leave town," she said.

"I'm not gone yet."

I HEARD THE SEA LIONS BEFORE I REACHED WHARF TWO. THEIR IN-cessant barks grew louder as I neared the harbor. By the time I reached wharf's end the cacophony was so noisy it made normal conversation almost impossible. The huge beasts congregated and clamored amid the pilings, as the boats of the Monterey fleet ma-neuvered close to the wharf, waiting to unload holds full of squid, mackerel, anchovies, and sardines. Brown pelicans lined the rail-ing, eager for a share of the ocean's bounty, even mingling with the fishermen and cannery employees who crowded the wood-plank surface of the wharf. Seagulls wheeled and screeched over-head, keeping their distance, as did the otters and harbor seals, but all of them still looking for an opportunity.

As I watched on this crisp clear October morning, a purse seiner sidled up to the pumphouse, where a hose like a giant vac-uum cleaner was lowered into the boat's hold. Several tons of fish were then pumped upward, electronically measured and weighed, and loaded into the cannery trucks backed up to the chute outside.

Someone clapped me on the shoulders. I heard Uncle Dom's rough and melodic Italian shouting over the sea lions as I turned. He introduced me to three old men I recognized from the bocce court, each as silver-haired and weathered as my great-uncle. Uncle Dom had been telling his friends about last night's adven-tures, embellishing the tale dramatically with each telling, I was sure.

The purse seiner finished unloading and I excused myself. I spotted Donna near the end, with one of her Fish-and-Game col-leagues. While he talked to some of the fishermen, my cousin watched one of the big brown pelicans. It sat on the wharf railing, interested only in food, so trusting and heedless of dangers posed by the humans who walked nearby.

"I hope the pelican mutilations stop," Donna said in my ear when I joined her. "Now that Lacy and Frank are in custody. Were they responsible? If they were, is there any way to prove it other than the dates?"

"I don't know," I told her. "It's another one of those theories I had. If the mutilations stop, maybe I'm right."

"If they don't, we've still got some sicko out there hurting birds. And somewhere down the line, next year or the year after, there will be another copycat." Donna sighed. "I hate to sound so cynical."

The pelican stretched his enormous wings and sailed into the air. It skimmed the water, blue sky its backdrop, then plunged into the depths, emerging with a silvery fish that had escaped the nets. Then it swallowed its prey as the sea lions barked all around us.

My cousin and I walked back up the wharf toward the pump-house, where another boat was unloading. Bobby was there now, talking with several of his contemporaries. He saw us, waved, and headed our way.

"You two make a hell of a crew," he said with a grin. "Not that I'd want to make a run like that every night. What time did the cops let you go?"

"Midnight, or thereabouts," I said. "Magruder and I went over it several times. How about you?"

"Eleven-thirty. And I've been talking to the Coast Guard since eight A.M. Been looking for you and Donna. The DA wants us in his office at one."

"My supervisor will be thrilled," Donna said wryly.

I looked at my watch and sighed. "Damn. I've said my good-byes to Errol and Minna and I've got my bag in the car. Magruder said it was okay for me to leave. I was hoping to go back to Oakland sometime today. At this rate I'll never get out of town."

Bobby's smile quirked. "Thanks, cuz. For figuring this one out. I guess it's finally over."

I shook my head. "You'll be surprised at how long and slow the legal wheels grind." I paused. "I saw Ariel's family this morning."

The smile left Bobby's face and his dark eyes turned somber. "They know I didn't kill her? That's important to me, even if they don't like me. Just so they know I loved her."

"They know." I put my hand on his shoulder. "Maybe after a while you can talk with them, about your memories of Ariel. It might help. They'll grieve for her a long time."

"So will I," Bobby said, so quietly I could barely hear him. He stuck his hands into his pockets and walked toward the end of the wharf.

"Have you talked with your mother?" Donna asked as we began walking toward land again.

I didn't answer right away. "She's on my list of people to see," I said finally. "Before I leave town."

"Don't let too much time pass," she said. I wasn't sure whether she meant between visits, or conversations.

I DIDN'T SEE MOTHER WHEN I WALKED INTO CAF° MARIE. IT WAS A quarter to noon and Rachel Donahoe was on the telephone in the office. The radio at the bar was tuned to the same station it had been before, playing songs from the Big Band era. When Rachel hung up the phone, she told me Mother was out talking to a prospective customer about catering a party, but she'd be back soon.

I wandered down the hall and into the kitchen, where the pastry chef was putting the finishing touches on something delectably chocolate. Julian Surtees stood at the chopping block, dicing vegetables with a knife. All the cooking smells kicked in.

"Any chance of getting some lunch?" I asked.

Julian scowled at me over his cleaver. "Do I look like a short-order cook?"

I laughed. "Julian, you're going to miss me when I go back to Oakland. Monterey will seem so dull."

Julian rolled his sharp brown eyes heavenward and drawled, "I count the hours." He set down the cleaver, crossed the kitchen to the big refrigerator, and pulled open the door. "I've got some smoked chicken ravioli with wild mushroom sauce. No mice."

"Sounds good to me."

Julian carried the container back to the nearest stove, emptied the contents into a large pan, and fired up a burner. Then he walked to the window separating the kitchen from the bar, reached for a bottle, and poured two glasses full of brown liquid. He handed one to me and I sniffed it before tasting it. Sherry, a very good one.

"Marie will miss you, even if I won't," he said after taking a liberal swig.

"Why do you say that?"

"She talks about you all the time." He picked up a wooden spoon and stirred the ravioli heating on the stove. "My daughter this, my daughter that. The famous detective from Oakland." He set down the spoon and reached for his glass. "I was almost looking forward to meeting you, after that buildup. Little did I know I'd wind up on the grill."

"But Julian, you made such a tasty target." I smiled and sipped the sherry. "With your attitude, you had suspect written all over your forehead."

"How about patsy?" he growled. I knew he was thinking about Lacy and how she'd used him. "Well, screw it. Water under the bridge." He swallowed another mouthful of sherry.

"So, my mother talks about me a lot," I said.

"Yeah. I got the impression she's proud of you."

He stirred the ravioli again. Then he walked to the shelf where the tableware was stored, grabbed a plate and a large spoon, and set them on the cutting board. He cocked one black eyebrow at me as he transferred my lunch from pan to plate. "Does that surprise you?"

I balanced the plate on one hand and used the spoon to bisect one ravioli. "If she's proud of me, why doesn't she tell me?" I asked him.

Julian retrieved the bottle of sherry from the bar and topped off our glasses. "Maybe it's because you're as prickly as I am," he said. He raised his glass and saluted me with his sardonic smile. *"Bon appétit."*

Mother came in just as I was polishing off the last of the ravioli. When she'd set down the leather case she carried, she glanced at Julian and me, then examined the label on the bottle of sherry. "The best in the house. It's a little early, isn't it?"

"It's never too early," Julian declared. He fetched another glass. I set my plate in the sink, picked up the bottle, and took Mother by the arm.

"Let's go into the dining room and talk."

We sat down at the table nearest the bar as Ella Fitzgerald sang softly in the background, accompanied by the steady rhythm of Julian's knife. I filled our glasses and Mother looked at hers, then picked it up and sipped the contents.

"I heard all about it, from Nick and Uncle Dom," she said. "And Karl, after he finished talking with the authorities last night. You could have been killed out there."

"But it didn't happen. We caught up with Lacy in time to prevent her from dumping the stuff. She killed Ariel, you know."

"It's hard to believe. Everything, from the restaurant to murder. You think you know a person and maybe you don't. And why? For money? For revenge?" She shook her head.

I'd covered this ground before, last night with Sergeant Magruder and again this morning. Besides, that wasn't why I'd come.

"I have to ask you about something Karl said when he left that night you and I fought. He said, 'You were right about her, Marie.' What did he mean by that?"

Mother flushed. She moved her sherry glass in a circle on the table's surface. "It was something I said earlier in the summer. About you."

"What about me?"

She looked distinctly embarrassed but she took a deep breath and plunged ahead. "I told him you're like a pit bull. When you get your teeth into something you don't let go until it's over."

I tilted my head to one side, not sure whether to put a positive or negative spin on the description. "Did you mean it as a compliment?"

"At the time, yes."

"Fine. Then I'll take it as one," I said, aware that the only reason Karl Beckman recalled the remark was because my teeth were sunk firmly into his ankle. "There's a lot of truth to the pit-bull analogy." Now it was my turn to take a deep breath. "Just as there's a lot of truth in some of the things we said to each other Friday night."

"I know," Mother said, meeting my eyes. "Your father once said you and I don't get along because we're so much alike. He's right. I wish we could be friends, Jeri."

"We can, I suppose, if we work at it. I'm willing if you are."

She smiled and reached across the table for my hand. "Of course I am. Even if we're at each other's throats, I'm still your mother. I do love you."

It still felt awkward, I thought. Maybe it always would. At least we were speaking to each other.

Someone pulled open the door of Café Marie and walked slowly toward the bar. It was Karl Beckman, his big shoulders slumped, his broad face tired and drawn. He looked as though he had been through every ringer the county had to offer. I got to my feet and stepped behind the bar, fetching yet another glass. When I returned to the table I pulled out a chair and beckoned to Karl.

"Have some sherry. You look like you could use it."

"I spent the morning in the DA's office." His hazel eyes looked stunned at the extent of the havoc his sister-in-law had wrought.

"I'm due there at one." I consulted my watch. "I'd better get going."

"Are you spending the night at Errol's?" Mother asked. "Or do you want to come back to my house? You still have the key, don't you?"

I started to tell her that I planned to head back to Oakland as soon as I was finished with the DA—or he with me, as was probably more the case. I thought about the key I was going to mail to her, my overnight bag in the Toyota, and my cat and the need to get back to work. But what was one more night?

"I'll have the teakettle on when you get home," I said.

JANET DAWSON's first novel, *Kindred Crimes*, won the Private Eye Writers of America Best First Private Eye Novel Contest, and was nominated for Anthony and Shamus awards as well. Dawson worked as an enlisted journalist in the Navy before moving to Alameda, California. A member of the Mystery Writers of America and Sisters in Crime, she is also the author of three other Jeri Howard mysteries, *Kindred Crimes*, *Till the Old Men Die*, and *Take a Number*. She is now at work on the next novel in the series.